A Matter of Chance

L.L. Diamond

Leslie
L. L. Diamond

A Matter of Chance

By LL Diamond

Published by LL Diamond

© 2013 LL Diamond

Facebook.com/LLDiamond
Twitter.com/LLDiamond2

Cover art: © 2013 by design

2

For my Brandon, who has become my biggest cheerleader, and for Brenna, Lainey, and Jacob, who, on a daily basis, inspire me.

Author's Note

After completing *Rain and Retribution*, I wanted something very different. I enjoyed writing Regency, but I had a scene in my mind and had already begun forming a story around it.

One of the first questions was where to place Meryton. I wanted it within the United States, but I wanted to base Meryton on a town with a lot of history and beautiful homes, like England. As a result, I loosely based Meryton on Natchez, Mississippi. The fictional Meryton is larger, but has the old Antebellum plantations around the area.

From there, I researched Antebellum homes and found some that I was very inspired by, including Monmouth, which I loosely based the exterior of Longbourn on. There are obvious differences, including the land around the home, but I loved the white pillars, the old oak trees, and the azaleas.

For the exterior of Netherfield, I was inspired by Palo Alto Plantation, which is actually in Louisiana, but I took a bit of artistic license and placed it in Meryton. I also mention Longwood plantation in the story, which was one of my favorites when I visited Natchez as a teenager. It was a fascinating place with its unfinished upper floors.

The story kind of took shape from there. I hope I conveyed what I wished when I wrote it, and I hope that you enjoy reading it.

L.L. Diamond

Prologue

"Happiness in marriage is entirely a matter of chance. If the dispositions of the parties are ever so well known to each other or ever so similar beforehand, it does not advance their felicity in the least. They always continue to grow sufficiently unlike afterwards to have their share of vexation; and it is better to know as little as possible of the defects of the person with whom you are to pass your life."
– Charlotte Lucas, Pride and Prejudice, Ch. 6

<u>June 15, 2005 (7 years earlier)</u>

Elizabeth Bennet stared at her reflection in the full-length mirror.

"Lizzy, you don't have to do this," Jane insisted, as she zipped the elegant white dress. "Mom and Dad's approval isn't worth it."

"What do you know? In our mother's opinion, you can do no wrong. You weren't the child who couldn't do anything right."

"You had our father's approval."

"Until I decided I wanted to be an artist, not a doctor or a lawyer, and then he looked at me in the same manner that our mother does. Greg was the only thing I've ever done that earned their favor, and for the first time, they are supportive of me," Lizzy sighed, as she turned to plead with her sister. "Please, Jane, you're my big sister and my best friend. I want you by my side today. I want to share this day with you."

Jane looked at her sister skeptically. "If you ever need anything, you know I'll be there. Aunt Mel too."

Lizzy laughed. "I know. She had the same conversation with me last week."

"It's just that you're so young. You're only twenty-one, and getting married to a man that I know you *do not* love." Jane grasped her hands and Lizzy looked up into her imploring eyes.

"What makes you think I don't love him?" she asked defensively.

"Because I know you. I see your face when no one's paying attention, and I hate it that you're sacrificing yourself for our parents' approval."

"I never said that I don't love him," Lizzy responded. "I'm happy. I finished my BFA and I begin my MFA in the fall. Mr. Wickham was wonderful when he discovered that there was a master's program where Greg would be attending law school. He bought us a small house. He's even paying my tuition."

Jane regarded her warily. "In all of that, you never once said that you love him."

"Please, Jane," she pleaded, "no more."

Her sister nodded reluctantly. "Fine, I promise, but I will always be here if you need me."

"I love you," Lizzy smiled.

"I love you too, sis," she sighed. "Well, let's go get you married."

April 14, 2010 (2 ½ years earlier)

During the still dark early hours of the morning, Lizzy climbed into the back of the grungy cab that had just pulled up to the curb.

"562 Netherfield Park Lane in Meryton," she told the driver as she closed the door. He seemed surprised when she said her destination, but said nothing. She noticed that he had seemed to scan the bruises and bleeding on her face before he turned to watch the road.

They pulled away from the curb as she thought about everything that had happened. Greg had been gone for so long this time that she hadn't thought he would return—she was wrong. He'd turned up that night drunk, and when he saw her, he'd become furious. She tried to plead with him, but he swiftly became so enraged that he was beyond reason.

She ran her hand over the swell of her abdomen as the latest contraction subsided, hoping she could get to Jane in time. If it wasn't for the pain she felt everywhere, she doubted she'd be able to remain awake. Looking up, she noticed the driver staring at her in the rearview mirror, but he averted his eyes as she caught his stare.

"Ma'am, are you sure you don't wanna to go to the hospital?"

"I *want* to go to the address I gave you," she replied in the strongest voice she could muster. He glanced back with an apprehensive look upon his face, but nodded before he returned his eyes to the road.

Running her hand across her face, she could feel the swelling and the blood that was caked into her hair. Her left wrist and her ribs ached, but she was most worried about her baby.

She'd been almost four months along the last time Greg had come home. He'd been drunk—but then he always turned up drunk—and had laughed that she was getting fat. While she knew that she was pregnant, at the time, she hadn't understood how he'd come to the conclusion that she'd simply gained weight, but he was rarely around and so incredibly intoxicated that she saw no reason to argue. Last night was the first time he'd seen her since, and this time there was no denying that she was pregnant.

> *"Whose baby is it, Elizabeth?! Because it sure as hell isn't mine!"*
>
> *"I've never been with anyone else," she cried as his hand delivered another agonizing blow to her head.*
>
> *"You lie! I won't be supporting another bastard's child."*
>
> *She'd tried to calm him, but he wouldn't listen. What did it matter anymore? "Like you support us now," she commented sarcastically.*
>
> *"What did you say?" She was pushed to the floor and began struggling to get up.*

She'd lost consciousness not long after. He was gone when she awoke, so she left as quickly as she was capable in the event he might return. She couldn't possibly carry any of her belongings, so she left everything. Her condition necessitated a trip to the hospital, but she was afraid Greg would discover where she'd fled. The last thing she wanted him to know was where she was.

No, she needed to get to Jane. Jane and her husband, Charles, would handle everything. They'd always said they would help her, but she'd always refused. She had known that her parents would be angry with her for leaving her husband, so she'd remained. However, she couldn't—wouldn't stay any longer. If her baby survived, she would need to ensure Greg kept away from them. She could only trust her dearest sister with that.

"Ma'am, we're here."

Her head snapped up all of a sudden. How long had she been asleep?

Looking out of the window, she saw her oasis and breathed a sigh of relief. She'd made it.

"It'll be ninety-three dollars."

Lizzy searched through her bag, finding nothing, and coming to the realization that Greg had gone through her purse before he left. Her shoulders slumped, and she looked up to find the driver staring at her with narrowed eyes through the clear plastic barrier.

"My sister will pay the fare. I just need to get her."

"You have no money!" he exclaimed indignantly.

"This is my sister's house. I promise she'll pay. Just let me get to the door. You can even come with me if you want." He angrily exited the cab as she opened her door. She gingerly got to her feet and winced when she put her weight on her ankle. Another pain gripped her abdomen and she prayed she could make it up the path to the front porch. Gritting her teeth, she began hobbling towards the steps where the driver stood waiting for her, impatiently tapping his foot. One step at a time, she managed to climb up onto the porch of the Acadian-style home, and stumbled as she reached the entry, catching herself on the edge of the screen door. She reached toward the glowing light of the doorbell, when the driver pushed it several times for her.

"We could be here for years, if I waited for you."

She tried to stop the tears, but they began falling from her lashes as she fought the fatigue and pain that threatened to bring her to her knees. The man pushed the bell again, impatiently pressing it several more times before he huffed. She was about to give up when the porch lights turned on, flooding the area with light and making her reflexively close her eyes. They were just opening again when the door opened and she saw Charles' face.

"Oh my God! Lizzy?" he exclaimed as he pushed open the screen and she tumbled toward him. "Jane! Hurry!" He caught her in his arms, gathered her up, and carried her inside.

The last thing Elizabeth heard as the world went dark was the sound of her sister's voice calling out her name.

"Lizzy?"

She heard her name permeate the blackness that engulfed her.

"Lizzy?"

There was a bright sliver of light that made it difficult to open her eyes, but she waited until it became tolerable, her vision slowly returning until she could make out Jane's teary face above her.

"Oh, Lizzy! Thank God!" exclaimed Jane, as she stifled a sob.

"My baby?" Lizzy croaked, barely recognizing her own voice.

"She's fine. Her lungs were a little underdeveloped, so she is in the NICU. But she's beautiful." Lizzy nodded and her sister squeezed her hand. "There's an officer from the police department waiting to ask you some questions."

"I don't want Greg here!" she cried with as much force as she could.

"It's okay. *I* called the police. We need you to give a statement, so they can call a judge for an emergency protective order. That will keep him away until we can make arrangements for a restraining order." Jane's face bore an implacable expression she'd rarely seen as she stated in a vehement tone, "He will *never* come near you or your daughter again, if I have anything to say about it."

Lizzy nodded, reassured by her sister's biting statement. She saw movement in the corner of the room and noticed Charles leave, presuming he was notifying the officer that she was awake.

"Lizzy," called Jane to get her attention. "What are you going to name her?"

Lizzy smiled, and then gasped and clutched at the pain in her face. She felt the cold plastic and rough closure of a wrist brace as her hand cradled her cheek.

"You're going to be sore for a while, but don't worry," said Jane. "You're coming home with us, and we *will* take care of you until you are back on your feet."

A weight felt as if it had been lifted from her chest. "Thank you," she replied with tears in her eyes.

"I told you I'd always be here for you. Charles has told you the same thing since I married him."

"I know. I hoped, but I still worried it would be too much to ask."

"That's nonsense. You'd do the same for me if our roles were reversed." Jane smoothed her sister's hair back from her face, and then reached over to the side table to grab her cell phone. She touched the screen a few times and then held it up to show a tiny pink-wrapped bundle with a pink and blue striped cap. "Now, what are you going to name your beautiful little girl?"

Lizzy finally managed to focus on the picture and began to sob. Jane's arms gingerly wrapped around her, and she spoke soothingly into her sister's ear until her tears were spent and she quieted. Taking a tissue, Jane carefully dried Lizzy's face and held up the phone once more.

"No more stalling," she joked. "This little girl needs a name." Lizzy chuckled, grimacing at the piercing pain in her stomach. "Mel . . . Melanie Jane."

Chapter One

<u>**Wednesday, September 26, 2012**</u>

William Darcy was sitting in his car in front of Netherfield, the old, Acadian-style home of his friend Charles Bingley; a part of him still wondering if he'd made the right decision returning to America.

He'd left almost three years earlier when his father and younger sister, Ana, had tragically perished in an automobile accident. A drunk driver had broadsided their car, and in one night, he'd lost all that remained of his immediate family.

William, the son of Andrew Darcy, a prominent British businessman, and the late Anne Fitzwilliam, an American debutante from an old and wealthy family, had dual citizenship. Devastated, he'd fled the United States to England, bound and determined to separate himself from anything and everything that reminded him of what he'd lost. He'd even sold the family home.

However, upon returning to London, William remembered why his parents had moved to the southern United States and away from Europe and New York City—the paparazzi. At thirty-four years of age, he was a relatively young, wealthy bachelor thrust into the CEO position of a multimillion-dollar conglomerate, and as a result, he was relentlessly followed and photographed. Some of the furor eventually calmed, but it wasn't enough to maintain the privacy William enjoyed living in Meryton.

So, here he was, returned to where he'd spent the majority of his life, back where it had all happened.

Opening his car door, he exited the vehicle. He'd begun walking to the door when he heard it open, and looked to see his friend Charles on the porch waiting for him.

"I was beginning to wonder if you were going to sit in that car all day," said Charles with a broad grin.

Despite the fact that they were as different as night and day, Charles Bingley and William Darcy had been best friends since kindergarten.

Bingley was of average height and athletic build with sandy blond hair and hazel eyes. His open manner had gained him instant popularity in school, and seemed to appeal to the shy and reserved Darcy. William was also athletic, but he was tall, over six feet, with dark, curly brown hair and brilliant sea-blue eyes.

William smiled and held out his hand as he reached the top step of the porch. "It's good to see you," he said. Grasping his hand, Charles wouldn't let it go with just a handshake. He pulled him into a hug and slapped him on the back.

"There'll be none of that formality. We're family."

They had been friends for so long that Charles was insistent that despite the lack of blood connection, they were related. William chuckled and shook his head.

"Of course," he replied. "I apologize."

"And you know that the apology isn't necessary," said Charles, as he turned and opened the door to usher William inside.

As they walked through the house, William studied the interior. The house had been in the Bingley family for generations, and had been given to Charles and Jane approximately a year after their marriage, when Charles' parents moved to Florida.

In the time since they had taken possession of Netherfield, very little had changed. Everything was virtually the same as on William's last visit almost three years ago, with the exception of the pictures scattered throughout the rooms and a new piece of furniture here and there. There were various portraits of Charles with his wife, Jane, as well as a woman and child he couldn't readily identify.

"You've been gone for so long that I can't believe you're here," Charles Bingley gushed, as he showed his childhood friend into the study of his home.

"You know why I couldn't stay here."

"I know," he said sadly. "I believe the last time I saw you in person was . . ."

"The funeral."

12

Charles nodded. "I believe it was."

A cry sounded from a baby monitor to the side of Charles' desk, and they both jumped.

"Melly is awake," said Charles. "I'll be right back."

William studied the room for a moment before his friend returned, carrying a toddler of about two years of age. She was a beautiful little girl with chocolate brown curls and blue eyes.

Darcy looked upon the child in shock. "Charles, she isn't yours?"

"What? Oh no, this is my niece, Melanie," he explained, as he returned to his seat and the little girl cuddled into his lap. "We talk on the phone at least once a week. Do you think I'd forget to mention that we had a baby?"

"I wasn't expecting a child to be here." He knew Charles was correct, but he still hadn't expected to find him taking care of a young child. "So you're babysitting?" William asked incredulously.

"Jane and her sister, Lizzy, take Pilates every Wednesday evening, and I keep little Melly Belly so Lizzy doesn't have to pay for child care." William stared at Charles as he paused for a moment. "Why are you so shocked?"

"I guess because I've never seen you willingly volunteer to babysit. I wish we would've known years ago; you could've watched Ana instead of Caroline," he joked with a smirk.

"Screw you," Charles replied before he looked down to find his niece staring at him. "Shoot! Look what you made me do. If she repeats that, Lizzy will kill me, and then when she's done, my wife will finish the job!"

"She hasn't said a word since you fetched her," said William, still laughing. "Do you really think she'll repeat it?"

"Wait 'til she's truly awake and you'll see. She's two and a half, and will even mimic a cough."

William regarded Charles with a confused expression. "I don't remember a Lizzy at the wedding?"

"No, she wasn't living in Meryton at the time and was unable to attend. She and Jane have always been very close, though."

William nodded as the front door opened and he heard Jane's voice call through the house, "Charles!"

"We're in here, hon!"

A minute later, Jane strode through the door. Jane and Charles had been the perfect couple at every party since their marriage four years ago. Her always perfectly styled blonde hair, blue eyes, and willowy figure invariably attracted looks, but combined with her husband's athletic good looks and similar coloring, they looked as though they could grace the cover of a magazine.

"Oh good, Melly is awake," she exclaimed.

"Auntie Jay!" Melanie grinned as she held out her arms.

"William! It's so good to see you." She picked up her niece and walked over to give him a hug. William stood and embraced Jane before she pulled back to look at him. "We saw by your car that you'd arrived, and Lizzy didn't want to intrude, so she's waiting in her car."

"She knows better than that," chided Charles.

"Yes, she does, but she claims that it was a long day and she wants to get home." Charles nodded as his wife exited the room.

"Where's your luggage? Jane will scold me for not settling you in earlier."

"It may take me a while to find a place to live, and I don't want to intrude for that long," replied William. "I'll just go to the Haye Park Hotel."

"You're just looking for somewhere to rent at the moment?" confirmed Charles.

"Yes, I don't want to buy anything until I'm sure of where I want to purchase."

"You don't regret selling the house, do you?"

14

"No," replied William softly, "I couldn't live there. It just wasn't the same after they were gone."

Charles nodded. "Have they ever been able to discover who was driving the car?"

"No, the police still just have a vague description, and that he couldn't have walked a straight line if he'd tried. They have the blood sample from the interior of the vehicle he'd stolen, but as of yet, it hasn't matched anyone they have on file." William frowned and looked down to study his shoes while he tried to prevent himself from becoming emotional.

"I'm sorry," replied Charles, "I probably shouldn't have asked."

"Don't be sorry. You asked because you care. I appreciate it." He looked up and Charles smiled.

"Well, let's go get your things and get you situated. Given the long plane ride, we'd thought a relaxed evening would be best. I'm going to grill steaks, Jane has already made an apple pie that we'll need to run a few extra miles to burn off tomorrow, and you can go to bed as early as you like."

William laughed. "Thanks, Charles," he said softly. Charles nodded as he followed his friend out of the door.

Elizabeth Gardiner arrived home and looked at the large antebellum home before her. Longbourn was beautiful with its white pillars, old oak trees draped in Spanish moss, and azaleas adding to the grandeur of the old house. The home had been in the Gardiner family for two hundred years. Lizzy's great aunt, Melanie Gardiner, had inherited the property, much to the vexation of Olivia Gardiner Bennet, Lizzy's mother. Olivia felt she should have received at least a portion of the old home since her father, Aunt Mel's brother, had passed away, however, Lizzy's great-grandparents knew that Olivia was a spendthrift, and were worried that she would run the estate into the ground. Aunt Mel loved the home where she was raised, so they were confident she was the person to entrust with the family's legacy. Therefore, Melanie, as the only remaining child, received the old plantation as well as the Gardiner money.

Aside from her sister Jane, Aunt Mel was Lizzy's closest confidant. Essentially, she was the closest thing to a true mother Lizzy had ever known, because Olivia Bennet couldn't claim that she'd ever treated her like a daughter. Due to the close nature of their relationship, her aunt wished to leave the entirety of her estate to Lizzy, and enlisted the help of Jane, an attorney, to make certain that it occurred. Both ladies had known it was only a matter of time before Lizzy's marriage ended, and they knew she would need a place to live. Jane didn't need it; she and Charles had Netherfield. They also ensured that in the event of a divorce, Greg Wickham would be unable to sell the plantation for profit or be awarded the property.

When Aunt Mel died four years ago, Lizzy was in a difficult place. She and Greg were living in Baton Rouge, and he was rarely there. He would come and go and although Lizzy worked, she rarely had money to spare a visit home, since Greg's debts and her bills often took precedence. Without her knowledge, he'd even taken out a mortgage on the house his father had bought for them, which he allowed to fall into default. She had been shocked when the foreclosure documents were served, and had been desperately trying to find a place to live on what little savings she had.

Lizzy didn't have much contact with her parents during the marriage, and had even distanced herself from Jane. When Jane would come to see her, Lizzy never liked seeing the sadness in Jane's eyes when she looked at her. Charles coming along had only made things more difficult. Jane still was saddened by Lizzy's marriage, despite the fact that she attempted to behave otherwise, and Lizzy envied her sister's relationship with Charles, who so obviously loved Jane with his whole heart. He was such a stark contrast to the man she'd married.

All of those factors had left Jane and Charles with little idea of how to reach her. Jane, therefore, acted as trustee of the estate until that fateful night when Lizzy showed up at Netherfield's door.

Lizzy turned to look at her now two-year-old daughter, who was still strapped into her car seat.

"We're home, Melly Belly." The little girl giggled, and Lizzy got out and removed Melanie from her seat. "Let's go inside, shall we?"

She and Melanie had one of their usual evenings. They ate dinner, colored on newsprint that Lizzy had rolled out onto the floor, and wrapped up the night with a cartoon before Melanie was put to bed.

Lizzy, however, was a bit melancholy that evening. She poured herself a glass of wine and seated herself in a wicker rocking chair on the back porch. Taking a sip, she stared at the fireflies at the edge of the forest and the heat lightning in the sky. Normally, she'd spend the evening painting or drawing, but tonight she wasn't in the mood. She was lonely, and simply didn't have it in her to attempt to channel it into her work.

Jane and Charles were wonderful. They always ensured she was included, and they always spent time with her and Melanie. She also had her friend, Charlotte Lucas. They had talked briefly on Lizzy's way home, but it wasn't enough. Truth was, she'd been lonely for years, even before the divorce. There were friends she'd known since she was young, but several of them were still single, and she was so busy with Melanie and work that she rarely saw them. Lizzy sighed as she watched the night sky flash brightly. No answer was coming to mind, so deciding to worry about it later, she returned inside and went to bed.

Chapter Two

William scanned the farmland interspersed with trees on either side of the car.

"Where are we going again?"

"Lizzy lives in an antebellum home named Longbourn, that's located just outside of town," replied Charles, who was driving.

Charles turned onto a paved road surrounded by trees, that quickly forked, and they steered to the left. When the woods cleared, there was a lake with what appeared to be a very large barn on the opposite bank. As he again looked to the left, he saw the large house. He stared at the home in awe. From what he knew of Jane's sister, he didn't understand how she could afford living in such a place.

"I thought you said your sister was an artist. How can she afford the upkeep on a house like this?"

Jane turned so she could see William in the back seat. "The house belonged to my great aunt, who left it to Lizzy when she passed away four years ago. For years, Aunt Mel had requests from people who wished to have outdoor weddings on the property. When our friend Charlotte became a wedding coordinator, my aunt began allowing her to book the affairs. It began small, with a tent for the reception and as the demand grew my aunt expanded a bit to make the venue more marketable. Now there are weddings here nearly year round."

Jane cleared her throat and gestured to the right. "The barn out by the lake is actually a reception hall with a commercial grade kitchen. The facility is very nice; wood floors, Doric columns, a bar. During the months when it's too chilly for an outdoor wedding, some choose to have their ceremony within the hall. The money made from the events has paid for the upkeep, as well as the main house's kitchen remodel last year."

"She doesn't find it intrusive?" William asked.

"Most old homes like this give tours, hold weddings, and operate as bed and breakfasts," explained Jane. "Lizzy values her privacy, so she's kept it to weddings on the grounds, although recently, the reception hall has been rented during the week for business functions, as well. There's parking out along the highway, and for events, a shuttle service brings guests from the lots to the property. Other than the catering trucks and a limo for the couple, there isn't a crowd of cars."

Jane pointed behind the pond next to the barn. "The fencing by the barn separates the wedding guests from the home, as does the pond. The pond narrows at the footbridge, but typically the bride and groom just take pictures on it, so that the house is in the background. There's usually a rope up with a sign not to cross."

She turned to face William once more. "By the way, you weren't incorrect—Lizzy is an artist, but she also teaches a few art classes at the local college." William nodded, truly impressed with the operation.

"Jane?" Charles asked, to garner his wife's attention. "Why is Lizzy mowing?"

"Oh no," Jane sighed. "I hope she hasn't run off Billy again."

Charles groaned. "Charlotte and I both had to convince him to come back after the confrontation they had last year. I don't know if I can persuade him again."

"I don't understand," interjected William. "Is she not supposed to mow?"

"With the reception area and the acreage around the house, there's too much for her to keep up on her own. We hire a landscaping service that takes care of the mowing and keeps everything looking a certain way." Jane chuckled. "Billy Collins, who owns the landscaping company, has had a thing for Lizzy since we were kids. Last year, he proposed marriage, and my sister didn't appreciate his attempt. She told him exactly where he could shove his offer, and the weekend after, we found her mowing around the house. Although, sometimes she does it when she's angry or frustrated about something."

Charles was laughing. "You have to understand. She and Billy weren't even dating. I don't think Lizzy had ever had an issue with him in the past, but she certainly wasn't interested in marrying the man."

Jane picked the story back up from her husband as they neared the house. "They were never really friends, but Lizzy had nothing against him. To be honest, his proposal was offensive. I won't divulge everything he said, but he actually said something to the effect that she could never expect that another offer of marriage would ever be made to her." William raised his eyebrows, wondering what it was that would cause someone to make that kind of a comment.

A dog came up and began trailing the car as they pulled to a stop, and Jane quickly got out of the car, striding to where Lizzy was attacking the grass with a vengeance. William watched as Lizzy halted the mower and began obviously explaining something with large hand movements. As she made a gesture, he noticed one of her fingers was bandaged, and she pointed to the injury as she finished speaking.

"The dog is Bear. You're going to want to wait until I get out of the car," explained Charles. "He's very protective of Lizzy and Mel." Charles stepped out, and began petting the old blue merle Australian Shepherd. He motioned to William that he could get out as well.

William opened his door and rose from the seat. Bear watched him carefully from where he was standing near Charles, and then came over to give him a sniff. William put out his hand for the dog to smell, but Bear backed away and took a place near Charles.

"His trust isn't easily gained, but once it is, he's extremely loyal."

Nodding, William turned his head to see Lizzy steering the mower around to the back of the house. He could see Jane chuckling as she made her way back to the car.

"Well?" Charles inquired.

"3-D design," explained Jane.

Charles began to laugh. "What happened now?"

Jane looked at William as she began to explain. "3-D design is a class Lizzy is teaching. She didn't like the class when she was required to take it, and she's even less enamored of the idea of teaching it. But the university has no one willing to teach the class—well, that and no budget to hire a new instructor—so they've put it on Lizzy's schedule for the last year."

"Why doesn't she like it?" asked William.

"Well, for starters, she isn't a sculptor. Add to that a healthy fear of power saws and the fact that she doesn't have a large amount of experience with the other power tools that are used in the class, and you have the general basis of her contempt." Jane took a deep breath as she removed her purse from the passenger seat of the car and closed the door. "My sister has worried since she began teaching the class that she or one of her students will accidentally cut off her finger in class. Yesterday, she was helping a student, and he shot her in the finger with a nail gun."

William and Charles visibly flinched at the idea. "Oh, no!" exclaimed Charles. "Is she okay?"

Jane laughed. "Yes, she's fine. She had her hand x-rayed at Dr. Ladner's office when the class was over. He also updated her tetanus shot."

"Wait a minute," paused William. "When the class was over?"

Jane nodded. "Uh huh," she replied. "The incident actually happened very early in the class, but Lizzy pulled the nail out and bandaged it up so she could finish teaching."

William's eyebrows lifted, surprised, and although he was reluctant to admit it, impressed.

"Is Melly napping?" asked Charles.

Jane smiled. "She should be waking soon. Lizzy's going to go shower while we finish up the garden."

Charles nodded. "I guess we should get to work then."

"Lizzy has all of the tomatoes and corn picked. She also brought out the tiller so you can turn under the plants that are done." Jane turned and smiled at William. "As I said before we left the house, you can sit on the back porch and read or bark orders."

Laughing, Charles grabbed a bag from the back seat and closed his car door. "There's an occupation where a Darcy excels."

As Jane brought the bag inside, William followed Charles as he began to walk toward the left side of the house. "Lizzy, Jane, and I have been sharing a small vegetable garden since Lizzy took over Longbourn. We often spend Saturdays working on it together, cooking or grilling dinner when we're done."

"How long has Lizzy lived here?"

"For almost two years now. She moved in when Melanie was about five months old."

William began to scan the property. He could see where the drive branched and trailed back. His eyes followed it to a building that he presumed was a garage set back and to the left side of the property where it wouldn't readily be seen from the front or the barn that was across the lake to the right of the house. A door on one corner of the garage had a path made of brick pavers that led through an arbor covered in wisteria to a courtyard behind the house.

As they rounded the corner of the home, the entirety of the courtyard came into view, and William paused to take it all in from right to left. There were pathways framing flowerbeds, and urns placed in a few of the beds. In the center of the maze stood a large fountain that didn't flow, although it appeared to be filled with water.

As his eyes trailed back, he noticed the house made an L shape. Attached to the back of the main building on the opposite side appeared to be the former slave quarters. The doors and windows had been converted to French doors to blend in with the main building. The porches were also all joined, and ran the length of the rear of the house.

The flowerbeds were filled with roses, day lilies, crepe myrtle, agapanthus, and other decorative flowers mixed with herbs, tomatoes, and peppers of different varieties and colors. Behind a small black wrought iron fence, to the back of the courtyard, was what appeared to be a grove of dogwood that eventually blended into the tree line of the forest.

To the left, William's view returned to the garage, and between him and that building was the vegetable garden. There were corn stalks, a couple of vines with some small pumpkins, what appeared to be small pea plants, a few watermelons, cucumbers, and squash. The plot wasn't exceedingly large, but seemed to be well planned.

Charles turned and smiled to his friend. "The courtyard is incredible, isn't it?"

A small smile graced William's face. "It's lovely."

"Jane told me that Lizzy and her aunt drew out the plans themselves when Lizzy was a teenager. Then once the pathways, arbor, fountain and fence were all in place, the two of them planted everything together."

William's eyebrows lifted. "It must have been a lot of work."

"Lizzy will complain about how much work it all is sometimes, but you can tell she loves it. It's the only part of the yard the landscaping service isn't allowed to touch." He looked around at the garden. "Well, I guess we should get going, or we won't be finishing today."

There was the sound of a door closing, and they both turned to find Jane coming to join them. Jane and Charles pulled some gardening tools out of the garage, and William extended a hand.

"What would you like me to do?"

Charles stopped pushing the tiller and studied William's face. "You didn't bring a change of clothes, and this is going to get pretty dirty."

William chuckled. "I'm not afraid of a bit of dirt."

"We brought you along for company, and to meet Lizzy, not work," explained Jane. Regarding her dubiously, he opened his mouth to speak, when Jane cut him off. "Before you get all half-cocked, we aren't setting the two of you up. We spend a good deal of time with Lizzy and our niece, so we thought it would be good for the two of you to become friends."

He relaxed, and Charles stepped closer. "You've been in the office all day every day since you returned from London. Take a break today."

"I'll feel lazy watching the two of you work," he complained.

"Then keep us entertained," suggested Jane.

He sighed as they put themselves to work and William found a swing hanging from an oak tree to the far side of the garden. He chatted with his friends until Charles began running the tiller, mixing the soil where the corn once was. He tried to read his book, but the noise was too loud, so he moved to a rocking chair on the back porch.

There was a light breeze, and he remained there for some time before he heard a voice to one side.

"I'll be right back, Melly!"

He looked up from his book to find Lizzy closing the door and walking over to a gas grill. She turned on the gas and saw him when she looked up as she was lighting it.

"You must be William," she said with a raised eyebrow.

"I am," he replied, "and you're Lizzy."

She nodded and looked under the lid of the grill to ensure it had lit. Her eyes were a brilliant color green, and she had coppery brown hair that trailed down her back in long curls. William thought she looked about five foot six or seven, and she had a pleasing figure that he could not help but admire. Her bare toes peeked out from a long flowing skirt paired with a fitted top that resembled an old-fashioned corset. His reverie ended when he heard a small voice.

"Mama?"

He looked to the door where her daughter stood in the open doorway.

"Hey, sweetie," Lizzy called as she began walking toward the little girl. "Did you get bored with the pots and pans?" Mel nodded, but

24

started when she noticed William. "It's okay. He's a friend of Aunt Jay and Uncle Charles."

William watched as she began to pull her mother, who turned and smiled apologetically, inside the house. As he heard the door close, he turned his attention back to his book, until he heard the door open again and the lilting voice invade his solitude.

"Are you going to help mommy?" Lizzy asked as the toddler followed her out of the door.

"Uh huh."

"Can you please close the door for me?" Little Mel did as she was asked, receiving a thank you for her efforts, and followed her mother, who was carrying a plate of something William couldn't identify out to the grill. He noticed that opening the lid would be difficult with her hands full, so he jumped up from his seat.

"Let me help you."

"Thank you," she responded, as he strode quickly over to where she was waiting.

He opened the grill and looked down at what looked like a tied-up bundle of twigs. "What is that?" he asked rather abruptly.

She paused and looked at him. "It's a leg of lamb," she answered. "The bone is removed and then the meat is seasoned with salt, pepper and garlic. It's wrapped in rosemary that has been soaked in water, then tied together, and grilled." She looked at him worriedly. "Jane and Charles said you like lamb?"

He was entranced, watching as her eyes sparkled as she spoke. "Um . . .I do, but I've never seen it prepared that way."

"Oh," she chuckled. "I saw it on a cooking show once and tried it. It has since become one of my favorites." She looked down to the plate in her hands. "Would you mind holding the plate for a moment?"

"Of course." He noticed that she lifted a work surface from where it was folded down the side of the grill before she took back the dish and set it on the makeshift counter.

25

"Thank you." Lizzy gave him a small smile and he nodded briefly. He then watched her use tongs and a large fork to place the lamb on the grill before she closed the lid. She picked up the plate and turned to face him. "I should go back inside. You're welcome to come in if you become too hot out here."

"Thanks," he said with a small smile.

Lizzy turned and walked to the door as her daughter followed at her heels once more. "Open the door for mommy?"

They were soon inside, and William was left to stare after her, realizing that he was attracted to this woman. He shook his head as he returned to his seat. She would definitely not do. She was an artist, after all, with an odd sense of style, and most importantly, a kid. No, the last thing William Darcy needed was to get involved with a single mother. Shaking his head as if to clear his mind, he returned to his book.

Lizzy eyed William as he sat across from her at the table. The lamb was wonderful, especially paired with the Greek salad she'd prepared on the side, and he'd graciously complimented her on the meal. He seemed everything that was proper and polite since his comment earlier, but she was still bothered by his attitude. He'd joined in the conversations with Jane and Charles; however, other than the compliment on the meal, he hadn't said more than two words in her direction the entire evening. She took a sip of her wine, and glanced around as her three guests chatted away.

"Would anyone like any dessert and coffee?" she asked in a cheerful tone.

"Oh, I saw your chocolate cake in there!" Jane gushed and turned to William. "Lizzy makes the absolute best chocolate cake!"

William gave a small smile. "Perhaps a little later?" he asked. "I'm full at the moment."

She nodded, and stood to begin clearing the dishes from the table. Her daughter picked up her own plate and followed her as she pushed through the swinging door to the kitchen. Lizzy set down the load in the sink and reached down for her daughter's plate.

"Thank you," she said, while Melanie smiled in return. "You're welcome?"

"You welcome," the toddler replied.

The kitchen door swung open, and Jane came in and swooped the little girl into the air as she burst into a fit of giggles. "Why don't I take this giggle box upstairs for a bath and a story?"

"Yay!" cheered Melanie, as Lizzy smiled.

"You don't have to, you know."

"I know," replied Jane, "but I enjoy it. Besides, you won't let her spend the night with us, so I have to get my Melly fix while I'm here." She began to tickle her niece as she was talking.

"What would I do while you took her for the night? Putter about this big house by myself?" Lizzy shook her head vehemently. "No, thanks!"

"You could go out with Charlotte—we could all go out. Have a girls' night out?"

"Jane, Charlotte goes out looking for men. I will not find a man I want to date in a *bar*!"

"You never know," Jane called out in a singsong voice as she carried Melanie out of the door.

Lizzy smiled and shook her head as she thought about her sister. She wouldn't have survived the last two years without her, but Lizzy wasn't a college student any longer. She'd never even been one to party much in college. While she was studying for her masters, there were a group of friends that she'd periodically go out with while Greg was who knows where, but the idea just didn't appeal to her anymore.

She loaded the dishwasher, pressed the button to turn it on, and cleaned up any remaining mess as she wiped down the counters. She hung the towel on the stove handle and walked out of the kitchen toward the living room. As she crossed the foyer of the house, she heard Charles speaking, and crept to where he and William couldn't see her. She knew she shouldn't be eavesdropping, but she wanted to understand what this guy's problem was. Charles praised him to the skies, and to Lizzy he came across as haughty and rude.

"It's called an automata," she heard Charles say. "Lizzy made it in her 3-D design class when she was studying for her BFA." She heard the telltale clicking of the homemade gears turning and knew her project was being tested out.

"It sticks a bit," was the arrogant sounding response.

"They're handmade gears made out of discs of wood and nails. Do you really expect it to operate flawlessly?" exclaimed Charles incredulously.

"It's tolerable for a first try, I suppose," said William in a snotty voice. "But she could hardly expect a serious art collector to buy it."

Lizzy drew herself up to her full height, incensed at the insult to something that she worked so hard to create. She paused as she heard her brother-in-law's voice once more.

"Really, Will?"

"What?"

"Well, you could be a little less critical. Lizzy would probably agree with you about the project. She was proud of the fact that she built it, but she would never presume to try to sell it. She's not a sculptor and she's not mechanically inclined. This was a difficult project for her."

Nodding, Lizzy mumbled, "Darned straight!" The conversation seemed to have ended, so Lizzy decided to remain a minute before she entered the room. She didn't want them to realize their conversation was overheard.

"Lizzy! Melly wanted a kiss good night before I put her in bed," called Jane, as she walked down the stairs, carrying her niece.

Lizzy had just leaned against the wall when she jumped. She whirled around, blanching at being caught listening, while Jane placed the toddler on the floor to run toward her. She lifted her daughter into her arms and rested her on her hip.

28

"I have a kitty," Melanie said happily to her mother as she pointed to her nightgown.

"Yes, you have kitty on your nightie," smiled Lizzy. She gave her daughter a big kiss on the cheek. "And what does a kitty cat say?"

"Mrow!"

Jane smiled and gave a little clap while the little girl beamed. Lizzy suddenly realized the men were standing in the foyer just outside the door to the living room. She turned and gave them a half smile.

"Is it bedtime?" Charles asked as he stepped forward to give his niece a kiss on the cheek. "Good night, sweetie." Melanie gave him a noisy kiss in return, and everyone smiled.

"Sweet dreams," William said with a small curve to his lips that almost appeared to be the beginnings of a smile.

Lizzy gave her daughter a kiss. "Sleep tight, and don't let the bed bugs bite," she whispered in Melanie's ear, hugging her tightly. "I love you, my Melly." The toddler returned the hug and gave her mother a kiss.

"Night night, Mama."

Jane reached out her arms, and Lizzy passed Melanie to her. The two proceeded back up the stairs, and Lizzy turned to face Charles and William.

"I'm thinking it's time for coffee and cake," Charles grinned, rubbing his mid-section.

Lizzy laughed. "I prepared everything earlier. Just give me a minute to go cut the cake."

The men returned to the living room, and she made her way back to the kitchen to dish out the dessert and place it and the coffee on a tray for the four of them.

The remainder of the evening passed similarly to the first. Charles and William reminisced a good deal about the past and Jane laughed and joined in by asking questions as well as making comments. However, while Lizzy's sister and brother-in-law included her in the conversation, William Darcy did not.

What was even stranger was that periodically, Lizzy would feel as though someone was watching her, and glance over to find William staring at her. He'd quickly look away, but it disconcerted her. She decided he must have found something he couldn't like about her, and looked at her only to find more of her faults. This continued until Jane and Charles declared they were exhausted from all of the work that afternoon and the three of them departed to go to Netherfield. Turning off the lights and preparing for bed, Lizzy decided that regardless of the why, she'd think of William Darcy no more and went to bed.

William was once again in the back seat for the return trip to Netherfield. "Why have I never met Lizzy before?"

"Hmm?" asked Jane as she turned in her seat.

"Well, the two of you seem so close, but she wasn't at your wedding." He knew he'd brought up the subject with Charles before, but he still found it odd that she hadn't been at such an important day in her sister's life.

"No, she wasn't." Jane rested the side of her head on the headrest. "She was unable to attend." He waited for a moment for either Jane or Charles to clarify, but neither did. "It's really Lizzy's story to tell, and I try to respect that. I hope you understand."

"Of course." He didn't really understand, but since he didn't feel like it was right to press the issue, he let the subject drop.

William reclined his head on to the headrest of the back seat, while Jane turned and began a conversation in soft tones to Charles in the front of the car.

When William had first seen Jane's sister mowing the yard, she was farther away, she'd had her hair pulled up on top of her head, and she was wearing ratty clothes. He hadn't spared her a second glance. But when she came outside after she'd taken a shower and changed, he'd been able to look at her—really look at her. Her hair was a brown color, but when the sun hit it, there were coppery red and blonde highlights that made it stand out from just simple brown. Her body seemed fit and she appeared to have just the right proportions in all of her assets.

Although, who knew what was hidden under those clothes—stretch marks, flabby skin? She did have a kid, after all. Speaking of her daughter, who was the child's father? She wasn't married, and neither Jane nor Charles had ever mentioned a husband, so she'd probably never been married. He didn't even want to imagine the criticism he'd endure from his family if they had any idea that he was even remotely attracted to her.

He'd realized the attraction during their first face-to-face meeting, but he still held fast to his belief that she was the last thing he needed. He even recognized that he didn't really believe any of the negative ideas about her, but he clung to them nonetheless, to squash the attraction. But what he couldn't get out of his head were her eyes—emerald green, warm, intelligent. Keeping his own eyes off of her had been impossible; his line of vision was continually drawn to her.

He closed his eyes and sighed. He couldn't avoid Lizzy in the future, especially while he resided with the Bingleys. He would just have to be very careful not to show her his admiration, or excite any expectation in her. William Darcy couldn't afford the distraction that Lizzy presented.

Chapter Three

"There you are!" Jane exclaimed, as Lizzy opened the door to the large kitchen and entered.

"Sorry we're late. There was a wreck on the highway."

A look of alarm crossed her sister's face. "I hope no one was hurt."

"It looked like someone tried to stop rather quickly at the intersection of Jennings Road and 240. I think the people behind him were following too close. The sheriff's department was there and I saw no ambulance, so I would imagine everyone is okay."

Jane appeared relieved. "That's good. Don't worry about being late. Dinner will actually be ready in about twenty minutes. Where's Melanie?"

"With Uncle Charles," Lizzy smiled. "He offered to play horsey, and she decided that he was much cooler than mommy."

Laughing, Jane gestured to where she had some wine glasses on the counter. "Would you like a glass of wine? I have that moscato you like so much."

"That's evil, Jane. You know I have to drive home."

"Nonsense, we have plenty of room. You can spend the night and go home tomorrow morning."

Lizzy chuckled as she shook her head. "You already have a guest. I wouldn't want to intrude."

"Will? A guest?" Jane questioned. "No, he's family, just as you are, and I'm sure he wouldn't care in the least if you and Melly stayed." Jane went to the freezer, took out the bottle of wine, and removed the cap from the top. She poured Lizzy a glass before she resumed cutting vegetables for the salad. "You've never had a problem staying with us for a night—guest or no guest—so why are you suddenly avoiding it?"

Grimacing, Lizzy tried to quickly think of an excuse. "Collins and his crew are coming early to mow and work on the landscaping in the front. I need to be there to put Bear inside. You know how he hates Billy."

"Elizabeth Grace Bennet, you're lying to me." Jane put down the knife and leaned forward on the kitchen's island. "Tomorrow's Sunday, and you know darn good and well that Billy Collins would have to be deathly ill to miss church."

"Gardiner," Lizzy corrected.

"I know it's Elizabeth Gardiner, but for twenty-one years, you *were* a Bennet. I do understand why you decided to use the name Gardiner though." Jane picked up the knife and put it back down. "You won't distract me that easily. Why won't you stay?"

Lizzy picked up a cucumber and took a small bite. She chewed a bit and swallowed. "I don't think Charles' friend likes me very much."

"William?" she asked, surprised. "I don't see why he wouldn't."

Sighing, Lizzy went through her encounters with him the week before, as well as told her what she overheard when she was in the foyer.

"So! He doesn't like your project. You don't like it either."

"That's not completely true," Lizzy defended herself.

Jane exhaled. "I don't know why he behaved that way, but he's a really nice guy. Promise me you'll give him a chance."

"Jane," whined Lizzy.

"Promise me!" she insisted, but Lizzy shook her head. "Lizzzzzzyyy, for me?"

"Fine! I promise! Happy?"

Laughing at the ploy that had worked since they were young, Jane resumed chopping as her sister rolled her eyes. "Yes," she smiled smugly

When she was finished preparing the salad, Jane stopped to pull the pork loin from the oven and place it on the dining room table while Lizzy went to call the men and Melanie from the living room.

"How were classes this week, Lizzy?" asked Charles, before taking a bite of his food.

"They went well, thanks."

William looked up from his plate as she answered the question. "I understand from Jane and Charles that you're an instructor for a design class. Do you teach any others?"

"I do teach a kind of introduction to sculpture class called 3-D Design, but I also teach two levels of watercolor, and a beginning drawing class."

"And can you do all of these things that you teach?"

Lizzy bristled and looked to Jane, who smiled encouragingly. Lizzy knew from experience that her sister was imploring her to be nice. "3-D design isn't my specialty, but I can make the projects required for the class. My degree is in painting, and watercolor is my medium of choice, so yes, I'd like to think that I'm slightly qualified to teach the watercolor class. As for drawing, I took drawing classes when I received my BFA, and when I was working on my masters some of the drawing professors would allow me to sit in their classes and take their classes for practice."

"Do you think drawing is important for a painter?" he asked.

"I'm sure there'd be some who would argue that it's not," she stated carefully. "I'd suppose that it depends on the type of paintings the artist produces. Personally, I find it to be invaluable."

She looked down to check on Melanie, who was eating her cucumbers quietly, and then looked back to the table. While she'd been distracted, Charles had asked William a question and they'd become engrossed in a conversation about work. She glanced to Jane, who gave a small smile. Realizing that Charles had deflected his friend after a silent communication from Jane, Lizzy gave a small chuckle.

"Thanks," she mouthed. Jane nodded and the meal continued. William didn't ask her any more questions, and almost seemed to forget she was there, with the exception of the occasional staring. Since it was no different than the way he'd behaved before, she tried not to let it bother her as she finished her meal. Jane and Charles sometimes would pull her into the conversation, but everything seemed to pass much like the dinner at Longbourn.

When dinner concluded, William and Charles went into the living room while the ladies cleaned up the table and the kitchen.

"Would you like a drink?" Charles asked as William took a seat.

"Scotch sounds good."

Charles fixed them both drinks, and after handing William his, took a seat across from him. "So, what's up with you and Lizzy?"

"What?" he choked out. "Nothing, why?"

"Well, the question you asked her at dinner," laughed Charles. "I don't often see you put your foot in your mouth the way you did. Of course, I haven't seen you around someone you're genuinely attracted to in years."

"I simply asked her a question. I don't see how I said anything wrong." William thought back to the question. He'd been genuinely curious. He often donated money to arts groups, and had been to his fair share of art openings as a result, but he knew very little about the education of an artist at the university level. Also, thinking back to some of those openings, he didn't think drawing was important to some of the work he'd viewed. "And I'm not interested in her."

"You basically asked her if she was qualified to teach her classes, something that's between her and the university." Charles took a sip of his scotch as he chuckled. "Not interested, my ass."

William looked up, surprised at Charles' statement.

"You stare at her whenever she isn't looking, and you almost exclude her from the conversation when we're all together. At first, I thought that perhaps you just didn't like something about her, but tonight I caught the way you watched her when she was brushing her hair back from her face, and realized you're *avoiding* her."

"Okay, so I *am* attracted to her," he confessed in a frustrated tone. "But I can't do anything about it."

"Why ever not?"

"She's a single mother and probably a bohemian for goodness sakes! Could you imagine my Aunt Catherine's reaction to that?"

Charles rolled his eyes. "So what? Do you think Caroline likes Jane? Do you honestly think I care that she doesn't? You need to live your life for yourself, not for others." He shook his head. "I'd forgotten what an insufferable snob you can be."

"Pardon?"

"Bohemian? Lizzy does not fit that description. She has her own sense of style, but I can assure you she's far from the free love, hippie type that you're accusing her of being." William gave a small humph. "Lizzy is very pretty, intelligent, and immensely talented. You barely know her; stop judging her."

They heard the ladies coming from the kitchen, and both took a sip of their drinks, acting as though they'd been sitting quietly the whole time. Jane came through the door followed by Lizzy and Melanie.

"Do y'all need anything? There's more wine in the kitchen."

Charles shook his head. "Thanks, hon, but we're both drinking scotch."

Jane smiled. "I've been trying to get Lizzy to play piano. She hasn't played for us in a while."

"I haven't had much time to practice lately."

"You still play well. I certainly never had the ability like you, and we have the piano that just sits there waiting for you to play since neither Charles nor I do."

Lizzy laughed. "You aren't going to let up, are you?"

"Nope," Jane said, smiling.

"I would begin if she did," Charles interjected. "You know how much we enjoy it."

William watched as Lizzy rolled her eyes and, handing her daughter to Jane, took her place at the piano.

"Do you have any preferences, Jane?"

"You know what I want to hear."

Nodding, Lizzy placed her hands upon the keys and began to play; the dulcet sounds of Debussy's Clair de Lune permeating the quiet of the room. William's initial thoughts were of his sister. He missed the sound of her playing, and while Lizzy's playing wasn't as proficient as Ana's, she had a remarkable sense of expression that he found compensated for any technical deficiencies. He remained captivated until the final strains echoed through the room and the piece was finished. After a brief pause, she began the second movement of Beethoven's Sonata Pathétique.

When she was done, she quietly stood and walked over to where Jane was sitting with Melanie sleeping in her lap. Lifting her daughter, she left the room briefly to take her upstairs. When she had disappeared, they began conversing freely, and Lizzy joined in when she returned five minutes later.

William was having difficulty attending to the discussion. The more he was around Lizzy, the more infatuated he became. He found it frustrating, although not as frustrating as when he discovered that she'd be sleeping just down the hall from him. Sleep took a long time to overtake him that night.

Wednesday, October 10, 2012

"So, let me get this straight. He doesn't like any of the rental properties he's seen so far, so he's asked to rent your guest house?" Lizzy asked Jane incredulously as she drove them to Pilates that Wednesday.

"He wants to pay rent, but Charles and I would never accept any money from him. He insists on paying a portion of the utilities though." Jane shrugged as she smiled. "It'll be nice to have him close by."

Lizzy rolled her eyes. "You and Charles are too nice, Janie."

"A nice lawyer is a contradiction—doesn't exist." Lizzy smiled at her sister's long time joke. "Charles will, of course, see him at the office, but we'll probably only see him for a meal on the weekends. Other than that, he'll be back and forth from work and whatever else he does. He's worked some pretty long hours since he's returned to the states."

"Is that unusual?"

"According to Charles, it is. William can work from anywhere, which is why he was able to relocate to England so easily after the death of his father and sister almost three years ago."

Lizzy looked surprised. "You've never mentioned that. How did they die?"

"They assume a drunk driver. Witness reports say that the individual responsible was driving erratically and that he fled from the scene, but it was dark, so there isn't much of a description."

"The police have never found the driver?"

"No, the car was stolen and the prints lifted from inside the car didn't match anyone in the database."

"How sad," said Lizzy. She may not have liked William, but she would never wish something like that on anyone.

"It was very tragic. His sister, Ana, had just turned eighteen and was leaving that fall for Juilliard. She was an incredibly gifted pianist."

"Does he have any family left?"

"His mother died of cervical cancer when he was twenty. He has aunts and cousins, but I believe he's only really close to one uncle, his wife and his cousin Richard." Jane took a breath. "I know he's been a bit of an ass to you."

38

"A bit?" Lizzy raised her right eyebrow.

"Okay, I know he's been an ass to you, but I think he's closed himself off to everyone for so long . . ."

"Don't go making excuses for him," said Lizzy, parking the car. "Yes, I feel bad about what happened with his family and that it's just him, but it doesn't excuse the way he behaves. He's not a child, and he *should* know common courtesy." She turned off the engine and pulled out the key, pausing before she got out of the car. "I don't want to argue with you about him. He's Charles' friend, and yours as well, but it doesn't mean that I have to like him. And, if we don't get into class, we're going to be late."

Jane sighed. "Let's go."

Saturday, October 20, 2012

Jogging on the treadmill, William looked through the panels of glass before him. Below, the indoor pool of the gym was an eye catching, brilliant blue. He watched the children playing in the small wading pool, and the adults swimming laps in the lanes as the music from his MP3 player drowned out the sounds of the machines surrounding him.

Running always seemed to clear his head, and he was determinedly attempting to put a certain siren with vibrant green eyes out of his mind, when the subject that pervaded his thoughts these days entered the pool area as if summoned.

Her daughter was holding her hand while she made her way to where a few toddlers were standing with some lifeguards. Lizzy laughed as she spoke with one of the older guards, and William smiled. The lifeguard then took Melanie's hand and led the children into the shallow pool for the toddlers. He watched with rapt attention as Lizzy removed her simple dress to reveal her swimsuit underneath.

He was mesmerized as he studied the curves he longed to explore. Her body appeared to be everything he'd imagined, but he quickly decided that there must be some imperfection that the one-piece suit covered.

He watched as she gingerly lowered herself into the pool, assuming the water must be cold by her hesitance. Once she seemed acclimated and put on her goggles, she began fluidly swimming back and forth through the water. He was spellbound, and jogged for much longer than he'd planned, when he realized the time. Shaking his head, he slowed to a brisk walk before he gradually tapered the machine to a stop.

"This obsessing is getting ridiculous," he muttered forcefully to himself. William turned his back on where the object of his fantasies was still gliding through the water. He made valiant attempts to put her from his mind while he worked on his weight training, but she hovered there, refusing to leave him despite his best efforts. Eventually, he gave up and retreated to the locker room for a cold shower.

Chapter Four

The week had been busy. William's cousin, Richard, had flown in from England on Monday, so due to his arrival in town and their work obligations, William had managed to avoid Lizzy until Halloween. Jane and Charles were planning a small get together, which included taking Melanie trick-or-treating, dinner, and spending an evening together. He'd hoped to politely decline, but Richard, not realizing his cousin's hesitance, accepted the invitation on behalf of the two of them before William could open his mouth.

As a result, he was in a bad mood as they walked from house to house, while Jane and Charles gushed over Melanie, who was dressed as a black and white cat. What was putting him in an even worse mood was watching his cousin ogle and flirt with Lizzy. Richard had stayed by her side since they left Netherfield, and William was relieved when Lizzy announced they were finished after five or six houses.

"That's it?" questioned Charles, who was eager to dive into Melanie's spoils.

"She's two, Charles! She doesn't need a boatload of candy, and Jane has dessert waiting at the house. I'd much rather have her Boo Brownies than those little fruit candies everyone's given her."

"Thank you, Lizzy," said Jane, laughing.

"Don't mention it."

Once they returned to the house, Melanie refused to let Lizzy take off her costume, so she sat at the dinner table next to her mother, occasionally meowing and giggling.

William sat and jealously watched Richard, who continued to talk to Lizzy. Meanwhile, he was relegated to the other end of the table, not included in their cozy conversation. He didn't like it. He didn't like it one bit. Why did Richard always have such an easy time conversing with people? Why did she seem to enjoy his flirting so much? She seemed reasonably intelligent. Couldn't she see through Richard's corny lines and innuendo?

When the interminable meal finally concluded, Jane and Lizzy went to the kitchen to clean up the dishes while Charles, Richard and

William went to Charles' study, where he handed them each a tumbler of scotch.

Richard laughed at his cousin, "William, the scowl on your face has been frightening tonight. You should watch out. Your face might stick that way."

Charles guffawed. "You do realize that he's pissed you're monopolizing Lizzy tonight."

William gave a warning glance to his friend. "Shut up, Charles," he growled. Richard, whose eyes widened as he regarded his cousin oddly, was surprised at William showing that much interest in a woman. Luckily, Richard hadn't had time to respond before Jane poked her head in.

"Honey, would you help Melly with her bath and getting ready for bed while we finish up?"

Smiling broadly, Charles nodded. "I think now's as good a time as any to get out of Dodge." Jane gave him a questioning look as they exited the room.

Richard waited until everyone had been gone for a few moments before sitting across from William. "If you like the woman, then why aren't you speaking to her? You're never going to get anywhere scowling at her."

"I don't scowl at her," groused William, "and I've no intention of going anywhere."

"Why ever not?" he asked incredulously. "She's intelligent, witty, and, not that I need to point it out, sexy as hell." He laughed when William glowered again. "Has she shot you down?"

William set his drink down on the end table with a thud. "No, but that's because I haven't asked her."

"Like I asked before, why ever not?"

"She's hardly suitable, Richard."

Richard was again visibly surprised. "You're serious!"

42

"Of course I'm serious. Plus, how would it look if I dated an unwed mother. Could you imagine your parents' reaction, or even Aunt Catherine?"

"First of all," began Richard, "what Aunt Catherine thinks should be irrelevant. Her opinions should *never* be taken into consideration, especially when making a life altering decision. I would've hoped that you knew that by now."

The corner of William's lips twitched as he attempted not to laugh. "Regardless..."

"As for my parents, have you forgotten about my sister?"

"What about Jessica?"

"She was only married a year ago, and Brit is two, remember. My parents may not have been happy when she became pregnant, but they accepted it and their grandchild. It would be pretty hypocritical of them to criticize you for dating a woman just because she was unmarried and had a child."

"I hadn't forgotten about her, but the situation is a bit different. Don't you think? I mean Jessica is their daughter, while Lizzy is someone I'd be dating. I believe they'd see the two as completely different. They really had no choice but to accept Jessica's situation." William raised his eyebrows, feeling he'd made a good point and that Richard's arguments wouldn't hold water.

"They're going to be more worried about whether you're happy and whether the woman truly cares for you. A child will be the least of their concerns. Besides, that little girl is adorable. She'll have my parents wrapped around her little finger in a matter of minutes." Richard observed his cousin closely. "It's more than just the fact that she has a child, isn't it?"

"She's also an artist. She could be a hippie, free-love type, for all I know."

Richard laughed. "You've never really spoken to her have you?"

"Well, no," William responded, "I didn't want to give her the idea that I was interested."

Rolling his eyes, Richard took a drink. "I know that I just met her, but I don't get the impression that she has much experience with men."

"Why would you think that?"

"There's just something innocent in the way she responded to my flirting tonight. While her responses were witty, she seemed kind of shy with her answers, as if she was unsure."

"Only you'd notice something like that," William commented before Charles walked back through the door. "I thought you were getting Melanie ready for bed."

"It doesn't take that long to bathe a two-year-old and put on pajamas," chuckled Charles.

A minute later, little Melanie came through the door wearing her favorite character pajamas and toddled up to William. She crawled up onto the sofa and maneuvered herself into his lap. "Hi Willyum," she said as she hugged him and gave him a kiss on the cheek.

He glanced up to see Charles and Richard suppressing laughter and then looked back down to the little girl's face. He remembered Ana sitting in his lap, and smiled sadly. As he studied her, he couldn't help but notice how much she looked like Lizzy. The resemblance was uncanny, with the exception of the eyes. Melanie had blue eyes, much like his own.

"Hello, sweetheart," he responded, as she nestled into his arms.

Richard seemed to study William, "When was the last time you were in a relationship?"

"What does that have to do with this?"

"You rarely dated after Aunt Anne died, and to the best of my knowledge, you haven't had any kind of a relationship since the accident. Frankly, you're probably so uptight because of how sexually frustrated you are."

Glaring at a chortling Charles, he exclaimed, "I've taken dates to functions."

"I'm not speaking of the uptight socialites that you brought with you to charity galas and such, or that date Aunt Catherine set up with Anne de Bourgh. I mean a real relationship. One that has lasted beyond a single date."

William huffed. "I just don't understand why it's relevant."

"It's relevant, because all of your excuses about why you won't ask out Lizzy are bullshit."

"Excuse me?" He looked down to see that Melanie had thankfully just drifted off to sleep.

"You heard me the first time." Richard leaned forward in his seat. "You took time to grieve, which is fine, but now I think you're looking for reasons to avoid Lizzy because you're afraid to become attached to someone. It's possible that you see her as someone you could lose your heart to, and that scares you to death."

William looked over to see Charles' eyebrows had almost reached his hairline. "I have to say, he makes a very good point." Charles took a seat and leaned toward William in much the same manner as his cousin. "Add to that your natural reticence toward anyone you don't know well, and it explains the ridiculous excuses you've fabricated."

"Aunt Catherine's reaction wouldn't be accepting, but she wouldn't accept anyone she hadn't hand-picked to marry you."

"Who said anything about marriage?" asked William, with wide eyes.

"Well, if you'd stop putting your foot in your mouth around her, who knows?" Charles looked down into his glass. "Beneath the scowling and the size twelve loafer between your teeth, you're a good man, William. She needs that."

He looked at his friend strangely, but didn't have time to react before Jane and Lizzy entered the room. He looked over to see an expression of astonishment on Lizzy's face, and wondered why it would be directed at him.

Lizzy was shocked when she came in the room to find her daughter sleeping soundly in William Darcy's lap. What was even more incredible was that he didn't seem to mind it in the least. In fact, he was stroking her hair softly as he spoke with Charles.

She'd noticed early on how handsome he was, but he'd often ruined her appreciation of his looks with his haughty demeanor. Now, he was sitting there, cradling Melanie in such a gentle manner, that she found herself genuinely attracted to him. What was it about a man holding a baby that could generate lust in the most frigid of women? Jane had commented after Melly was born how sexy she found Charles when he held the baby. Lizzy had never seen Charles as anything more than her brother, so she hadn't truly understood the comments until now.

Unfortunately, the sexy man now holding her daughter routinely made her wish to slap him. His eyes left Charles and met her own as he gave her a small smile. If she hadn't known that everyone was already in the room, she would've turned to look behind her to see who he could be smiling at. She made her way across the room and leaned over in front of him.

"I hope she hasn't been a problem. I'll take her upstairs to bed."

He frowned, "She's fine. I was happy to put her to sleep." Her gaze left his to study her daughter as she slept, only to find William tilting his head to catch her eyes. "She's only been asleep for a few minutes though, so you may want to wait a bit to move her."

"I couldn't let her bother you that way."

He smiled. "She's not an inconvenience. I promise."

Lizzy straightened up and looked to find Jane watching her with a small smile. What was even more unsettling was the way William Darcy was smiling at her. Puzzled, she took a seat next to Jane, and proceeded to speak with her sister over their plans for the holidays. After about ten minutes, she gathered up Melanie and took her upstairs. She returned after tucking her in to find everyone discussing her upcoming show.

"Lizzy paints landscapes from photographs that she takes," explained Jane, as Lizzy re-entered the room. "She even included some of her photos in her last show."

46

"It wasn't many. Most of the photography belonged to Dalton."

"Your photography isn't abstract like Dalton's, so it's pretty easy to tell them apart," laughed Charles.

"You've said that you prefer watercolors. Is that the kind of work you're going to display?" asked William.

"They're all watercolor, and like Jane said, a few photographs."

William thought back to what he remembered of Meryton before he had moved. "I wasn't aware that Meryton had much of an art community."

"We have quite a few artists, but most of the locals would prefer to go buy their artwork at the local home décor store than to shop at a gallery." Lizzy wasn't sure why he seemed interested, but she figured she would go ahead. "My friend Charlotte's father, Alan Lucas, bought the old train depot several years ago, and renovated the place in order to save the historic building from being demolished. It's probably as old as Netherfield and Longbourn, but no one had ever bothered with it. He often rents it for small musical performances, parties, and such, but for two months before Christmas, he allows my friends and me to have a show and to leave our work up for the season. Downtown Meryton has a big tourist trade at Christmas. People come to see the antebellum homes decorated for the holidays, and we sell a good bit to them. Occasionally, we sell a work to someone who attended a party or a performance there."

"Do you have an official opening?" questioned Richard.

"Next Friday is an official reception that will open the show."

"Excellent," he exclaimed. "I don't leave until Saturday, so I can see your work."

"You assume it's open to the public," said Darcy, with an edge to his voice.

Lizzy bristled at his tone. "Anyone is welcome. The reception is even advertised in the local paper." She watched as William seemed to clench his teeth, but he nodded.

"Jane and I were already planning on attending," interceded Charles with a smile. "We could all have dinner beforehand, and perhaps go out for drinks after."

"I would need a sitter if we do that."

"Melly loves Mrs. King, and she lives just around the corner," Jane suggested. "The two of them could stay here, and the two of you can spend the night."

"I don't know, Jane," she replied. "You know how I feel about leaving her."

"She'll be fine," reassured Jane. "I'll call Mrs. King tomorrow and ask."

Lizzy exhaled. She knew that Jane felt she should get out more than she did, but other than the university childcare program, Lizzy really only trusted Jane and Charles with her daughter. Mrs. King had watched Melanie a few times when she was younger, but she was an elderly lady, who didn't get around well. Now that her daughter was more mobile, it made Lizzy nervous. "It's getting late, and I teach a morning class tomorrow. I think I should say good night."

"It's still early," exclaimed Jane. "You can't go to bed yet."

She looked around to find everyone watching her. She gave Richard a small smile, and out of the corner of her eye, saw his cousin with a frown on his face. Suppressing the urge to roll her eyes, she leaned over to hug her sister. "I'm sorry, but I'm tired. I'll see everyone at breakfast. Good night."

As she was walking out of the room, she heard Jane say in her usual happy voice, "Will, we're going to expect you and Richard for breakfast in the morning."

Lizzy sighed. She'd had a firm idea of what she thought William Darcy was, and then tonight he surprised her by willingly holding her daughter. She was supremely uncomfortable with how attractive she found him in that moment, and then he ended the night by giving her that glowering look. *Perhaps the incident with Melly was an aberration, I'm sure I'll find him just as disagreeable as ever in the morning.*

48

Meanwhile, William had tuned out everyone around him as he nursed his second scotch of the night. Two years had passed since his father and Ana had died, and he was tired of being alone. Could Richard be right, and he was making excuses? Did it really matter that Lizzy already had a child? There was also the question of the father. Who was he, and was he a part of Melanie's life?

As he gave it further thought, he came to the conclusion that Melanie was an adorable child, and he'd always wanted children. What would it hurt to include her in their number? Would Lizzy want to have more?

Lizzy was intelligent, articulate, and she seemed to have no problems making friends, if her manner with Richard was typical. He thought that she'd probably do very well at a business dinner or charity event, since there were times that he couldn't avoid attending those sorts of functions. Perhaps he should reconsider, and give Lizzy a chance?

He was absorbed in his thoughts when he was suddenly brought back to reality by the voice of Richard. "Earth to William?" Looking up, he found everyone staring.

"I'm sorry. I must've zoned out for a bit. You were saying?"

"I was thinking of calling it a night," explained Richard. "If you aren't ready to return to the guest house yet, I'd appreciate a key."

"No, I'm ready." He stood as Jane and Charles led the way to the backdoor. They made arrangements for what time they would meet for Lizzy's show, and everyone exchanged goodnights before William and Richard made the trek to the small house at the back of the property.

The next morning, everyone was chatting casually as they ate breakfast, comparing their days and making plans for the next week.

"Mama," came Melanie's voice from next to Lizzy, as she was eating her bacon.

"Yes, Melly."

"My ceweal is fwustwated."

"What?" Lizzy looked to Jane, who was suppressing the urge to burst into a fit of laughter.

"My ceweal is fwustwated," Melanie repeated, as if she couldn't understand what was unclear about it.

Charles coughed in an effort not to laugh and Lizzy looked up clearly amused. "Do you know where this came from?"

"I think she heard that word last night," Charles responded, as he looked to Richard and William.

Based on the looks the guys were giving each other, she could only assume that they were discussing something that wasn't suitable for Melanie, and fortunately, she'd only picked up the word, frustrated. "I really don't want to know, *gentlemen*. Just do me a favor, and in the future, make sure the subject matter isn't something I'd mind her repeating."

"Yes, ma'am," said Charlie, still muffling a chuckle.

"Of course," replied William, who was eyeing Richard.

She rolled her eyes and turned back to her daughter to discover she was eating her cereal despite its "frustrated" state, deciding that if she was eating, she should leave it alone. Lizzy returned her attention to her own breakfast as she continued her conversation with Jane.

When breakfast was over, Lizzy grabbed her overnight bag and placed it in her car. She came back for her daughter, who was showing William her stuffed kitty.

"She's very pretty," Lizzy heard him say, as Melanie gave him a huge grin and hugged her toy close to her. Watching, she was still rather dumbfounded at how someone who had been so disagreeable could be so sweet with her child. Why was he normally not like this?

"Come on, Melly Belly, it's time for school." The little girl ran and jumped into Lizzy's arms and turned to wave at William.

50

"Bye."

"Bye," he said as he waved back, then looked inquisitively to Lizzy. "She goes to school?"

"The childcare center on campus is kind of like a preschool. They have classroom time, so we call it school." He nodded as he gave Lizzy a small smile. "I apologize, but I really need to go." She gestured toward the door.

"Oh, of course," he replied, as he opened the door for them. "I'll walk you out."

She heard him say it, but it still did not lessen the shock. He must've seen Melanie's seat in the back of her ancient compact car, because he jumped forward to open the door that made a loud grinding noise as he pulled. Wincing at the sound, Lizzy buckled her daughter in, and he closed the door and stepped back to open hers.

"Thanks," she replied in an awkward manner, as she stepped into her car. He closed the door for her and moved away a bit as she put the key in the ignition, attempting to figure out what had come over the man. When she turned the key, her car wouldn't start. Lizzy made several attempts, but no matter what she tried, the engine wouldn't turn over. Managing to contain the urge to curse, she hit the steering wheel, and opened the door to find William still standing there.

"Why don't we move your things into my car, and I can give you a ride? The university isn't far from my office."

"No...thanks," she responded, "I can get a ride with Charles or I can call a cab. I don't want to put you out."

"Charles and Richard have a morning meeting with a client, so Charles won't be on that side of town until later this afternoon. And a cab is just silly when I'm already going in that direction." He pulled his keys from his pocket and unlocked his car.

She exhaled heavily. She didn't want to feel indebted to this man, but he didn't seem to want to take no for an answer.

"I thought you said that you really needed to go."

"I do," she bristled.

"Then I don't see that you have much of an alternative."

With a huff, she opened the door to the back seat and began unbuckling her daughter. "Let's go, Melly. We're riding with William to school." Melanie gave a cheer, and she stood next to her while she unstrapped the car seat. When she got everything unhooked, she pulled it out to find William's outstretched arm.

"Let me get that for you while you grab anything else you need."

She handed him the seat and dug out the messenger bag that served both as a purse and an art bag, slinging it over her shoulder as she walked toward what appeared to be a sporty, black electric sedan.

"Wait a minute," she exclaimed, as she saw him beginning to put the car seat on what she suddenly realized were probably leather seats. She grabbed something out of her car and ran to where he was standing by the rear door to his vehicle. "Let me put this under it, so it doesn't ruin the leather."

He shrugged in a nonchalant manner. "I doubt it would, but thanks." He stood there for a moment before running a hand through his hair. "I'm going to go let Jane and Charles know about your car and that I'm giving you a ride. They might worry if they find it out here later."

She nodded as he placed Melanie's seat back in the car, and she moved forward to begin strapping it back in while he walked inside. By the time it was installed and she'd finished securing her daughter, he'd returned.

"Jane said she'd call Mr. Long and see if he could look it over today."

"Thanks," she responded while she closed the back door. She then watched as he walked around the front of the car, beating her to her door, which he opened. Lizzy thanked him again, rather softly, and took a seat with her bag on the floorboard in front of her.

He climbed into his seat and turned on the car, which with its electric motor was very quiet. She watched him for a few minutes as he pulled out of the drive and turned to look at her for a moment.

"Is something wrong?"

"No," she replied. "Thank you for the ride."

"You're welcome," he checked traffic before he made a turn. "Jane indicated that your car breaks down a lot. Perhaps it's time to get a new one."

"I'm sure it is, but I'm still saving for it."

"The repair bills have got to be eating away at whatever you're saving. A car note would be preferable to continuing to put money into a car that needs more and more work. Plus, what if you and Melanie get stranded on the side of the road during the night?"

Lizzy turned toward the window and watched the passing buildings as they made their way closer to town. She didn't want to explain that her credit was shot due to her marriage to Greg. She'd once checked into a loan co-signed by Jane and Charles, but the interest rate was still through the roof, and she was unwilling to pay that when it would only take her another year or so to save the remainder of the money. As she was pondering the dilemma, a question from William interrupted her thoughts.

"I'd be happy to take you out car shopping this weekend if you'd like." With that statement, she could no longer restrain the incredulous expression that had been threatening to emerge since she first saw her daughter in William Darcy's arms.

"What?" he asked.

She noticed he was looking at her out of the corner of his eye, and she turned to check on Melanie briefly before her gaze returned to him. "Nothing, um...I appreciate the offer, but I just don't have it to buy a car right now. I'd rather wait and buy one outright than to deal with a loan."

"I could buy it, and you could pay me back as you get the money," he offered.

"What? No! I couldn't ask you to do that!"

"You didn't ask. I'm offering."

Lizzy shook her head determinedly. "It's too much. I do appreciate the offer, but I can't." She heard him sigh, and wondered why he was being so stubborn about this. He was being kind, for a change, but she couldn't understand what had brought on this transformation. She was silent for a while, as she thought before she checked their surroundings and found that they were entering the front gates of campus.

"Follow this road to the split, and the childcare center is on the left."

He nodded, and she watched the scenery outside of the car until he pulled up to the small brick building that served as a daycare and preschool. "Thank you for the ride," she began as she was unbuckling her seat belt.

"I can bring you to your building."

"I can walk, but thanks anyway."

"What time will you be done? I'll come pick you up."

She stopped to look at him, attempting to gauge whether he was in earnest. "I'll figure something out."

"I don't have a busy schedule today. In fact, I'd considered leaving a bit early. Why don't you let me take you home?"

"I..." she began, not really knowing how to answer him.

"What time are your classes?"

"I teach watercolor from ten to twelve forty-five. Then I'm meeting my friends, Dalton and Gavin, for lunch at Gouldings."

"Why don't I pick you up around two then?"

Being unable to think of any other excuse, she nodded and got out of the car. She unbuckled Melanie, and they both waved to him as they walked through the white picket fence in front of the center.

William ensured Lizzy and her daughter were safely inside before he left to drive to the office. As he drove, he thought about their discussion since they'd left Netherfield. He'd found it rather obvious that she didn't want to discuss her finances or affording a new car. She'd also been rather reluctant to accept a ride from him. Deciding that part was probably his imagination, he shrugged it off and didn't give it another thought as his mind drifted to the possibility of dating Lizzy.

Richard was correct in his assessment. He was making excuses, and that was going to stop now. His only dilemma seemed to be how to proceed. Should he try being friends with her first, or should he simply go for it? He considered his options carefully. He didn't really want to delay dating her. If they didn't work out, then they could be friends, but now that he'd decided to ignore his former misgivings, he was determined to throw caution to the wind.

They hadn't spoken to each other much, but they'd been in company together. He knew that Jane and Charles would've praised him and said how great of a guy he was. Yes, he'd definitely ask Lizzy to go to dinner with him that afternoon when he brought her home. She'd say yes, and he'd finally have a chance at happiness. There would be no more persuading himself otherwise. That was the plan and in his mind he was committed. There would be no going back.

Chapter Five

<u>Thursday, November 1, 2012</u>

Dalton and Gavin were waiting when Lizzy dismissed her students, and the three of them left as soon as the last student had finally finished cleaning his brushes, packing his belongings and wishing her a good weekend as he walked out of the door.

Lizzy had known Dalton and Gavin since she was working on her bachelor's degree. Gavin had dated one of her roommates, and the four of them were part of a large group that would go to bars and parties together. She and Dalton both finished college with art degrees, but Gavin's degree was in English literature, and he was currently an instructor in the English department.

She couldn't help but laugh as she rode in the back seat of Dalton's old sedan to Gouldings, a coffee shop near campus that served the best sandwiches in town. Since it was a warm day for November, the sunroof was open and they were blaring 70's disco music as the two men danced like John Travolta in the front seat; their arms reaching out of the sunroof when they pointed up.

If there was one thing that she could count on from Dalton and Gavin, it was a laugh. They'd continued to exchange emails and kept in touch after her marriage to Greg, and when the marriage ended, Gavin recommended Lizzy for the teaching position at the university. Dalton had also helped her get her work included in some of the art shows around town after Melanie was born. At first glance, the guys were silly and loved to have a good time, but they were good friends.

The restaurant wasn't far from campus, so they arrived in very little time and quickly ordered. Their food was delivered swiftly as they conversed, Lizzy enjoying the company as she always did. Her two friends were always wonderful for lifting her spirits, and when they heard about her car, they obviously decided to do just that. She found it amazing that she'd been able to eat through all the laughing she'd been doing at their antics. The trio was just finishing their meal when a strange expression came over Dalton's face. "Hey, Betty, there's someone staring at you."

"What? Who?" She turned around and saw William standing near the door. He gave a stiff smile and put up his hand to kind of wave or signal to her. She did the same and turned back to her friends. "That's William. He gave me the ride to school today. We'd agreed he'd pick me up at about two, but I thought it would be at the childcare center." She turned to see William walking toward their table.

"I can give you a ride home, if you'd prefer," offered Dalton, as he eyed William carefully.

"I appreciate the offer, but really, he's okay." He gave a brief nod as William reached where they were seated.

William turned toward Lizzy as he spoke. "I realize I'm a bit early, so please take your time."

She gestured to her friends. "William Darcy, these are my friends Dalton Breaux and Gavin Smith." Lizzy regarded William warily; worried he'd give the appearance of the insufferable snob she was accustomed to. Dalton and Gavin would pounce on that in a heartbeat, and she really didn't want to have to deal with their jokes for the next few weeks.

"It's nice to meet you," he replied affably, although he lacked a smile as he spoke.

Her friends each shook his hand as they all stood to leave. "Are you sure?" Dalton asked her with a concerned look upon his face.

"I'll be fine. Thanks, hon."

She hugged each of the guys goodbye, and they waved one last time and called out, "Bye, Betty!" before they walked out of the door. She laughed and shook her head, wondering if those two would always be so carefree and silly.

"They call you Betty?" asked William as the barista handed him a cup of coffee in a to-go cup. "Would you like something?"

"No, thank you." He motioned toward the door and opened it for her to exit ahead of him. "And yes, they've called me that since I met them nine years ago."

The car was parallel parked along the curb, and he stepped ahead to open her door. "Because your name is Elizabeth?"

"No," she smiled. "My name is Elizabeth, but it actually has nothing to do with it."

He looked puzzled as he closed the door and walked around to get into the driver's seat. "May I ask why then, or is it private?"

"It isn't private. I first met them through Lisa, a friend and college roommate. According to Lisa, Dalton couldn't remember my name for a while after we met, so he began calling me Betty. It caught on, and soon the entire group began calling me by the name."

"That didn't bother you?"

"No, I found it funny, so I didn't mind. You'd probably have to know Dalton to understand." She watched the buildings pass as they drove back to the university.

"Is this the same Dalton you were saying is in the show with you?"

"Yes, he's a photographer. His works are often stark contrasts of light and dark, so you can't always tell what the object truly is."

When the car pulled to a stop at the childcare center, Lizzy exited and went inside. She came out a few minutes later, carrying her daughter on her hip. William jumped out of his seat and opened the rear passenger door.

"Hi, Melly," he greeted the toddler, who cuddled closer to her mother.

"Thanks," she said as she leaned in to put Melanie in her seat. When she had her all buckled in, she straightened and faced William. "I'm sorry she didn't say hello, but she hasn't taken a nap yet, so she's tired."

"An apology isn't necessary. Perhaps she'll fall asleep in the car?" She nodded, and William closed the door before he walked around to open the door for Lizzy. She gave him a small smile as she got in, before he walked briskly around the front to his side. He took his place, started the engine and backed out of the parking spot. "Did your class go well?"

She turned toward him and gave a non-committal shrug, "Sure."

"Are your students working on anything specific at the moment?" he asked, hoping to begin a conversation.

Out of the corner of his eye, he noticed Lizzy peer back at Melanie before her eyes returned to him. "It's a mixed class of watercolor one and two. The beginners are working on a landscape of their choice. They bring in several pictures, and I help them sort through what would probably work the best for the medium as well as their strengths. Then they draw out and paint the image we choose. The upper level students choose a theme at the beginning of the term and work on a portfolio of pieces to be completed for the end of the semester."

"Do you teach specific techniques, or do they just paint and you make corrections as they require it?"

"The beginners initially learn basic techniques—washes, brush techniques, tints and shading, and then there are a series of styles they're required to paint—a still life, a painting with text of some kind, an abstract, and a landscape. Once they've completed those, they pick a theme and paint a minimum of four paintings. I then help them by teaching further techniques that might help with their projects, or give them tips, more on a one on one basis."

"Do students sometimes not complete the minimum?"

"It's rare. If they don't, it's usually because they've picked a pretty detailed image to reproduce, and I don't fault them for that as long as they've been working steadily throughout the class and don't waste their time. Periodically, I do have a student who doesn't care, and I have to explain to them that they must complete the minimum to pass the class."

He nodded, realizing she was probably a pretty flexible instructor. They fell silent for the remainder of the trip, and he enjoyed simply being alone with her—well, almost alone. They reached Longbourn, and she got out of the car, where Bear was waiting for her, his docked tail wagging furiously. William then exited to quickly open the door so she could retrieve her daughter, who was sound asleep. He marveled how the child could sleep with her head in that awkward position before Lizzy leaned over to unbuckle and lift her from her seat. As Lizzy was lifting to straighten up, her bag fell from her shoulder and he caught it.

"Here, why don't you let me take this for you?"

"Thanks, but I can get it." She awkwardly tilted her body to attempt to get the strap back on her shoulder.

"Lizzy," he said, catching her eye with an earnest expression. "I know you can get it, but let me help you."

She seemed to search his face for a moment before she nodded. "Thank you."

He dipped his chin in acknowledgement, put the bag over his shoulder and leaned forward to unbuckle the child seat from his car. He closed the door with his hip, and carrying the bulky safety equipment, he made his way to the front door where Lizzy had just entered, the dog following at her heels. The load was placed against the curved stairway in the foyer, and he stood awkwardly with his hands in his pockets until Lizzy came down from putting Melanie in bed.

"I really appreciate the ride," she began as she took the last step. "Jane had to be in court today, so you really saved me."

Bolstered by her gratitude, William took a deep breath. "I was wondering if you and I could go to dinner sometime?" He hadn't looked at her face when he asked, so he missed the startled expression his question prompted.

"You want to take me to dinner, like a date?"

Meeting her gaze, he shrugged. "Well...yes, a date. I know it took me a while to ask, but I've admired you for some time. In fact, I think you're beautiful, but I was unsure of whether you'd be suitable to be a part of my life." He noticed her eyebrows shoot to her hairline, but didn't give thought to why she would react in such a way. Instead, his nervous energy manifested itself by further explaining his reservations. "You're an unwed mother. I also initially felt I shouldn't ask because I was concerned my family wouldn't approve—well, I know my Aunt Catherine won't, but that's beside the point. I'm also obligated to consider how a relationship with you would appear to my stockholders and the board of directors. I can't afford to have someone sully my reputation and by association the company's." He took a breath. "There's also the matter of your family."

"My family?" There was an unusual glint in her eye, but he took it as a positive sign and forged ahead.

"Yes—well, Jane and Charles are fine, and so is Melanie, of course. I was referring to your parents and sisters."

"When would you have met..."

"At Jane and Charles' wedding," he interrupted. "Their behavior was far from proper. Your mother is...well...vulgar and crass, your two youngest sisters seem to emulate your mother while they throw themselves at any available man within a two mile radius, and your father seems to sit by while he laughs at it all. Your other sister, I don't remember her name..."

"Mary."

"Yes, I believe that's her. When she didn't have her nose stuck in a book, she was trying to convince people to donate money to some missionary group."

"I see..." she said curtly when William ended his speech. "I can only imagine that most women have thrown themselves at your feet when you asked them out—especially given your obvious talent at the endeavor—but I certainly have no intention of doing so."

"Pardon?"

"I've never sought your company, and until this morning, you've avoided mine at every opportunity."

"Are you saying no?" His face showed the shock he felt at her rejection. A woman hadn't dismissed him since Susan White stomped on his toe in second grade when he tried to hold her hand, and he'd just not expected it.

"Yes, I'm most definitely saying no."

"May I ask why?"

"I can't believe that you need to ask," she said angrily.

He stood there waiting, just looking at her. Finally, she burst.

"You've been rude and condescending since the first day I met you. I've caught you watching me with a disdainful look upon your face, so I'm sure you are just looking for something else to find wrong with me, especially given the myriad of failings you just listed—I'm still trying to comprehend why you felt *that* was even necessary. *And* you intentionally exclude me from conversations."

Affronted, he pulled a hand out of his pocket and pointed accusingly. "*That* is most certainly not true."

"Really? Is that why after a period of staring, you've practically turned yourself so your back is to me? That's happened at almost every occasion where we've both been in attendance. You also bring up topics that seem designed to shut me out. You, Jane and Charles all have law degrees, but I don't, and I can't keep up with the entirety of your discussions. They at least make a point to include or ask me a question and then you proceed to change the subject."

"I never meant for you to feel excluded. I found myself bewitched by you, and I guess I avoided you to a certain extent because I felt you were inappropriate." He paused for a moment as he rubbed his hand back and forth across his forehead. "In the end, I couldn't stop myself."

Her face became a mixture of amazement and anger. "There is another reason, right there. Why would you ask me to date you while insulting me so abominably?"

"I did no such thing!"

"You did! You basically said that you liked me against your will, and despite your better judgment!"

William, realizing what he'd unwittingly said, paled. "I didn't mean it that way."

"Oh, then please tell me how you did mean it? Did you mean to insult me when you criticized me for having a child, which, I might add, isn't uncommon when someone was once married."

His jaw involuntarily dropped as he just stood there speechless. He thought back and realized that no one had ever said that she'd been married, so he'd assumed. Internally berating himself for his misconception, he was startled when she continued her tirade.

"As for *my family*, I more or less agree with you, which is part of the reason why I have nothing to do with them! I will not discuss with you the other motivations. They're none of *your* business."

"I doubt any of this would've mattered if I hadn't brought up my reservations to a relationship with you. If I'd flattered and pursued you instead," he blurted out in frustration. Bear came through the kitchen door and growled when he heard the tone of William's voice.

"Bear, NO!" yelled Lizzy. "In the kitchen!" She pointed back through the door as the dog obeyed, and she closed the swinging door behind him, rounding to face William and walking forward to her previous spot. "I still would have refused!"

"I don't believe you!"

"From the first day I met you, your manners only proved to me how conceited and rude you are! I wouldn't go out with you if you were the last man on Earth!"

Taking a step back, he reeled. He'd spent all of this time fighting his attraction to her and had alienated her in the process. Dejected, he couldn't continue with the argument and decided to retreat while he still had a modicum of dignity. "Please, no more...I understand... I...I'm sorry to have bothered you."

Lizzy had watched him almost stagger backwards and noticed the lost, almost heart-broken expression, and immediately bit back more angry words that she'd been about to release. She looked down to the floor, barely registering his parting words, and when her gaze returned to the door, he was gone.

Dropping down onto one of the bottom steps, she put her elbows on her knees and her head dropped into her hands as she began to cry. She had no idea how long she'd been sitting there when her cell phone rang. Without even looking at who it was, she pressed the button to answer.

"Hello?"

"Lizzy?" came Jane's concerned voice, "are you okay?"

"Yes, of course." She wiped the tears from her eyes as if her sister could see them.

"Don't lie to me, Lizzy. I can tell by the tone of your voice that you've been crying."

"It's nothing. What's up?" She tried to sound upbeat, but if anyone would notice she was faking, it would be Jane.

"I understood that William dropped you at work this morning and brought you home. I wanted to see how things went. It was very sweet of him." Lizzy could hear a hopeful tone to Jane's voice and sighed.

"It was very nice of him," Lizzy agreed, hoping her sister wouldn't press any further.

"Have you heard from Mr. Long yet?"

"No, and that worries me. Usually, he calls me within an hour or two to tell me what's wrong, but I haven't heard anything. I'll call him when I hang up with you."

"Good, you know that Charles and I are more than happy to co-sign a loan if you need it."

"I know, sweetie, but I can't afford the interest rate." She heard Jane sigh. Her reliance on her sister had truly come to bother her in the last year. She knew that Jane and Charles didn't mind helping her, but she couldn't continue to inconvenience them the way she was. She wasn't lying about the loan. The interest rate was too high, but even if it wasn't, she couldn't ask them to co-sign.

"There are times I want to strangle that man," said Jane in what was, for her, a menacing voice.

"I know, I do too, but we'd have to know where he is. I'm still amazed you found him for the divorce papers."

"I consider it a stroke of luck."

Lizzy laughed, but it came out sounding strained.

"Are you sure you're okay?"

She sighed. Jane had always known how to get Lizzy to talk about what was bothering her. The next thing she knew, she'd unburdened the whole of the day to Jane. She even gave her the entirety of William's botched request.

There was a long silence before her sister began. "Do you know how long it's been since he's dated anyone?"

"So what are you saying, Jane, that he was right to say the things he did?"

"No, of course not, but I also know what a tough time he's had. He's also extremely reserved, and not comfortable around people he doesn't know. Charles and I have seen first-hand how awkward he is in social situations, and he's only become more reserved since Ana and his father died."

She exhaled heavily, knowing Jane would be disappointed in her. "I became so frustrated that I lost my temper."

"Lizzzzyyy! You told me everything he said, but left that out. I can only imagine what you said."

"I hope the friendship you and Charles have with him isn't affected by the situation."

"I sincerely doubt it will be. William detests Charles' sister, Caroline. In fact, he has a restraining order against her, and she hasn't caused problems between them."

"Yes, well...even Charles likes me better than Caroline. I can only imagine the way she would fawn all over William. He seems like he'd be her ideal man."

"*Her* ideal man, yes, but she's far from William's ideal woman. She made him miserable, not to mention broke a few laws in her pursuit."

Lizzy laughed. "I may have misjudged him if he dislikes *dear Caroline*."

"Be nice," she chastised. "The point is that the problems with Caroline haven't affected their relationship, and your disagreement with him is a pittance by comparison." Lizzy shrugged. "Look, you need to call Mr. Long before he leaves for the day, so I'm going to let you go. I'll check in later tonight."

"Okay, Jane, I love you."

"I love you, too."

Lizzy pressed the end button and went through her contacts list to find Long's Garage. Locating the number, she hit send, and two rings later heard the familiar sound of Larry Long's voice.

"Allo?"

"Hi, Mr. Long. It's Lizzy Gardiner. I was just wondering if you had word on my car."

"Sorry I haven't been in touch yet. I ran a couple of tests and then called a friend of mine who works for a dealership over in Vidalia."

"Okay, so what's the damage this time?"

"Darlin', there's no easy way to say this, but that car is toast."

"What?" she exclaimed. "No! I need a car. There isn't anything that can be done?"

"We replaced the alternator and the battery a few weeks ago, and now it appears to be the same problem. That was why I called Davey. I told him everything I've done in the last couple of months, and he agrees that the computer system is shot. They don't even make the computer system for that car anymore, so you'd have to go searching through junkyards to find one. I called around to the three closest to us and came up with nothin'. I'm sorry."

She sighed. "Thanks for picking it up. I'll be in as soon as I can to settle the bill."

"No charge this time. I figure I've made enough money off of that old car. Keep it to help buy a new one."

"Thank you," she replied, relieved.

66

"For what it's worth, two of the junkyards I called are interested in your car. I could call them back tomorrow and see how much they'll give you for it."

"I'd appreciate it."

"Don't mention it. You have a good evenin'."

"You, too." Lizzy ended the call and dropped her head back into her hands. She'd bought that car in the hopes that it would last her until she could save enough to buy another newer model. She just needed one more year to save, because she didn't want to purchase a car that would require constant trips to the mechanic like this one had.

Her moping was interrupted when she heard Melanie chatting away to her stuffed animals upstairs. She stood up, brushed off her clothes and made her way to her daughter's room with the best smile she could muster on her face. The last thing she wanted to do was let her mood affect her daughter.

Melanie went to bed at her usual time, and Lizzy returned Jane's call. They didn't speak for long, but Lizzy informed her of Mr. Long's diagnosis of her car. Her sister patiently listened and promised that between them and Charles, they'd figure something out. The call was short, and when she'd hung up, she grabbed a glass of wine and her sweater and headed out to sit in the swing on the back porch.

Despite her aggravation over the car, Lizzy thought about William the most. She wasn't sorry that she'd turned him down, but she was remorseful about losing her temper. Some of the things she'd said to him were rather harsh, and the mournful expression on his face as he walked out of the door had only served to make her feel guilty for her cutting words. Not to excuse his part. He could've asked her to dinner in a way that wasn't offensive, but she didn't have to lash out as severely as she had.

The evening was cool, which prompted her to return inside sooner than she probably would have normally. Instead, she cuddled up in her bed, but her mind would not turn off so she could sleep. With no other occupation, her mind warred between her car and William, and neither would give her a moment's rest.

She went back through and dissected the entirety of her acquaintance with William from her first glimpse of him to their argument that day. As she recalled the first time she saw him on the back porch, she remembered how she found him extremely handsome. What disturbed her most was when she realized that she'd wanted him to notice her—to look at her—and when he didn't, her pride had been wounded. His comment about her project had only added fuel to the fire.

"Now, how will he behave around me?" she wondered aloud just before she finally drifted off to sleep.

Chapter Six

William arrived at the guesthouse at about five. He'd driven aimlessly around the area, and only returned because his car battery was running low. He hooked everything up to charge in the garage, entered the house, and immediately went to the kitchen for a scotch. Taking a sip, he swallowed and attempted to relax. His mind hadn't stilled since he left Longbourn, and as a result, he was emotionally drained. William sighed as he raked his hand through his disheveled hair.

He'd really put his foot in his mouth, and despite how much thought he put into it, he couldn't come up with any ideas of how to repair the damage. While driving around the countryside, he remembered that Charles had mentioned once that he was ignoring Lizzy, but he'd failed to heed his friend's observation.

He took a seat on the sofa, sipping his drink until he heard Richard coming in the door and switching on the lights.

"Why are you sitting in the dark?"

William didn't turn. He simply took another sip and responded, "Because I feel like it."

"I thought you'd be in a good mood after spending time with Lizzy today." His cousin appeared before him and surveyed him from head to toe.

"All I did was give her a ride to work and then to her house."

Richard gave him a puzzled look. "I thought you would've tried to take her and her daughter to dinner. Instead you're sitting here moping in the dark. What happened?"

"I don't want to talk about it," he mumbled.

Richard's eyebrows lifted and he appraised William carefully. "I'm going to put my briefcase in my room and I'll be back in a minute. Maybe we can order a pizza or some Chinese food for dinner?"

William lifted one shoulder in a kind of half-hearted shrug, and took another drink. When his cousin re-entered the room, William hadn't noticed. He continued to stare straight ahead when the sound of a knock echoed around the room.

Richard strode to open the door, and Charles entered, glancing immediately to his friend who hadn't moved a muscle. "Hey, Jane was wondering if y'all wanted to come over for dinner. It isn't fancy, just chicken and salad, but you're both welcome." He took a seat across from William and studied him carefully. "Jane talked to Lizzy on the phone this afternoon."

William's head bolted to face Charles. "You know?"

"No," he replied. "Lizzy confided in Jane, but all I know is that you and Lizzy argued. My wife wouldn't tell me any more than that."

Nodding, William's brow furrowed. "She hates me."

"Lizzy isn't one to hate people. If you really like her, just be yourself from now on, and don't be the imbecile you've shown her since you returned."

"Was I really that bad?" Out of the corner of his eye, he noticed Richard take a seat on the other end of the couch, but continued to look at Charles, waiting for an answer.

"If I didn't know you," began Charles, "I would've probably been offended by your behavior as well."

He sighed. "So you think I can fix things?"

"I'm not guaranteeing you anything, but while Lizzy and my wife may seem strikingly different, they're very similar in some ways. They're both exceedingly forgiving women, although Lizzy is slower to trust than Jane."

"May I ask why you've never mentioned that Lizzy was married? I'd even commented to you that she's a single mother."

"Oh no, you didn't assume..."

"*Yes*, I assumed, and she was furious. I think the only thing that seemed to infuriate her more was when I criticized her family."

70

"The Bennets?" At William's nod, Charles cringed. "You really did do a good job of stepping in it this time." Charles rubbed the back of his neck with his hand and exhaled heavily. "Her marriage was far from easy, and ended very badly—to put it mildly."

William sat forward. "What do you mean?"

"That's a story for Lizzy to share, if she wishes—as is her relationship with her parents. I *will* tell you that she uses the name Gardiner, which was her mother's maiden name. She took it from her great aunt though." He gave William a meaningful look and patted him on the shoulder. "Don't give up. I saw the way she looked at you when Melly was asleep in your lap last night."

Looking puzzled, William took a sip of his drink and sat forward. "I don't understand."

Charles laughed. "One thing I've learned since that munchkin was born is that most women find a man with a baby or small child sexy." He lifted his eyebrows a couple of times as he donned a wide grin.

Richard began guffawing, and William became affronted. "I will not use her child to earn her affections."

"That's not what I was implying," chuckled Charles. "She gave you a look very similar to what Jane gives me when I'm holding Melly. Trust me, it's a good thing. She's not indifferent to you."

Richard wore a wide grin as he gave his cousin a hearty slap on the back. "Hang in there, cousin. She may just take a while to win over. Look at it this way, you know she's not after your wealth, otherwise, she wouldn't have cared how much you insulted her."

Charles nodded. "Let's go get some dinner, and perhaps Jane can give you a pep talk. She's good at those."

William gave a small smile as he followed Charles' lead and stood. "Are you sure she won't be angry with me?"

"She knows you well enough to know that you'd never intentionally hurt her sister. You're safe—in this instance, anyway. Just don't play around with Lizzy's affections. Jane would never forgive you for that."

"We know that isn't William's style, so it shouldn't be a problem," interjected Richard, as he opened the door.

"Exactly," exclaimed Charles.

The three men walked to Netherfield, where Jane was awaiting them with dinner. The meal was very informal, so everyone served themselves before they were seated around the large kitchen table. The conversation was also very relaxed as they discussed mainly some of the local events that would be happening in Meryton leading up to the holidays.

When they finished their meal, the results of the day's meetings were discussed as the men cleaned the kitchen for Jane. She'd insisted it wasn't necessary, but William was adamant, since she'd ensured he was invited to dinner at least once a week and he knew that she'd often put a great deal of work into the menu.

Once the kitchen was spotless, everyone retired to the living room, where they found Jane on the phone with Lizzy. Charles served William and Richard some scotch as Jane wrapped up the call.

"Her car can't be repaired," she said to Charles as soon as she hung up the phone.

"Oh, no," he said in an exasperated tone. "She's still refusing to let us co-sign a loan, isn't she?"

"She claims it's because of how high the interest rate would be, but I suspect that's not the only reason."

Charles furrowed his brows.

"I think she's trying not to lean on us as much as she has in the past," Jane continued. "It's silly, really. Lizzy is for all intents and purposes independent, so I'm kind of worried about how far she'll take this."

William listened closely to the conversation, his mind attempting to formulate ideas to help. "I'd asked about getting a loan this morning, but she claimed she couldn't afford it."

Jane sighed. "She could afford a car note, but the asshole that she was married to ruined her credit along with his. Despite the fact that they were divorced almost two years ago…"

"It takes longer than that for her credit to clear," William finished as the three boys chuckled a bit over the rare sound of Jane cursing.

"Exactly, and Lizzy refuses to accept the interest rates they're offering," she continued, ignoring them. "She'd prefer to save for another year and buy a car outright that would admittedly be newer than the model she was driving, but not necessarily in that much better condition."

"I offered to buy a car and she could pay me back, but she refused."

"I can't say that I'm surprised," Charles chimed in. "She's been allowing us to help her less and less. I think she wants to prove that she can handle things without us, but I don't see how she can get any kind of car without either taking the loan or accepting our help."

"She's done everything on her own since she began living at Longbourn," explained Jane. "The money that came with the estate and the earnings from the events is strictly used to renovate and keep the house in good shape. She pays for everything else out of her paycheck, *and* she paid us back for the few months we helped her out in the beginning."

"Despite the fact that she was told it wasn't necessary," Charles interjected.

Richard whistled. "It's admirable that she wishes to be so independent, but she has to have a car."

An idea suddenly coming to his mind, William smiled as he looked at Jane and Charles. "I have an idea, but I'll need your help to figure out the particulars—especially, how to persuade her to accept it."

"Well, let's hear it," said Charles as he leaned forward in his seat.

Luckily, Lizzy didn't have classes on Friday, so she didn't have to worry about finding transportation to work. She knew that she'd need a few groceries by the next day, so she planned on calling Jane that evening to see if her sister could give her a ride into town.

She and Melanie both painted that morning. Lizzy worked on her last landscape for the show, and her daughter with her finger paints on her own little table in the corner, playing with some toys that remained in that room when she was bored with painting. They'd eaten a late lunch, and Lizzy had just put Melanie down for a nap when the knocker on the door sounded and Bear, who happened to be inside for a change, began barking.

"Hush, Bear! You'll wake Melly!"

Puzzled at who it could be, she checked through the leaded glass on the side of the door. She was unfamiliar with the man who was standing there, so she opened the door carefully while she kept the screen door locked. Bear stood at her feet, growling in a low tone.

"Can I help you?" she asked warily.

"Are you Ms. Elizabeth Gardiner?"

"Yes, I am."

"I have a delivery for you, but I'm required to ask you for some identification."

She lifted one eyebrow and eyed him curiously. "What's the delivery? I'm not expecting anything."

"I was given strict instructions that you should sign for the delivery before I'm allowed to divulge the contents."

The whole situation seemed strange, and she was finding it frustrating, but in the event it was about a check for her old car, she nodded. "Okay, I'll be right back." She closed and locked the door while she went to the mudroom off the kitchen where she kept her purse. As she pulled out her wallet, she wondered what on earth this could be about. A part of her was concerned with whether she'd have to hand the man her identification, not to mention why he needed it in the first place. When she reopened the door, Lizzy held up her license to the screen.

74

He made a note on his papers and then looked back to where she was standing. "I just need you to sign here," he indicated with his pen.

She opened the screen and he slipped her a clipboard through the gap. The document only said that she acknowledged that she received the delivery designated by a long alphanumeric code. She signed her name and passed it through the gap when he handed her a manila envelope.

"I'm sorry, but I don't understand."

"I believe your answers are in the package. You have a good day, ma'am." The man smiled, and she watched as he walked down the steps to where two cars were waiting to one side of the circle in the front of the house. One of the vehicles, a minivan with a logo for Meryton Automotive emblazoned on the side, had someone waiting in the driver's seat. The man stepped into the minivan, and it pulled out as soon as he was safely inside.

"Wait!" she called, running out on to the porch, "you forgot your car!" Bear took off and followed the strangers until they passed through the front gates and then doubled back to inspect the tires on the vehicle remaining in the drive.

Confused, she examined it carefully, and noticed a brand new floral car seat strapped into the backseat. Suddenly, she had a feeling that the car was supposed to be left, and that *it* was the delivery. Whoever had planned this had known that she wouldn't just readily accept it, and had strategically schemed for her agreement before she learned what the "package" truly was.

Everything added up. The way the cars were to the side of the house—she wouldn't have been able to see them with the door cracked or from the leaded glass. She also realized that the alphanumeric code was more than likely the VIN number.

Sighing, she took a seat on the edge of the porch and opened the manila envelope. A stack of papers fell out along with the keys and what appeared to be a letter. She placed the documents and keys next to her while she opened the envelope, scanning down to where the name William Darcy was signed at the bottom. Dumbfounded, she returned to the top, and slowly read the words he'd written out in an even script.

November 2, 2012

Dear Lizzy,

I'm aware that I'm probably the last man in the world you would be prevailed upon to accept anything from, but I'm still going to try. I was at Jane and Charles' house last night when I learned that your car is unfixable. Remembering our conversation about buying a new one that morning, I took the liberty of making the arrangements for your use of this vehicle for as long as you have the need of it. I've had the paperwork put in your name, and you may look on it however you feel most comfortable. I would very much like you to accept it as a gift, but I know that you're unlikely to agree to such a present. If that is the case, then you may look on it as a loan, until you can make arrangements to purchase your own, or you can consider me the bank and pay me back. In this case, I insist on the stipulation that I will not accept any more than what you have already saved.

I'll abide by whatever decision you make, so long as you use it. The thought of you and Melanie in an unreliable car like what you were driving concerns me. I understand it took you from point A to point B, but I would be terrified if the two of you were stranded on the side of the highway at night, as would Charles and Jane. If for no other reason, please take it to ease their minds.

While I have the means at my disposal, I must apologize for my thoughtless words yesterday. I'm sorry. I never meant to insult you or wound your feelings, and it pains me to know that I did just that.

I admit that I've admired you from the first moment I saw you. I've never been particularly at ease with people who are unfamiliar to me, but I now know that my behavior toward you was unacceptable and rude. Regardless of the excuse, I was wrong, and I couldn't be more sorry.

76

Please understand, I will never press you for an intimacy that you don't wish to have. I respect you too much for that, and I would never wish for Charles and Jane to feel as though they had to choose between us because we can't remain civil to one another. I look forward to the opening of your show, but I also understand if you would rather I not attend.

Fondest regards,

William Darcy

Lizzy closed the letter and wiped the tears that had begun to fall from her eyes. After the argument yesterday, she wouldn't have expected him to help her at all, but he was being exceedingly generous. Jane had tried to tell her several times that he was a good guy, but Lizzy had refused to listen. She groaned—Jane was right.

As she thought about their last encounter, she still didn't know why she'd let him get to her. If it had been anyone else, she would've laughed and let it go, but not William Darcy. Instead, she stewed and fumed over the way he'd behaved toward her. She exhaled heavily and wiped at her eyes with the backs of her hands.

A brand new high-end crossover hybrid wasn't what she would've been able to afford with the money she'd saved so far. She'd purchased her last car with less than four thousand dollars, and she'd only been able to save a bit more than that so far. She didn't even want to think about how much William had spent on this one. Why wouldn't he buy a less expensive model? She'd have to give him her savings and then try to persuade him to take payments, but even then, it would take her years to pay him back for it.

Reaching down for the paperwork, Lizzy flipped through the parts of it she would need to file, and noticed Jane's notary seal on the bottom. She should've known that her big sister and best friend would have a hand in this. She was scanning through the documents one last time, paying a bit more attention to detail, when she noticed the year and mileage on the car.

"Nine thousand miles," she mumbled to herself. The fact that the car was two years old did give her a bit of relief—the price wouldn't be quite as high as a new one.

Deciding she couldn't do much about it at the moment, she put the forms back in the envelope and looked at the car in the driveway. Lizzy sighed, walked over, and sat in the driver's seat. Judging by the amenities on the dashboard, it seemed more of a mid-range model, which combined with the fact that it was used helped alleviate some of the guilt that he'd bought her a car.

Looking in the back, she found the expensive car seat that he'd purchased for Melanie. She recognized it as being top rated, and smiled at William's effort to ensure Melanie's safety.

Lizzy placed the key in the ignition, pressed the start button, and pulled the car around to the garage. When she automatically looked up for the remote for the door, she noticed it was clipped to the visor, and realized that they must have retrieved it from Mr. Long's. Once she pulled inside, Lizzy closed the door behind her, turned off the car, and returned to the house. Melanie was still sleeping, so she began some rosemary bread that she'd been planning to make. She had just set out the dough to rise when her phone rang.

She noticed her sister's name on the screen and answered. "How could you, Jane?" She heard her sister chuckle.

"It wasn't my idea. William came up with the entire plan, and I only agreed to it." Lizzy rolled her eyes. "You need the car, and he wanted to ensure that you and Melly were safe. From what you've told me, you only have a small bit more than the last car's purchase price. If you'd purchased a car with the money you'd saved, there would've been no guarantee that it would be reliable."

"But it would've been *mine*," she exclaimed. "I would've done it myself. As for being reliable, it would've been an improvement over the last one."

"I know, honey, but this way, we all know that you're safe when you drive home."

"How can I face him?" came the question that had been plaguing her mind since she'd first read the letter.

"He doesn't want to make you uncomfortable and he doesn't want recognition. He just wanted to do something to help you."

"I misjudged him so badly."

"He made it easy. Don't beat yourself up too much," said Jane, causing Lizzy to smile. "Settle things with the car and then start anew—as friends. I think he'd like that."

"How can I give him what I have saved? It's nowhere near what that car costs!" She began furiously cleaning her stand mixer with her phone propped on her shoulder. "I mean, if he had to do this, why such an expensive model?"

"We went to several dealerships today. He wanted to get you a hybrid to help save money on gas, and that model was the most family friendly. We both agreed that it was the best choice. For what it's worth, he wanted to buy one brand new. I insisted on the used model. I knew you'd be just as happy with it, *and* I hoped you'd be more willing to accept it."

"I was relieved that it was at least used. It's a great car...If I didn't know any better, I would think it was brand new."

"It was a lease trade-in. The dealership had just put it out on the lot." She could tell that Jane was proud of her find, but Lizzy still felt guilty about accepting it.

It still would never fall within my price range." She heard Jane exhale heavily.

"Lizzy, he did this without telling you because he knew that you have a lot of pride about doing things on your own, and yet, you needed the help. He just wants you to accept it."

"I'll think about it."

"Don't overthink this. Just let things happen."

"I don't know if I can," she said sadly, and stopped wiping the mixer to bite the fingernail on her thumb.

"You can be friends, which he'll accept happily. He knows you're going to be busy between now and the opening, so take some time to accustom yourself to the idea of everything that's happened. He'll be at the show, and you'll have some time to get to know him."

"How do you know that he'll be there?"

"He was concerned that you wouldn't want him to come, and I assured him that it would be fine. I think he's really interested to see your work. Is that okay?"

Lizzy paused while she considered whether it would bother her to see William at her opening and sighed, worried about the situation being awkward. She couldn't avoid him forever, and how could she exclude him after his help with the car?

"Yes, it's okay," she responded as she nodded.

"I love you, sis."

"I love you, too." Lizzy ended the call and proceeded to make a grocery list. Coming to a decision about the car, she realized that at least she wouldn't have to wait to go to the store. She called her insurance company to ensure the vehicle would be covered. The cost was higher, but then the replacement on this one was significantly more, so it shouldn't have come as a surprise.

An hour later, Melanie awoke, and the two of them tried out the new car on a trip into town. She ran a few errands, and they drove back to the house for the evening. Her mind hadn't stopped turning in circles since the car had been delivered, and she was emotionally exhausted as a result.

She and Melanie spent a quiet weekend at Longbourn, and Monday they returned to their usual routine. Lizzy received a call from Mr. Long, so she stopped by his garage on the way home. He was surprised to see what she was driving, and seemed a bit sad as he handed her the check from the junkyard for her old car.

The remainder of the week was rather normal. Lizzy had her classes, and her daughter went to the childcare center while she worked. They set up the show on Thursday afternoon, and Jane and Charles came by to see if they needed a hand, bringing pizzas and beer for everyone who was pitching in. Finally, Jane and Charles put Melanie in a car seat they had for her and took her home to

Longbourn, allowing Lizzy and her colleagues to finish hanging everyone's work.

By the time everything was completed and completely ready, Lizzy returned to the house exhausted. Jane and Charles had already given Melanie her bath, read her the almost dozen books she had requested, and put her to bed. They even had a bottle of Lizzy's favorite wine chilled and waiting for when she finally returned. They popped the cap and toasted the show, enjoying the cool night under the stars in the courtyard.

When their glasses were finished, Jane and Charles returned to Netherfield, and Lizzy was left alone with her thoughts. The next day, she would see William for the first time since their argument, and she was nervous. She dragged herself upstairs, and despite the whirring of her mind, she climbed into bed, falling asleep as soon as her head hit the pillow.

Chapter Seven

Lizzy kept the day of the show pretty low key around Longbourn. She cleaned house and baked bread before Melanie's nap. While her daughter slept, Lizzy showered, dried her hair, and then stepped into her closet to decide what she would wear.

Last year, all of the artists had made a joke out of what they wore by donning black turtlenecks. They'd been teasing one of the art history professors who always quipped in his classes that it was the attire of all stereotypical artists. Everyone in the department had had a chuckle about the look on Professor Dunbar's face when he'd entered the old depot to see the seven of them decked out in black. Lizzy had even worn a black beret.

This year, they hadn't made any arrangements, so she began looking through her clothing with a discerning eye. Thirty minutes later, she was no closer to deciding, and almost all of her clothes were strewn across her bed. At least she wouldn't have to clean it since she was staying at Jane's tonight!

As she plopped down on the edge of the mattress, she suddenly remembered a dress that Jane had given her last Christmas. She'd fussed that it was far too expensive and that she had nowhere to wear it, but her sister had insisted. Lizzy had put it in her closet, but a few months later, Melanie began to play in there, trying on her mother's shoes and such, so Lizzy moved it to the wardrobe.

Making her way to the large, ornately carved doors, she pulled open the right side to reveal a grey garment bag that she took out to lay on the bed. She unzipped the closure, removed the dress, and before she had time to second-guess herself, slipped into it. Studying herself in the mirror, she smoothed the fitted skirt over her hips anxiously. Her nerves were worse than they had ever been before a show, and she was at a loss as to why.

"It's just a show, Lizzy. Just like last year," she muttered as she opened the other side to pull a shoebox off of the shelf. She put on her stockings and then slipped on her black pumps. When she was dressed, she styled her long, curly hair to trail over her left shoulder before applying a bit of mascara and tinted lip balm. Stepping back, she took one last look in the mirror to ensure she was ready to go.

Hearing Melanie stirring in the next room, Lizzy grabbed her robe and threw it over her dress to get her daughter out of her crib. When she walked in Melaine's room, the little girl bounced up and down.

"Oooohh, Mama pweddy!" she exclaimed.

"Thank you, sweet pea." Lizzy picked her up and brought her downstairs where she pulled a peanut butter and jelly sandwich that she'd prepared earlier out of the refrigerator and waited for her daughter to eat. Then she quickly cleaned Melanie's hands, dressed her in pajamas, and placed some of their belongings into a bag.

She loaded everything into the car, and Lizzy was about to get in when she realized she was still wearing her robe.

"Crap!" Looking back to see if her daughter heard her, she was relieved to see that the car door was closed, and she ran just inside the front door where she swapped her housecoat for her long coat in the event it was chilly.

She made it to Netherfield at approximately five o'clock to find Mrs. King already there and chatting with her sister. When Jane noticed her enter, she smiled and came over to tickle Melanie.

"Melly, do you remember Mrs. King?" she asked happily. The little girl eyed the older lady up and down and cuddled closer to her mother's leg, obviously needing to become reacquainted.

Mrs. King was Jane's nearest neighbor, and didn't get around very well. She'd always been happy to babysit Melanie, but it was easier for her to make it to Netherfield than Longbourn. The few times Lizzy was out with Jane and Charles, Melanie was usually asleep by the time they returned, which was why Lizzy and her daughter spent the night. There was no use waking Melanie just to drive to Longbourn.

Lizzy leaned down and whispered in her ear, "She's a nice lady, and guess what?" Her daughter looked at her with wide eyes. "She likes to play, and I'd bet that she would love to meet your kitty."

The older lady leaned forward. "I thought we could play with the toys your Aunt Jane keeps for you, and I would love to meet any little friends that you brought." Melanie tilted her head and watched Mrs. King for a bit before she held out her stuffed cat for the grandmotherly woman to inspect. "Is her name Kitty?" she asked.

Melanie nodded, and Jane walked over to the television to press play on the DVD player. "Guess what I have for you and Mrs. King to watch?" The Parisian music that indicated the beginning of Melly's favorite movie began to play, and Melanie cheered. She ran over and dropped onto her beanbag, and Mrs. King grinned.

"We'll be fine," said the older woman. "You have a fun evening."

Lizzy smiled and walked to where her daughter was paying rapt attention to the three kittens playing on the screen, leaning over to kiss her on the temple.

"I love you, Melly," she whispered as she drew back. Her daughter looked over and gave her a peck on the cheek before her gaze was drawn back to the movie.

Jane beckoned to Lizzy and they met Charles in the kitchen. "Y'all were quick."

"Once I hit play on the DVD, she was glued."

He chuckled and retrieved his coat from a hook near the door. "Are we ready then?"

"I think so," replied Jane. She looked to Lizzy, who, due to how warm she had become, was untying her coat and slipping it from her shoulders. A huge smile broke out on Jane's face, and Lizzy checked the front of her dress, smoothing it.

"What?"

"Why are you so dressed up?" her sister asked in a teasing way.

"Because I have a show tonight, and we're going out."

"You wore a black turtleneck and black dress pants last year. For the faculty show, you wore a long skirt and a top. Is there someone you want to impress this time?"

"Nooo," she exclaimed using a tone that caused Charles to chortle. "You bought me the dress, so if you don't want me to wear it, just say so."

Jane stepped forward and hugged Lizzy. "I'm sorry if I'm making you uncomfortable. You look beautiful."

"Thank you."

Rubbing his hands together, Charles smiled widely. "Well, let's get this show on the road, or we won't make it to Acadiana for our dinner reservation."

William and Richard were waiting at the bar when Lizzy entered with Jane and Charles. His cousin was facing away from him when William saw them, so he missed the awestruck look on William's face when he first laid eyes on Lizzy. She was stunning. The red velvet dress she was wearing clung to every curve, while the asymmetrical neckline draped around the top and the notched sleeves made the dress as unique as she was. She had a simple ruby pendant that sat in the hollow of her throat, with matching studs in her ears. He motioned to Charles and Jane, who began moving toward him as she followed behind. He couldn't help but notice a slight sway to her hips as she walked, and noticing her stockings, William caught himself wondering if she was wearing garters under her dress.

Redirecting his thoughts before he embarrassed himself, he offered everyone a glass of Chardonnay, while Richard turned to greet them. Since she was driving, Jane declined, so he handed Charles and Lizzy a glass, his hand brushing hers as she accepted it. He'd thought he felt her shaking as their fingers touched, but he decided he must have been mistaken. The sensation of her touch lingered on his skin, and he gave her a small smile in an attempt to appear unaffected as he turned toward Charles.

"I take it the meeting went well today?"

"Went off without a hitch," said Charles. "Are we waiting for our table?"

"The hostess said she'd seat us when the entire party arrived. Did you say anything when you passed her?"

"No, I didn't realize. I'll go let her know." Charles turned to walk back up front and William noticed Jane speaking with Richard. He wanted to talk with Lizzy, but he was unsure of where to begin.

"You must allow me to thank you," he heard Lizzy say as she stepped forward. "I should've called you or sent a note earlier, but, honestly, I had no idea what to say...how to apologize." Her hands were gripping each other fiercely, making him well aware of how uneasy she was. He only hoped it wasn't because she didn't want him there.

"I don't require either an apology or a thank you. As long as you like the car, I will be satisfied."

"It's wonderful, and Melanie adores her new seat. It's very girly."

"Just like she is," he said with a small smile. "I thought of her when I found it online. Luckily, the local baby store had one in stock." He looked down into his glass of wine for a moment, returning to find Lizzy holding an envelope out to him.

"I know it doesn't come anywhere close to what you paid, but I'd like for you to have it." She paused for a moment. "And I'd like to continue to make payments somehow. What's in that envelope isn't...near..."

He took the proffered item from her hand. A part of him was disappointed that she wouldn't accept it outright as a gift, but he'd expected her to attempt to reimburse him as much as possible. In fact, he'd already discussed with Jane the particulars for putting the money into a trust fund for Melanie.

"This isn't necessary, you know."

"Yes, it is. Especially after I abused you so abominably to your face. It probably isn't even one-fourth of what that car cost, but I'd be uneasy if you didn't take it."

"I'd prefer that you leave it in your savings."

86

She shook her head. "I didn't take everything from my savings. I have an amount that I always keep in there, and then there was what I was setting aside for this." She pointed to the envelope, and he nodded as he tucked it into the inside pocket of his suit jacket. "I reserve the right to pester you about taking more money."

He noticed one side of her lip curved up a bit and he chuckled. "Good luck," he replied.

She seemed a bit more relaxed as she lifted one eyebrow. "Is that a challenge?"

William laughed and shrugged. "If you like."

His vision returned to his glass for a moment before he looked back to study her expression. "You're certain the car is okay?" Jane had been so adamant that the used car was the best option, but he was simply accustomed to buying new. He worried that she would be disappointed. "I mean...you don't mind that it isn't new?" Her smile finally appeared and he relaxed a bit.

"No, I don't mind. I already feel guilty that you bought me something so expensive, but I would've felt much worse if it had been new. It's much nicer than anything I would've bought on my own." She then paused for a moment, swallowing nervously. "Again... about the other day, I'm sorry for losing my temper the way I did." Her eyes left him for a moment to where Charles and Richard seemed to be having an animated discussion while Jane looked on.

"You had every right to be angry with me. I was a daft prick, as my Aunt Adelaide would say."

His heart leapt to hear a laugh bubble up from Lizzy's lips. "Aunt Adelaide?"

He beamed at the sound of her melodic laughter. "Richard's mother."

"Oh," she responded as the hostess came to escort them to their table. William held out a chair for Lizzy and she thanked him as she sat. He then realized the only place left at the table was the one to the right of Lizzy, and took his seat.

"When did this restaurant open?" he asked.

"About a year ago," responded Charles. "Everything is wonderful. Just pick something."

As he studied the menu, Lizzy's voice interrupted him. "Jaaaane, split the blackened snapper pasta with me?"

"Charles and I are already splitting the shrimp scampi. Just order it, and if you can't finish it, we'll get the rest to go."

"And then it sits in the car for a few hours." She made a face that showed her disgust.

He glanced down at the item she mentioned—sautéed crawfish, onion, mushrooms, and bell peppers in hollandaise poured over blackened red snapper and pasta. He could live with that. "I'll share with you, if you'd like."

"Really?" she exclaimed. She gave him a large grin. "Thanks, you won't regret it. It's wonderful, but the portion sizes are so large that I can't eat it all."

"She also wants to make sure she gets some of the appetizer," laughed Jane. "There is hollandaise sauce on the fried green tomatoes also. I don't know how she eats so much of it in one sitting."

"They are my two favorite dishes on the menu, and I'm not ashamed to admit that I'll eat all of it if you set it in front of me." Everyone chuckled as the server returned to take their order.

William couldn't complain about the meal. The food was some of the best he'd ever eaten, and he was enjoying the company immensely. The time flew by, and Charles mentioned skipping dessert so they could have Lizzy at her show on time.

"No," she objected. "Have whatever you like. I'll just walk down to The Depot, and you can come when you finish here. After all, I have to be there until nine, and it won't take you two hours to look at the work." Lizzy took out her wallet to pay her share, but William beat her to it, placing enough to cover everyone's food and wine on the table.

"I'm actually quite full, and would rather not have dessert. May I walk with you?" William asked as he stood from his seat. He thought she looked a bit surprised, but he didn't think she appeared displeased.

"Yes, of course," she replied softly. They made their way out of the restaurant, and began walking down the sidewalk.

"Thank you for dinner. I hope I didn't put you into a hollandaise-induced stupor."

He laughed. "I wasn't sure about that much, but splitting the entrée helped, since the food was so rich. I'd never had fried green tomatoes, but with the lump crabmeat and hollandaise, they were very good."

"Good, I'm glad. Those are my two favorite items on the menu, but it's a lot of food, and I always try to persuade Jane to share. Melly will eat the pasta and crawfish, so now I have her to split the plate with me when Jane shares with Charles."

He grinned. "Did your daughter have any problems with the sitter?"

"No," he noticed her less than pleased expression, "Jane had everything arranged. She turned on a movie, and she never even noticed that I walked out of the door."

"You shouldn't leave her with Mrs. King if you are uncomfortable with it." He couldn't imagine leaving his own child if he wasn't at ease.

"She just doesn't get around very well, and while I don't think Melly would get into any trouble, I worry unless she's at school or Jane and Charles are watching her."

He nodded as she veered toward the light pouring out of a set of glass double doors. He noticed "The Depot" etched at eye level, and Lizzy put a hand on his arm to stop him before they entered.

"Mr. Lucas can be very...well, verbose. I think I remember Jane saying that the local paper ran a feature on your return to the Meryton offices?"

William knew he had a confused look upon his face, but he was trying to understand what the article had to do with Mr. Lucas. "Yes, I allowed the Meryton Register to follow me for a day."

"Mr. Lucas studies the paper so he remains up to date on who's who in Meryton. I've watched him monopolize the time of unsuspecting people in the past because they were featured in the paper. As far as he's concerned, it's all about who you know."

His eyebrows raised and he wondered if there was any way at all to avoid the man for the entire evening.

"I'll survive, but I do appreciate the warning," William replied. "Perhaps we should get you inside." He stepped forward to open the door for her.

"Thank you."

"Lizzy," he heard a boisterous voice exclaim as they made it inside. "We were just waiting on you to place the "open" sign outside of the door." The man gestured to an employee in a black skirt and white button down blouse, who went and fetched a folding sign that she then placed on the sidewalk.

"I'm sorry I wasn't earlier, Mr. Lucas. We went for dinner at Acadiana, and it was packed.

"Not a problem." He dismissed her with a wave of his hand and a broad smile. He positively beamed when he realized the man standing next to Lizzy was none other than William Darcy. "Mr. Darcy! I'm so pleased to have you join us tonight."

Thanks to Lizzy's warning, he'd been prepared, but William never cared for the preferential treatment he received in many places. He wanted to be just like everyone else, but he glanced at Lizzy, who was regarding him with a mischievous grin, and took a deep breath. Despite how uncomfortable he was, there could be no hint of conceit or disdain, so he attempted a pleasant face as he held out his hand.

"William Darcy," began Lizzy, "this is Alan Lucas. He owns The Depot, as well as The Lodge."

"The lake resort out on six-eighty?"

"The very one," declared Mr. Lucas, puffing out his chest. "I'm also an investor in my daughter, Charlotte's, event coordinating business. Perhaps you've heard of it?"

"In passing," said William, as he remembered that was who scheduled the events at Longbourn. Mr. Lucas seemed pleased, and he noticed Lizzy's eyes were indicating how amused she was. He heard one of her friends call her over to speak with some people who'd come in during the introduction.

"Excuse me," she said as she turned to walk away. He watched her for a few moments before he heard Mr. Lucas clear his throat.

"You must allow me to show you around."

"Oh, that's not necessary, sir."

"I insist, young man. Why don't we start over here with Dalton's photographs? I don't quite get them myself, but I've heard several people comment about how intriguing they are." William remembered that Lizzy hadn't thought it would take two hours to view the exhibit, but he was sure that if Alan Lucas had been allowed to continue his tour, it would. He was extremely thankful when a young woman came over to inform the man that he was needed in the office. Mr. Lucas quickly introduced his daughter, Charlotte, and began to sing her praises when she tactfully reminded him that his presence was required elsewhere, and led him away.

William glanced around the room for Lizzy. The Depot was a large building, with all of the inner walls, and even some temporary dividers, displaying work. As he turned a corner, he swiftly located her speaking to some people in front of a painting, occasionally gesturing toward the piece as she spoke.

He could see where her work began, noticing a sign with her name and a small biography.

> *Elizabeth Gardiner is a native of Meryton. She graduated magna cum laude with a Bachelor of Fine Arts in painting and a minor in art history at the University of Meryton, before receiving her Master of Fine Arts at Louisiana State University. While studying for her master's, she had her first solo show at Hill Gallery in New Orleans, Louisiana.*
>
> *In 2008, Elizabeth was an artist-in-residence at the Bemis*

Center for Contemporary Art in Omaha, Nebraska. She has
worked as an instructor at Southeastern Louisiana
University and the University of Meryton...

Darcy skimmed the list of shows and honors Lizzy had received
before moving on to her first painting. He glanced down the wall,
and noticed she seemed to have preferences for landscapes of the
gulf coast, and there were a few that he was sure were the local Hart
and Ford lakes. As he took in each work, he noticed that she tended
to show her brushstrokes with lines of color in some places. The last
work, a monochromatic still life, showed this to an even greater
extent, the wine bottle being composed of different shades painted
in lines in an attempt to try to capture the play of light and shadow
on the smooth glass surface.

He had to admit that his initial reaction to the work she had around
her house was grossly incorrect. Lizzy was extremely talented. She
was now chatting with Charles and Jane, so he made his way to join
them.

"I'm going to go look at your work now," said Jane.

Lizzy laughed. "You see everything as I paint it. Nothing has
changed since then—except maybe that I've signed it."

"But it wasn't hung on the wall in a show, Lizzy. That makes a big
difference."

William heard Lizzy's lilting laughter as she cast a glance in his
direction. "Are you enjoying yourself, Mr. Darcy?"

Chuckling, he pivoted so that he was standing in front of her. "I am.
I like your work very much."

"Ooooh," she said with a glint in her eye, "you mean that it's
tempting enough for a collector, or perhaps even you, to buy it?"

Suddenly realizing why the phrase sounded familiar, he closed his
eyes in mortification. "I never knew that you'd heard that
statement. I owe you an apology."

"Yes, I heard it, but I wasn't saying it to receive an apology. I was
teasing. Please don't make yourself uneasy."

"I should be uneasy. I was horribly rude. You had every right to react the way you did that day at Longbourn."

"Let's not quarrel as to who shared the greatest portion of the blame on that day. I don't believe either of us was at our best."

He nodded and gestured toward the bar. "Would you care for a glass of wine?"

She glanced over and stepped closer as she indicated she wanted to whisper something in his ear. "The wine is terrible. Mr. Lucas buys the cheapest he can find and sells it for five dollars a glass." At the feel of her breath near his ear, goose bumps erupted down the back of his neck and he became warm.

He laughed in an attempt to hide his reaction. "In that case, my palate thanks you."

"My pleasure," she smiled shyly.

For the first time, he noticed what Richard had mentioned about her seeming self-conscious. As he opened his mouth to say something, he heard Mr. Lucas calling out over the crowd.

"I would like to thank all of you for coming out to support the artists in our show this year." William watched as he pointed out each artist around the room and called them by name. "Dalton Breaux, Ellesandra Jennings, Jackson Wright, Elizabeth Gardiner..." Lizzy put her hand up with a wide grin adorning her face, "and Josie Lagasse." If you are interested in any of the works displayed here tonight, please come by the office, and someone will be happy to help you take it home...for a price, that is." When he was finished, the crowd gave a chuckle and resumed their mingling.

"There you guys are," said Richard, as he came striding toward them. "Your work is lovely, Lizzy." He leaned in to give her a kiss on the cheek, and William scowled.

"Thank you," she replied before she turned her attention to William. "You've been so pleasant all evening. What brought that on?" His cousin chortled, and William's lips turned up on one side as he shrugged.

Jane and Charles came up and each hugged Lizzy. "I think this year's works are better than last year's," Jane gushed.

Lizzy rolled her eyes. "You say that at every show."

"Well, it's true!"

Lizzy smiled and shook her head, and William noticed the crowd seemed to be thinning since Mr. Lucas's announcement. He wanted to buy one of her paintings, but he thought he would return later in the week to have a longer look before he made a final decision. "How long are you required to stay?" he asked.

"I'm only required to stay until nine, and I believe he thanked everyone at about five minutes before." She glanced around him where a clock on the wall read five after nine.

Charles clapped his hands together and rubbed them excitedly. "Shall we go then?"

"Where are we going?" asked Lizzy.

"On the walk here, Jane and I noticed The Balcony has a jazz band and dancing tonight. We thought it might be fun."

Inwardly, William was groaning. *Why dancing*? He was a horrible dancer, not that he'd been much better at speaking lately. Richard and Lizzy enthusiastically agreed, and they walked back to where Acadiana was and took the steps up the side of the building to the jazz club upstairs.

"Would you like something to drink?" he asked Lizzy once they were inside.

"I would love some moscato, but I don't know if they have any. I've never been here." He felt like he shouldn't be surprised, but he was. They made their way to a large table to one side of the dance floor and took a seat. A waitress in a white tuxedo shirt, black skirt, and cummerbund quickly appeared, and William and Charles began to order.

Once Charles had ordered for Jane, William leaned forward. "Do you have moscato?"

94

"No, sir, but we do have champagne." He saw Charles subtly shake his head, so William pulled out his wallet and casually removed and handed the woman a hundred dollar bill so that Lizzy didn't see.

"I believe there's a liquor store on the next block that carries the lady's favorite." With his eyes, he beseeched his friend to help him. Charles leaned forward and whispered the name of the wine to the waitress, and she noted it on her pad. "The money should cover the wine and the remainder can be split between you and whoever you send."

The waitress's eyes widened, "Yes, sir."

He ordered himself a scotch, and she took Richard's order before she made her way back to the bar.

Charles leaned forward, laughing. "You should realize that Lizzie's moscato costs about eleven dollars, so you just tipped the waitress and the barkeep she sends over forty each."

William chuckled. "Then hopefully we'll get good service for the evening." He looked at his friend earnestly. "You can't say you wouldn't do the same for Jane."

Charles chuckled. "I've never put my foot in it as badly as you have, so I've never needed to. Besides, Jane prefers merlot, which most places carry." He felt a hand on his arm, and turned to find Lizzy attempting to get his attention, a worried expression on her face.

"Did you order my drink? She never asked me what I wanted."

"Yes, I took care of it." Lizzy nodded and smiled. He noticed Jane and Charles rise and move to the dance floor. That was when he decided that bad dancer or not, he would swallow his pride and ask Lizzy, but he was too late. As he leaned forward to ask her, she stood and began following Richard onto the dance floor. She looked back and gave him a shy smile before his cousin took her in his arms.

William glowered and waited for the song to be over, but all that happened was Richard and Charles swapped partners. Deciding that his friend was less of a threat than his cousin, he relaxed some, waiting for his chance. When the song ended, Richard walked toward the back of the club, and Jane made her way over to him.

"Come dance with me."

"Jane, I'm a horrible dancer."

"I doubt you're that bad. Plus, I *know* you want to dance with my sister, and sitting over here with a sour expression the entire night won't put her in your arms." She wrapped her hand around his forearm and pulled. "Come on!"

He stood and walked with Jane out to where there were about five couples swaying to the music. He put his arm around her, and she took his other hand as they began to move.

"Relax, Will. You're doing okay, but you're stiff as a board." He took a deep breath and exhaled.

"I haven't tried to dance since high school."

Her expression was incredulous. "Why not?"

Shrugging, he continued to concentrate on his feet. "I stepped on my date's foot at prom, and I was so embarrassed that I always refused to dance at any function after that."

"It couldn't have been that bad."

He grimaced. "She had small feet, and my foot only caught a portion of hers. Her foot became somewhat swollen..." He was surprised when Jane let a chuckle escape before she managed to stifle it.

"I'm sorry. I really shouldn't laugh, but I can only imagine." She looked down at their shoes. "Keep your feet close to the floor like you are now, and you might bump my feet, but you won't hurt me." He nodded. The song soon ended, and Jane looked over to Lizzy. "I think I'll take my husband back now," she said with a grin.

William looked to Lizzy and held out his hand. "May I?" He noticed the blush that accompanied the almost shy smile that she seemed to be using only with him. She stepped forward, and he wrapped his arm around her and took her hand, pulling her closer than he had held Jane. They were a hair's breadth from touching, and he wished he had the right to draw her the remainder of the distance.

"I was under the impression that you don't dance." She raised her face to him with her right eyebrow raised.

"Who told you that?"

"I didn't like the idea of leaving you on your own at the table, but Richard assured me that you never dance. He also said that you wouldn't expect us to keep you company."

He smiled. The statement sounded like something Richard would say, and typically he would be correct. At work and charity functions, he typically found business associates to speak with while most couples danced. "I don't expect anyone to remain behind to entertain me if they'd rather be dancing, so he isn't incorrect."

"Why don't you dance?"

"Because I'm horrible at it," he laughed. "You can be honest."

"I don't see any problem with your dancing, but then I'm no proficient. Jane was the dancer growing up. I was the tomboy who liked to draw and paint."

"You were a tomboy?" he asked, genuinely surprised.

She shrugged. "I liked to dress up in pretty things, but I'd go out and play in the mud, climb trees, and ride horses. My mother didn't know what to do with me, because I'd come home with my dresses torn and stained, my hair flying in all directions and tangled with twigs. She cut my hair to about my shoulders, so when it dried, the curl bounced up without the weight of the length, and it was to my chin. Then she bought me jeans at the local thrift store."

"Did you complain?"

"About my hair—yes, not that she listened. She just pulled it into a tight ponytail so it looked like I had a poof of curls on top of my head." He bit his lip to keep from chuckling. "It's okay. You can laugh. Everyone does when they see pictures of me from when I was a kid."

"You'd never know to look at you now. You look lovely."

"Thank you," she responded as she averted her eyes.

He was beaming by the time the song ended. She'd seen fit to tell him a story about herself. It meant a lot to him that she was sharing those experiences with him. She wrapped her hand around his arm and he escorted her back to the table, where Richard was looking at him with an amused expression.

The waitress returned with their drinks, opening Lizzy's wine and serving it at the table. "You bought a bottle?" she asked with wide eyes when it was placed in a container of ice near Lizzy's seat.

"The bottles are half the size of most wine bottles, and you usually drink the entire bottle at Jane's."

"Yes, but I don't pay restaurant prices there."

He put his arm on the back of her chair as he leaned in a bit further. "Don't worry, I've already taken care of it."

Her shoulders slumped a bit, and she looked at him defiantly. "I don't need to be taken care of."

Leaning farther in, he looked directly in her eyes. "I know you're an intelligent and capable woman. Tonight is a special night, with the reception for your show. I just wanted to treat you."

"But with the car..."

"The car is so that you and Melanie have safe transportation, and has nothing to do with this. You also paid me for the car."

"I still owe you though."

"No, you don't," he said adamantly. "Drink your wine. We're supposed to be celebrating." He watched one of her eyebrows quirk up as she lifted her glass to follow his directions.

"Yes, sir."

"That's better," he stated with a grin, and noticed her lip turn up on one side. They watched the band perform while they enjoyed their drinks for a bit. When Lizzy had finished her glass, most of the band members exited the stage area for their break, leaving the pianist and the singer. They began a song that he eventually realized was one he'd heard before and he leaned over and asked her to dance.

He enjoyed the faint blush that appeared on her cheeks, and once he felt her relax in his arms, he gently eased her so that their bodies were touching. Her breath was warm on his neck as he touched his cheek to her silky hair.

The next number was faster, and he led her back to the table where he filled her glass with the remainder of the bottle. They watched Jane and Charles dance, and spied Richard dancing with Lizzy's friend, Charlotte.

When the music slowed down again, William persuaded Lizzy to stand up with him again. Unlike before, he could tell that she was feeling a little tipsy from the wine, since she leaned against him a bit more than she had the last time they danced. The song ended, and he drew back to brush a few curls from her eyes. "Are you ready to leave?" He realized he was being rather forward, but was relieved that Lizzy didn't seem to object. The last thing he wanted to do was to push. Somehow, he didn't feel that she would respond well to it.

"I am, but it doesn't look like anyone else is."

He looked over and saw Charles and Jane beginning to dance to the next song as Richard joined Charlotte and her party at their table. Placing his hand on the small of her back, he steered her over to Charles and Jane. He leaned in to Charles' ear so he could hear them over the music. "Lizzy is ready to go, but I'd be happy to drive her if you'd like to stay longer."

Charles gave him a knowing look. "We aren't quite ready, but we'd be happy to drive Richard to the guest house if he'd like to remain."

"I'll ask him, thanks."

Richard wasn't ready to leave, so after Lizzy said her goodbyes to everyone, William pointed out where his cousin was seated to Charles before he steered Lizzy outside. The weather had cooled considerably since they'd arrived, and she inhaled and folded her arms across her body as they descended the stairs. When they reached the bottom, William shrugged off his suit jacket and draped it over her shoulders.

"Thank you," she said softly. "I guess I shouldn't have left my coat in the car. You aren't cold, are you?"

"No, but I have sleeves."

She laughed lightly as he unlocked his car and opened her door. "Always the gentleman," she quipped with a grin as she stepped into the car.

He pulled away from the curb and began driving toward Netherfield, Lizzy pivoted her body toward him. "I really enjoyed this evening, thank you for everything."

"I had fun as well. I'm glad you weren't repulsed by my dancing." He smiled as she began laughing.

"I don't think you're as bad as you think you are. I found you to be a charming dancer."

"Miss Gardiner, flattery will get you everywhere." She smiled, and they fell into a comfortable silence for the remainder of the ride.

When they arrived at Netherfield, William found that Lizzy had fallen asleep while he'd been driving. He knew he would have to wake her, but he took a few minutes just to watch her as she slumbered. She was so natural, and he thought, beautiful. She couldn't be called a classic beauty like her sister, but he loved the way the moonlight coming from the window reflected off of her hair, and he wanted nothing more than to run his hands through it. He reached out and gently pushed a curl from her eyes, running his fingers down the soft skin of her cheek, when her eyes fluttered open.

"Are we there?" she said softly, as she turned forward in the seat.

He quickly exited and opened her door. When she stepped out, he straightened his jacket that still rested upon her shoulders. She wrapped a hand around one of his arms, and he led her into the house. Mrs. King was happily knitting and watching television when they walked into the living room, and Lizzy disengaged herself from the warmth of his jacket and handed it to him.

"I didn't expect you so early, dear. From what your sister said, I thought she would keep you out until at least midnight."

"I haven't had the inclination to be out that late for a few years, ma'am." Lizzy reached into her purse and attempted to hand the grandmotherly woman a few bills.

"Oh no, your sister took care of that before you left." She put her knitting in her bag and put it on her shoulder. "She had a cup of milk during the movie, I read her a few books, and she fell right to sleep. That little girl of yours is a perfect angel."

Lizzy chuckled. "I don't know about angel. She knows exactly how cute she is."

Mrs. King giggled. "They always do. I'll show myself out. Good night."

They both said goodnight, and Lizzy made a trip upstairs to check on her daughter while William poured himself a glass of scotch. When she returned, she seemed surprised to see him still there. "You're still here?"

"I was going to stay until Charles and Jane returned."

"I'll be fine on my own. I stay at Longbourn by myself with Melly."

"You also have Bear. Charles tells me that he's a pretty good watch dog."

"So you're staying to be my watch dog?" She raised her eyebrow.

"I...I didn't mean it that way." She burst out laughing and he shook his head. "You're welcome to go to sleep if you're tired."

"I won't leave you down here on your own. Just let me change out of this dress, so I don't ruin it." He nodded as she went back upstairs. He took a long sip of his drink, and made himself comfortable on the sofa. She wasn't gone long, and returned wearing a pair of yoga pants and a long sleeve shirt.

"So you've got some of Charles' scotch. I'll go see if Jane has something in the kitchen." He rose and trailed behind her, looking in the refrigerator while she looked where Jane kept the liquor. They laughed when they found a bottle of her wine already chilling. "She's always prepared," smiled Lizzy.

William opened the bottle and poured her a glass. They went to the living room, and he started a fire in the fireplace. They spoke of the art at the show, and Lizzy explained some of the other artists and their work. She asked him about D&F, and he told her how his father began the company. He'd turned to stare into the fire when he was speaking of his father, so he didn't notice when she dozed off. When he realized she was asleep, he put down his scotch and carried her upstairs to the room where she'd always stayed. He lay her down, covered her with the quilt, and trailed the backs of his fingers down her cheek before he turned to leave the room.

Noticing the crib in the corner, he stepped over and peered inside. Melanie was sleeping in the same position that Lizzy had curled into when he'd placed her on the bed. He smiled tenderly as he glanced back at Lizzy one more time, and returned downstairs to wait for the Bingleys to return.

Chapter Eight

Lizzy snuggled deeper into the quilt when she woke the next morning. As she lay there, she tried to remember coming upstairs to bed, but the memory was just not there. The last thing she could recall was William telling her about his father.

"Oh no," she groaned, "I fell asleep on him."

She couldn't help but give a dreamy sigh as she thought about the remainder of the evening. William was very sweet, and she still couldn't believe that he'd danced. She'd seen him scowling when Richard escorted her to the dance floor, but his cousin had assured her that William never took part in the activity. Her surprise when she saw Jane pulling him out with them had been considerable.

Peering over the covers, she noticed Melanie was still breathing evenly, and smiled. She would have some time to just lie there and relive the previous night. There was so much of it that she wanted to indelibly imprint in her mind so that she could replay it whenever she wished.

The way it felt to be in his arms was something she'd never experienced before. His large hand pressed firmly to her back as he occasionally rubbed with his thumb. The touch lingered long after he'd released her, and she experienced the same sensation when he placed his hand in the small of her back as they left the club. A part of her was a bit mortified at how relaxed she became after the second glass of wine. She hadn't intended to dance so closely or touch her temple to his cheek, but she was so comfortable that she'd forgotten herself.

Then when they returned to Netherfield, she drank the other bottle of wine. Granted, one of her bottles was half the size of a regular bottle, so she'd only drank one bottle by most people's standards. But the amount was more than she was accustomed to drinking. She'd been truly interested in hearing about the company; the wine had sabotaged her.

She was just beginning to doze off once more when she heard rustling.

"Mama?" She lay there for a moment, not moving, in the hopes that Melly was talking in her sleep. "Mama!"

She pulled herself up to see her daughter standing in the crib with one leg thrown over the side. "Don't you dare, young lady!" she cried as she scrambled out of bed. Melanie pulled her leg back, and Lizzy looked her straight in the eye. "You don't climb out of your bed. You could get hurt. Big owie, okay?"

Her daughter looked at her and nodded. "Okay."

Lizzy held out her arms and swung Melanie out of the crib and into her arms. "Let's take you potty and then go see if Aunt Jane is up and cooking breakfast yet."

The girls arrived downstairs to find that they seemed to be the first two up, so Lizzy began the coffee and rummaged through the pantry to see what there was for breakfast. Once she'd decided what she was going to cook, she put Melanie in her seat and cut up a banana on her tray. She made her daughter some scrambled eggs and toast and then began cutting vegetables for an omelet. Once she cooked down some onions and garlic, she added some frozen asparagus and let it heat through. As she pulled the pan off the stove, she heard a faint knock at the back door.

A blush diffused her cheeks when she realized it was William, and swiftly opened the door to let him inside. "I didn't expect to see you this morning."

"I had to take Richard to the airport early, and Jane insisted that I come by for breakfast."

Lizzy laughed. "She's not even awake yet, but I was just making the filling for omelets if you're interested."

He beamed at the invitation, and Lizzy felt a flutter in her stomach.

"Do you need any help with anything?"

"If you'd like some toast, you can make that while I make the eggs." He nodded as she handed him a loaf of sourdough bread. "It may sound like a strange question, but when you eat fried eggs, how do you like them?"

"Over easy, why?"

"I can make an omelet the traditional way, but I like my eggs over medium, so I make them that way, and then fill them with the ingredients."

"I'm not sure..." He looked at her skeptically.

"How about I make one and you can try it? If you don't like it, I will make you a more traditional omelet."

He agreed, and so she took out the eggs. She sprayed the pan with cooking spray and poured in enough egg whites to cover the bottom, cracking one egg on the top. When it had set enough, she carefully flipped it, pleased she had managed not to fold it in the process. Then she put some Monterey jack cheese and the asparagus filling and folded it in half with the yolk up so it would not overcook. As soon as the cheese melted, she placed it on a plate and set it in front of William.

He looked at it dubiously and she laughed. "Pop the yolk, spread it around and try it. It's good. I promise." She watched while he did as he was instructed and took a bite, chewing completely and swallowing before he looked up at her.

"It's really good!" he exclaimed in a surprised voice.

"I told you! Would you like some coffee?"

"I'll get it. Make yourself one and come sit with me."

He rose and prepared his coffee while she put on some milk to warm for her own, and began her eggs. When she finished making hers, he placed a piece of buttered toast on her plate and she sat down next to him with her cup of café au lait.

"I'm really sorry that I fell asleep on you last night. In my defense, I can't remember the last time I drank that much."

He chuckled. "I presumed as much. Don't make yourself uncomfortable. I wasn't offended."

"I do have one question though. How did I get to bed? I don't remember."

Shrugging, he swallowed a bite of toast. "You were sleeping so peacefully, and I didn't want to wake you, so I carried you."

Lizzy choked on her drink. Did he really carry her to bed and she never woke? "I appreciate your doing that, but you should've awakened me. I wouldn't want you to hurt yourself." He began laughing and she regarded him questioningly. "What?"

"You weigh next to nothing. I won't hurt myself."

"Thank you," she said as she blushed. He nodded and she heard Melanie calling her. Lizzy took her out of her high chair and cleaned her up. Her daughter then ran over to where she had a basket of toys in the corner and began to play.

"What do you have planned today?" he asked as she returned to her seat.

"I need to finish my Christmas shopping."

He grinned. "I'd be happy to go with you."

"And normally I'd accept, but Jane and I had planned to go together."

"What did we plan on doing together?" Lizzy started when she heard her sister's voice.

"I was just telling William that we we're going Christmas shopping today."

"Actually, I have some paperwork I need to complete for Monday, so I can't go."

Lizzy noticed Jane was playing with her necklace, a telltale sign that she was lying. Lizzy stood and walked over to her sister, removing Jane's hand from the charm. Her sister winked at her and she shook her head.

"I'll make your breakfast."

Jane grabbed her arm. "I can make my own. You and William are going to have to stop by Longbourn to feed Bear, so you should probably get dressed so you can get on the road."

Lizzy stared at her sister. When had Jane turned into milder version of her mother? Olivia Bennet would match her daughters with whomever she thought was best for them, which was usually based on money not character. Jane hugged Lizzy and whispered in her ear. "I just want you to get to know him. I'm not saying you have to marry him, but he deserves a fair chance at winning your heart."

She kissed Jane on the cheek and looked in the other direction so that William wouldn't notice that she was suppressing her anger. Lizzy had been enjoying William's company, but she felt Jane's matchmaking was going too far. She didn't like feeling pushed or manipulated.

Lizzy's attention was drawn back to the present by her sister's voice. "Leave your dishes on the table. Melly and I can load the dishwasher later."

"I need to get dressed, and then we can go." William nodded and Lizzy hurried upstairs and into the shower. She quickly bathed and dressed in the jeans and blouse she'd brought with her. Once she'd put on her shoes, she packed up her dress in its bag and re-packed her overnight bag. Bringing it all downstairs, she placed her belongings at the foot of the stairs while she said goodbye to her daughter. When she returned, William was waiting for her with her things.

"We'll need to take my car for the hatchback," explained Lizzy. He nodded and they loaded everything in her car. "Would you like to drive it?"

"I drove this one, and several other models before I bought it."

She regarded him curiously. "What made you choose this one?"

"The rest seemed rather small for a car seat." He shrugged as he continued. "I know it's just the two of you, but it seemed the most practical."

She smiled and shook her head while they took their seats. They drove to Longbourn, where he helped her unload her bags, and let out Bear. Lizzy filled a metal bowl from a plastic bin of dog food in the laundry room and placed it next to the fresh water she had on the porch.

"Won't he want to come inside?" asked William curiously.

"He does come in sometimes during the day, but really he prefers to be outside. I keep him in at night because he likes to roam, and I don't want him to find his way to the highway. During the day, he stays closer to the house, really only venturing into the woods behind the garage."

"I wonder why," he mused aloud.

"I don't know," Lizzy responded, shrugging. "I do bring him inside more during cooler weather, and sometimes he'll follow me in when I first arrive home. Other than that, he'll sit at the door to go outside." She brushed her hands against each other as she glanced around as if she was double-checking that she had accomplished everything. "I'm ready when you are."

William followed her through the house, where she picked up the keys she'd left on the table against the wall in the foyer, and they departed.

William had hugged and kissed Jane on the cheek the moment Lizzy stepped out of the kitchen. He was thrilled to be spending the day with her. A part of him wished he could call it a date, but he knew that being together even as friends was a big step.

He also derived a great amount of satisfaction from seeing her drive the car. She seemed to have adjusted to the differences from her old clunker, and he smiled seeing her campus parking pass and MP3 player in their places.

The first stop was a boutique that sold bath and skincare products, where Lizzy picked out a gift box of rose scented products for Jane. As she was looking, William realized, listening to her speak with the sales associate, that she came in periodically. Hearing a product mentioned, he smelled a bottle of almond body oil and realized it was the scent he'd come to associate with her. Motioning to another sales associate, he had them wrap up a box of the different items in that line. He then had a box of the lavender products wrapped up for Mrs. Lyla Reynolds, his family's former housekeeper.

He paid, and then waited for Lizzy as she completed her purchase. When they turned to leave, she looked at the bag, surprised. "You found something?"

"Yes, I bought a present for Mrs. Reynolds. She was our housekeeper since just before I was born."

"That long?" He nodded. "Is she here in town?"

"Yes, her family lives here. She insists that I come to dinner every couple of weeks. If I ever find a place to live that has enough room, I hope she'll come back."

"Does she want to work again, or is she happy being retired?"

"She doesn't need to work. My father set her up with a great retirement, but she keeps saying that if I ever have need of her, she wants to return." They put their bags in to the back and they took their seats. "Where to now?"

"The toy store," she responded as she pulled out.

"What are you getting Melanie?"

Lizzy smiled. "She's getting a toy kitchen from Santa. Then I'll get her a box of dishes, a book, and some things for her stocking."

"She's not a tomboy like you were?"

"No, she's definitely a girly girl, but she has a mischievous streak that you could say is like me. Fortunately, she doesn't seem to be much like her father."

"Is he a part of Melanie's life?"

"No, he was...angry when he discovered I was pregnant. I haven't seen him since the night before she was born." He noticed she had a strange expression, and felt there was something to the pause in her statement. As much as he wanted to ask, he had the distinct impression that she wouldn't want to discuss it, and he didn't want to ruin their day.

She glanced at him briefly as they were turning into the toy store. "I'm sorry. My marriage wasn't good. He wasn't around much, and, well...things ended badly."

"He wasn't around much?" William couldn't imagine. All he wanted was to be with her all of the time.

"We were married just before he left for law school. He was accepted into LSU, and his father bought us a house in Baton Rouge. Initially he was around, but as time went by, he began spending a few days at a time away, then a week or so. After his father died, he'd disappear for months."

William was astounded. He now understood why Charles had said that she needed someone she could rely on. Jane's motives for helping him were also becoming clearer.

She turned off the car and had turned to face him. "I wasted enough of my life with him, so I'd rather not discuss him anymore, if you don't mind."

He nodded and they exited the car. As they walked toward the entrance to the store, she grabbed his arm. "Despite what I said, I don't want you to think that I regret my daughter. She's the only good thing that came from that time." Her hand relaxed its grip on his shirt, and he took it between his own.

"I would've never thought that of you." He kept her hand in his as they entered the large glass electric doors, and Lizzy led him to an aisle where they had several toy kitchens. She stopped at a pastel pink, vintage style kitchen, pointing to it with her free hand.

"Here it is."

William took one of the tags for it and turned to her. "Perhaps we should go find the other items." She nodded, and they quickly picked up everything plus a pair of dress up shoes for Melanie's stocking.

"What should I get her?" he asked before they checked out.

"You bought her the car seat. She doesn't need so many toys that she can't play with them all." He became aware that he must have a pretty dejected look on his face, because Lizzy began to chuckle.

110

"I'm going to feel guilty if you keep spending so much money on us. The car alone was more than enough."

"Lizzy," he said earnestly, "I take care of those who I care about. That includes you. The money doesn't matter."

"I understand your point of view. Please try to see it from mine?"

He wished she would just accept that he wished to do things for them, but he acquiesced. She paid for her purchases and pulled the car up to the front so an employee could load the kitchen into the back. They quickly returned to Longbourn, and William helped her bring the presents into the house and hide everything where Melanie wouldn't look.

When they had begun driving again, William turned toward Lizzy. "Why don't we go to lunch somewhere?"

"I think Jane is expecting us back soon. She probably has something planned."

He nodded, disappointed, as he attempted to gather the courage to try again. They were pulling into the driveway at Netherfield when he finally burst out, "I'd be happy to help you put the kitchen together." He saw her smile, and couldn't help but grin widely.

"Do you doubt my carpentry skills, Mr. Darcy?"

He laughed. "I have every faith in your skills, Ms. Gardiner, but it might help to have an extra set of hands."

She switched off the car and faced him. "I'd like that, thank you."

"Let me see your phone." She looked at him questioningly, but handed it to him. He dialed his number and pressed send. Once his rang and he stored her number, he saved his to her contact list.

When he returned her cell phone, she had an amused expression on her face. "You could've just asked for my phone number."

Enjoying her teasing, he smiled, and he felt his face become warm. "I could've but this way, I know you have mine as well. There are no excuses for not calling me."

Lizzy smiled and shook her head as she exited the car. He met her when she came around to the passenger side, and he gently grasped her hand. "I enjoyed going with you." He took great pleasure in watching her cheeks pink. She averted her eyes towards the windows of the house for a moment, and when they returned to his face, she leaned forward and placed a quick kiss on his cheek.

"Me, too."

William was sure he was still grinning from ear to ear when he stepped foot into the house. Charles looked at him curiously a few times, while Jane seemed to appear as happy as he felt. He did question whether she might have been watching through the window, but decided not to worry about it. She seemed to be his greatest supporter when it came to a relationship with Lizzy.

After a late lunch, Lizzy announced that she and Melanie would be returning to Longbourn.

"Why don't you stick around while Melly takes her nap?" Jane cajoled.

"If I leave now, she'll fall asleep in the car, and then I can clean house while she naps."

"The house is always immaculate, Lizzy."

"Because I clean it!" Lizzy laughed and hugged her sister. "I love you, but you and Charles need to have time to yourselves. When was the last time the two of you spent an afternoon in bed?" she asked softly. William hadn't meant to overhear, and looked out the window, pretending he had no knowledge of their conversation.

"Don't answer that!" Lizzy continued. "I don't want to know. It was just meant to make you think."

Turning in time to see Jane's expression of shock and embarrassment, William couldn't help but chortle. "I didn't mean to eavesdrop. I'm sorry, but I turned in time to see Lizzy's face when she told you not to answer." Jane reddened. "I think I'll be going as well." He watched as Lizzy wrapped her daughter in her sweater and hugged Jane.

"Call me when you come up for air."

"LIZZY!"

They all were laughing when Charles returned from his study. "What's so funny in here?"

"It's nothing, really." William said as he hugged Jane and shook his friend's hand. Melanie gave her aunt and uncle each a kiss on the cheek and they walked out to the car. "You embarrassed your sister on purpose, didn't you?"

She grinned while she buckled her daughter into her seat and stood to face him. "I truly did enjoy shopping with you today, but my sister deserved a bit of retribution for putting me on the spot this morning."

Shaking his head, he donned an expression of mock reproof. "You should be ashamed of yourself, young lady."

One side of her lips turned up, and she began to fidget nervously with her hands. "I just think that whether we become simply friends or more than that should be something that happens on its own. That we shouldn't be pushed by others." By the end of her statement, she was looking at her fumbling fingers. He brushed a few curls behind her ear and tipped her chin up to look him in the eye.

"I wouldn't want you to ever feel like you are being pressed to be someone you aren't or to feel something that you don't." He felt her body relax with the tips of his fingers that were resting on her neck. She gave him a shy smile and reached up to wrap her arms around his neck to hug him. Wrapping his around her body, he pulled her just a bit closer and breathed in her scent while he had the opportunity. When she drew back, she planted a kiss on his cheek and got into her car.

He watched her pull away, and then walked back to the guest house with a feeling of hope he'd been scared to let loose until now. After all, that kiss had been a bit longer than the previous, and she'd hugged him. It was most definitely progress.

As Lizzy pulled out onto the highway, her mind was still full of William. He was so perfect the night before, and she was still amazed that he would want to go shopping with her. What man *wants* to go shopping if he can avoid it?

She then realized that she didn't have a Christmas present for him. Moreover, she'd no idea what to give him. He, no doubt, had enough money to ensure he could purchase anything he ever wanted, and at more expensive prices than what she could afford.

When she reached Longbourn, she put Melanie in her bed and opened her laptop. She had no clue what she was searching for, but deciding that anything might help, she searched his name and waited to see what would appear.

After twenty minutes of hunting through useless articles on his business, she was about to give up when she noticed a headline that piqued her interest.

'Pemberley restoration to remove 200 years of grime.'*

Clicking on the link, she found a photo of a beautiful British estate with scaffolding and drapes covering a large portion of the walls.

'A £15m project at the famous Derbyshire estate is restoring the limestone exterior to its original splendor. The work, which includes cleaning and replacing the limestone on the exterior of the grand home, will not only remove grime, but will also turn back the clock on nearly 200 years of weather damage.

"It's exciting to see Pemberley as it must have looked to my ancestor, Fitzwilliam Darcy, who rebuilt the estate after a fire in 1820," said owner, William Darcy, who ensured the limestone for the restoration came from the same quarry as the stone for the 1820's project...'

An idea coming to mind, she opened a new window and conducted an image search for Pemberley. Finding, a view she liked, she printed a photo and toyed with the idea of having it printed larger at an office supply store.

"I'll make do with this for now," she muttered to herself, deciding she'd have a larger poster size made if she required it. She'd used

114

print-your-own poster websites, but there were always portions of the photo missing, and it made it difficult to draw.

She closed her laptop and stared at the photo, then she walked through the mudroom off the kitchen to where she had her studio. Her largest drawing board was placed on her worktable, followed by a large sheet of watercolor paper. Using art tape, she immobilized the paper on the board and then tacked the photo to the wall next to her. Sitting on her stool, she pivoted it so she was facing the picture and leaned the drawing board against the wall.

An initial sketch for a watercolor didn't always take very long, but she took her time, checking her angles and measuring to ensure she managed to recreate the image as close to the picture as possible. She'd just finished the house when she heard Melanie through the baby monitor two and a half hours later. Pleased with what she'd accomplished so far, she placed the drawing on her worktable, and returned after her daughter went to sleep, only going to sleep herself once the initial sketch was completed.

Information on the restoration is adapted from a BBC article reporting on the recent restoration of Chatsworth, in Derbyshire, England. http://www.bbc.co.uk/news/uk-england-derbyshire-17285696

Chapter Nine

Lizzy had wanted to have a discussion with Jane about the shopping trip, but the chance didn't arise until they went to Pilates on Wednesday. Not wanting to possibly argue before class, she suggested a trip to Gouldings for some coffee before they returned to Netherfield. When they'd ordered and taken a seat, Lizzy took a deep breath.

"I want to talk to you about Saturday."

Jane looked puzzled. "What about it?"

"I know that you and Charles are friends with William, but I don't appreciate being put on the spot the way I was that morning."

"You like him and you know it. I'm just trying to help you along."

Lizzy didn't like her sister's response and became defensive. "I don't know how I feel, but I do know that I don't want to be pushed."

"We aren't trying to push you, Lizzy. He's a good guy, and I think you should give him a chance." She took a deep breath. "I probably shouldn't tell you this, but he was so happy to be going with you, he hugged me when you left to take a shower."

She couldn't help but smile at the image. After taking a sip of her coffee, Lizzy leaned forward and looked Jane directly in the eye. "Regardless, I want to figure this out with William on my own. The other day, I felt like when I would come home from college for the holidays and mom would have my whole vacation scheduled with dates with Greg." Jane sighed and Lizzy sat back in her chair.

Her sister groaned. "I knew you were probably a bit annoyed with my deception, but I hadn't thought about that. I'm sorry."

"I wasn't sure if you remembered. I'm not angry anymore. I just didn't like the feeling that being with William is expected of me."

"I know that mom and dad always had unfair expectations, and I don't want to put the pressure on you that they did." Jane's hand reached out to take hers. "I love you regardless of who you have a

116

relationship with. Please understand that Charles and I only want you to be happy."

Smiling, Lizzy blinked back the tears that were forming in her eyes. "Thanks, sis. I love you, too."

Jane stood and pulled up Lizzy to hug her. When she drew back, Lizzy saw Jane wipe a tear from her eye. "Now, I think we should head back to the house. Charles will worry if we're running late." Both picked up their cups of coffee, and once they had been on the road for a while, Jane suddenly furrowed her brow. "Why don't you know how you feel?"

Lizzy sighed. "Until about a week ago, I couldn't stand the man. I understand why I felt that way, but then there's the way I feel when I'm with him now."

"Initially, I think you wanted his attention, and you felt he was dismissing you." Jane was smiling widely and Lizzy began to laugh.

"When did you get a degree in psychology, Dr. Bingley?"

Jane began laughing with her. "It makes sense though. You usually laugh people like that off, and every time you were around him, you became increasingly more hostile toward him. There's a reason why people say it's a thin line between love and hate." Jane checked her mirrors and then glanced at Lizzy. "What about now?"

"I don't know if I want to say," said Lizzy as she blushed and faced the window.

"Spill!" she demanded with a wide grin.

She rolled her eyes and remained facing her window. "When he places his hand on my back, I feel it even after he has removed it. When his breath hits my ear and neck, he…"

"And when he holds you in his arms, you're home."

"I thought it would sound silly," confessed Lizzy as she turned to face Jane.

"No, honey, you just described how I feel about Charles." Jane pulled into the garage and turned off the car.

Lizzy shook her head. "But you knew Charles for a couple of years before you were married. I doubt you felt this way from the beginning."

"Actually, he took me dancing for our third date and I knew. Don't judge all men by the exceedingly paltry experience you have with them...well, with *him*. William would never be like him, and would never hurt you the way he did."

"I know," Lizzy said softly, "but I'm just hesitant. I guess I want to know this time."

"You knew it was wrong last time, and you can't tell me that you didn't."

She sighed. "I did, but I never would've admitted it. I just wanted mom and dad's approval, which was short-lived. Mom quickly decided that I shouldn't be pursuing my MFA, and that I should be barefoot and pregnant."

Both women were startled when the side door to the garage opened and Charles walked in. "Are you ladies going to sit in the garage all day?"

They laughed as they exited the car and followed him into the house, where Lizzy found William sitting on sofa reading books to her daughter. Melanie was seated comfortably in his lap, her head resting against his chest as his deep voice smoothly narrated the story.

She startled when Charles appeared at her side. "She saw William, and I became obsolete, it seems. He's been reading to her for the last half hour." Charles wore a warm smile and she nodded just before he left to go find Jane. As she turned back, William finished the book and closed it. When he discovered Lizzy watching, he grinned broadly and stood, carrying Melanie with him.

"Hi Melly Belly," she said as she held out her arms. Her daughter didn't lean toward her as usual, but instead, she snuggled in closer to William, angling herself away from Lizzy.

He looked at her guiltily. "I'm sorry."

118

She shook her head. "Don't be. She's comfortable with you, and obviously likes you. I'm glad she has Charles, and I wouldn't be upset if she had you as an important part of her life, as well."

He was visibly pleased by her statement, and Lizzy was relieved that he wasn't averse to the idea. After all, if he was interested in her, she and Melanie were a package deal.

"We should go. I need to get Melly her dinner soon."

"I'll walk you out."

She nodded, and after saying bye to Charles and Jane, they walked out to where Lizzy's car was waiting. William buckled Melanie into her seat and gave her a kiss on the cheek. "Bye bye, Melly."

Her daughter giggled. "Bye bye."

He stood, closed the door, and turned to face Lizzy. Leaning in, he kissed her on the cheek. "Would you call me to let me know you made it safely?"

"Yes," she said softly, "of course." Her cheeks were warm and she wondered if she was blushing. She gave William an awkward little wave, and climbed into the car. He watched her pull out of the driveway, so she never saw him return to the house before she left.

The drive home was uneventful, and when she got there, she texted William that she would call him as soon as her daughter was settled in for the night. Melanie was showing signs of fatigue after her bath, so Lizzy sat in a chair in her daughter's room until she fell asleep, about thirty minutes before her usual bedtime.

Once she was sure Melanie was dreaming away, Lizzy cuddled in a blanket on her own bed and called William. She became suddenly nervous when she heard the phone ring, but wasn't able to worry for long.

"Hey," he said warmly, "is Melanie sleeping already?"

"Yes, she took a rather short nap this afternoon, so she was pretty wiped by the time she had her bath." He chuckled and her anxiety dissipated.

"What do you usually do after she falls asleep?"

"It depends. Some nights I read and others I paint. I watch TV at times, but that's rare. Most of my TV time is spent watching cartoons."

"I would imagine you watch a lot of cartoons about kittens."

"She has other movies, but that's her favorite, so yes…What were you doing when I called?"

He exhaled. "I was going through some paperwork for a meeting tomorrow."

"You don't sound like you're enjoying it."

"We're firing executives to a subsidiary because they deliberately went against a directive from corporate."

"What did they do?"

"They were told six months ago to begin adhering to the new environmental laws that will be put into effect in a few years. Richard toured the facility before he arrived here, and discovered that they hadn't even begun to take the necessary measures. We spent the last few weeks making arrangements for the first phase of the upgrades and interviewing for replacement of upper management."

"Would you like to change the subject?"

"Very much so."

She smiled. "I want to have Saturday dinner over here. Jane is having Thanksgiving at her house, and we've been going over there a lot lately. Do you want to come?"

"Of course," he said with a pleased tone.

"I'm going to let you get back to your work though." He groaned, and she smiled.

"Don't leave me to my papers!"

"I'm sorry, but I have some work I want to do as well."

"Okay." She couldn't help but laugh at his rather morose tone.

"Bye, Will," she said softly.

"Bye."

When she heard the click from his side, she ended the call. As she crept down the stairs to her studio, William pervaded her thoughts. She couldn't deny that she already had feelings for him. He was really very sweet, and she found it endearing that he seemed to want nothing more than to take care of her. His purchase of the car, walking her to her show, and carrying her upstairs to bed when she fell asleep were evidence of his affection.

In a way, she felt her feelings were moving quickly—that they were moving forward quickly. The idea frightened her some, but she didn't know if she wanted to slow things down. How do you slow your feelings? Allowing her fear to overtake her wasn't an option. She'd allowed that when she remained married to Greg for all of those years. No, she wouldn't give in to fear.

Entering the studio, she decided that she might try to slow their relationship, but in her heart, she knew that the effort would be futile. She was falling, and falling fast.

The watercolor of Pemberley was still laying where she'd left it last, on her worktable. She turned on several lights and filled a cup with fresh water. Dabbing the dried watercolor pigments with some water, she let them sit for a moment while she checked to see which colors she would need more of on her palette. When she had everything prepared, she sat down and mixed the color she wanted, testing it on a small sheet of watercolor paper that was next to her.

The painting was coming along nicely. Lizzy had laid in the background washes and then some of the variations in color. Tonight she was going to lay in some of the final detail work. She hoped to have it finished before Thanksgiving, so that she could take it to be framed. Hulin's had always framed Lizzy's work when she needed it, but she didn't like asking for a rush job if it wasn't absolutely necessary. She painted until midnight, and then showered before she went to bed, falling asleep almost the moment her head hit the pillow.

William pulled up to Longbourn a few hours earlier than he knew Jane and Charles would be arriving. He and Lizzy had spoken on the phone for almost an hour the night before, and she'd said he could come whenever he liked but he was nervous that she might have changed her mind.

Stepping out of the car, he heard a growl, and looked down to see Bear displaying his teeth. "I didn't realize you were out," he said to the protective dog. He got back into his car and called Lizzy on the home number she'd given him when they spoke on the phone Thursday night.

"Hi William," she answered happily.

"I'm out front, and your dog won't let me out of my car." He heard some rustling as she laughed.

"I'll be right there." She was at the front door a minute later, and Bear left the driveway to sit next to her on the porch.

He stepped out of his vehicle and made his way over to her. "Thanks, I hadn't even noticed he was outside until I went to get out, and he let me know that I was unwelcome."

"You aren't unwelcome," she explained as she smiled. "He just wants to ensure that I know you before you come to the door. He'll trust you after a while." William nodded, and she turned to lead him into the house. As they were walking, he admired the way she looked in the jeans she was wearing, as well as how the black wrap-around top accentuated her curves. Her long hair was down around her shoulders, falling in loose curls down her back. He was fascinated with the way the sun highlighted the coppery-red color in her hair.

"What's in the bag?" She gestured toward a shopping bag he held in his hand as she removed his attention from her hair to what he was carrying.

"Oh, I brought wine."

"You didn't have to do that."

"I know, but you're making dinner, so I thought it was the least I could do."

William enjoyed the warm smile that came to her face. Bringing him into the kitchen, she patted the beige granite countertop of the island. He set the bag down as he surveyed the room.

He remembered Jane mentioning the kitchen had been remodeled within the last two years. The architect had accomplished his job well. The kitchen, while completely updated, didn't seem out of place in the old plantation home. He found that the liked the feel of the room very much.

"This is lovely," he said earnestly.

"Thanks." She smiled. "Charles had an architect come out and render some sketches and plans. Then Jane and I went shopping for everything and his contracting crew did the work."

William looked toward the rear of the house where a windowed door led to a small room with another door off the other side. "Where do those doors lead?"

"My great aunt remodeled the former slaves quarters so that they were attached to the house. She had a mudroom, laundry room, and art studio put back there. The upstairs was remodeled into storage on one side, as well as a modern master bathroom and walk-in closet just before Melanie and I moved in."

"I'd love to see your studio," he stated, as he turned back to face her. She paused from pulling wine out of the bag as an expression he couldn't identify appeared on her face.

"It's a wreck right now with the leftover mess from the show. Would you mind if I showed it to you another time?"

"No, I don't mind." He took the remaining bottles out of the bag, and she began looking at the labels.

"You didn't have to buy me more moscato."

"Isn't it your favorite?"

"Well, yes, but I drink other wines as well. It's just that we're having lasagna, and I think red wine would go better with the meal."

"So save it for later, or when you're in the mood for it."

"Are you sure?"

He could see that she was concerned that she might offend him, and ensured that he smiled. "Positive."

"I'll save it for when you're here."

He laughed. "I don't expect you to do that."

"But I'd prefer it that way." He loved that she wished to wait for him, despite the fact that it was unnecessary.

William watched as she picked up the two bottles and put them on a wine rack that was built into the upper cabinet. A bottle of red wine was removed and placed on the counter. "The merlot you brought will work with dinner, so we can drink those."

He picked up the bottle she'd taken down. "This is cabernet."

"Just in case." She moved to a bottom cabinet and pulled out a pot. "I was going to get the sauce going, so it can simmer on low heat for a while."

"I'd be happy to help if you need it."

Lizzy rummaged around in a cabinet, pulling out a food processor that she assembled on the counter. "Do you know how to operate one of these?"

"Ummm...not really, but if you teach me..." His heart stuttered as she laughed and gave him a quick lesson on how to use the appliance. Onions, garlic, carrots, mushrooms and spinach were quickly chopped and placed in bowls for her to use when she required them. They chatted about the house and her Aunt Mel as they worked comfortably with one another. When he was finished, he placed the blades and bowl in the sink, and glanced over where she was cooking the vegetables in with the meat. "I don't think I have ever had carrots in lasagna."

"You don't really taste them," she explained. "Melanie is still kind of finicky when it comes to vegetables, so I try to mix them into dishes where she won't find them."

He smiled. "You're a step ahead of her then."

Chuckling, she began adding sauce to the meat. "I try." Their laughter dwindled down and Lizzy gave him an inquiring look.

"You never speak of your parents," she commented. "What were they like?"

Caught off guard by the question, he paused for a bit. "I would imagine they were like most parents." He glanced up to see her turn down the heat on the sauce and give him her undivided attention. The subject of his mother and father was usually avoided, but he wanted her to know him, which meant learning about his parents and Ana. Unfortunately, there would be no escaping the conversation.

Lizzy reached out and placed a hand on his arm. "I was just curious about what you remember. You don't have to tell me anything that makes you uncomfortable."

"No, I don't mind," he stumbled out. "My mother...my mother was beautiful. She had this long, flowing blonde hair—like wheat. I remember how soft it was when I would hug her." He paused as he tried not to break down. "She was always trying to help others—charity functions, volunteer work—she did it all, until she couldn't any more.

"My father was a firm businessman, but he liked to take me camping. He also loved history, so we would visit museums."

When his eyes returned to her face, she was regarding him with a concerned expression. "They sound wonderful," she said softly, reaching up and embracing him. He remembered that her relationship with her parents was nothing like what he experienced, and despite the sadness he retained when he thought of his parents, he was thankful. He'd had a wonderful childhood, wonderful parents.

She stepped back and began attending to her cooking again, seasoning the sauce that had begun to gently bubble. When that task was completed, she began grating Parmesan. The conversation had moved on and she had been telling a humorous story about one of her students when he heard her inhale sharply.

"Are you okay?" William asked, stepping forward to see if he could help.

"Yes," she grumbled, as she ran her hand under some cool water. "I just tried to grate my hand is all."

He grabbed a towel and gently dabbed where he saw blood coming from the joint of her index finger. "Do you have any bandages?"

"In the cabinet next to the refrigerator."

He left her to hold pressure on it while he retrieved the box. When he returned, he pulled off the towel and applied the bandage. "Perhaps I should finish the Parmesan."

She nodded as she looked up to his face. Still holding the injured hand in his, he brushed her hair back from her face with the other. Slowly leaning forward, he saw her glance at his lips and back to his eyes. She wet her lips with her tongue, and he could resist no longer. He closed the remainder of the distance, brushing her mouth with his as he cradled her face in his hand. She sighed and he captured her lips once more before he drew back.

As her eyes opened, she blushed and looked down at her hand. "Thank you...for the help, that is."

He chuckled and kissed her forehead. Taking the grater she had placed beside the sink, he washed it and finished the cheese. Once it was stored in the refrigerator, he took Lizzy's hand and entwined his fingers with hers. "How much longer will Melly sleep?"

She looked over his shoulder to the clock. "Probably until four, so approximately another hour."

"Would you feel comfortable walking around the yard?"

"We can do that. Let me grab a sweater." When she returned, they left out of the mudroom, and began by strolling through the courtyard hand in hand. She showed him the three-hundred-year-old oak tree she'd climbed when she was little, pointed to the

126

portion of the woods where she had had a fort, and then they sat in the porch swing for a while before they decided to head back inside.

Lizzy checked in on Melanie, who was still fast asleep, and then put on the noodles to boil. William helped her to get everything ready, layer the lasagna, and put it in the oven. She'd just poured him a glass of merlot when they heard the knocker on the door.

"That'll be Jane and Charles," she said as she put the cork in the bottle.

"Why don't I go let them in while you finish pouring the wine?"

"Okay," she said with a smile.

He made his way to the foyer and opened the door before they could even knock. "You're here early?" exclaimed Jane as they came inside and began taking off their jackets.

He nodded, although he didn't elaborate on how long he'd been there. "Lizzy's in the kitchen, pouring the wine."

Charles beamed as he put his coat in the small closet off the foyer. "Great!"

He followed them through, and found Lizzy holding a glass of wine and three glasses in front of her. "Help yourself."

"Thanks, but I took some medicine for a headache earlier, so I'm not drinking," said Jane, as she picked up a bottle to examine the label. "I'm surprised you bought this though, Lizzy."

"Why's that?" William asked before Lizzy could interject.

"Because she hates merlot," laughed a clueless Jane.

He looked over to Lizzy, who closed her eyes. "Jane, William brought the merlot."

"Oh?" Jane looked up at the two of them. "Oooh." Everyone heard Melanie's chattering come through the monitor. "Why don't I go get her?" she said, as she placed the bottle back on the counter and escaped the kitchen with Charles laughing, following closely behind his embarrassed wife.

"Is that why you took down the cabernet?" She nodded, a guilty look on her face. "Why didn't you just say so?"

"I didn't want to offend you." She bit her bottom lip.

"I want to be a part of your life, so I would've discovered it eventually."

She lifted one shoulder and looked into her glass. "I guess I'd hoped that by the time you figured it out, you would've forgotten about today."

He took her glass and placed it on the island, as he pulled her to him with the other hand. Once she was in his arms, he tilted her face so she was looking him in the eye. "You wouldn't have offended me. I don't want you to be polite. I want you to be yourself."

She gave him a sheepish look. "I poured the merlot for Jane, Charles, and you. Mine is cabernet."

He chuckled. "You're a sneaky thing. I'm definitely going to have to keep a close eye on you." She opened her mouth to protest, but he captured it with his own. Her hand wrapped around the back of his neck and, deepening the kiss, he touched his tongue to her lips. He felt her tongue timidly touch his, and he pulled back just as he heard Charles' voice carrying through the door.

Lizzy backed away to the oven and peered in at the lasagna just before Jane and Charles re-entered the room with Melanie.

"Willyummm!!" Melanie exclaimed as she saw him.

"Hi sweetheart." His heart warmed as she ran and he swooped her up into his arms. He was hugging her when he looked over to Lizzy, who had a wistful expression on her face.

"Are you okay?" he mouthed.

She nodded and, after watching them for a moment, proceeded to start the garlic bread, while Jane prepped the salad. Soon they were all seated at the table in the kitchen, instead of the formal dining room. The hardwood floors, oak cabinets, and warm colored walls made it very homey, and the table and chairs in the kitchen were more comfortable than the original antique dining room furniture.

128

Melanie could also easily move to her toys when she was finished eating, so the adults could dine without interruption.

The meal was enjoyable—good food, good company, and Melanie insisted on sitting between William and her mother, which made him feel part of their family. That feeling was something that he realized he'd been missing for a long time.

Jane and Charles took Melanie up for a bath when everyone was finished, while William and Lizzy cleaned up the kitchen.

"You don't have to," she protested as she loaded the dishwasher.

He just continued to wipe down the table and the counters, ignoring her protests. When he was finished, he wrapped his arms around her from behind and kissed her ear. "I'm content as long as I'm with you." He heard her sniff, and looked around to see if she was crying. He really couldn't tell as she pulled away to put the dessert in the oven to warm and started the dishwasher. When she had set the ice cream on the counter to soften, she walked over and wrapped her arms around his waist. "Are you okay?" He felt her nod and ran his hand up and down her back.

They remained that way until Jane and Melanie returned. Jane gave him a questioning look, and he mouthed "It's okay," so she wouldn't worry. Melanie immediately demanded his attention, and he took her to the living room where they colored until she decided it was time for him to read.

The fireplace in the living room had a beautiful, roaring fire, thanks to Charles, and they all had their dessert, an apple crisp with ice cream, as they watched the flames dance in the grate.

When they were done, Jane collected the dishes and finished cleaning up the kitchen while Charles tucked Melanie into bed. Lizzy had at some point begun leaning against William, and he wrapped an arm around her shoulders. "You don't mind them tucking her in?"

"No," she said softly through a yawn, "I put her to bed most nights, and they seem to be so happy to do it. I think they missed her when we moved out."

"You lived with them?"

"I had nowhere to go when Melanie was born; Charles and Jane took me in."

"Your aunt had left you Longbourn though."

"I'd been unreachable after Aunt Mel's death. Longbourn was also left to me with very specific terms, so that Greg couldn't get his hands on it or any of Aunt Mel's savings."

"Can you tell me what happened?"

She turned and looked him pleadingly in the eye. "After my sister goes home."

He nodded, and stroked her hair as he stared into the fire. He wanted to know what happened that ended her marriage, but a part of him was also afraid of that knowledge.

Jane and Charles left soon after Melanie was asleep. William helped Lizzy turn off the lights in the kitchen and outside before they settled in on the sofa before the fire. William remained quiet, hoping that Lizzy would just begin when she felt comfortable. He had his arm wrapped snugly around her, and she was leaning into his side. He'd almost begun to doze when he heard her shaky voice begin its narration.

"I met Greg when I was sixteen. My parents were friends with his father, and they began pushing me toward him."

"At sixteen!" he said incredulously. "Why?"

"I was daddy's little girl when I was young. Jane thinks he saw something of himself in me, and decided that I'd succeed where he had failed. He'd never had the money to pursue the degree he wanted and worked his way up at the local bank. As a result, he pushed me toward becoming a doctor or a lawyer, but ultimately it wasn't what I wanted."

She took a deep breath, and he kissed her hair in the hopes that it would help dispel any nerves she had confiding in him. "By the time I was sixteen, I was already rebelling and Aunt Mel was helping me with my pursuit of being an artist. My mother decided that if I wasn't going to become a professional, then I should get married as

130

soon as I graduated high school. I think my dad just didn't care to argue with her.

"She'd arrange dates, and I guess I never saw the harm in it at the time. I also found that I enjoyed the acceptance I gained by giving in to them, so it continued through college, until Greg proposed the Christmas before I graduated. We were married that summer. I'd just turned twenty-one."

"You graduated college when you were twenty-one?" He knew it wasn't unheard of, but he did find it surprising.

"My father made me take college courses in the summer my junior and senior years of high school, so I had college credit when I officially began my degree." He nodded. "I discovered later, Greg's father had agreed to pay for law school, my masters, as well as buy us a house if he married me. I believe that he thought I'd be able to calm Greg down."

William furrowed his brow. "I don't understand."

"I'm not sure how he made it into law school with his GPA, but apparently he'd been quite the partier while he was getting his undergraduate degree. Mr. Wickham had hoped that being married to me would somehow curtail that. Greg's father died two years later, and that was when he became worse."

"Worse? How?"

"Do you remember how I told you he would disappear, at first for a few days, then for a few weeks, and finally for months at a time?"

William nodded.

"The house was foreclosed upon a few months after Mr. Wickham died. Unknown to me, Greg had taken out a mortgage on the property and had failed to make the payments.

"That and his car loan were how he ruined my credit. My name wasn't even on either of the loans." She was obviously still angry about the situation, and he couldn't blame her.

"I ended up shipping most of my valuables to Jane so they wouldn't get lost in storage, and I took a residency at the Bemis in Omaha.

They have studios with living quarters, which gave me a place to stay as well as a living allowance. Fortunately, I had just enough money for bus fare."

"I'd sold several works and managed my money well for the three months of the program, so I had enough for a down payment for a studio apartment when I returned. Greg had been in touch, and began the same behavior as he always had."

"Was he abusive?"

"Mostly, he was just never around. When he did show up, he was always drunk, and sometimes I'd wonder whether he was on drugs." She kind of shrugged one shoulder. "Greg was verbally abusive a few times, yelling at me about money, and he did threaten to hit me once or twice toward the end of our marriage."

"He felt you overspent?"

He could see her tense as she remembered. "He couldn't hold down a job, but I usually managed to keep one, so he'd felt that I should always have money for him when he showed up. If I didn't, then I'd usually wake to find something missing. Jane, at one time, offered to return my things that I'd sent her, but I was concerned he'd sell my belongings."

He began rubbing her arm. "You hadn't thought to leave him?"

"I was barely scraping by, and I was too embarrassed to go to Jane."

Nodding, he was thankful that he'd never been in a situation where he didn't have the family or money to obtain the help he required.

She took a deep breath, and he could feel as her body tensed. "I was certain he wasn't faithful, so I avoided being with him as much as possible during the last few years of the marriage. I also ensured he wore a condom when I wasn't successful."

William began to feel like he was going to vomit. He wasn't sure where she was going with the story, but there was no way it was going to end well. "He forced you?" he gritted out through clenched teeth.

132

"Not exactly, he was usually extremely drunk and I just let him, so that he'd leave me alone. That was how Melanie was conceived."

"Why did you remain with him for so long?"

He felt her shoulder lift and realized it was a shrug. "It was easy, I guess. He was rarely there. I worked and paid my own way. I couldn't go back to my parents. My mother told me when I was married that if I were smart, I would keep Greg interested and not screw it up."

He was horrified at her mother's callous disregard for her own daughter. "But you still had Jane?"

"As I said earlier, I was embarrassed. I didn't want to rely on her or be an inconvenience."

"Did you see him again after Melanie was conceived?"

"Yes." She reached over to the hand that was resting on his leg, and entwined her fingers with his. "He showed up at the apartment when I was between three and four months pregnant. He didn't try anything, and instead made jokes about me getting fat."

William was appalled, but he hoped it wasn't obvious in his expression. "He thought you were just gaining weight?"

"Again, he was very intoxicated. He was gone before I awoke the next morning, and he'd cleaned out my wallet. Then Greg returned once more when I was eight months along." Her hand squeezed his in almost a vice-like grip. "There was no denying I was pregnant, and he became enraged. He swore it wasn't his and he screamed at the top of his lungs. It wasn't until he punched me in the side that I became afraid for our lives. That night, he beat me until I passed out. When I regained consciousness, he was gone again with everything in my wallet. I left as quickly as I could and took a taxi to Netherfield."

"Where were you living?"

"Across the river, in Vidalia."

"By the time you traveled through Meryton to Netherfield, the fare must have been..."

"A hundred dollars."

"I was going to say outrageous."

She shrugged. "I couldn't stay there. I was having contractions, and I didn't want Greg to know where I was."

"He wouldn't have thought to go to Jane first?"

"He may have, but he didn't come looking for me."

His mind was reeling. "You said you were having contractions, but you were eight months?"

"Yes, Melanie was born sometime the next day. She was four and a half weeks early and required a bit of help at first, because her lungs weren't fully developed."

He looked over and noticed a tear trailing down her cheek. Releasing her hand, he lifted her into his lap and held her tightly to him. "What happened to him?"

"I haven't seen him since that night. There's a warrant out for his arrest—because of the beating. There's also a restraining order that says he can't come within a certain distance of Melanie or me."

He brushed the hair back from her forehead with his fingers, and softly kissed the newly exposed skin.

"Jane hired an investigator to find him, and had him served the divorce papers. When the process server returned and confirmed Greg was there, she called the police. They sent officers the next day. I guess they figured he wouldn't disappear again, but by the time the police showed up, he was gone."

"Does he have any claim to Melanie?"

She shook her head. "No, thankfully. Jane was brilliant. She included a waiver of his parental rights with the divorce papers. He insisted the process server wait while he signed the documents, and then immediately handed them back."

"Did he understand what he was signing away?" William couldn't imagine signing away his own child, but he had to admit he was thankful Wickham had.

"Yes, the server was someone that Jane uses often. Since most of the time people don't sign them and give them back, he returned to the office to show Jane before they were filed at the courthouse. Apparently, Greg made a comment that he wanted to make sure he never paid a penny of child support for some other man's child. Of course, Greg's words were cruder."

William suddenly understood so many things; Charles' comment that she needed a good man in her life, her unwillingness to be called Bennet, and her fierce desire to stand on her own two feet. He wanted to kill Greg Wickham, but his respect for Elizabeth Gardiner had grown exponentially. She'd accepted help when it was necessary. She'd also done everything she could to become independent and raise her own daughter.

"Is your marriage why you weren't at Jane and Charles' wedding?"

"Yeah," she answered softly. "We were living in a small town north of Baton Rouge at the time, and I was barely making ends meet. I've always regretted that I missed it. They came to see me periodically, but luckily Greg was never home at the time. I always met them somewhere anyway. I would've never brought them to where we lived."

He was rubbing her back when he heard her voice, small and timid. "William?"

"Yes."

"Whenever I've had to speak of this in the past, I've had nightmares."

"Would you like me to stay here with you tonight?"

She looked into his eyes. "I can't...I'm not..."

Suddenly understanding what she was trying to say, he brushed the backs of his fingers down her cheek. "I only meant to sleep."

Nodding, she squeezed the hand that had returned to her thigh. She rose and held out her hand, leading him up the stairs to her room. He turned as he looked at the antique bedroom set that reminded him of a bit of Pemberley. She took something out of her dresser drawer and walked over to a door on the other side of the room.

"I'll be right back."

He was unsure of what to do. Should he take off some of his clothes so that he was more at ease, or would it be better to leave them on for Lizzy's comfort? When she returned, he was sitting on the foot of the bed, waiting.

"I put out a new toothbrush for you."

Nodding, he entered the bathroom, prepared for bed, and brushed his teeth. He then reentered the bedroom, where she was sitting on the bed wearing a pair of floral pajama pants and a fitted tank top, waiting for him. He took a seat beside her, and she looked at him with an amused expression.

"Are you going to wear your jeans to bed?"

"I wasn't sure if taking them off would make you uncomfortable."

She smiled softly. "I'll be okay."

He nodded and he rose to remove his jeans, throwing them on a nearby chair. He then tugged his thermal Henley over his head, to reveal a white t-shirt and boxer briefs underneath. She lay down, and he crawled in and spooned behind her, pulling her close. "Good night, Lizzy."

"Good night, William," she responded sleepily.

Chapter Ten

<u>**Sunday, November 18, 2012**</u>

William didn't move as he slowly became aware of his surroundings the next morning, smiling when he realized Lizzy was tucked to his side. Her leg was thrown over his and her head was resting on his shoulder, the warm cadence of her breath tickling his neck. In an attempt not to disturb her, he shifted awkwardly trying to reposition himself so that he was more comfortable. His effort soon proved useless, so he tightened his embrace just a bit, enjoying his presence in her bed probably a bit more than he should.

His fingers carefully trailed from her temple, pulling her curls away from her face. She seemed to be sleeping peacefully, which relieved him. She'd indeed had a nightmare at some point in the early hours of the morning, and her thrashing had awakened him. He rubbed her back and spoke soothingly to her, but when she began talking in her sleep, he couldn't take anymore. To hear her plead for that lowlife to stop was difficult enough, but when she began to cry that she'd never been with anyone else it became sheer torture. He began gently shaking her in an attempt to wake her. Lizzy's relief when she opened her eyes to see his face was as heartbreaking as it was heartwarming.

Pressing a soft kiss to her forehead, he heard a sound like the rustling of sheets. Unsure of the origin, since neither he nor Lizzy had moved, he looked over to find Bear lying on a dog bed in the corner of the room still fast asleep. A few minutes later, he understood what the noise had been when the baby monitor on the bedside table began emitting the chattering of a now awake two-year-old.

Lizzy groaned and rolled over, so William used the opportunity to turn the unit off. He carefully pulled himself to sit on the edge of the bed, and then stood. She was still sleeping when he turned to check, so he followed the chatter to Melanie's room. She was playing with her stuffed animals when he peered in, so he took a minute to go to the bathroom.

After he had taken care of personal matters and brushed his teeth, he put on his jeans and shirt. Then he woke Bear, who all but ignored him at first, but reluctantly came when he realized William was going to put him outside. With Bear's needs taken care of as well, he made his way back up the stairs to retrieve Melanie from her crib.

William hoped she wouldn't be upset that he was getting her out of bed rather than her mother. He carefully opened the door and peered in to where she was sitting in her crib, talking to her stuffed cat. A wide smile adorning his face, he took a few steps in when Melanie jumped up to stand in her bed.

"Willyum!" she cried excitedly.

"Shhhhhh," he said with his finger over his lips. "Mommy's still asleep. Why don't we let her sleep in this morning?"

He picked her up and put her on his hip while he considered what he needed to do next. Was she potty trained? If she needed a diaper, where did Lizzy keep them? As he scanned the room, taking in the faintly pink walls with white furniture, Melanie began squirming to get down.

"Potty," she mumbled when he began to lower her to the floor. She ran on her tiptoes to a door on the side of the room and he followed. When she was standing next to the toilet, he was surprised when she took off her own diaper and climbed up onto the toddler seat. Feeling awkward, he waited just outside of the door until she came running out to her dresser, where she opened a drawer and took out a pair of panties. She sat on the floor to get them over her feet and then stood to finish pulling them on. When she was done, she looked up at him as if she were waiting for something.

"Don't you need to wash your hands?"

Melanie giggled as she returned to the bathroom. William couldn't help but chuckle when, after putting soap on her hands, she began loudly singing her ABC's. She rinsed when she was done singing, and he helped her dry them.

She held out her arms and he carried her downstairs to the kitchen. When he walked through the swinging door, William stood there, lost for a moment, while he tried to figure out what she ate for breakfast, eventually deciding that he might have some clue by opening the refrigerator.

138

As they stood in the open doors, she leaned forward, took a bottle of organic drinkable yogurt, and handed it to him.

"Yo-gurt, pwease."

He smiled as he tried the cabinet where Lizzy had retrieved the wine glasses the night before and found a few lidded sippy cups. Once he figured out the insert that was set in the lid of the cup, he poured in the contents of the bottle and handed it to her. He then placed her in her high chair and grabbed a pear off of the fruit bowl on the island.

"Do you like pears?" He was relieved when she nodded, and the fruit was swiftly cored, sliced and placed on her tray. She seemed fine as she took a bite, so he pulled out the eggs and bread. He buttered a piece of toast and placed it in front of her.

While Melly ate, he located the French press and made coffee. He began drinking his first cup as he poured the remainder in a travel mug he'd found to keep it warm. He was startled when Melanie suddenly yelled, "Done!"

After taking a glance at the mess she had created, he grabbed the kitchen towel and dampened it to clean her hands and face. "Let's get you dressed in some clean clothes," he suggested, as he gingerly lifted her out and placed her standing on the floor. As soon as her feet hit the floor, she went running out of the kitchen, and he followed her to her bedroom where she opened her closet. William drew closer and she pointed up to a red and green plaid jumper with a white lacy collared undershirt.

"Is this what you want to wear?" he asked, removing the dress.

"Uh huh!" Melanie smiled widely and ran to grab a pair of tights from her dresser. She returned quickly, and he helped her dress before she searched out a pair of black patent leather Mary Janes that were to the back of her closet.

Once she had her shoes on, the pair returned to the kitchen where Melanie immediately ran to some toys she had in one corner, chattering as she played, while William made Lizzy breakfast. The problem was that he wanted to serve her breakfast in bed, but had no idea where he might find a tray, if there even was one. Rummaging through the cabinets, he found what he was sure was a decorative wooden serving tray that would work, so he wiped it and arranged the plate and cup of coffee.

"Melly, do you want to help me bring Mommy breakfast in bed?"

"Yeah," she responded as she jumped up.

He handed her the napkin to carry, and they made their way back upstairs. When he opened the door, Lizzy's eyes fluttered open and she smiled radiantly as her daughter jumped up on the bed.

Lizzy woke to the sound of her door creaking, and she propped herself on her elbow as Melanie bounded on the bed.

"Here, Mama," she said as she handed her a napkin.

"Thank you, but what's all this?"

"Beckfast."

"Breakfast? In bed?" When Melanie nodded, she arranged her pillows so she could sit against the antique headboard. "You're going to spoil me," she said as she tickled her daughter. She looked up at William, who was chuckling as well, before she turned back to Melanie. "Do you want to watch TV?"

"Yes, pwease," said Melanie, as she bounced on the bed.

Lizzy turned on the television while William placed the tray on her lap. "That omelet is huge," she gasped.

"It's for us to share. I hope you don't mind, but I thought it would be easier to have one than to carry several trays of food up here."

"Oh good. I'd be stuffed if I ate it all," she said, relieved.

"I hope you like broccoli and cheddar."

"It's great, thanks. I do need to get up for a minute first though."

He helped her move the tray to the bed, and she went in the bathroom. She took care of a few early morning necessities, including brushing her teeth and checking her appearance in a
140

mirror. She made an attempt to tame her hair, but eventually gave up, returning within a few minutes. Soon everything was once again situated with the tray on the bed in front of Lizzy, and William took a seat beside her.

As she swallowed her first bite, she turned to face him. "This is good. I wasn't aware that you could cook."

"I get by, but I'd never have my own cooking show."

She laughed as she considered that he was much more handsome than any television chef she'd seen. She looked toward Melanie, concerned whether she was hungry. "Melly, do you want some toast?"

"No," the little girl answered, her eyes never leaving the television screen.

"I gave her breakfast right after she woke up. She had a bottle of that yogurt from the fridge, a pear and a piece of toast."

Lizzy shook her head. "I just don't understand why I didn't wake up. I'm so sorry about that."

"When I heard Melly, I turned off the monitor so you could have some more time to sleep."

She swallowed and turned his face to kiss him lightly on the lips. "That was very nice of you. I hope you didn't have any problems."

"Honestly, she helped me quite a bit." He saw Lizzy's raised eyebrows and laughed. "No, really. She told me she needed to potty, she found her own clothes, and she asked for the yogurt."

Lizzy chuckled. "She always wants to wear that dress." She picked up her cup as she pointed to it. "You fixed me coffee."

"I warmed the milk and added two spoons full of raw sugar."

Impressed, she took a sip. "How did you know?"

He grinned. "I was with you last night when you made coffee. I paid attention."

She was just sitting back into the pillows, cradling her cup in her hands, when the sound of a cell phone ringing resonated through the room. William grabbed it off the bedside table and looked at the screen before answering.

"What's going on, Richard?"

She drank her coffee as he placed his free arm around her. Snuggling into the warmth of his shirt, she could smell the remnants of his cologne from the day before and sighed. Her dreams had been fitful all night. Fortunately, she'd only seemed to wake him the one time. His face had appeared a combination of anger and worry when she opened her eyes, but he'd been wonderful, rubbing her back until she fell back to sleep.

She was brought back to the present when she heard him groan. "I'm not at home right now…You're a prat, Richard…I'll have it to you in an hour or two…Goodbye…I'm not going to discuss this with you, Goodbye." She was giggling when he hit end and, putting his phone in his pocket, leaned over to look her in the eye. "Just what's so funny?"

"He was giving you a hard time?"

"He was being a shithead." She slapped his arm. "What?" She pointed to Melanie and his expression became apologetic. "Sorry."

"It's okay. I know it can be easy to forget." She entwined her free hand with his. "You have to leave, don't you?"

"Yes, Richard needs some papers I have at the guest house. I need to scan and email the documents to him so he can review them before he goes to bed tonight." She nodded, disappointed that he wasn't staying longer. "I'm not leaving until you've finished your coffee though." He placed a kiss to her temple and she leaned back against him.

Melanie's show was over and a new one beginning by the time Lizzy finished the cup. She placed it on the tray and turned her face into the side of William's chest. His arm came around her shoulders as he held her to him. He kissed her forehead and said in a low voice near her ear. "I'll help you take the tray back to the kitchen, and then will you walk me to the door?"

142

"Okay," she said, her voice muffled against his shirt.

He stood and then helped her to rise. She retrieved a sweater from the closet, finding Melanie in William's arms when she returned.

"I have to go home, so do I get a goodbye hug?"

Lizzy smiled as her daughter threw her arms around him. She gave him a big, smacking kiss on the cheek, and he placed her back on the bed.

"I'll be back in a minute, Melly," she said as she led the way from the room.

"Bye, Willyum!"

They dropped off the tray in the kitchen, and made their way to the front door where William pulled her into his arms. "I'll call you tonight."

"I'd like that."

He held her a bit closer and brushed his lips against hers, holding her close for a few moments. "Will you be okay tonight?"

"I hope so."

"I can come back," he said with a hopeful tone to his voice.

"A part of me would love that, but this is already moving kind of quickly. I think it would be better if you didn't."

She could see a bit of disappointment in his eyes while he shrugged his shoulders with a small smile. "I had to ask."

Lizzy laughed as she drew back and kissed him tenderly. Their foreheads still touching, she brushed her hand down his cheek. "Bye."

"Bye." He backed away and opened the door. She followed him out onto the porch where watched him as he got into his car. Once he had the engine running, he waved one last time before he pulled away. Remaining on the step, her eyes followed him until he disappeared into the trees. Lizzy then pulled her sweater closed and crossed her arms over her stomach as she walked back into the house.

The few days of classes leading up to Thanksgiving were busy for Lizzy. She'd managed to finish the painting of Pemberley on Sunday, and with a day off on Wednesday; she planned to bring it into town so that it could be framed. Jane and Charles offered to keep Melanie for the day, so once she dropped off her daughter, she set off into Meryton to run a few errands.

Her last stop for the day was Hulin's. Joslyn, the manager and a friend, immediately came forward to help her when she stepped through the door. "Lizzy!" she exclaimed as she came up and hugged her, "I just saw your work over at The Depot. It looks great." When she took a step back, she gave Lizzy a look. "When are you going to let us frame your work for those shows? The mounting and matting is okay, but they would look so much better fully framed."

Lizzy laughed. "I know, but a lot of customers take the paintings and reframe them. I actually sell more with them mounted and matted than I do in a fancy frame. Don't forget that I brought my work for the last faculty exhibit to you."

"I know," said Joslyn. She gestured to the large art bag in Lizzy's hand. "What did you bring me today?"

She walked to the table and pulled the painting from between two drawing boards that were protecting it to set it on the surface. "It's a Christmas present for a friend. Do you think you can have it finished in time?"

"This is lovely." Joslyn looked up and smiled. "I can have it finished..." she ran her finger across a small calendar taped to the table. "Actually, I can have it the ready the tenth." She reached behind her and pulled out a rack of matting and set them on the surface. They picked out a dark green to bring out some of the finer detail work in the landscaping with a wider antique-looking frame.

Joslyn had just written up the work order when Lizzy's phone rang. "Hey, you don't usually call me during the day."

William's chuckle was the first thing she heard. "You usually have class, and I usually have work."

"True, so is something wrong?"

"No, but I'm done for the day, and I thought you might want to have lunch."

Lizzy was sure she had a ridiculous grin, because her friend was laughing as she sang "Bow-chicka-wow-wow" low enough that it couldn't be heard through the phone. She looked at Joslyn with wide eyes as she shook her head, prompting her to chortle. "Did you have something in mind?"

"Well, I just finished having coffee with the mayor, so I'm on Main Street. Where are you?"

"I'm at Hulin's."

"I think...I just passed it..." he said in a distracted fashion.

Realizing he was probably backtracking, she began frantically motioning to Joslyn to put everything away. Lizzy watched her as she gathered up the painting and samples and took everything to the back room. She was just breathing a sigh of relief when the bell sounded to the front door. Turning quickly, she found William striding toward her as he turned off his phone. She pressed end on hers just before he leaned in to kiss her softly on the cheek.

"How are you?" he asked near her ear before he drew back.

"Good, just finishing up actually."

"Here's your copy of the ticket," said Joslyn, who'd returned to the room, and handed her a slip of paper. Lizzy noticed her friend's eyes rake up and down William and stifled a chuckle.

"Thanks, I'll definitely see you on the tenth then." She felt William's hand take hers and noticed her friend's eyebrows lift. "William," she said as she glanced at him, "this is my friend, Joslyn Quinn. We went to high school together. Joslyn, this is William Darcy."

"It's nice to meet you," greeted William as they shook hands.

"You, too. It sounded like the two of you were making plans when you called, so don't let me keep you." Joslyn walked off and began picking up and straightening.

"Is there a particular place you would like to go?"

Lizzy turned to face William. "We could walk down to Riverside?"

He smiled. "Sounds good. Are you ready then?"

"Yes," she said as he turned toward the door and she followed. She turned once to yell goodbye to Joslyn, but instead saw that her friend was not standing far behind them, grinning like the Cheshire cat. "Nice ass," she mouthed. Lizzy could feel the heat in her cheeks, and not really sure what to say, lifted her hand in a small wave as they exited the shop.

The day was fair and the sky was blue, so once they placed her bag in her car, they walked hand in hand to their destination. Upon their arrival, they were seated at a table that overlooked the Mississippi river.

"Is Melanie in school?" William began, putting his napkin in his lap.

"No, she's with Jane and Charles." She picked up the menu and placed it to the side of the table.

"Do you know what you want already?" he asked, surprised.

"I always get the crab and corn bisque and a side salad."

William thought for a moment before set his menu to the side next to hers. "That sounds really good. I think I'll do the same." He took a sip of water and set the glass back on the table. "Do you return to school on Monday?"

"Yes, but since I hold my portfolio reviews the week before finals, it's only for two weeks. Do you have to go to work on Friday?"

"No, the U.S. based offices all have off until Monday. Speaking of holidays, do you have plans for Christmas yet?"

She laughed. "Christmas is a month away. Do you have anything planned?"

"No, but I know that I would like to spend it with you."

She couldn't help but smile at his hopeful expression as she bit her bottom lip. "I'd like that. If Jane and Charles are going out of town, then we could spend the day at Longbourn."

"Do you think they will?"

"It's a distinct possibility. They haven't visited Charles' parents since they moved to Florida. They also haven't been to see...the Bennets for a while also." His brows furrowed and he looked confused for a moment.

"I thought you were from Meryton."

"I am, but my father was offered a better position with a company in Atlanta six years ago."

"I know you changed your name, but do you ever see them?"

"No, my mother came to Jane's once after Melanie was born, and she...well, let's just say that I didn't appreciate her comments and orders."

"Orders?"

"She wanted me to go back and beg Greg's forgiveness." She could see the revulsion on his face and sighed. "My parents are a subject better left alone. Let's go back to planning Christmas."

He smiled. "Do you want to cook, or should I order dinner from somewhere?"

"No, I'll cook, but it probably won't be turkey and dressing. By Christmas, I'm usually all turkeyed out."

Laughing, he leaned back as their food was served. "That's fine. Between the Thanksgiving potluck we had yesterday at work, the Christmas party we'll have next month, and tomorrow at Jane's, I'm sure I will be, too."

"Can I ask you a question?"

"Sure," he responded, just before taking a spoonful of his soup.

"Why do you have D&F's corporate headquarters in Meryton? It isn't a large town, and it must make some things terribly inconvenient."

"My father moved the company's main office to Meryton before I was born. He and my mother liked it here. My mother didn't want to live in London, and I think the historical feel of the town appealed to him, reminded him of home. We would spend a portion of the summer in New York and England, but the tabloid press was a constant pest—especially in London."

"I assume you went to Catholic High like Charles did?"

"He nodded. Where did you go?"

"I was on the south side of town. I graduated from Meryton South High."

"I'm surprised I'd never heard of you, especially after Jane won the Young Miss Meryton pageant. She was known all over town, but no one knew she had a sister so close in age."

Lizzy swallowed and exhaled as she brushed her hair over her shoulder. "My mother pushed Jane into all of those pageants every summer until she went to college, while my father was putting me in math and science curriculums. I was in a few clubs in high school, but nothing that met outside of school, because he didn't want my study time taken up with what he called 'useless nonsense.' I didn't go to football games or to most of the dances. Prom was an exception." She left out that she'd gone with Greg. The omission wasn't to hide it from him, but due to the fact that she was finally away from him, and didn't want to have him keep coming up in conversation.

"I'm sorry. You asked to leave the subject of your parents, and I inadvertently steered the subject right back to them."

She shrugged. "I guess it's unavoidable if you want to learn more about me."

"Yes, but I think we can take that a bit at a time."

Lizzy smiled at how thoughtful he was being and took a long look at him. "What kind of a child were you? Somehow I can't see you

148

being mischievous, but then you might have had a bit of a naughty streak."

He laughed at her teasing. "You'd have to ask Mrs. Reynolds about that. She could tell you more."

"Maybe I want to hear some from you. I can find out if you're being honest from Mrs. Reynolds later." She smiled mischievously and he lifted his eyebrows.

"You think I would lie?"

"I never said that, but I'm certain it'll be fun to hear it from her point of view."

Shaking his head, he began telling her a few stories that he explained were the ones he remembered his mother telling when he was younger. She thoroughly enjoyed lunch, and was disappointed when it was time to walk back to her car.

He took her hand, and they entwined their fingers as they strolled leisurely through the older market area of Meryton. She pointed to some of the more festive holiday window displays that had already been arranged.

When they reached where she had parked, William squeezed her hand. "Why don't I pick you and Melanie up tomorrow?"

"But Netherfield isn't that far, and I don't mind driving. Plus, my sister is insisting that I spend the night, so that I'm not on the road late."

He gave a kind of nervous half shrug and a small smile. "I know. I was thinking that I can drive you home too, and we can spend the day together Friday."

She bit her bottom lip as she smiled. "That sounds nice."

"Okay, then I'll pick you up around ten?"

"That sounds good. I'll be able to help Jane with the last of the cooking."

He leaned forward and placed a warm, soft kiss on her cheek. "I'll see you tomorrow then," he whispered near her ear.

She nodded and brushed her lips against the corner of his mouth as he pulled back. One side of his lip curved to reveal a dimple, and she looked to the side as she blushed. "Bye." She unlocked her car door, and he opened it for her, closing it once she was seated and buckled. He raised his hand to wave as she backed out of her parking space. Then after waving back, she drove away, already anticipating seeing him the next day.

Chapter Eleven

<u>**Thursday, November 22, 2012**</u>

Early Thanksgiving morning, William was humming as he pulled away from the guest cottage. Since he'd let go of the foolish notions he'd had when he first met Lizzy, he'd been happier than he'd been in a long time. He passed Netherfield and wondered at the unfamiliar car in the drive, but assuming Jane had invited someone from her law firm, he didn't give it another thought as he continued on to Longbourn.

Lizzy and Melanie were ready when he arrived, and she had him pull his car into the extra space in the garage. She was afraid of spilling the casserole she was bringing in his, but he laughed when he saw how tightly it was covered, and led them to his car after all.

He buckled Melanie into the seat that he'd bought earlier in the week for his vehicle, and opened the door for Lizzy when she finally made her way to the garage with everything she needed. They were soon on the road, and he was content listening to Lizzy and Melanie giggle as they sang silly songs. Melanie's versions were mispronounced and missing words, but nonetheless, he laughed along with them.

They reached Netherfield, and he pulled into the drive alongside the vehicle he'd seen earlier. "Whose car is that?" asked Lizzy as he put the gearshift into park and shrugged.

"I don't know. I saw it as I passed earlier, but I wasn't aware that Jane or Charles had invited anyone. I just assumed Jane probably asked a co-worker at the last minute."

She nodded and they gathered everything and made their way inside. William was carrying Melanie, following Lizzy in through the backdoor, when a shrill cackle sounded, and he almost bumped into her as she froze in her tracks. She slowly turned to face him.

"Shit!" she mouthed. He furrowed his brows and she whispered, "That's my mother's laugh."

His eyes widened. He couldn't understand why the Bennets would be there. Jane and Charles knew that Lizzy didn't wish to have her parents in her life. He stood there watching while she leaned back against the wall with a tense expression. Finally, with a huff, she strode purposefully through the hall and into the kitchen. Jane gave a worried smile, and took the dish from her sister's hands.

"Hi, Lizzy," said Jane as she went to hug her. Lizzy backed away.

"You have to know that I heard our mother's laugh, Jane. How could you?" She was harsh, but William felt that it wasn't unwarranted, and he noticed that Jane was nervous.

"I didn't know they were coming. They showed up about an hour ago—I swear." He felt Jane was telling the truth, but he couldn't understand why neither she nor Charles had bothered to call.

"You know why I don't want to be around her, but you also know that I don't want *my* daughter within a mile of either of our parents. Yet you didn't call me to tell me!" Lizzy emphasized the last word with her hand on her chest.

Jane appeared near tears, and her shoulders slumped. "Mom hasn't stopped going since they walked in the door. I haven't had the chance!" William was sure his eyebrows were in his hairline as he thought that it only took a minute to pick up a phone. Surely, one of them could've handled a simple call.

"Why would she just show up? I thought you told her that you were going there for New Years?"

Jane exhaled heavily. "I did, but when she came in, she was going on and on about how I couldn't possibly have meant it. I honestly didn't know what to do. Was I supposed to make them stay in a hotel, or drive back to Atlanta on Thanksgiving?"

"No! I don't expect you to do that, because I know that you would feel terrible for it. I do expect you call me so I'm not blindsided! Is everyone here, or just mom and dad?"

"Lydia and Katie are here. Mary is on a missionary trip."

Lizzy turned toward William. "Would you be upset if we spent the day at Longbourn?" He was on the verge of telling her he'd do whatever was necessary to make her happy, but Jane's voice prevented him.

"You and Melly can't spend today alone. Just give her a chance," pleaded Jane with a distraught look. "For me?"

"That's emotional blackmail, Jane." Lizzy's hands were on her hips, and she was shooting daggers with her eyes at her sister.

William wasn't sure what to do when Mrs. Bennet came striding through the door. "Well! There you are, Elizabeth. We were beginning to think you wouldn't show."

He hadn't seen Mrs. Bennet since Jane and Charles were married, and he'd forgotten that as long as she didn't speak, she was actually an attractive woman with strawberry blonde hair highlighting her pale skin and blue eyes.

"Why is that?" Lizzy asked as William placed a hand on her back in support.

"You don't bother to keep in touch, and Jane won't tell me anything."

Lizzy rolled her eyes. "Enough of the melodrama. You made it clear years ago that I was to go back to Greg, or you would never speak to me again. I may not have attempted to contact you, but you've never attempted to contact me, so don't pretend you're the injured party here." Her mother humphed, but William could see that Lizzy didn't let it faze her. "As for Jane, it's unfair for you to put her in the middle. She and Charles don't discuss my business with anyone."

Mrs. Bennet's expression was indignant. "Well!" she exclaimed shrilly. "I can tell where I'm unwelcome." She turned on her heel and stalked out of the room.

"Lizzzzy," Jane cajoled. "Please, just try to get along today."

Lizzy stepped up with her finger pointing toward Jane. "For you, I'll stay, but if either of them begins insulting me, I *will* leave." She pushed the sleeves of her blouse up her arms and began cutting and peeling sweet potatoes that had been sitting on the counter. "I can't believe I'm doing this!" she muttered to herself.

After bearing witness to the first confrontation, William was determined not to leave Lizzy or Melanie unprotected for the entirety of the day. He set Melanie down, removed her sweater and then they played together with the toys she had in a corner of the kitchen until Charles entered about five minutes later.

He kissed Jane on the cheek as he surveyed the food she and Lizzy were preparing. "Everything looks wonderful. When are we eating?"

"About two hours?" estimated Jane.

William watched as Charles glanced worriedly at Lizzy, who'd given him a short greeting when he entered the room. "How are you, Lizzy?"

She turned around as she casually brandished the large knife she had been using in front of her. "What do you think?"

Charles, who'd never been good with confrontation, visibly startled at her acerbic tone. "Look, we didn't know..."

"I don't want to hear it," she interrupted. "Jane told me what happened this morning, but it doesn't mean that I have to be happy about it."

Exhaling, he made his way to where he saw William with Melanie. "I was wondering when you were going to get here. Why don't you come watch football with me and Mr. Bennet in the den?"

"No thanks, Charles," he responded curtly. "I think I'm fine here."

His friend gave him a strange look. "Okay...if that's what you want." Charles then disappeared back through the door, and William returned to the puzzle he'd been putting together with Melanie. He felt a hand on his back and started.

"You can go with the guys," Lizzy said softly near his ear. "I'll be fine."

"No, I'm not leaving you while they're here."

She smiled and kissed him softly on the cheek. He watched her hips sway just slightly in her charcoal grey slacks as she walked back over to where she'd been working.

154

Jane had been correct when she'd said that they would be eating in about two hours. William helped Jane and Lizzy carry the food to the table that was set with the Bingleys' good china. Once she was seated, Mrs. Bennet praised Jane and how she was able to "catch" Charles. How fine the house was. How Jane would always have the best of everything. William was losing his patience with the woman by the minute. Did she have even an inkling of how offensive she was?

When everything was set, Lizzy brought in Melanie, while Jane went to go get Charles and her two sisters, Katie and Lydia, who'd been watching television in one of the upstairs bedrooms.

They all were soon seated at the table, and once Mr. Bennet had said the blessing they began dishing the food out onto their plates. Everyone had been unusually silent, the only sound coming from the clinking of china and cutlery—the calm before the storm.

Lizzy was seated at the end next to Jane, with her daughter next to her. William seated himself on Melanie's other side in the hopes that he could help shield her from anything that might be said.

"So, where exactly is Mary?" asked Lizzy, directing her question towards Jane. Lydia snickered as she rolled her eyes.

"She's on a missionary trip to Uganda," said Jane, as she glanced nervously around the table. The silence descended again, and Lizzy turned to help Melanie with her spoon.

"So I finally get to see my grandchild. I had no idea what she looked like until today." Mrs. Bennet's voice resonated across the room from where she was seated beside Charles.

William watched Lizzy, whose jaw clenched just before she responded to her mother's comment. "She was in the kitchen earlier, but then you probably weren't paying attention." Mr. Bennet made a small choking noise, and William was certain he had needed to stifle a laugh.

"Well, I'm not the one who decided she was too good for her family."

"No, *you* decided that I wasn't good enough for you."

William looked at Charles, who was staring into his plate, and then to Jane. She had her elbow on the table and her forehead in her hand.

"When I decided that I didn't want to be a doctor or a lawyer, I was no longer worth any effort on your part except to marry me off, and when that didn't work out, you told me that I was to go back to him. You didn't even care *why* I left."

"Fine, Elizabeth, *why* did you leave?" asked Mrs. Bennet in a dramatic fashion. She noisily dropped her utensils on her plate before she crossed her arms over her chest.

"Mom, I don't think we should get into this right now," interjected Jane, attempting to diffuse the situation.

Dismissively waving her hand at Jane, Mrs. Bennet's gaze returned to Lizzy. "We're waiting?"

Lizzy, for some reason, seemed stunned that her mother asked. "He hit me. He beat me so badly that I went into early labor."

William watched Mr. Bennet actually look up from his plate to where Lizzy was sitting. "I seriously doubt that," her father reproached with the tone of his voice. "I knew Leonard Wickham for twenty-five years. He was one of my best friends. There's no way he or his son would have laid a finger on anyone."

"Dad," Jane tried to interject, but Mrs. Bennet steamrolled right over her.

"I agree! Greg was always such a nice boy. He would've never laid a finger on you," Mrs. Bennet began as if she had first-hand knowledge of the subject. "You were the one who ran around on your husband."

William noticed Charles lean forward in his seat, "Now, Mrs. Bennet, I know..."

Mrs. Bennet ignored him and instead leaned toward Lizzy, pointing. "I certainly never did anything like that. I don't blame him for divorcing you. That little girl looks more like Charles's friend here than Greg." Her pointed finger turned to William, and Lydia snorted loudly, not even attempting to disguise she was guffawing, while Katie giggled.

"Mrs. Bennet," interrupted a wide-eyed Charles, obviously desperate to change the subject, "have you tried the stuffing? Jane makes it from scratch..."

"I don't know where you got that idea, but I never cheated on Greg." He could tell that Lizzy was internally seething. William didn't know how she was as composed as she seemed.

"That's not what he told Lydia," her mother rebounded.

Jane's head jumped up and she leaned forward. "When did you see him, Lydia?"

Their sister who had been too busy laughing was now defensive. "I wouldn't tell you that, because it's my business. He says y'all are going after him for child support for your little bastard over there." She pointed to Melanie, who was becoming visibly upset at the raised voices.

"That's it! I've had it!" Lizzy jumped up and leaned on the table so that she was eye to eye with her youngest sister. "You can say whatever you want about me, but if you ever call my daughter that again, I will not be responsible for my actions."

Lydia gulped loudly and Mrs. Bennet gasped. "Elizabeth Bennet! You sit right back down! You will not speak that way to your sister!"

The hair on the back of William's neck stood on end at the tone of Lizzy's voice, but what had amazed him most was how she ignored Mrs. Bennet, pushing aside her anger in order to calmly whisper something to her daughter. He watched as she gently took the spoon from her hand and picked her up. William stood and moved around beside her while she turned toward her youngest sister. "I would steer clear of Greg Wickham if I were you."

Lydia stood and began yelling. "He told me everything. How you cheated and then left him. That you have people looking for him because you want to sue him for child support." Jane jumped up during her youngest sister's outburst and grasped Lydia's arm, startling her and temporarily stopping her tirade.

"You know nothing!" yelled William, unable to restrain himself any longer. He felt Lizzy's hand on his arm and looked down to see her shake her head. Until that moment, he'd held himself back because he knew he couldn't fight Lizzy's battles for her, no matter how much he wished he could, but he simply couldn't handle sitting back and doing nothing anymore.

Mrs. Bennet, noticing their silent communication, pointed at William. "You are Melody's father!"

Lizzy rolled her eyes. "Melanie! Her name is Melanie—like your aunt."

"You won't get anything from Greg, you know," interrupted Lydia in a snotty manner.

"I don't want anything from that man," Lizzy gritted through her teeth, startling Lydia with her vehemence. "I don't want to even lay eyes on him again for as long as I live." She then glared at Jane as she walked by her and through the door.

William was close behind until he heard Charles call his name. "Are you going to leave, too?"

Surprised and furious, William faced him and gestured toward the dining room table. "There are two of you, and it only takes one person to pick up a phone and make a call. You should've warned Lizzy first!" He turned and walked into the kitchen where Lizzy was holding back tears as she tried to put her daughter's sweater on her. Striding to where she was, he took her in his arms and rubbed her back as he attempted to calm her. They had only been standing there for a moment when he heard Jane clear her throat behind him.

Lizzy stepped back, and he leaned over to help Melanie finish putting on her sweater.

"I'm sorry I begged you to stay earlier," said Jane sadly. "We'd already planned today, and I just didn't want you to spend the holiday alone."

Lizzy sighed. "You always want our mother to be someone she isn't."

"Charles and I were planning to tell y'all after dinner that I'm pregnant." Jane shrugged her shoulders up with a hopeful expression.

Lizzy exhaled heavily. "I'm happy for you, but that doesn't excuse keeping me here with our mother."

Jane sighed as she despondently shrugged her shoulders. "I suppose I was hoping that if the two of you could make it through Thanksgiving, we wouldn't have a problem with the christening. Charles and I want you and William to be the godparents. How are we going to have the service if you and mom can't be in the same room without arguing?"

"How far along are you?" asked Lizzy.

"Nine weeks."

"Then we have roughly seven months to figure that out. Just not today, because I need to leave before our parents decide to move the argument in here."

"You can't just leave," implored her sister. "It's Thanksgiving, and I don't want you to be alone."

William, who'd taken Melanie to get a roll from the counter, came up behind Lizzy and placed a hand on her back. "She won't be."

"Are you sure?" Lizzy turned to ask him.

"Positive."

Jane sniffled. "I'm so sorry, Lizzy. I love you."

"I know that you didn't mean any harm, but you should've warned me before we came over. This wasn't fair to me. I don't deserve the way she treats me. I never did."

Her sister crossed her arms in front of her. "No, you didn't. Dad was hardly fair either." Lizzy and Jane stood there awkwardly for a moment before Lizzy turned to face him.

"Are you ready then?"

William nodded, and soon they were quickly loaded into the car, pulling out of the driveway. "Back to Longbourn?" he asked.

"I guess so. Thanks for grabbing the bread for Melly. At least she won't be starving by the time we manage to make something to eat."

He wrapped her hand in his, and could feel her shaking as she sat, quietly taking in the landscape outside of the window. His cell phone began ringing and he released her to check the caller ID. Seeing it was Mrs. Reynolds, he answered and put it on speakerphone.

"Happy Thanksgiving, Mrs. Reynolds."

"Same to you, dear. I hope I haven't interrupted your dinner."

"No, ma'am. I'm actually driving right now."

"You better have me on Bluetooth or speakerphone, young man."

"Yes, ma'am," he said. He glanced at Lizzy and noticed she was smiling widely at Mrs. Reynolds' scolding.

"Good, but why are you on the road? I thought you were spending the holiday with the Bingleys."

"That fell through." He looked toward Lizzy, and hoped he wouldn't have to give any lengthy explanations over the phone.

"That Caroline didn't show, did she?" she asked with an angry tone.

Both Lizzy and William were unable to control their laughter. "No," he managed to get out. "Caroline had nothing to do with this."

"That's a relief! Well, if you aren't going to the Bingleys', then what are you doing today?"

"We're heading back to Longbourn, and then I think we're going to figure out what to cook for lunch."

"How many is we?"

He chuckled at her hopeful tone. She'd scold him when she discovered that he hadn't wanted to spring three extra people on her

160

for Thanksgiving dinner. "Myself, Lizzy, and Melanie, her two-year-old daughter."

"Well, wherever you are, you can turn right around and drive over here. You know that I cook enough to feed a small army, so there's plenty of food."

"We couldn't intrude at the last minute," Lizzy interjected worriedly.

Mrs. Reynolds didn't skip a beat. *"Nonsense, William and his friends could never be an imposition."*

"We'll be there in a half an hour." He peered over and noticed Lizzy's nervous expression.

"We'll see you soon then."

"Thanks, Mrs. Reynolds."

"There'll be none of that. You just drive safely."

"Yes, ma'am," he responded, and pressed the end button. Reaching over, he took Lizzy's hand and squeezed. "She wouldn't invite us if she didn't mean it."

"I've never met this woman, and I have nothing to bring. We can't just show up empty handed."

"She's like a mother to me, and she doesn't expect us to bring anything." He laughed at the face she made while he took the first road that would lead him in the direction of Mrs. Reynolds' house. During the drive, Lizzy noticed an open liquor store and persuaded him to stop. She ran inside and returned five minutes later with a bag containing several bottles of wine.

As a result of the stop, they were slightly over the half hour when they pulled up to the red brick home where Mrs. Reynolds lived. He stepped out, opened the door for Lizzy, and unbuckled Melanie, lifting her from the car. Melanie seemed to want her mother, so William took the bag of wine while Lizzy took her daughter from his arms. They were just turning to go to the door when an older woman emerged from the home and waited for them to make their way to the porch.

"I'm so glad you came," she exclaimed as she hugged William.

He eagerly returned the gesture before he turned to face Lizzy. "Mrs. Lyla Reynolds, I'd like you to meet Lizzy Gardiner and her daughter Melanie."

"Hello, dear," she said as she moved over and waved away Lizzy's outstretched hand to embrace her. "There'll be none of that. I like to give hugs."

Lizzy smiled as she returned the gesture. When Mrs. Reynolds drew back, she patted William on the arm. "Now, we're eating in about two hours." She turned toward Lizzy. "I like to have an early dinner. That way no one goes to bed uncomfortable. So, does this cutie need a snack to tide her over?" Melanie had her head on Lizzy's shoulder, and didn't respond like William felt she would've normally.

"She ate a roll in the car on the way over here," said Lizzy as she rubbed her daughter's back. "But I think it might be a good idea to let her eat something before she takes her afternoon nap."

Mrs. Reynolds gave a motherly smile. "Of course. Let's go into the kitchen then." They followed her inside, where Lizzy met Mrs. Reynolds' two sons and their families.

Once everyone had been greeted, Mrs. Reynolds ushered William, Lizzy and Melanie into the kitchen, where William handed her the bag of wine. "This wasn't necessary," she scolded.

"Actually, it's from Lizzy."

The older woman smiled. "Thank you, but you don't ever have to bring anything to one of my dinners."

She gestured to a stool by the counter that had a child's booster seat. Lizzy placed Melanie in the seat while Mrs. Reynolds took a slice of ham that she'd already prepared, and added a bit of steamed sweet potatoes, and green beans to a plate for Melanie. Once Lizzy had ensured Melanie was eating well, she asked about a bathroom. Mrs. Reynolds showed her where it was, and swiftly returned.

"She's very pretty, William. How long have the two of you been seeing each other?"

162

"Not long," he responded. "We met through the Bingleys. She's Jane's sister."

"What on earth happened this morning that she wouldn't want to spend the holiday with her family?" He couldn't help but grin at the way she asked as she folded her arms across her apron-clad chest.

"It's a long story, but she doesn't have a good relationship with her parents. They showed this morning without warning, and neither Jane nor Charles called to warn us. She attempted to make the best of it, but things devolved pretty quickly. It was best that she and her daughter remove themselves from the situation."

Mrs. Reynolds nodded as she added some more green beans to Melanie's plate. Then claiming he would be in the way if he remained, she shooed William to the living room, where her sons were watching football. He left reluctantly, with the feeling that there was more to her excuse than she let on, and worried that Lizzy would be either uncomfortable or upset that he didn't remain. Soon after, his concerns were relieved when he heard the sound of the laughter he loved through the connecting door.

Lizzy took her time and just leaned against the wall for a bit as she attempted to collect herself. She knew that her mother could be demanding, but she still couldn't believe that Jane hadn't called her. The incorrect and vile assumptions that spewed from her mother's and Lydia's mouths were what she'd always wanted to protect Melanie from hearing. Her only consolation was that her daughter was too young to have any long-term memory of it.

She took a deep breath and washed her hands, steeling her courage as she opened the door and stepped into the hall. When she returned to the kitchen, she immediately checked on Melanie, who was just finishing her early dinner, and scanned the room. "Where's William?"

Mrs. Reynolds turned off the faucet where she'd been washing some potatoes, and leaned against the counter to face her. "I sent him to watch football with Michael and Brian. I have some work to do on dinner, and he'd only get in the way."

"He's helped me cook before," defended Lizzy in a good-natured manner.

"Oh, no, it's nothing like that. He helped me when he was younger, but this kitchen is small, and he's like a wall that I have to move around."

Laughing, Lizzy handed Mrs. Reynolds the plate Melanie had been using, and unstrapped her from the booster. "Is there something I can help you with?"

She scrutinized her for a moment before handing her a bowl of potatoes. "You could peel and cut these up so I can steam them for mashed potatoes."

Nodding, Lizzy took them out of the bowl and placed them upon the counter. Mrs. Reynolds handed her a cutting board, a peeler, and a knife. She then walked over to a corner cabinet that she opened to reveal some old pans, plastic bowls and spoons.

"Melanie, I have a special place for you to play. Would you like to cook like Mommy?"

Lizzy took her hand and showed her a few of the items. "What do you think, Melly?" She watched as her daughter took a bowl and sat on the floor as she began to rummage for a spoon. Standing, Lizzy looked over and smiled. "Thank you."

"I have grandchildren, dear. Every room in this house has somewhere for a little one to play." Lizzy smiled and picked up the utensil to begin peeling.

"Your daughters-in-law don't help you with the cooking?" Lizzy found it strange that neither was present.

Mrs. Reynolds rolled her eyes. "They're sweet girls, but if I let them chip in, we'd be eating chicken nuggets and macaroni and cheese from a box."

Lizzy chuckled. "I'll confess to cooking that from time to time. Mainly for Melly, but sometimes I eat it too."

"But you wouldn't make it for Thanksgiving."

164

"No, I wouldn't." She glanced over to ensure her daughter was still playing happily, and continued with her task.

"Where did she get the nickname Melly?"

Lizzy stopped for a moment and looked at the motherly woman. "When she was about six months old, I would blow little raspberries on her stomach. She would just giggle and giggle. One day I said 'I'm going to get Melly's belly.' It was a spur of the moment thing, but Jane, and even Charles began calling her Melly Belly."

Mrs. Reynolds gave a warm smile. "William mentioned that your sister is married to Charles Bingley. I've always liked him. He was such a happy boy."

"He still is," Lizzy replied with a grin. "William has told me some stories from when he was a boy, and he always seems to blame Charles for the times when he was naughty."

Mrs. Reynolds gave a hearty laugh. "Don't let my boy fool you. When the stories were told from all sides, William was usually the one with the ideas, with Richard and Charles helping him to instigate the plan. He just wasn't one to try them on his own. Without those two, he was more likely to disappear, and we'd find him hiding somewhere with his nose in a book. He'd be so engrossed in the story that he wouldn't hear us calling him." She shook her head. "His poor mother would be beside herself with worry."

"He was quiet then, as a child?"

"Unless you really knew him. I heard the kids sometimes refer to him as a snob, but I saw none of it." She sighed and placed her bowl on the counter. "Since his father and sister died, he's withdrawn further into himself. I've been so worried about him, but today has given me reason to hope."

Lizzy looked puzzled. "Why's that?"

"Because he brought you here, dear," she said with a wide grin, as she began mashing sweet potatoes. "He hasn't brought a girl home since before his mother died. The fact that he was willing to bring you here speaks volumes to his feelings for you."

She felt her cheeks burn, and she began vigilantly concentrating on cutting the potatoes. "I..."

"I didn't mean to make you uncomfortable. I just wanted you to understand that he's not one to go leading on young ladies."

Lizzy nodded, and finished the potatoes. Melanie seemed to be flagging so she picked her up and rubbed her back as she held her. She and Mrs. Reynolds continued to chat, but more about cooking and children, remaining more light-hearted than serious. By the time Mrs. Reynolds had put the sweet potato casserole in the oven and taken the potatoes off of the stove, Melanie had fallen fast asleep.

"I have a toddler bed in Michael's old room, if you would like to lay her in there," suggested Mrs. Reynolds when she noticed that Melanie had nodded off.

She hated to put her in a strange room, but she was getting rather heavy. Lizzy also couldn't help Mrs. Reynolds with a sleeping child in her arms, so she left the kitchen and was going to ask where to go, when William noticed them.

"Would you like me to hold her while she sleeps?"

"Mrs. Reynolds had suggested a toddler bed in Michael's old room, but I was unsure of which room it was."

William stood and placed a gentle hand on Melanie's back. "You don't think she'll be upset if she wakes by herself in a strange room?"

"I'm not sure. I hope not..." She stopped as he took her daughter from her arms and situated her in his own.

"Now you won't need to worry about it." He leaned forward enough to plant a kiss on Lizzy's forehead, and then seated himself back where he was on the sofa, reclining so that Melanie was sprawled across his chest.

She took a step back and then stopped to watch them for a moment. William was so good with Mclanie, and it warmed her heart. One side of her lips quirked up into a small smile and she returned to the kitchen.

When it was time to eat, William continued to hold her at the table, despite Mrs. Reynolds' protests. Dinner was wonderful, and Lizzy marveled at the number of dishes. Turkey, ham, dressing, gravy, sweet potato casserole, mashed potatoes, homemade cranberry sauce, sweet peas with pearl onions, and green beans with almonds were all served, and Lizzy had no idea where she would put dessert. The choice of desserts was equally impressive, and neither Lizzy nor William knew how they would be able to move when the meal was over.

When everyone had eaten more than their fill, Lizzy rose to help with the dirty dishes, when Mrs. Reynolds stayed her with a hand. "We cooked, so my boys and their wives do the dishes."

She and William followed Mrs. Reynolds to the living room and they all took a seat around the now silent television. Mrs. Reynolds embarrassed him with a few more stories of his childhood, until her family returned from the kitchen and football was once again playing loudly. Lizzy rested her head against William's shoulder, and he took her hand in his.

"Lizzy," she heard William's voice as she felt his hand gently brush down her cheek.

"Hmmm?"

"It's time to go," he chuckled. She felt her arm get flung up and down followed by a "Wake up, Mama!" from Melanie.

She opened her eyes, and suddenly remembered where she was. "Oh, I'm so sorry!" she exclaimed, worried of offending Mrs. Reynolds. "How long have I been sleeping?"

He brushed the hair back from her face and smiled. "About an hour?" he said as he checked his watch.

"Oh no," she said as she sat up. "I didn't mean to fall asleep."

"You're fine, dear," came Mrs. Reynolds' voice from behind her. "I want you to make yourself at home here, so please don't worry about napping. It wouldn't be Thanksgiving if someone didn't indulge in a turkey coma."

Lizzy laughed and rose from the sofa. The sky was dark, and she set about putting on Melanie's sweater. When she was ready, she took her daughter's hand and walked over to where William was giving Mrs. Reynolds a hug. The older woman gave him a peck on the cheek.

"Next time, you just come over here. You know that you're always welcome."

He smiled as he picked up Melanie. Lizzy was surprised when her daughter leaned forward to embrace Mrs. Reynolds. "You take good care of your mommy, and I'll read to you some more the next time you visit."

Melanie cheered, and Lizzy stepped forward to give Mrs. Reynolds a hug. "Thank you so much for inviting us."

"It was really not an imposition, and you're welcome to join William for Sunday dinner here anytime. Perhaps I'd see him more if you do." Both ladies laughed and William turned bright red. "Drive safely," she said seriously to him. "You're carrying precious cargo." She glanced at Lizzy and Melanie, prompting William to smile.

"Yes, ma'am."

Melanie was quickly buckled, and as they pulled away, Lizzy looked back to wave at Mrs. Reynolds, who was watching them as they began to drive. When she turned to face the front once more, she noticed William had a content expression on his face. "She likes you, you know."

Lizzy smiled. "I hope so, because I like her, too."

William took her hand. "Do you have any place you'd like to go before we return to Longbourn?"

"No, home sounds wonderful. Are you going to stay, or return to the guesthouse?"

"I'd like to stay as we originally planned. Is that okay with you?"

Her cheeks became warm, and she glanced at their hands as his sight veered from the road to her for a moment. "Yes...yes, I'd like that."

168

Chapter Twelve

Friday, November 23, 2012

William groggily opened his eyes and flexed his legs before he spooned back against Lizzy's curled form, enjoying the feel of her in his arms.

After spending the afternoon at Mrs. Reynolds', they'd returned to Longbourn for a leisurely evening. Melanie ate a small dinner, and then Lizzy bathed and dressed her for bed. They colored, which he enjoyed once he realized he didn't have to actually be able to draw, and watched a classic Christmas cartoon before tucking Melanie in for the night.

The two of them then settled on the sofa to watch a movie, falling asleep not long after it started. William could only assume that the final credits woke Lizzy (since she was the one who shook him awake), and the two of them stumbled half-asleep upstairs to her bedroom, where they both randomly shed articles of clothing before passing out once more.

As he lay there in nothing but boxer briefs, her leg rubbed against his when she moved, and he realized that she wasn't wearing pants. What else had she removed? He seemed to recall a contortionist maneuver in which she removed her bra without taking off her top, but it was hazy.

"Mmmmmm..." she groaned, as she wiggled attempting to cuddle closer. "You're so warm."

He chuckled. "Are you usually cold?"

"Not always, but it's so nice to wake up and be cocooned in a toasty bed." She rolled over, buried her head in his chest, and entwined her legs with his. "What time is it?"

"I'm not sure. I didn't want to roll over to see the clock."

She smiled. "Melly will be awake soon."

"Do you think we'll get a reprieve and she'll sleep in?"

"Not likely. She has an internal clock that rarely allows her to sleep later than eight." He grinned as she pulled back and he could see her face. She looked lovely—her eyes sparkling and her hair tousled. He leaned down and softly kissed her. His lips caressed her upper lip and then bottom before he drew back.

"It might be a good idea if I brushed my teeth." She pouted and wrapped one of her legs around his.

"But I don't want you to get out of bed yet."

"I don't want to either, but I'd like to kiss you a bit more without having to worry if I have dragon breath." She grinned and withdrew her legs from his. When he sat up and threw his legs over the side of the mattress, he shivered at the difference in temperature between the bed and the room. "It's chilly."

"It was supposed to freeze last night," commented Lizzy as he stretched.

"Do we need to make sure Melly is warm enough?" He turned to see her with a large smile.

"She's got on that thick footed sleeper, so she should be fine."

William nodded, and stood to make his way to the bathroom. Once he'd taken care of the necessary business, he opened the door and began brushing his teeth. He'd just finished when Lizzy walked through the door and proceeded to put toothpaste on her own toothbrush. He was disappointed to notice that she'd donned her pajama bottoms; he had liked the feel of her bare legs against his. He was contemplating her soft skin and the way her legs entwined with his when Lizzy suddenly captured his attention by waving her hand in his face.

"Hellooo? Earth to William?"

He looked up and she was laughing. "What has you so distracted? You've been staring at my pants for a few minutes."

Shrugging, he pulled her into his arms and began to lean in.

"Umm...I need a few minutes first," she said as she put a hand on his chest. She lifted her eyebrow and he reluctantly released her.

170

"Of course, I'll be waiting for you in the bedroom."

Lizzy nodded, and watched as he exited the bathroom. He was so kind to her and especially considerate of Melanie, that she realized just how differently she thought of him since their argument. The evening of her show, she had decided to give him a chance as a friend, but by the time they had returned to Netherfield, she had wanted him to kiss her. The feeling surprised her at the time, but now, looking back, he'd been there for her unconditionally since her car died. His support yesterday at Jane's had been exactly what she'd needed.

Regardless, her feelings had made such a material change that they were completely opposite of what they had been before and a part of her was scared by them. What if he changed his mind? With Greg, they began as nothing more than friends, so while his abandonment bothered her, her heart wasn't broken. This was a different situation entirely.

She finished what she needed to do and returned to find that he'd gotten back in bed.

"It's not quite seven yet. We have a bit more time to be lazy if you want." Smiling, Lizzy climbed back in with him. As she cuddled up, he flinched. "How did your feet get so cold so fast?"

"Yours feel so good," she purred as she attempted to warm them with his.

He wrapped his arms around her, pulling her close. She felt his hands roam around her back and waist. "I liked it better when you weren't wearing these pants," he pouted.

She laughed nervously, but removed them and entwined her legs with his. "Better?"

"Much," he murmured. He leaned in and kissed her lips softly.

Lizzy had never felt the way she did at that moment. In the past, she'd initially found the kissing agreeable, but after a while, she'd just wanted Greg to finish so he would leave her alone. There had always been the question in the back of her mind whether it would be different with someone she cared for, but at the same time, she'd worried it would always be so unfulfilling.

She wound her arms around his body to pull herself flush to him, while a heat traveled through her body to her core. Her top leg slid up his while his hand stroked its way up to her thigh, gripping her to him as she tentatively tasted his mouth with her tongue. She heard him moan and felt her own body respond.

Though instead of continuing, he seemed to slow things down, brushing his lips up her cheek to plant small kisses on her closed eyes and forehead. He then wrapped his arms around her and just held her. She could feel the very evident proof of his desire for her bulging against his boxer briefs while the sound of his heart pounding filled her ears.

"Being in bed with you is too tempting," he whispered. "Perhaps we should go make breakfast."

She smiled as she drew back from him so that she could see his face. "I thought I'd make pancakes. They don't take very long, so it'd be better to wait until Melly wakes." His large hand rubbed her back, and an idea came to her mind. "There's something I've been wanting to know, and it might help with the situation."

His expression was curious, but she was a bit wary of asking him. "Jane had mentioned it before, but after Mrs. Reynolds said something yesterday, I've been wondering." She bit her lip as he closed his eyes, seeming to understand what she wanted to know.

"You want to know about Caroline?"

Lizzy nodded and she felt his erection slowly begin to recede as he sighed. "Please?"

He exhaled heavily, and she could tell by his expression that Caroline Bingley was probably the last person he wished to think about, much less speak of. "I've known her since she began school the year after Charles. She was a sweet little girl, but when we became older, she began making me some pretty blatant offers. I think she was probably about fifteen when she tried to sneak into my bed during a sleepover at Charles' house? I was never interested in her—not in that way, but she never seemed to take no for an answer."

172

Lizzy was astonished. Until her mother had begun setting her up with Greg, she hadn't dated, much less thought of offering herself up in the manner he was suggesting. When she'd gone to college, she'd been too busy with her classes and friends. She was occasionally kissed, but nothing serious. The marriage proposal from Greg had even come as a surprise, since they'd never been exclusive.

"Then I went to Princeton and Charles to Stanford. We made a point of meeting up during holidays, and Caroline always found a way to tag along with him. I tried to be polite because I didn't want to offend the Bingleys, who were friends of the family, but she went off the deep end about four years ago when I was working in the New York offices. She began stalking me."

"You have got to be kidding me?" she exclaimed.

"I wish I were. She lied about being a client, and tricked my assistant into a meeting. As soon as the door closed, she opened her coat to reveal she was wearing nothing underneath but garters and stockings."

"I could've gone my whole life without having that image in my mind," Lizzy said with obvious distaste.

He chuckled and ran his hand through her hair, lightly kissing her lips. "You and me both. Security removed her from the building, but she showed up at our family's penthouse a few days later. She managed to get past security by claiming she was a decorator, and then somehow made it inside."

"What did you do?" she questioned with wide eyes. She'd always thought that Caroline had a screw loose, but this was worse than she'd ever imagined.

"My father notified Grant Bingley, Charles's father, and he came to New York. I called the police and Caroline was arrested. With the help of her father, she was convinced to accept a deal where she agreed to abide by the terms of the restraining order I had issued, and in return, I'd drop the charges."

Lizzy whistled and chuckled, "I thought she probably annoyed you with her excessive flattery or some such nonsense. I didn't know that she needed to be committed."

"I understand that Grant paid a great deal of money to get her professional help after that, but I still won't go anywhere near her. I take it you don't like her either?"

"She came to visit Jane and Charles when Melly was about a year old. Caroline acted as though Melly would attack her or was contagious, and when Charles said I was an artist, she said, 'Oh, how quaint.'" Lizzy mimicked the high-pitched tone that Caroline had used. "She just rubbed me the wrong way, and whenever I hear about something she's said to Charles or Jane, I still get annoyed. I know she doesn't like Jane, but she should keep her mouth shut."

William rolled his eyes as he continued to comb his fingers through her hair. "Can we not discuss her anymore? She's the last person I want to discuss while we're in bed together." He leaned down and captured her lips. He'd just begun to deepen the kiss when she heard her daughter call her through the monitor. He broke their connection and they both began laughing.

"I think it's time to make breakfast." Lizzy grabbed her pants off the side of the bed and slipped them on under the covers. As she moved to a seated position, she couldn't help but sneak a peek as William rose, appreciating the sight of his sculpted back and his boxer briefed behind.

He caught her off-guard when he turned to face her. "Why don't I get Melly out of bed while you let out Bear and start breakfast?"

She glanced to where Bear was now awake and watching them from his bed in the corner, and then tilted her head when she turned back to William. "He didn't want you to take him out last time, did he?" she asked with a grin.

"No, he went, but he was rather reluctant."

She laughed that he'd rather deal with a two-year-old than a dog, but agreed. Once she'd made it to the kitchen, she took out a bowl and began mixing the ingredients for pancakes, just pouring the first batch on the griddle as they entered the room.

William took out a bottle of yogurt, put it in a cup for Melanie, and then began making coffee while Lizzy flipped and plated some pancakes for each of them. She served her daughter first, she and William taking their seats a few minutes later. They chatted over

174

their breakfast, sipping their coffee long after Melanie decided she was done and it was time to play. Lizzy couldn't help but think how domestic they seemed.

"What do you want to do today?" he asked after swallowing a sip from his cup.

"I want to be lazy, but I had someone who sought me out to paint a couple of landscapes, and I should really work on those."

"That sounds interesting. Do you often take commissions?"

"Not really, but the offer paid well, and they are a Christmas present, so I decided to take the work."

His face took on a look of concern as he placed his hand over hers. "Are you short of money?"

"No!" she insisted, holding out a hand in front of her. "I'm fine. I promise." They both laughed and William entwined his fingers with hers. As she took a sip of her coffee, Lizzy noticed he seemed a bit hesitant. "I know you'll probably want to go home to change, but you could spend the day here if you'd like." A brilliant smile diffused his features and he leaned over and gave her a brief kiss on the cheek.

"I hope you won't think me presumptuous, but after the last time I stayed here, I put an overnight bag in the back of my car. I'd wanted to spend the day with you then, but I couldn't."

"I understand," she said, standing to put her cup in the dishwasher. "Why don't you go get your bag, and I'll show you where everything is?"

He nodded as he stood and left to go out to his car. When he returned, Lizzy quickly pointed toward the door that led to her studio before she brought him upstairs. She showed him where to find towels so he could shower, and then departed with Melanie to her studio where she began sketching out the first painting. Thirty minutes later, he appeared in the door, his hair still damp and his face cleanly shaven.

He walked over to see what Melanie was coloring before he came to stand behind Lizzy. He'd been there a while when she turned to look over her shoulder. "Are you going to watch me from there the entire time?"

He chuckled as he lifted a book from his side. "I didn't know if you could talk while you painted, so I brought something to read."

"I can talk, but I work faster when I don't." William nodded, leaning in to capture her lips in a brief kiss before he took a seat in a large chair set off in one corner.

William tried to read, but wasn't getting very far with the distraction that Lizzy presented. He'd probably read the same paragraph three or four times, and was once again staring at her while she worked.

She'd changed into what appeared to be an older top, but remained in her pajama bottoms. He loved seeing a bit of her everyday life that he hadn't been privileged to before, making note of every nuance. He noticed the way her eyes surveyed the photo, darting back and forth between it and what she was drawing—the small line that sometimes appeared between her eyebrows when she was holding out her pencil and checking her angles, the careful yet methodical way she applied her pencil to the paper.

Glancing over to Melanie, he noticed she was playing blocks instead of coloring, and moved across the room to help her.

By eleven o'clock, Lizzy, had most of the sketch done and decided to take a break. She showered and changed so they could cook lunch and spend the remainder of the day together. William found that he was content with whatever Lizzy suggested, whether it was playing a game with Melanie or holding Lizzy as they watched a movie during her daughter's nap.

As much as he wanted to remain that night, he knew that they weren't ready for him to stay on almost a nightly basis, so he reluctantly kissed her, wished her sweet dreams, and made his way home, considering the day a great success.

On Wednesday, William knew that Lizzy would be going to Pilates with Jane, so he ventured over to see Charles for the first time since

Thanksgiving, hoping to get a bit of time with her for himself. His friend let him in, and they went to his study where they both took a seat.

"Jane said you took Lizzy to meet Mrs. Reynolds on Thanksgiving," Charles began uncomfortably. "I hope y'all had a nice time."

William couldn't help but give a forbidding sounding laugh. "Whatever it is you want to say, just say it."

Charles took a deep breath as he fidgeted in his seat. "I wanted to apologize for allowing what was an extremely uncomfortable situation."

William leaned forward and put his elbows on his knees as he looked Charles directly in the eye. "I think you owe Lizzy an apology more than you do me. Especially for just sitting there while Mrs. Bennet and her daughter attacked her. I know it's probably not my place to say this, but you need to put your foot down with that woman, or she'll just continue to walk all over you and Jane."

"What do you mean?" asked Charles as he furrowed his brow.

"What I mean is that she showed up here without an invitation and with no doubt of her acceptance into your home. She'll do it again, Charles, and I would wager that it will be worse once the baby is born."

Rubbing the back of his neck, Charles winced. "When she showed up, I hoped that she wouldn't be horrible to Lizzy like she'd been in the past."

"Why would that be any different?" asked Will, frustrated. "She doesn't contact her own daughter, and from what I understand that woman has said dreadful things, especially when you consider what that man did to Lizzy. I don't see how you would believe that would simply change."

"Lizzy told you?" Charles had an expression of surprise on his face with his eyebrows lifted until he saw William's anger and backpedaled. "Not that she shouldn't, but I'm just surprised that she told you so quickly.

"Well, she did, and it infuriated me to listen to that ignorant woman's assumptions while you and Jane did virtually nothing to stop her. Did you consider Melanie during the argument? She was obviously upset." Charles closed his eyes and exhaled heavily as William leaned a bit further to ensure he caught his eyes when they opened. "That sweet little girl was called a *bastard* at your dining room table, and you just sat there."

"I know I messed up," he interjected, "but you've known for years that I'm terrible with confrontations."

"I do know that. It's a good thing you're excellent at contracts and negotiations. I've never really understood how, considering your dislike for arguments."

Charles furrowed his brow and thought for a moment. "I guess it's because I'm supposed to do it," he said, shrugging. "I don't have a personal relationship with the clients when I negotiate a deal. It's business."

William shook his head and exhaled heavily. "Anyway, Lizzy deserves better than the way she was treated that day—by everyone. You and Jane took her in, you helped her get on her feet, and then you abandoned her to Mrs. Bennet."

Charles began to raise his voice a bit. "The Bennet's visit wasn't planned, and when they showed up at the door, we weren't sure what to do. Mrs. Bennet and Lizzy haven't seen each other in two years, so we hoped that things would be different—that time would've made a difference."

"That's a pretty unrealistic wish, Charles."

"We did try to interject."

"You didn't try very hard," said William while he leaned forward. "I can tell you one thing. Lizzy was very upset when we left here. She's cut the Bennets out of her life because of their treatment of her. If you do this to her again, she might just sever her relationship with you as well." His friend blanched.

"She told you that?"

"She didn't have to. Why would she continue to put herself or Melanie through that? What you did was extremely unfair to her."

They heard Melanie's chatter through the monitor and Charles stood while William rose as well and stepped into his path. "I said that day that it only takes one of you to make a phone call, and I stand by that. There is no excuse, *no excuse* for not warning Lizzy in advance. She should've been allowed to decide whether she wanted to see the Bennets, not you making that choice for her."

Charles nodded glumly. "I'll be right back." William nodded as Charles stepped around him, and then listened to the sound of his friend entering the room upstairs. He heard him softly say "I'm sorry," and despite the fact that Melanie probably had no idea why Charles was apologizing, William felt a certain amount of satisfaction at his attempt. He then heard what he was sure was the sound of Charles giving her a soft kiss followed by a large smacking kiss and Charles laughing. "Thanks, Melly," he said as he chuckled.

All sound disappeared for a few minutes, until he heard Melanie singing her ABC's and realized she was washing her hands. The monitor then clicked off and Charles appeared with her a minute later.

"Willyum!" she cried as she wiggled down her uncle's side to climb into William's lap.

"Hi, sweetie." He gave her a kiss on the forehead as she settled against him.

"You and Lizzy seem to be seeing a good bit of each other," began Charles carefully. "Are the two of you a couple?"

William shrugged while he shifted to get comfortable when Melanie was settled. "As far as I'm concerned, we are, but I haven't spoken to her about it yet. It wasn't that long ago that she hated me."

Charles grinned as he took his seat. "I wouldn't say she hated you. Otherwise, she wouldn't have been so annoyed over your idiotic behavior."

William shrugged. "Just out of curiosity, what happened after we left Thanksgiving?"

Charles rolled his eyes. "Mrs. Bennet ranted for a while, and then she acted as if nothing had happened—except that she continued to bring it up every five minutes or so until Jane's father told her to stop."

"What exactly was she ranting about?"

Chuckling, Charles shook his head. "Lizzy and your departure along with the usual nonsense. Jane tried to talk to her mother after dinner, but she told Jane she didn't want to hear anything bad about Greg and walked away. She also tried with Lydia, but that went worse than her attempt with her mother."

"What was the point? We had already left."

"She hoped that Lydia would screw up and say something that would tell us where Greg is hiding. Lydia is also stupid enough to trust him. Jane doesn't want to see her hurt."

"And did she say something?"

Charles shook his head. "She became irate and then Mrs. Bennet came in and scolded Jane for upsetting her sister." William rolled his eyes and cuddled Melly a bit closer. If he had anything to say about it, she wouldn't ever have to deal with that family.

Their talking ceased when they heard female voices. A moment later, Jane walked in, followed by Lizzy. "Hey, Melly Belly," said Lizzy as she came over and gave her daughter a kiss. "Do I get a hug?" Melanie leaned forward enough to hug her mother, and then reclined back against William.

She gave William a shy smile as she straightened and turned toward Charles. "Has she been awake long?" While she'd been at ease with him and Melly, Lizzy had become a bit stiff when turned to address her brother-in-law, and William couldn't blame her.

"She just woke up a few minutes ago." He shifted nervously in his seat before he rose to stand before Lizzy. "I know Jane has apologized for what happened Thanksgiving, but I owe you one as well. I'm sorry." Leaning forward, he hugged Lizzy as she gave William a stunned look, with her arms awkwardly around him and patting his back.

180

"Thanks, Charles," she said softly. She released him and took a seat next to William.

Charles returned to his seat and stared at Lizzy and William sitting side by side for a moment. "Why don't Jane and I keep Melly for a little while tonight? The two of you can go out to dinner or something."

Smiling nervously, Jane walked over and sat down next to Lizzy on the sofa. "We'd love to keep her for a few hours."

William cautiously looked at Lizzy. "What do you think?"

She glanced at her workout clothes. "I'm not exactly dressed for a date."

"I don't mind. We'll just do something more casual." He took her hand, rubbing his thumb over the top as she seemed to consider the situation.

"Okay," she said after a moment. "Sure, why not."

"Great!" exclaimed Jane, "Melly, do you want to go help me make supper? I have macaroni and cheese." Melanie cheered and went with Jane while they stood to leave.

William and Lizzy made their way to his car, and were soon driving toward town.

"How was Pilates?" he asked, breaking the silence. Lizzy sighed and turned to face him.

"It was okay." He raised his eyebrows and she rolled her eyes. "Things are pretty awkward between Jane and myself. She apologized again when I arrived, but I'm so angry with her, I could spit nails."

"You should be," William responded after noting her shocked expression. "I don't know why you look stunned. I mentioned last night on the phone that I was surprised you were even going to Pilates this week. I mean I understand that your family took Jane and Charles off guard, but they should've called." He could see Lizzy shrug out of the corner of his eye and reached out for her hand, squeezing it gently.

"But, *I* know how my mother is, and I *know* Jane has never stood up to her in her life. Is it unfair of me to think she should've this time?"

William exhaled heavily. "No, I don't think it's unfair. From what you've said, Jane knew exactly what your mother has said in the past—knew the potential of what could be said that day, and did nothing to prevent it." He made the next left and turned to face her for a moment. "We're getting into town, so where would you like to go?"

Lizzy thought for a moment, biting her lip. "Why don't we go to Gouldings?" He nodded and took the next right to go downtown. She sat there quietly for a moment, staring out of the window, while he attended the road until he suddenly heard her begin again. "I let Jane have it on the way to the gym this afternoon."

"Good! I said something to Charles before you arrived." She smiled and laughed a bit.

"Is that why he hugged me?"

"Probably, he apologized to Melly when she woke up from her nap." Lizzy smiled and shook her head.

"In all honesty, I did want to back out of Pilates today, but I went because Melly loves her afternoons with her Uncle Charles. I didn't want to take that away from her. My parents would be the only reason I don't trust them with her and they left on Friday."

"Has Jane ever tried to tell your parents about the night before Melly was born?"

"Once," she responded, "when my mother came that time after Melly was born. Olivia shut her down pretty quickly, and Jane has never pushed the subject again."

"I did say something to Charles that I feel you should know about." Lizzy turned to him with a puzzled expression.

"What's that?"

"I basically told him that you'd cut ties with your parents, but that if there was ever a repeat of Thanksgiving, I could see you severing your relationship with them, too."

182

"I told Jane something similar," she confessed after a sigh. "I don't want to. I mean she's been my best friend for as long as I can remember, but I'm not going to put myself through that again."

"How did she take it?"

"She was crying when we reached the gym and spent half the Pilates class in the ladies locker room."

They stopped speaking so William could parallel park the car and went inside, where they quickly ordered and were seated. He took in her appearance for a moment across the table. Her hair was pulled back in a low ponytail with a few escaped strands curling softly around her face. Even in her workout clothes, he thought she looked stunning.

"You're staring," she said as she blushed.

"You're lovely."

She couldn't hold his gaze and fidgeted with her silverware. "They changed my class schedule around next semester," she stated, changing the subject.

Concerned, he leaned forward. "How so?"

"They want me to teach the night section of 3-D design. I can turn it down, but then I lose the salary that I make for that class. If I take it, then I have to worry about childcare for Melly."

Concerned for her safety, he frowned as he considered the options she had. "I'll be honest. The idea of you being on campus at night worries me, but ultimately this is your decision. As for Melanie, you know that you have several childcare options."

"I have Jane and Charles," she interjected.

"You have me, too."

She looked surprised. "You wouldn't mind?"

He leaned forward and placed his hand over hers. "I know we haven't discussed it, but I already consider us a couple."

"I didn't want to assume," she said shyly. "And I didn't want to presume that you'd be so accepting to Melly. I mean, we're a package deal, and I wasn't sure you'd be interested in the possibility of being a father to another man's child."

William gazed at her earnestly as he gently squeezed her hand. "I realized before I ever asked you out that I wouldn't mind having Melly as a daughter. She's an adorable little girl." He smiled warmly, hoping to reassure her. "I would've thought I was rather obvious, but I want both of you in my life." The gentle grip he had on her hand slackened, and he began caressing the top of her knuckles with his thumb as he watched several emotions play out across her face.

"I'm crazy about both of you. I want nothing more than to spend all my time with my favorite ladies." He loved the way one side of her mouth turned upwards, indicating that he was saying the right things. "So, I wouldn't have a problem helping out—your daughter isn't exactly difficult."

Lizzy was a bit nervous when William mentioned being a couple. They hadn't really discussed it, but it did seem as though they were together already. She wasn't seeing anyone else, so things really wouldn't be any different. Their relationship needed to move forward, and although a part of her was wary, she couldn't go turning everyone away for that reason. She would be alone forever if she did.

"I do," she said softly, "I would like for us to be official—I guess would be a way to put it." She laughed a bit at how the conversation seemed a bit silly, despite the fact that it needed to be discussed.

"Taking care of Melly isn't always easy," Lizzy said with a smile. "She has her moments."

"I have yet to see one."

"Well, if you're going to take care of her, then you'll definitely witness a tantrum eventually. Just when you do, walk away."

"Walk away?" he asked, bewildered.

"You'll understand when it happens, but it's the quickest way to deal with it. Trust me."

He smiled and leaned back as their food was placed on the table. "Okay, then how many nights are you teaching?"

"Just one night, five to ten. The department head promised me that this is the last semester I'll have to teach that class, and I pray that he keeps his word. There's a rumor floating around that Braiden Younge has agreed to teach a few sculpture classes beginning in the fall."

"Braiden Younge?"

"He's a local sculptor who moved to San Francisco for a time, but he's apparently decided to return to Meryton."

"Didn't he succeed there?" asked William interestedly.

"No, from what I understand he did well. Perhaps he just missed home," she suggested, shrugging. "I've never met him, so I don't know."

The discussion turned to other topics until they finished, William paid the bill, and they walked out of the door. Settled back into the car, the ride back was for the most part a comfortable silence. Lizzy turned toward William as she studied the profile of his face in the small amount of light coming from other cars on the highway. She thought he was so handsome, and found herself wondering why he was interested in her and not someone who looked more like Jane.

"Are you going to watch me the entire drive?" he asked with an amused smile when they were almost to Netherfield.

"I'm sorry. I was just watching the play of the light on your face— the way it affects the appearance of your profile." She blushed and turned toward the front of the car.

Laughing, he reached out and took her hand in his. "You aren't going to draw me, are you?" She could tell by the tone of his voice that he was teasing her.

She smiled. "My portraits aren't great, so no."

"Why do you say that?" He had an interested even earnest expression on his face.

"There's usually something that isn't quite right about them. It also takes me forever because I'm so careful, so I hate working with a model."

"So there *is* something you don't do perfectly?" Lizzy noticed the mischievous grin return to his face as they turned into the driveway.

"There are a lot of things I don't do perfectly, Mr. Darcy. I'm not great at portraits, I don't excel at sculpture, I could never be a lawyer, and I'm horrible at math and chemistry. Oh, and I usually cut myself at least once every time I shave my legs." She watched the dimples that had appeared on his face as he laughed, feeling a flutter in her stomach.

Once the car was parked, he turned to face her. "Nothing tragic then," he said softly as he gently stroked her thigh. "Except the damage you inflict on your legs."

Lizzy chuckled and glanced up to find him leaning toward her. She closed her eyes as he delicately claimed her mouth in small feather-like touches. She sighed in contentment and he deepened the kiss, his hand curling into her hair beneath her ponytail until he suddenly drew back.

"This isn't going to work," he grumbled as he unbuckled himself, then Lizzy, and pulled her across the car to his lap. She heard the whir of the seat being moved back as he brought her closer to his body.

"Are you sure you want to be this close to me?" He looked at her questioningly and she gestured toward her workout clothes. "I haven't showered since Pilates, remember?" He unzipped her jacket, dropped his head to her chest and sniffed as she squirmed and laughed. "What are you doing?"

He sat up straight as his arms snaked under the now open garment. "I find nothing offensive about the way you smell tonight." His thumbs were stroking her stomach, which was making her increasingly warm all over.

186

She placed her palm on his chest and grazed her lips against his. The kiss progressed quickly as Lizzy straddled his lap for a more comfortable position. One of his large hands wrapped around her hip to grasp her behind as the other slipped under the back of her shirt, pressing her closer to him as his fingers gripped her around her waist.

One of her hands had made its way into his hair, and she shifted down, which suddenly caused him to press warm and solid between her legs. She gasped at the unusual ache that manifested itself. The sensation was something new—something that had occurred only since being with William. She rocked a bit on her knees and he groaned as he broke the kiss and leaned his head back against the seat.

"As much as I'm enjoying this, I think we need to stop. I don't want to make love to you here in the driveway at Netherfield."

Lizzy smiled and inwardly hoped that Jane or Charles hadn't looked out of a window while they were embraced. She nodded as she felt his hand withdraw from her top, her skin still tingling where his fingers had been grazing along her back. She put her forehead on his shoulder and breathed evenly in the hopes of regaining some of her composure before facing her sister.

His hand moved up and down over the back of her shirt and she felt a light kiss at the nape of her neck. Pulling back, she carefully climbed over to her seat, and he entwined his fingers with hers. She looked across the car to where he was watching her with the same expression he'd always used in the past. How could she have not recognized it for what it was? A thought came to her mind and she began to chuckle.

"What's so funny?" he asked as a dimple made an appearance.

"It's just that I'm an adult with a child, and I'm making out like a teenager in a car in my sister's driveway."

He laughed and rubbed the back of her hand with his thumb. "You act as though you've never made out in a car before."

She thought for a moment, furrowing her brow. "I actually haven't."

He regarded her strangely. "Not even? ...Never mind..."

"It was never like that, even after we were married. I think at first it was because it was expected, and then because I happened to be available." She noticed his jaw tense, so she brought her hand up to caress his face. "It's over, and he's gone."

"I detest the way he treated you."

"I know, but he won't ever do it again."

Chapter Thirteen

<u>**Saturday, December 15, 2012**</u>

William was excited for the winter season. He remembered enjoying the holidays when he was young, but they hadn't been a source of joy for what felt like a long time.

The Saturday evening after their date at Gouldings, he'd taken Lizzy and Melanie to the town's annual Christmas tree lighting. They'd had a wonderful time, full of smiles and laughter. He dearly loved seeing the look of wonder on Melanie's face at the large tree and the joy on Lizzy's as the lights glittered in her eyes.

Since it was also Lizzy's last week of school, he even surprised her after class one day, taking her to lunch at Riverside before they picked up Melanie and took her to the park until it was time for her nap.

That morning, however, he was standing in the midst of a tree lot, surveying the selection, anticipating the look on Lizzy and Melanie's face when the perfect spruce tree came through the door. Lizzy had confided that the previous year, she'd found a small pine sapling in the woods behind Longbourn that she cut down and used for Christmas. She equated it with a little tree in one of the Christmas television specials, the small limbs bowing under the weight of the ornaments.

This year, since it was the first where Melanie would be more of a participant, Lizzy wanted to buy a small tree from a lot, so he'd decided to surprise them. The foyer of Longbourn had extremely high ceilings, so he knew that she wouldn't have problem with fitting any of the trees the lot had in the house. The only problem he could foresee would be getting Lizzy to accept it.

He opened his wallet to pay for his purchase and did a double take. Shaking his head and chuckling, he began counting to see how much money Lizzy had sneaked in there. For some time now, she'd been attempting to get him to accept more money for the car, first offering him a check and then covertly putting it places where he might find it and mistakenly think it was his. The last time, she'd placed it into his coat pocket. He'd found it quickly and had slipped it into her purse before he left, but she was a bit more devious this time. She'd even sorted the bills, mixing them in with his own money.

Once he'd figured out how much extra there was, he paid for the tree and made arrangements for it and a stand to be delivered that afternoon, since he couldn't strap it to the top of his car. He then went to the bank, depositing Lizzy's money, so he could put it into Melly's account and then to the storage unit where he kept some of his family's belongings, putting a few items in his trunk before heading over to Longbourn.

When he arrived, he looked around, and not seeing Bear, stepped out of the car. William continued to watch for him, but didn't notice him until he stepped up onto the porch at the same time as the old dog ambled around the corner of the house. He was unsure of how he would react, but he only came and sat watching him sternly until Lizzy opened the door.

"There you are!" she exclaimed. "I was expecting you earlier."

"It's only ten-thirty," he laughed as she let him in the house. "I had a couple of errands to run on my way here. For example, someone put a rather large sum of money in my wallet and I had to go to the bank to deposit it." She smiled widely as she closed the door.

"I'm glad you're finally giving in," she said with a bit of a flirting manner.

"No," he chuckled, "I'm not giving in completely. You just kept adding more money, and I don't like the idea of you keeping large sums of cash around the house." He found the competitive gleam in her eye sexy and, surveyed her attire, a fitted top and yoga pants, while he leaned in to give her a brief kiss. "Were you painting?" He was changing the subject, but his mind was taking the two of them upstairs to her room, which wasn't a great idea at the moment.

"Uh huh," she responded. "I heard Bear's barking coming from the woods, so I thought I'd see if you were here. I'm at a good stopping point though. I need to let everything dry before I continue."

Out of the corner of his eye, he saw Melanie come through the kitchen door. "Hi Melly Belly!"

"Willyummmm!" She ran and jumped as he caught her.

"What've you been up to, sweetie?"

"Blocks!" she exclaimed.

He gave her a kiss on the cheek and put her down on the floor. "Why don't you show me?"

She led him to the studio where she proudly displayed the towers she had been making from the different shaped wooden blocks that were strewn all over the floor. Once he told her how wonderful they all were, he made his way to Lizzy's table, where he studied the painting she'd been working on.

"It's not done yet," he heard Lizzy explain as she walked in behind him.

"I think it looks amazing." He turned to see her beaming at his praise. "This is the second photo, isn't it?

"It is. Since I put all of my grades in the computer earlier this week, I've had a lot more time to work on them, so I've been able to get a lot done." She moved over to her daughter's mess and began throwing blocks in a laundry basket along the wall. "Let's get these cleaned up!"

Melanie and William helped her, and when they were finished, they moved into the kitchen to work on lunch. Lizzy washed her hands and pulled the towel off of a bowl of dough that had been rising. "What kind of pizza do you like?"

"I pretty much like all pizza. Is that what we're having?"

She nodded, and put him to work chopping vegetables that she sautéed while he grated the Mozzarella and Parmesan. When lunch was ready, they had a large pizza that was mainly vegetables, with a quarter of it that appeared to be just cheese for Melanie.

"Have Charles and Jane ever made definite plans for the holidays?" asked William as Lizzy handed him a plate with a slice on it. "Last I heard, they were planning on staying here after the whole Thanksgiving incident."

"They decided this week to go to visit Charles' parents for Christmas."

"I think they've changed their minds four or five times, at least," he said, shaking his head.

"Originally, they'd planned to go to Atlanta and visit our family, but after mom decided to just drop in for Thanksgiving, Jane called and told them they would be going to visit the Bingleys instead."

"I doubt Mrs. Bennet took that news well."

"No," chuckled Lizzy, "I shouldn't be laughing, but Jane was wishing she could drink after that conversation." She shrugged as she took a sip of her water. "Are you still coming here?

He beamed at the idea. "Of course."

"We should plan on you staying for Christmas Eve, so you won't have to get here so early. I have a feeling someone won't want to wait to open their presents."

He laughed as he nodded in understanding. "I heard from Mrs. Reynolds the other day. She extended an invitation to Christmas dinner, but I told her we were planning a quiet holiday after Thanksgiving." He noticed Lizzy's worried expression. "She understood, although she insisted that I make sure you knew that we'd be welcome. She also offered to babysit one night, so I could take you to dinner or a movie. What do you think?"

She blushed and glanced over at Melanie, who was eating quietly, before turning her attention back to him. "I'd like that."

"You'd feel comfortable with Mrs. Reynolds watching her?"

"I like her, Melanie likes her, and you've known her since you were a child. I can't think of better recommendations."

He knew that his smile was probably ridiculous, but he couldn't help it. Thoughts began whirling around in his mind of where they could go and what he could arrange. "Is there anything special you'd like to do?" he asked, interested to see if she had any different ideas.

They discussed several possibilities while they finished lunch and cleaned up the kitchen. Melanie had woken up early that morning and was flagging, so Lizzy put her down for a nap.

"Would you mind if I put in some more work on the painting?" she asked worriedly.

"Not at all," he responded. She returned to her studio while he grabbed his briefcase out of his car. He joined her when he reentered the house, and took a seat on the chair by the window.

"You brought work with you?" she asked, smiling.

"I know that job needs to be finished, so I thought I'd bring something to do in the event you needed to paint."

She nodded before she leaned over and gently applied the brush to the paper. He turned his attention to his documents, managing to concentrate on the report he was reading until Lizzy rose to change out her water at the sink in the laundry room. He then set the papers aside and stretched, glancing outside where he noticed Bear running toward the front of the house barking.

"I wonder what that's all about?" Lizzy asked as she peered out of a window.

William stepped forward and kissed her on the cheek. "Why don't I go find out?"

She nodded, so he quickly walked to the front of the house, calling Bear when he stepped out of the front door. He saw the truck from the tree lot coming up the drive, and took out a package of sliced turkey that he'd stolen from Lizzy's refrigerator, quickly luring the dog into the front living room. Happy with his success, he then shut the doors and rushed back out on the porch as the vehicle stopped in front of the house.

The trunk had been trimmed before they left the lot, so once it was in the stand with the netting removed, they were done. William tipped the men handsomely as they gathered up the trash and left, closing the door behind them.

He was just moving to release Bear from the confines of the living room when Lizzy came in through the entry to the kitchen, her eyes widening as she took in the tree. "What on earth have you done, William Darcy?"

Turning, he smiled as he stepped up to take her in his arms. "I wanted to surprise you."

"Well, you certainly did that!" she said as she laughed. "Melanie's only two. She doesn't need a—what is that? A ten to twelve foot tree?"

"But you have to admit, she'll adore it." She was shaking her head at him, and he was loving every minute. At that moment, Bear let out a bark, and he moved to let the dog out of the living room, shrugging at Lizzy.

"Of course she will, but that's beside the point. That's an expensive tree." She turned toward the blue spruce that her dog was sniffing curiously.

Realizing her concern, he turned her face gently with his hand so that she was looking at him. "I'm not having a tree at the guest house, and I'm spending Christmas here. I hope to spend a lot of the holiday at Longbourn." She smiled radiantly and he grazed his lips against hers. "Besides, you wouldn't let me buy Melly a present."

She burst out laughing, and wrapped her arms around his chest. "It does look lovely with the high ceilings in here, but I don't think I have enough ornaments. Aunt Mel stopped replacing the ones that would break as she got older, and just bought smaller trees."

"I have some ornaments in the car from my parents, and I thought we could use some of those. I also have lights. New ones. You mentioned that your aunt's were antique, and the ones I had in storage were rather old as well."

She gave him a lingering kiss before she pulled back. "I would imagine it needs water, so let's get that, and then we'll put the lights and the ornaments on the top half of the tree before Melanie wakes."

"I don't understand," he said with furrowed brow.

"We're going to need ladders to reach the top. Melly climbs the step stool whenever it is out. I shudder to think of her scaling a ten foot ladder."

"Got it! You don't have to say anymore," he exclaimed at the mental image she created. "How much time do you think we have?"

"It depends...she woke up really early this morning, and she could make up for that, which would be at least another two hours, or she'll wake up in a little over an hour."

He nodded and they set to work. Melanie didn't give them any extra time, but fortunately, they'd managed to put away the ladders just before she woke. Lizzy held her hand as they walked down the stairs, leading her around so she could see the entire tree before pointing it out.

"Look at the tree, Melly," she said.

Her daughter looked up and gasped as she smiled from ear to ear. "Pwetty!" She immediately moved to an open box and grasped an ornament. Lizzy came to help, but Melanie gave her a stern look and turned to keep the bauble away from her mother. "I want to do it!"

After a bit of persuasion, Lizzy and William were able to take turns helping her put non-breakable ornaments on the tree. Lizzy had planned that those would be kept around the bottom, so that if Melanie played with them, they wouldn't have to worry about broken glass all over the floor.

When they were finished, they spent the remainder of the day simply spending time together. They colored and played with Melanie, ate dinner, and watched a new Rapunzel cartoon before Lizzy bathed her daughter and put her to bed. William hadn't been too sure about watching the animated movie, but he'd found himself chuckling at a good bit of it. Of course, hearing Lizzy laugh made it worth sitting through just about any film.

She arrived back downstairs after Melanie was asleep, turned off all of the lights but those on the tree, and sat down with him on the sofa. He'd been watching an old sit-com while she was gone, but it wasn't as interesting now that she'd returned.

"What are you watching?" she asked as she cuddled up to his side.

He put his arm around her and looked down into her face. "I wasn't really. I was just waiting for you."

She placed her hand on his cheek, winding it back through his hair to pull his face down to hers. Her lips stroked his and he returned the kiss as he slipped his tongue in to caress hers. His free hand roamed up her leg to her hip, where he wrapped it around to her rear.

He hadn't, as of yet, tasted her skin, and so he skimmed his lips down her cheek where he began placing small tender kisses on the sensitive skin of her neck, suckling a spot just under her ear. She moaned, and he pulled her closer, reclining so that he was laying over her. He loved the way she felt—her body was firm, yet the skin of her face and neck was so soft. Her curves seemed to conform to his perfectly, and he took a deep breath attempting to calm himself before he overwhelmed her.

Her leg slid its way up his, and the one simple move shredded any restraint he had been trying to maintain. He swiftly reclaimed her mouth, and she matched his ardor as his fingers found the edge of her shirt, moving inside and spanning her abdomen with his hand. He traced his fingers along the velvety skin on the underside of her bra while her hands moved to his backside to pull him closer. Their bodies pressed firmly together as they were was sweet torture. William groaned while his fingers happened upon the front closure to her bra, which easily gave way to reveal her soft breasts to his fingers.

His thumb skimmed her nipple, and she gasped as he felt it harden on his palm, cradling the entirety of her breast in his hand. He returned to her neck, hearing her uneven breathing. He loved that she seemed as turned on as he was.

Her silky skin beckoned to be stroked, so he continued to caress her breast until he heard her breathe out his name. William could tell by the tone that she felt they should stop, but he just wanted her to know—he wanted to show her how much he cared for her.

"I know we should stop, but I just want to touch you...please? I promise that we won't go any further." He gazed into her eyes as she nodded. He kept his eyes locked on hers while his hand moved beneath the elastic waistband of her yoga pants then panties. William ached for her, but he wanted to give her this. He was sure that her needs were probably never met in the past, and more than anything, he wished to put her first.

196

She inhaled sharply, closing her eyes, as he began to run his fingers along her sensitive bundle of nerves. He watched her initial reaction to be sure she was well, and then he began kissing her again, deep, hungry kisses that she returned eagerly. Her response to him didn't take long to intensify and he pulled back from kissing her, keeping his forehead pressed to hers. She was writhing against his hand as she panted and whimpered, and he felt his heartbeat accelerate just watching her. Her climax came quickly, and she cried out his name just before she arched up into his neck and tensed all over. He continued long enough to ensure she was complete before he kissed her passionately. "You're so beautiful."

She relaxed back against the sofa as he studied her expression. William could see desire and possibly love in her eyes, but he was sure he saw a bit of fear. He maneuvered so that he was on his back with her curled to his side. "Are you okay?" He felt her nod against his shoulder, and moved so that he could see her face. "Are you sure?"

Lizzy's body was still on fire when she heard William say she was beautiful. Lying back on to the cushion, she saw him gazing into her eyes, and attempted to suppress the fear she felt. She'd just had the most intense sexual experience of her life, and they hadn't even had sex. She was falling in love with him—an idea that terrified her. She truly had very little experience with men and sex. What if she wasn't enough? What if he wasn't satisfied with her?

His voice asking if she was well intruded on her thoughts, and she felt him move so that he was able to see her face.

"Yes," she responded as she cuddled closer. She didn't wish to talk about her insecurities, or else Greg would inevitably be mentioned. The last thing Lizzy wanted was to let that man ruin her evening, much less the rest of her life.

He pulled back from her so she could see his face. "You can always tell me no. I don't want to push you to go too quickly." His expression was so earnest, so loving, she felt herself fall just a bit deeper.

"Everything has been fast, but I wanted you to touch me." A part of her wanted to roll her eyes at the wide grin he wore at her admission, no matter how cute it was. "What about you?" she asked softly. She leaned in and gave him a small kiss where his chest was exposed by the neckline of his shirt.

William's hand brushed through her hair as she pulled back to see the endearing smile that he wore. "I'm fine." She propped her head on her hand as he combed her hair behind her ear.

"Are you sure?" He nodded and she blushed. "Then would you mind if we watched TV upstairs?" she suggested shyly. "I'm tired, and all I want is for you to hold me while I fall asleep."

"That's one request I will happily grant." He rose and offered Lizzy his hand to aid her in standing. When she was upon her feet, she entwined her fingers with his and led him up the stairs.

Lizzy woke during the early hours of the morning and, despite being warmly cocooned in William's arms, couldn't return to her dreams. She was restless, and fearful of waking him if she remained, so she slipped on her sweater and ventured down to her studio. The moonlight was shining through the windows, eerily illuminating the room, when she stepped through the door and turned on the lights. She took a seat, situated herself in front of her worktable, and studied the painting for a few moments, deciding where to begin. When she'd made a decision, she added water to the dried pigments, and began carefully laying in some of the detail to the scene in front of her.

She'd worked for close to an hour, carefully alternating areas where she was working so that there was no bleeding between colors. When she came to a point where everything was too wet, she reached up to stretch her arms and back.

As she began to relax, a pair of arms circled her stomach to embrace her from behind. "I missed you."

"I woke up and couldn't go back to sleep, so I came down here."

"What's wrong, Lizzy?" Something in her eyes and tone of voice must have made him suspicious. Of course, there was also the fact that she was painting in the early hours of the morning.

She turned within his embrace, wrapping her arms around his solid torso. "Why do you think something is the matter?"

"I know that I haven't stayed over much, but you've never mentioned waking up this early to paint," he said with a knowing look.

She sighed and drew back. "Sometimes I think too much and I need to stop—painting helps."

"I wish you'd talk to me," he stated earnestly. He gently brushed the hair from the side of her face behind her ear.

"I'm tired of Greg coming up in conversation. I feel like he ruins things, and I don't want to give him that power anymore." Her tone showed her irritation as she vented only part of what had bothered her.

He pulled her back within his arms and touched his forehead to hers. "Last night you said you were fine, but you seemed a bit afraid. Are you sure I'm not pushing you into more than you're ready for?"

She drew back and shook her head. "No, I already feel more for you than I have anyone. It's just difficult to trust..." She tried to shrug nonchalantly as she looked down to fidget with the waistband of his pajama pants. "It frightens me to think that you might leave."

"Sweetheart," he crooned as he placed his hand on her cheek, lifting her face so she could see his eyes. "I *love* you. I have no plans of going anywhere."

She choked back a sob, and he held her close while she wept out her fear and relief. When she'd calmed, she slowly pulled back a bit, embarrassed that she'd lost her composure in front of him.

"Lizzy," he said softly. Her eyes met his crystal blue ones and her stomach fluttered. "You need to talk to me next time instead of bottling all of this up. There's no reason to be embarrassed. I'll understand."

"How'd you know that I'm embarrassed?" she asked in almost a whisper.

"Because your face is beet red," he said, smiling widely. She groaned and buried her head into his chest that shook a bit as he chuckled. "Let's go back to bed," he said softly in her ear. She nodded, and he hooked his index finger through hers to lead her back upstairs. When they were snuggled back under the covers, he drew her against his body and held her closely until she faded back to oblivion.

Lizzy woke again when the sun was shining through the windows, to find she was still nestled within William's embrace. She could feel him lightly rubbing his thumb on her shoulder, and sighed as she buried her face in his neck.

"Good morning," he whispered.

"Mmmm, it's too early," she mumbled.

She could feel his chest shake as he laughed. "It's eight o'clock."

Drawing back so that she could see his face, she frowned. "Melanie isn't awake yet?" She began to rise to check on her daughter, and he pulled her back to him.

"I just looked in on her a little while ago and she was sleeping peacefully." He seemed to appraise her carefully. "I want to know what you meant last night by saying that you didn't like Greg ruining things."

"He just seems to come up in conversation a good bit, and it's beginning to bother me. I'm sure you don't want to hear about him, and I'd rather not discuss him."

William tilted her face so that she could see his frank expression. "I want to know you—all of you—which means that he'll be mentioned from time to time. He was a part of your life for years, and we can't just pretend it never happened. I know that you don't like speaking of him, and I understand." He pulled her to him and hugged her close. "Don't worry on my account though. He won't scare me away."

"You must think I'm ridiculous," she mumbled into his neck.

"Not at all," he reassured her. "I think it would be strange for you to come out of that relationship without any scars."

"Scars?" she asked, as she pulled back so that she could see his face.

"Baggage, battle scars," he said, softly brushing her hair behind her ear.

She nodded, and lifted herself up on her elbow. Placing her hand on his cheek, she leaned in and brushed her lips against his. She tugged gently at his top then bottom lip before he leaned her back into the pillows. He deepened the kiss while his hand made his way to her hip, and she sighed at the feel of his hand on her body. He had just moved his soft lips to the sensitive skin of her neck when the sound of Melanie's chattering coming through the monitor caused him to cease his actions.

"She's awake," he groaned.

"She's okay for a few minutes." Lizzy reached up to pull his lips back to hers. She heard him moan as she ran her hands around his sides to his back. Her desire was to make him as aroused as she was—to know that she wasn't the only one who wanted more. She felt his hand just begin to snake its way under her top when she heard a creaking, followed a minute later by the bed shifting and a loud "Boo!" resounding through the room.

William was so surprised that he nearly fell from the bed due to how quickly he jumped off of her. "She can get out of her crib?" he exclaimed, his voice hitting a pitch Lizzy didn't know he was capable of achieving.

Lizzy looked from him to where her daughter was crawling up the bed with a self-satisfied expression. "I caught her trying to crawl out once, but she's never actually done it. I told her it was a no-no." She sat up as her daughter plopped herself in her lap, glancing to where William was attempting to prevent the covers from tenting. "I'm sorry," she said as she tried unsuccessfully to stifle a laugh. "In the past, she's always just played for a bit with her animals."

He looked at her with a mischievous smirk on his face. "So you've left Melanie in her crib while you were with other men?"

She gasped loudly and pulled a pillow to hit him. "I can't believe you just said that!" He picked up his and retaliated, prompting her to yell, "Get him, Melly!"

He looked affronted as he yelled, "That's not fair!"

Her daughter was not deterred by his exclamation. She ran over, gigging loudly, and began hitting him with her stuffed animal while Lizzy alternated with her pillow. William was quick though, and it didn't take long before he had grabbed Melanie around her waist with one arm and took down Lizzy with the other. They all wound up lying in a heap on the bed, laughing. She turned toward William, who was lying on his back, sporting a fully dimpled smile.

His arm moved around her shoulders and she shifted so that her head was on the side of his chest. As she felt him kiss her on the temple, she couldn't help but think how perfect he fit in with her and Melanie. She cuddled them both as close as she could, realizing that in that moment, she was happier than she'd ever been.

Chapter Fourteen

<u>**Monday, December 24, 2012**</u>

William started the dishwasher and made his way to the spare bedroom. As he wound his way up Longbourn's staircase, he smiled at how well things had gone the last few weeks.

The day of Melanie's escape from her crib, now known as Melly's Climbing Expedition, Lizzy had decided that the day for a toddler bed had arrived. Aunt Mel had given the original bed for that room to Lizzy's mother, so a day of shopping had been planned. After one store, William frowned and took his ladies to the storage facility where his family's belongings were kept. His little sister's antique bedroom set wasn't being used, and was perfect for Melanie. Lizzy had required some persuasion, but after he commented that it would just sit in storage if she didn't use it, she relented. She did insist that he'd only have to ask for it to be returned. He couldn't, however, convince her to let him buy a new mattress. She instead took one from another bed at Longbourn.

Saturday night, they'd attended the annual D&F holiday party while Mrs. Reynolds watched Melanie. He'd worn his sleek black Armani suit and red silk tie, while Lizzy, at his request, wore her red velvet dress—he dearly loved the way she looked in it. That evening, she charmed everyone she met, even James Wattingly, his curmudgeonly head of accounting who had a propensity to hate everyone. Looking back to the excuses he made when they first met, he could only shake his head at the thought that Lizzy would negatively impact him with the board or the company. How could he have ever taken that notion seriously?

He turned the corner into the spare bedroom that was the farthest from Melanie's, and closed the door. Opening a drawer on the bureau, he pulled out an old fashioned key and unlocked the closet where they'd hidden Melanie's Christmas presents. He removed the packages, one by one, and the kitchen that they'd put together during her nap Sunday, and set them by the door. He was just putting his hand on the doorknob when the door suddenly opened to reveal the object of his thoughts.

"She's asleep," Lizzy exclaimed wearily. "I still can't believe she took so long to go down."

He laughed as he took her into his arms. "You're the one who read her all of the different versions of *The Night before Christmas* and then told her that it's Christmas Eve like the tale."

She smiled as she reached down to pinch his side. "I just wanted her to be excited tomorrow. Besides, I wasn't the only one reading her those books. You even bought her a new one when we purchased the safety railings for her bed."

He kissed her quickly. "Guilty, as charged."

Laughing, she moved to one side of the pastel pink kitchen. "Let's get these things downstairs so we can go to bed."

"Is that meant to be an incentive for me to hurry?" he asked, grinning widely.

She rolled her eyes and lifted one side as he picked up his. "You're incorrigible, Mr. Darcy."

They brought down the kitchen, and while Lizzy arranged it under the tree, William brought down the remaining gifts. She filled the stockings, surprising William by filling theirs with apples, oranges, and pears. "We'll eat them, and I don't have to buy something I really don't need," she explained. He could think of a number of things he'd like to see in Lizzy's stocking, but he knew that she'd probably fuss at him for the gift alone. He'd have to remember to buy something to put in there for next year.

Lizzy then disappeared for a few minutes, allowing him to pull the box of body supplies from his bag and place it under the tree. He was just putting out a small box for Melanie when she brought out a large, rather flat wrapped package from the direction of the kitchen.

"What's that?" he asked curiously.

"You'll find out tomorrow." She had a mischievous smile, and he came closer to attempt to discern what she'd done. "Nah ah ahhh," she sang in a flirtatious manner, "you have to wait until tomorrow, or Santa will put coal in your stocking." She leaned it against the wall by the tree as he drew near, and then turned and put a hand on his chest to push him back.

He chuckled and pulled her to him by the waistband of her pants. "But I want to unwrap a gift," he growled. Her eyes widened, and he worried that perhaps he'd taken the joke too far.

"You'll have to catch me first," she exclaimed as she propelled herself out of his grasp and up the stairs. Truth be told, William was a bit shocked at first, but with a large grin, he took off after her, his longer legs helping him to catch up quickly. He reached her as she made it to the top of the stairs, and grabbed her by the waist as she let out a squeal.

"Shhhhh," he said, throwing her over his shoulder, "you'll wake Melly."

He strode into her room, dropped her onto the bed, and crawled over her. She met his gaze, and, for the first time, he didn't see any trepidation in her eyes. William peered down to see her begin pulling his shirt from the waistband of his pants. She removed it and tossed it over his head, placing her hands on the solid plane of his chest. His eyes closed in contentment while her fingers traced the contours of his muscles. Wanting her to feel comfortable, he remained still, allowing her to explore for as long as he could manage before he dropped his forehead to hers.

"Lizzy," he growled. "I..."

She put her finger over his lips and looked him unreservedly in the eye. "Make love to me."

He lifted himself up, his face showing his surprise. "Are you sure?" His mind was reeling at the implied feelings of the words she chose.

"Yes," she whispered as she nodded.

Still having a hard time believing that he was going to finally be with Lizzy, he lowered himself to claim her lips softly, one at a time, before he took full possession of her mouth. Her tongue slid in to meet his, and he moaned as he reached down to find the edge of her top, parting long enough for him to bring it over her head. His eyes roamed down the smooth expanse of skin and her white lace bra, which was easily unhooked to bare her to his sight. Only his hands had ever made their way under her tops in the past, so he remained where he was, indulging himself in a long look. The room was not well lit, but he thought she was more lovely than he had dreamed.

When his sight returned to her face, he noticed that she appeared unsure, so he ran the back of his hand from her shoulder to her waist before curving its path back up to cup her breast.

"You are stunning," he murmured. He lowered his head to kiss the tip, which caused her to inhale sharply, and he felt his heart begin to beat faster. She ran her hands up his arms to wind them in his hair as she pulled him back down. Taking her nipple into his mouth, he suckled and nibbled until he heard her breathing become heavier. Her fingers were wound through his hair, alternately gripping and caressing, and when he released her, she grasped him to pull his mouth to hers.

The intensity of their kissing increased and William realized that it was different than before. The glimmer of fear that he'd seen in her eyes must have always held her back, and tonight, she was baring herself completely to him—body and soul.

Her nails trailed down his back, gently scratching until they reached his rear where she gripped him and pulled him down onto her. All thought seemed to disappear, and he released her mouth to kiss and lick his way down her body to the top of her slacks.

William couldn't remember ever being so nervous, and his fingers shook as he attempted to unfasten her pants, so he could pull them from her legs. He'd backed off the bed as he worked, and Lizzy sat up, gently pushing him to stand and removing his jeans so they could join her clothes on the floor.

Her hair brushed his hip when she reached back up to remove his boxer briefs, and he wove his fingers into her hair, enjoying the silky strands flowing through his fingers. She trailed her hands back up his legs, and raised her face as she viewed his body.

Lizzy studied the contours of William's stomach and chest for a few moments before she stood to kiss him. When their mouths met, she trembled and pressed herself against him, wanting nothing more than to hold him as close as possible. Her tongue reached in to caress his while he lifted her and maneuvered them to the center of the bed where he covered her body with his. She'd never felt as comfortable with intimacy as she did with William. Nothing felt forced, and she didn't feel as though she were mechanically going through the motions as she had in the past. She was nervous, but she was turned on and actually enjoying herself.

He turned his attention to her neck, and when he suckled on one spot, just below her ear, she moaned, instinctively lifting her knees until he was cradled between her thighs, his weight melding their bodies together. She stroked his hip as she moved to cup his backside, attempting to pull him in to quench what was becoming a familiar aching need.

"I've been tested, but do we need protection?" he managed to get out between kisses to her neck.

She attempted to form a coherent thought as he moved to lave her pebbled nipple. "I'm...ummm...my last test was negative...I'm..." she whimpered as he once again took it in his mouth and gently nibbled the tip. "I'm...pill...on...the pill."

He wore a large grin as he reclaimed her mouth, running his fingers between her legs. She cried out softly and he continued to manipulate her while he slipped one of his fingers inside.

She arched her back and closed her eyes as he made her feel as if she were aflame. She couldn't control the whimpers and moans she was making while her hips began involuntarily moving in response to the work of his fingers, eventually crying out as she fiercely gripped his hair. He continued his ministrations, which drew out her orgasm until she could take no more, and began pulling his head down to kiss her.

His lips softly touched hers before he moved down to spread soft kisses up her stomach and chest until he was lying on top of her. She ran her hand along his cheek as he held her gaze. "I love you, Lizzy," he whispered while he joined with her. She gasped, and he stopped, appraising her worriedly.

"It's been a long time."

"Are you sure..."

"I'm fine," she reassured him. She kissed him passionately while she wrapped her legs around him and guided him the remainder of the way.

"You feel so good," he moaned when he parted from her lips. She kissed his nose and smiled so he'd know she was well before he began moving in long strokes, maintaining eye contact between kisses as he slowly quickened his pace.

Lizzy was having a difficult time not becoming emotional at the storm of sensations and feelings she was experiencing. The same warmth she'd felt earlier was spreading throughout her body, and she knew that he'd overwhelm her again. As her orgasm bore down, she dug her fingers into the flesh of his back while she climaxed so hard she felt tears leaking from her eyes.

When the roar in her head subsided, she could hear him moan, and needing to tell him her feelings, she placed her hand on his face. "I love you," she said artlessly just before he involuntarily closed his eyes and cried out as he tensed over her. He collapsed onto her body soon after, and she lightly brushed his curls back from his face until he could prop himself on an arm over her.

"Did you mean it?" he asked with wonder.

"Yes," she said with a small smile, "I love you."

"How long?" he asked with an almost excited tone. "How long have you felt this way?"

"I'm not sure," she said, trying to remember when her feelings had deepened. "I think I was in the middle before I knew it had begun." He held her close and pulled her with him to his side. Wanting to remain as close to him as possible, she wrapped her top leg around his body and nestled her head just under his chin.

"I love you, too," he whispered as he lightly ran his fingers over her back.

The feel of his hands on her bare skin felt so nice that it was all she could do not to purr with contentment. Being with him like this was so natural to her. She turned her face into his chest and kissed him lightly before the feel of his strong hands softly caressing her back lulled her to sleep.

Lizzy woke to a darkened room and glanced around, briefly disoriented. The lights hadn't been on when they came up to the room, but the hall and tree lights had still been burning brightly. She could only assume that William must have risen after she fell asleep to turn everything off.

Needing to go to the bathroom, she carefully unwound her legs from his so she could rise. He mumbled in his sleep as he rolled to his back, and she stifled a chuckle at his hair sticking up in every direction.

The room was cold, so she grabbed her robe from the inside of her closet door before she tiptoed to the bathroom. When she returned, she threw the robe over the end of the bed and gingerly climbed back under the warm covers. She curled against his side with her head on his shoulder and was scooting her legs closer when her foot brushed his calf.

"Good night!" he suddenly gasped out, "how are your feet like icicles?"

"I'm sorry," she whispered, "I needed to get up for a minute."

"Is everything okay?" He pulled her on top of him, where she could feel him pressing insistently on the inside of her thigh.

"Fine, I just needed to use the bathroom."

"Oh," he mumbled. He ran the backs of his fingers from her temple to her chin, his other hand splayed across one cheek of her behind. He spent a few moments simply holding her and caressing her face before he reached around to wind his hand into her hair, pulling her face down and kissing her urgently. Their lips and tongues seemed to meld together, much like their bodies did, before they once again fell into a deep slumber.

William woke early to the first rays of the sun peeking through the sheer drapes of the window. He carefully stretched out his legs while he took in the vision of Lizzy sleeping curled against his side. He gingerly rose from the bed to close and lock the bedroom door.

He loved Melanie, but he wanted some warning if she was going to burst into the room as she had before. Then he crawled back under the covers and slowly rolled to his side, entwining his legs with Lizzy's as he ran a hand under the comforter to caress down the curve of her hip. She sighed in her sleep and he smiled, biting his lip, as he reached up and pulled the covers down to bare her to him.

"Oh, it's cold," she murmured. She opened her eyes to see the comforter down around her waist, and grabbed it to pull it back. "What are you doing?"

"I want to see you." He buried his head into her neck, brushing small kisses from the bottom of her ear to her shoulder.

"But it's so bright," she mumbled, blushing bright red.

"That's the point. I saw you last night, but the room was dimmed with the only light coming from the hall.

She whimpered and closed her eyes while he pulled the sheets back to her thighs, lifting himself so he could study her every curve.

"You're lovely," he whispered as he reverently ran his hands down her body. He reached her stomach and saw a small patch of stretch marks at the very base of her abdomen. He ran his fingers across the three or four faded scars before he glanced up to view her expression. Seeing her apprehension, he leaned over to brush his lips against the spot, working his way back up to her face. When his lips found hers, he claimed her mouth, and proceeded to demonstrate his love for her without words.

Their interlude was perfect. The entire night had been perfect in his mind and when William finally collapsed against her, he felt her skimming her lips and bestowing small kisses up his shoulder, her soft voice bringing him back from oblivion. "I love you."

"I love you, too," he responded. "Merry Christmas."

She chuckled. "Merry Christmas."

Her legs wrapped around him, and he lifted up on his elbows as they softly and repeatedly brushed their lips together, William sometimes giving small kisses to her nose and eyes before returning to her mouth.

210

His hand trailed down her side and she gave a small giggle. "Are you ticklish?" He grinned as she squirmed under his fingers.

"I don't like to be tickled, so please..."

His hand cupped her hip, and he was just planting a kiss to her neck when they heard Melanie begin talking to her stuffed animals, prompting Lizzy to grab the covers in a frantic attempt to cover them. "What are you doing?" he laughed.

She looked at him as though he had lost his mind. "She can't see us like this!"

"I know," he responded calmly, "that's why I locked the door." William rolled off of her, and she exhaled in relief when she noticed the door was indeed closed. They both rose from the bed, and she put on her robe while he grabbed his sleep pants before heading for the bathroom.

"William," she called before he reached the door. "Where's Bear?"

He looked over to the empty bed and shrugged his shoulders. "I don't know. I just assumed he came up with us." He continued into the bathroom as he heard the bedroom door unlock and open behind him.

When he returned, he heard Lizzy's laugh from the other room, and smiled in contentment while he moved to her dresser to remove a shirt. As he had begun to stay over more and more, his things that remained continued to increase, and she had recently moved some of her belongings around so he had a place to keep them. Lizzy came back as he was pulling on the t-shirt, and kissed him on the cheek.

"Did you find Bear?" he asked.

"He was sitting downstairs by the door in the kitchen. The swinging door between there and the dining room slid closed last night, and I think he was trapped in there. He has a bed, food and water in the laundry room, so he was probably perfectly happy." He nodded and she turned to dig for some clean pajamas in her dresser before she closed herself in the bathroom.

William strode one room over as Melanie finished putting on her panties. She turned and stretched her arms up to him.

"Did you wash your hands?"

She ran over to the bathroom and he followed to help her with the sink and the soap. He smiled as she sang her song then helped her to turn off the faucet. While she dried her hands, he quickly straightened the covers, making her bed, until he heard her come padding into the room behind him.

"Merry Christmas, sweetie!"

She trotted up on her tiptoes and jumped into his arms, hugging him when he lifted her. "Hi Daddy," he heard her say as he held her to him.

His heart swelled, and he kissed her on the cheek. "I love you, too, Melly."

Figuring she must have picked it up from the other children at her school, he wondered if she would continue to call him that, or if it would be a one-time event. Regardless, calling him daddy was a huge deal to him. He found that he loved it. He only hoped Lizzy wouldn't mind.

Asking Lizzy to marry him was only a matter of time. He knew it was what he wanted, but he was also very aware that she wasn't ready, and would require time before he proposed. He hoped that once they were married, he could adopt Melanie and make her officially his daughter, but that was entirely up to her mother.

Melanie returned his kiss with a big smack, and he grinned widely. "Should we go get your mama?"

"Yes, pwesents!" she exclaimed while he chuckled at her enthusiasm.

They walked around the corner and into the bedroom as Lizzy was coming out of the bathroom dressed in a pair of pajamas. "Are we ready to go see what Santa brought?" Melanie bounced in his arms, and he beamed when Lizzy's laughter reached his ears.

His hand found Lizzy's and they entwined their fingers, making their way downstairs, where she plugged in the tree lights before he set Melanie down in front of the presents. They watched her survey the colorfully wrapped gifts and shiny bows as her eyes made their way to the pastel pink toy kitchen. She gave a high-pitched squeal and ran over, opening the refrigerator and turning the knobs.

"Melly," called Lizzy, "why don't we see what else is under the tree? You can play with your kitchen while I make breakfast."

She sat on the floor and her daughter came over and plopped down in her lap. William took a seat facing them, and reached under the tree to pull out a present since Lizzy couldn't reach. He'd never seen someone rip through wrapping paper so quickly. She only had two others from Lizzy, pots and pans and a set of dishes, her stocking, a doll from Jane and Charles, and a box of play food from him.

"I told you getting her a present wasn't necessary," scolded Lizzy.

"I know, but I wanted to have something for her under the tree. Besides, you bought everything but the food."

"And you bought the tree and claimed that it was because I wouldn't let you buy her a gift. Besides, she could pretend," she laughed. "Can you say thank you, Melly?"

"Thank you," her daughter mumbled as she attempted to pull a pot from one of the boxes, her face contorted with the effort. William helped her open the box and she eagerly left them where they were sitting to play with her toy.

Lizzy pointed to a gift that was beneath the tree next to William. "I don't remember putting that there last night?"

"Perhaps Santa left you a present."

She gave him an amused look while he handed her the decorated box from the bath store. "I can smell the almond scent from here. How did you know?" she asked as she pulled off the decorative band and opened the lid. Her eyes bulged when she looked inside. She was obviously aware that he had given her a very expensive gift set. He'd learned since their trip to the store that she usually bought an occasional bottle as a treat, and used it very sparingly.

"I heard you speaking with the sales associate." He shrugged as if it was perfectly normal for him to eavesdrop on her conversation. "When I smelled the body oil, I recognized it as what you wear. I know you told me not to, but I wanted to have a present for you." She ran her fingers over the large bottle of shower oil while he continued to speak. "I honestly prefer that scent than most perfumes. I love it on you."

Lizzy blushed as she placed the lid back on the box. "It was very thoughtful, thank you."

He'd expected her to be upset with him for buying her a present, and so he was surprised she accepted it so readily. "You aren't angry?"

She studied him with her eyebrow raised. "Do you want me to be?"

He laughed and leaned forward to kiss her on the lips. "No, but I understand why you didn't want me to spend more."

"I know you're going to want to do things for us. I'm not saying that I'm always going to accept it, but I'm trying not to overanalyze. I just don't want you to ever feel like I expect any of this."

"You don't expect it, and that's one of the reasons why I like to do it."

He leaned forward and captured her lips once more. "Stay right there," she ordered as she jumped up and strode over to Melanie. She whispered in her daughter's ear just before she pulled the large, flat present he'd seen last night from behind the tree where it was propped against the wall.

He smiled when Melanie grabbed one side so that she was helping her mother bring it to him. "Here, Daddy," she said happily just before she dropped into his lap.

He glanced up to see Lizzy's shocked expression, and he kissed the little girl's cheek. "Thanks, sweetie. Do you want to help me open it?" She nodded, and he made a small tear down the front that allowed her to strip away the remaining paper, revealing a large watercolor of Pemberley.

He swallowed hard as he tried to maintain his composure. "When did you do this?" he asked almost to himself.

"Do you remember when you came for dinner and I wouldn't let you see my studio?"

He nodded as he admired not only her work, but also how well the deep green matting and frame set off the colors in the painting.

William heard her chuckle. "You almost saw it a few weeks ago. I was ordering the frame that day when you came into Hulin's."

Melanie decided that it wasn't as interesting as her new toy, so she toddled off to play. Meanwhile, he was so absorbed in staring at the work that he hadn't noticed that she began to appear doubtful.

"If you don't like it..."

He started and rose from where he was seated on the floor while she still held the painting propped in front of him. "I love it!" She still looked skeptical, and he moved it to the side so he could take her in his free arm. "You surprised me, but I promise you that I love it." He pulled back so that he could see her face. "I'm going to hang it in my office at work, where I can see it all day every day. I can show it to everyone who comes in and say 'Look at what my talented girlfriend made me.'"

Her musical laughter rang out and he breathed a sigh of relief. He'd never wanted to overwhelm her by mentioning his family's ancestral estate, so how did she know? "Did Charles tell you about Pemberley?"

"No, I wanted to do something for you, but I had no idea what, so I ran an internet search on you to see if I could get any ideas. An article on Pemberley's restoration came up, and from there, I searched for images online. You're sure you like it? You can be honest. I promise I won't get upset."

William took the painting and leaned it against the wall so he could embrace Lizzy with both arms. "I was stunned when I opened it. I'm sorry if my silence made it seem as though I disapproved of it somehow, but I was amazed at the detail and time you put into it." He could feel his eyes dampen as he fought tears. "That present means more to me than anything you could've purchased in a store."

He lifted her up so that they were face to face and kissed her passionately. When he released her lips, he placed her feet back on the floor as she glanced uneasily at Melanie.

"I still don't understand how you weren't shocked when she called you daddy?" she asked softly.

"She said it upstairs before we came down."

"You don't mind?" she asked in wonder.

"Are you kidding?" he asked incredulously. "An adorable little girl wishes to call me daddy. I'd be honored to fill that position in her life as long...as long as you want me to, that is?"

"It concerns me with how quick everything has moved, but even if we corrected her, I'd worry that she might become upset. We once tried to get her to call Jane, 'Aunt Jane' instead of 'Aunt Jay,' and she pitched a fit." She turned to watch Melanie for a moment before she turned back to him a wary expression on her face. "You're sure?"

"I told you before, I have no plans to go anywhere. I won't desert her or you."

He noticed her becoming emotional, and caught a tear with his thumb as it landed on her cheek, gently brushing it away. "She's lucky to have you," Lizzy whispered. She wrapped her arms around his chest so he could hold her close. As he held her, he looked over her shoulder, where he could see the gift that she had painstakingly created for him. Marveling that for the first time since his father and Ana died, he felt as if he belonged somewhere—he felt like he was home.

Chapter Fifteen

<u>**Thursday, January 10, 2013**</u>

Lizzy turned off her car and exhaled, relieved to be home. This evening had been the first night class of the semester, and she disliked that she hadn't been there for her daughter's bedtime. She trusted William, who was at that moment waiting for her inside, but she wanted to be there with both of them. She missed him as well.

She exited the car and the garage, making her way through the courtyard, which was illuminated by the outdoor lights. Of course, William had remembered, but then she smiled and doubted that he'd ever forget anything if it kept Melanie and her safe.

As Lizzy let herself in the back door, she turned off the flood lights, placed her coat on a hook, and took off the black steel toe work boots she wore to class.

Taking a quick look around, the house bore no signs of a mishap or battle, so she took that as a hopeful sign that things had gone well. The kitchen was spotless, the foyer was clear of any toys that her daughter might have thrown down the stairs, and she could hear the sound of the television coming from the living room.

She took a few more steps to where she could see William sitting in his usual spot on the end of the sofa, and smiled. He had a tumbler of scotch in one hand, unusual for when he was at Longbourn, while he stared at the news program on the screen.

Lizzy quietly came up behind him and began to massage his shoulders. Initially, he started, but his head soon dropped back with his eyes closed. "Mmmmmm, you're home."

She loved it that he called Longbourn home, and rubbed her arms down his chest as she leaned over to brush her lips against his. Taking her arm, he led her around the side of the sofa and pulled her into his lap.

"What are you wearing?" he laughed, scanning her old beat up overalls.

She propped her hand on her hip and pretended to be affronted. "You don't like them?"

"I would love you in a potato sack, but I've never seen you wear these." Lizzy's act melted away and she grinned.

"They're so I don't ruin my regular clothes with sawdust, plaster, and wood stain." She watched as he nodded, and she then gestured to the drink in his hand. "You don't usually have scotch unless Jane and Charles come over. Did you have a bad day at work?"

"Actually, I witnessed one of your daughter's temper tantrums tonight." He shook his head with a puzzled expression. "I don't understand though. She was so happy to see me when I picked her up from school, but things just...devolved once we got home."

"She didn't want to go to bed?"

He took a sip from his glass and chuckled. "She didn't want to eat what I made for dinner, which was nothing more than grilled cheese, but she became worse when she decided you were to give her a bath."

Lizzy bit her bottom lip while she fought her amusement at the expression on his face. "What did you do?"

"I put her in the tub and bathed her while she screamed," he told her as he grimaced.

"Oh, no," she chuckled. "I'm sorry."

"Then I wrapped her in a towel and brought her to her room. I tried to help her put on the training pants you bought her for at night, but she fought me tooth and nail. I finally just left her there, and sat on your bed." Swirling the amber liquid, he leaned his head back on to her arm, which was wrapped around his shoulders.

"She came out a few minutes later in her Marie nightgown, which is summer, so I asked her to put on a pair of leggings I found. She pitched a fit, but somehow I managed to put them on her, despite her kicking and flailing. By the time she was dressed, there were still thirty more minutes until her bedtime. I took a chance that her tantrum might be because she was tired, and I decided to put her to bed."

"Did she go down easily?"

218

"No," he responded in a low, drawn out manner. "She cried and wouldn't let me lie with her like you do, so I sat on the trunk at the foot of the bed until she fell asleep."

Lizzy was disheartened. She knew that Melanie might have tantrums, but she never expected anything to this extent. "Now I don't know what to do about next week," she thought aloud.

"What do you mean?" asked William with a confused expression.

"I'm not going to continue to put both of you through this..."

He put his glass on the end table and took her hand. "Lizzy, she wasn't traumatized by any means—neither was I, for that matter. I need to put her to bed more often when I'm here, so she'll adjust."

"But..."

"She needs to get used to me being more like a parent, not just William who comes over to play and for dinner. Don't you think?"

Lizzy carefully considered what he was saying. "I know you're right, but I'm just not used to doing things this way."

"I know, but we'll be fine. I think as long as I take care of her at bedtime when you're here, she'll become accustomed to it, and it won't be so different for her when you're in class."

"I hope so. I certainly don't want you to go through this every Thursday night."

He shrugged and squeezed her hand. "I'm certain I won't. We just need to be patient with Melly, and let her adjust."

She leaned in and kissed him softly. "You're very sweet with her, you know."

"She's an adorable little girl. Plus, she's practically a carbon copy of a woman that I love very much."

Lizzy pulled away in an attempt to stand, and he wrapped an arm around her legs, preventing her from rising. "Where are you going?" he asked.

"A shower. I demo'ed the saws and power sanders tonight. I think I even have sawdust in my hair."

He looked into her curls, noticing the small flecks of wood, as he brushed a hand through them. "Would you care for some company? I'd be happy to wash your hair and scrub your back," he suggested with a devious gleam in his eyes.

She stood and gently tugged his hand. "I think that sounds like a wonderful idea. Having someone to shampoo my hair sounds heavenly."

He quickly rose with an eager expression, and she laughed. Obviously, he didn't have to be asked twice.

Thursday, February 14, 2013

William hummed to himself as he put the finishing touches on the surprise he'd arranged for Lizzy and stood back to survey the room. Since she'd had to teach classes on Valentine's Day, he couldn't take her to a nice restaurant for dinner, so he'd decided to celebrate when she came home that evening. When he was certain everything was arranged the way he wanted, he returned to the kitchen to finish Melanie's dishes and wait.

She walked in the door not long after, and he grinned widely. "I'm so glad you're home." He enjoyed the beatific smile that graced her features, at the same time noticing her sawdust covered hair and clothes. Quickly turning off the light in the dining room, he ushered her up the stairs and into her bathroom, where he began running hot water into the large antique tub in the corner. As it filled, he began adding some of her shower oil to the water to create a bubble bath.

"I was going to take a shower," she protested. "The sawdust comes out of my hair easier with the spray."

"So we'll wash your hair and rinse you off in the shower and then climb in here." He finished removing her overalls, and set to work on the remaining garments, while she wore an amused smile. When she was undressed, he turned on the water in the shower and removed his clothing. He washed her hair, which had been part of their Thursday evening ritual since she had begun night classes, and then led her to the tub.

"This feels wonderful," she groaned, as she sunk into the warm, bubbly water.

He opened the linen closet door where he had hidden a bucket of ice with a bottle of her favorite wine. He poured them each a glass, and strode back over, passing one over her shoulder. He then lit some candles he had brought up earlier, before he climbed into the bath with her.

"Candles? Wine in the bath?" she asked. "You're going to spoil me."

A smile graced his lips as he made himself comfortable. "Good, you deserve to be pampered."

She took a sip from her glass, and leaned it against the edge of the tub. "Mmmmm, I haven't had any moscato for a while."

"I still can't believe you saved those bottles I bought in November for over a month."

"I told you that since you bought it for me, I'd only drink it when you were here. Then we toasted in the New Year with the second bottle."

He picked up her foot and began kneading as her head lolled back along the side of the tub, where William had placed a rolled-up towel. "You don't usually get this extravagant on Thursday nights."

"Most Thursdays aren't Valentine's day," he said simply.

Her eyes opened wide. "I'd completely forgotten!"

"How do you forget?" he asked, laughing.

"I knew it was coming, but I totally blanked on today's date. It was such a busy day." She took a sip of her wine, and her head returned to its previous position. He noticed that she was peeping at him through almost closed eyes. "I'll make it up to you. I promise."

He grinned widely. "I look forward to it, but I don't want you getting extravagant. Perhaps you could surprise me when I get back from London," he said nonchalantly.

Her head darted up as her eyes opened fully. "London?"

He knew that she wouldn't be pleased that he had a business trip, but he also knew he couldn't put off telling her for much longer. They'd been spending more and more time together since Christmas. In the beginning, he was spending just a night, then the entire weekend, but once he'd begun watching Melanie on Thursday nights, he was living at Longbourn at least four nights a week.

"My uncle, who runs the London offices, requested that I come for some important meetings being held around the end of this month. I would love for you and Melanie to come with me."

William had known the answer, but his heart still dropped as she shook her head. "I can't. Not only do I have classes, but Melanie and I don't have passports."

"We'll definitely need to get those, so you can go with me next time." He watched her smile at the idea, and he lifted her other foot out of the water to kiss her big toe before beginning to knead that one as well. She laughed and the sound somehow made him feel better. "I hope you know that I wouldn't go if it weren't necessary."

He wasn't sure by the expression on her face, but he'd felt she might need reassurance. "I know you wouldn't. How long will you be gone?"

"Two weeks," he answered, "but I *will* call every night." He took another sip of his wine, and set his glass on a small cabinet she had next to the tub. Crawling over to where she was sitting, she lifted her eyebrow.

"What are you up to, Mr. Darcy?"

He shifted and slid in behind her. "Only this," he replied, softly kissing her shoulder. His fingers set to work kneading her shoulders, arms, and neck and he smiled when he heard her sigh. He loved hearing those little signs that indicated she was affected by his touch. Occasionally kissing along her neck and shoulders, he continued to massage her back, leaving her relaxed and limp. He then turned her around to massage her thighs while she leaned against his shoulder.

222

Eventually, she lifted her face and looked him in the eye, running her hand into his curls to pull him in to another kiss. When he was finished, he slowly maneuvered her off of his legs, unplugged the drain, and rose to grab a towel that was hanging close by. He dried off and wrapped it around his waist before he took the other that he'd set aside for Lizzy. He helped her to stand, and enfolded her in the large, fluffy towel.

"Where did these come from?"

"I bought them when I moved into the guest house. You don't have very many, and I thought they'd get more use here." He brought her into his arms and kissed her gently before he placed her glass of wine in her hand. "Why don't you go into the bedroom, and I'll be there in a minute."

She walked through the door, and he blew out the candles, taking one to light more inside the bedroom. When he turned, he couldn't help but inhale deeply at the sight before him. She'd removed the towel, and was provocatively seated on the comforter. "I don't need all of the candles. I only need you."

She was a vision, and his eyes greedily perused her body as he stepped to the edge of the bed where she moved to meet him. On her knees, she stripped off his towel and ran her hands up the solid plane of his chest followed closely by her lips.

"Lizzy, I wanted to..." He stopped to moan as she scraped her teeth down his ear lobe, her warm breath causing goose bumps to erupt up behind his ear and into his hair.

"I just *want* you," she breathed against his ear. He turned his face and hungrily claimed her mouth as she began to maneuver backward to the center of the mattress. He eagerly followed, pressing her back into the pillows while he caressed every inch of soft skin that beckoned to him.

Looking back, he had no idea how he'd held on for as long as he had. Her voice telling him that she needed him inside of her, combined with his heightened state of arousal, only served to make his control harder to maintain.

"I love you," he murmured. She was lying partially on top of him, and he was brushing his lips in gentle kisses along her shoulder and neck.

"I love you, too," she responded shakily.

He was just going to shift up onto an elbow when he felt something cold and wet on his hand. Lifting up, he glanced over to find Bear resting his head on the side of the bed.

"Bear, go lie down!"

"What?" Lizzy exclaimed, turning so that she could see the dog. She burst out into peals of laughter at the sight of his furry head resting on the edge of the bed.

"He nosed my hand," William complained. "Was he watching us the entire time?"

"If he was, I was too preoccupied to notice." He could tell she was trying her best not to continue laughing. "Bear," she said sternly, "go lie down!" At first the old dog just stared, but after a second command, he reluctantly obeyed his mistress, curling up on his bed before William returned his eyes to Lizzy.

He ran his hand up her arm to her face and cradled it in his hand. "I know I have a week before I have to go, but I don't want to leave you." He wrapped both arms around her body, and held her as close as he could. He rolled them to their sides, her one leg still wrapped around his hip.

His fingers brushed up and down her side as they faced each other on the pillows. "I don't want you to go either." Her words were sincere, and he could see a certain amount of fear in her eyes.

"You know that nothing will prevent me from returning," he reassured, taking a guess at what was bothering her. William knew his suspicion was on target when she cuddled closer and her embrace became a bit tighter.

"I'm sorry," she whispered. "I know it's silly. You're nothing like him, but it's what..."

224

"It's what you were accustomed to for six years." He felt her nod against his chest, and carefully drew her back so that she could see his eyes. "But unlike him, I *need you*. I'm in love with *you*."

He watched as she held back tears and ran her finger along his jawline. "I'm sorry."

"Don't apologize. We've been together for roughly three months, and I'll just need to reassure you until it's understood that there's nothing in the world that would prevent me from returning to you."

She bit her lip, and he kissed her forehead. He was just laying his head back on the pillow when he heard her stomach growl loudly. "You should've told me you were hungry."

"I try not to eat this late," she protested.

"Yes, but it is Valentine's Day, and I have a treat for you." He rose from the bed, put on his robe, and headed downstairs to the kitchen. When he'd grabbed a second bottle of wine and the surprise from the refrigerator, he made his way back up to her room.

Lizzy watched William stride out of the room, admiring his well-toned rear end through his robe as he disappeared through the door. She leaned back into the pillows and sighed. He was so sweet to have planned all this, and she wondered what else he had in store for the evening.

"Are those what I think they are?" she asked when he came back through the door. He set the tray down on the bed before her and she grinned. "Oooh, I love chocolate covered strawberries."

He quickly refilled their glasses, and removing his robe, he slipped back between the sheets as he pulled her next to him. "I thought you might." He picked up one and held it before her mouth. She sank her teeth into the luscious berry and juice began to trickle down from her lip.

She lifted her hand to catch it, but he stayed it and leaned in to clean the mess by gliding his tongue up her chin. He kissed her, tugging at her bottom lip, before he finished the strawberry. She took a sip of her wine, and leaned against him with her head resting on his shoulder.

"Mmmmmm, they're dark chocolate, too," she said with the flavor of the dessert still on her tongue.

A slight chuckle resonated through his chest. "Of course, that's your favorite."

"It's your favorite, as well." She smiled, and lifted her head so he could continue to feed her. They shared the remaining strawberries on the plate with their wine before he blew out the candles and they settled back into the sheets, spooned together, her back into his chest.

The only problem was Lizzy wasn't tired, so she reached behind her to knead his buttock and thigh. She smiled as she rocked her hips back into his groin.

"Lizzzzy," he groaned. "I thought you'd be tired."

"No," she whispered, looking over her shoulder. "I'm not ready to go to sleep."

His lips crashed into hers, and Lizzy never had a chance to catch her breath from that moment on until the roaring in her head was subsiding and William collapsed atop her.

She felt his hand stroking up and down her side, and she grasped it, entwining her fingers with his. "I love you."

"I love you, too. Better?"

"I think so," she responded. She heard and felt his low chuckle as he rolled them back to a spooning position.

"Just let me know if you're not. I'll happily take care of it," he said sleepily.

She chuckled, "You're incorrigible."

He murmured something that she couldn't quite make out, and realized that he'd fallen asleep. She grinned as she rubbed the arm

226

that was draped across her middle, slowly drifting into her own dreams that stretched straight through until morning.

Lizzy woke early to find William in his boxer briefs while he sprayed his cologne on his chest. She glanced at the clock, and then turned back to face him, admiring the view. "You're up early. It's not even seven yet."

He started and smiled when he saw her. "Charles and I have an early meeting. I'm sorry if I woke you."

She shook her head as he crawled under the covers with her, enfolding her in his arms. "No, you didn't," she said as she snuggled further into his embrace. His fingers began dragging up and down her back, and she sighed, enjoying the fresh smell of his cologne.

"I forgot to tell you last night that I spoke with Mrs. Reynolds about when I'm in England, and she said she'd be happy to watch Melly as much as you need."

"I'm not sure," she hesitated before deciding to elaborate. "I'd meant to speak to you about something last night before I was...sidetracked." She felt him laugh a bit, and he pulled back so they could see each other's faces.

"Nothing bad, I hope."

"No," she responded. "Last year, Anita, the book arts instructor, and I made paper periodically throughout the year, but most of it was made during a couple of weeks around this time."

"Handmade paper?"

"Yes, Anita has the know-how, we split the supplies, and I help her get everything done. Last year, we took part in the spring craft fair, and sold most of what we made, splitting the profits fifty-fifty. I've been picking up old cotton and linen clothes and sheets at the local thrift stores, but I didn't want to assume that you'd be willing to watch Melanie as much as I would need for those two weeks.

"Anita came to me yesterday, asking if I wanted to get together like before, and I told her I'd need to speak with you first. Now, I'm thinking the two weeks you're gone would be the perfect time, but I wouldn't feel right about Mrs. Reynolds being at my beck and call without paying her. Unfortunately, that takes any profit out of it."

William took her hand and squeezed. "She's loved taking care of Melly when we go out on dates. I'm sure she'd be happy to do it."

Lizzy looked skeptical. "Last year, Jane and Charles took care of her, and then I stayed at Netherfield for those two weeks. They even came out here and fed Bear for me. I didn't want to rely so much on them this time, but asking Mrs. Reynolds to drive across town so much isn't fair either."

"Perhaps she could stay here while I'm gone. You could work as late as you needed, and she wouldn't be on the road after dark." He ran a hand through her hair and pressed his forehead to hers. "It would ease my mind to know that there's someone here when you come home so late."

"I don't know."

"At least let me speak to her about it. She might love the idea."

She reluctantly nodded, and he kissed her lingeringly.

"I need to get out of this bed, or I'll never want to leave." He gave her a peck and shuffled to the closet where he began pulling on his trousers.

Lizzy lazily watched him from the warmth of the covers, until he was completely dressed. "I should get up to make you breakfast." She pulled on some pajama bottoms and moved to the dresser, where she was pulling out a tank top when his arms snaked around her middle.

"We're going to have coffee and pastries at the meeting, so I'll be fine."

"You're sure?"

She felt his wide smile on her shoulder, and leaned her head back so that it touched his. "I love croissants and coffee. As much as I love your cooking, this morning won't be a hardship."

She laughed and turned to embrace him. "You eat too many, and I won't be able to wrap my arms around you."

"I'll just do some extra running this evening when I go to the gym." He brushed his lips against hers one last time. "Enjoy your day," he whispered, before he strode out the door. Melanie wouldn't be awake for a bit, and Lizzy didn't feel like getting dressed just yet, so she decided to read. She sat down in bed, propped in the pillows, and opened a book. Soon she heard his car's tires crunch the gravel on the drive as he departed for work.

Chapter Sixteen

<u>**Sunday, February 24, 2013**</u>

"Hi," called Jane as Lizzy walked through the back door of Netherfield. "You have just enough time to take a quick shower before we sit down to eat."

Lizzy looked down at her damp, rather smelly clothes and nodded. "I'll be right back." She made her way up the stairs to the room where she usually stayed, and after peeling off her dirty clothes, entered the shower. The mess from the paper pulp was embedded into the thin hair of her arms, so she took a soapy bath sponge and began to scrub. The problem with pulp wasn't that it was difficult to get off of the skin, but that it was harder to see when it was wet, which meant she couldn't tell if it was all off until she was getting dressed. So, Lizzy showered as thoroughly as she could, washing her arms several times in the hopes that they would be clean when she was done.

When she'd changed into some clean, comfortable clothes, Lizzy went to pick up her dirty jeans, and was surprised to find that everything was gone. As she stepped down the stairs, she heard the washing machine running and smiled. Lizzy then took a deep breath, inhaling the aroma of the enchilada casserole Jane had just taken out of the oven. Not only was her big sister washing her clothes, but she was feeding her as well.

Her stomach growled, and Jane chuckled. "Please tell me you've eaten something today."

"I had a small bag of pretzels and an apple during breaks," she said defensively.

Jane shook her head. "By the way, your clothes are in the washer."

"I figured as much, thank you," she responded. She sliced herself and Melanie sections of the casserole, and put them on plates. Lizzy then set them on the table while Jane called through the door for Melanie, who'd been playing in Charles' study. She came running in a minute later.

"Mama!" she cried as she ran and jumped at Lizzy. She put her daughter in her booster seat, not buckling her because she had begun fighting her on it.

Jane took her own seat and Lizzy regarded her curiously. "We aren't waiting for Charles?"

"He's been on the phone with his parents for close to an hour. He won't expect us to wait on him."

"Everything's okay, I hope."

"I'm sure it is, but I think it's important, or he wouldn't have waved and mouthed to go ahead."

Lizzy glanced down at Melanie, who was picking through her food, and then back to her sister, her now rounded abdomen very visible, even sitting at the table. "When's your next OB appointment?"

Her face glowed as she stroked a hand over her belly. "Next week we're having an ultrasound."

"Are you going to find out what you're having?"

"I want to. We would've found out a few weeks ago, but this little bugger was sitting on his feet." They both laughed.

"The baby's okay, isn't it? I mean, is a second ultrasound this soon normal?"

"They didn't find anything out of the ordinary, but it was still a bit early, which made it difficult getting the images of the heart that they wanted. I'm sure you had more than one ultrasound of Melly?"

Lizzy shook her head. "I was going to the free clinic. They only gave me the one to make sure everything was okay. After that, they checked her heart rate, measured my belly and then lectured me on my eating."

"Oh," said Jane, who'd never asked a lot of the specifics on her time with Greg unless they were needed for court papers. She always just let Lizzy tell her as she was comfortable. "How are things with you and William?"

Lizzy's eyes jumped to Jane's face and she blushed. "Fine, why do you ask?"

"I'm just curious. He spends very little time at the guest house these days."

She was sure her face was crimson as she began to fiddle with her food. "He's very sweet, and Melanie loves him."

"Do *you* love him?" Jane cocked her head to the side, and Lizzy knew that she was studying her reactions.

Nodding, she put down her fork. "Yes, I do." The next thing she knew, she was pulled up and engulfed in a hug, Jane's belly bulging into her own.

"I'm so happy for you!" she exclaimed. "I'd hoped the two of you could get past your differences!"

"Jane!" she laughed, "you act as though he's proposed!"

"It's only a matter of time!" she exclaimed, releasing her.

"Do you really think so?" Lizzy was beginning to find the idea of being married to William appealing.

"Sweetie, the way he looks at you. Charles doesn't even look at me with that expression."

Lizzy grinned. She knew the look her sister was witnessing, and now that she knew the meaning of it, the desire in his eyes made her want to find a secluded spot with him.

"You should see the look on your face right now," her sister teased. "I think it would rival William's." Lizzy bit her bottom lip in an effort to stifle her grin, but it seemed useless. "Charles said that William now has a picture of you and Melanie on his desk at work."

Her eyes bugged out and she swallowed hard. "He's taken his camera out a few times, beginning with the town tree lighting, but I didn't know he'd done that." She wondered what the picture looked like.

232

"We could go snoop in the guest house. I bet he has one in there, too."

"Jane Olivia Bennet Bingley! We will not go spying in his things!" She did her best to sound affronted, despite the fact that she was itching to see if he did indeed have a copy there.

Her sister guffawed and Lizzy stuck out her tongue. "You know you want to," she sang tauntingly.

"Oh, well, it doesn't matter. He probably took it with him to London anyway." Jane fiddled with her food for a moment. "I've also heard that he has two of your paintings in there too." Lizzy knew her eyes were probably as round as saucers, especially when Jane began to laugh again.

"Which ones?"

"I believe the scenes that you did of Longbourn pond."

"The footbridge set?"

Smiling, Jane nodded her head. "I believe there was one painting from the spring and another from the summer."

Lizzy was amazed. He'd never mentioned buying any of the paintings at the Christmas show.

Jane was still giggling gleefully and Lizzy could feel her cheeks burning from Jane's teasing. "I'll get you back for this one day, dear sister," she said, pointing across the table.

"If you say so." Things fell silent for a moment while they both took a bite, chewed, and swallowed.

"I was wondering if you could help me with something." She waited for Jane to nod curiously before she continued. "Would you mind taking a trip to the mall with me one day during your lunch break?"

"We have such different styles that I'm not sure how much of use I'd be."

"I want to go to the lingerie stores, and I don't know what William would like."

"And I do?" laughed Jane.

"No!" exclaimed Lizzy. "But you know more about what a guy would like than I do, and I've never bought anything like that before."

She noticed her sister's countenance change, and wondered if she should've brought it up. "I'm sorry. I can do it myself. I just wanted to knock his socks off."

"No, I don't mind shopping with you. Although as your big sister, I feel I must tell you that the idea is to knock him out of much more than just his socks."

The nervous tension that Lizzy had pent up was released with Jane's comment, and she burst into a fit of teenage giggles. Jane joined her until Charles walked in, grabbed a plate of food, and took a seat.

"Is everything okay?" Jane asked.

He rolled his eyes. "Dad was just giving me a heads up with some business pertaining to Caroline. I'd really rather not talk about it at the table though. It'll ruin my appetite."

Lizzy took her last bite and placed her fork on her plate. "I wanted to ask the two of you a favor." Jane and Charles both set their utensils down, and she decided to plunge ahead. "You know that William gets back Friday the eighth?" They both nodded. "I was hoping that maybe Melanie could have her first sleepover here that night."

Charles leaned over and put his hand on her forehead. "Are you sure you're not ill?"

She batted his hand away and rose to put her dishes in the sink. "Y'all and Mrs. Reynolds have been keeping her some in the evenings, so I thought it might work. I do trust you, but I think I'll always worry if she's not with me."

Jane stood and walked over to take Lizzy's hands. "I'm sure that's perfectly normal. I also think that it will be good to let her stay over here and let the two of you have some uninterrupted time together. If you wait until the honeymoon to do this, then it'll be a nightmare."

234

"Jane!"

Charles laughed as he sat back in his chair. "William's always been pretty tight-lipped when it comes to relationships—not that he's had many—but I've also never seen him as happy as he is with you. It's only a matter of time."

She felt as though her cheeks had been warm all evening. Glancing at the clock, Lizzy began cleaning up her daughter's mess. "Thanks for dinner, but we've got to get back to Longbourn. Mrs. Reynolds is coming over tonight, and I don't want to have her waiting on me."

"You warned her about Bear, didn't you?" asked Jane.

"Of course," responded Lizzy. "I wouldn't want him to hurt her."

"He's always had a better disposition with women than men," Charles interjected with a thoughtful expression. "Mrs. R. will probably have him eating out of her hand within an hour."

Jane took her seat next to Charles while she watched Lizzy continue to clean up. "I'm surprised she's coming over tonight. She could just pick up Melly at school tomorrow."

"When she discovered that campus childcare charges by the hour, she insisted on keeping her at Longbourn with her all week. She mentioned baking cookies with her and all kinds of things. They should have a great time."

"Sounds like it!" exclaimed Jane. "Maybe I should take off for the week and hang out at Longbourn."

Lizzy nodded her head in agreement as she laughed. Then she and Melanie each kissed Jane and Charles on the cheek before hurrying out of the door. Settling into the drive, Lizzy thought about everything that was said during dinner. She was surprised that she was not more disturbed by the thought of William proposing, but as she contemplated it more, she realized that she'd always feared a marriage like her last. William was proving daily that their relationship would be different.

Since William had left on Friday, he'd called her nightly so he could tuck her in over the phone. She'd checked the time difference and was sure that he was waking up in the early hours of the morning to place the calls, but so far he hadn't missed a night. He even promised to call several times during the week to talk to her daughter. Her love for him was growing, and she was beginning to envision a longer future with him, possibly even a sibling or two for Melanie.

As she pulled into the driveway, she was relieved to see that Mrs. Reynolds hadn't arrived yet, and hurried inside to straighten up a bit before the older woman knocked at her door.

Mrs. Reynolds showed at about seven. Lizzy let her use William's remote, so she could park her car in the garage, and then she and Melanie helped her get her things inside. Once she was all settled in one of the spare rooms, Lizzy bathed her daughter, and Mrs. Reynolds read Melanie several books before she was tucked in for the night.

When the two of them returned downstairs, Lizzy glanced toward Mrs. Reynolds as she pulled down a bottle of cabernet. "Would you like a glass of wine?"

"A small amount would be lovely, dear."

Lizzy poured her about half a glass, and they moved into the living room.

"Have you heard from William yet?" she asked.

"Yes," Lizzy replied with a smile, "he called me briefly when he landed, and he checked in on us yesterday and this morning."

"And I'd venture a guess that he'll be calling tonight before you go to bed," she said with a knowing smile.

Lizzy tilted her head a bit. "How'd you know that?"

"His father was the same way when he'd have to leave them behind for business trips. He'd usually try to bring them along, but once William was in school, it became more difficult. That's why they spent part or all of the summer in England. It allowed Mr. Darcy the ability to check on that office, and they'd schedule any annual meetings the London branch required during that time."

"Did Mrs. Darcy work?"

"Not really, not in the conventional sense anyway. She did volunteer work, helping to plan charity functions and bringing in donations, but she didn't have a job that she went to daily." The grandmotherly woman appraised Lizzy carefully. "I would imagine that he hasn't spoken much of his parents."

Lizzy nodded and took a sip of her wine before Mrs. Reynolds continued, "His mother's death was very hard on him. He watched her grow sicker and sicker, at first from the chemo, and then because the treatments stopped working. It took a while for his father to learn to handle everything on his own."

"He wasn't on his own. He had you."

"That he did," she responded warmly. "Anyway, then his father and sister were killed, and he retreated into himself further. I'm very thankful he found you." Mrs. Reynolds was teary-eyed as she took her last sip and began to stand. "I would imagine that Melanie wakes rather early in the morning."

"Seven to seven-thirty," answered Lizzy, as Mrs. Reynolds acknowledged her response.

"Then I'll be off to bed. I'll see you in the morning."

"Yes, ma'am. Good night." Once she heard Mrs. Reynolds' door close upstairs, she made her way through the house, checking the doors and turning off lights. She brought her glass of wine with her to her room, where she changed into her pajamas, and began reading a book while she waited for William's call.

Her phone finally rang at about nine-thirty, the suddenness of the noise startling her. "Hey," she said softly.

"Hi, beautiful," came a groggy voice over the line.

"You sound tired."

"I fell asleep pretty early, but I had an alarm set so I could call you before bed."

"What time is it there?"

237

"Ummmm..." She heard him shift and figured he must be checking a clock. "Three-thirty."

"William! You're going to be exhausted if you keep waking every night to call me."

"I'll be fine. I promise. I just needed to hear your voice."

She could make out the longing in his tone and found tears coming to her eyes. "I miss you, too, but I think you need to go back to sleep. You have meetings tomorrow, if I remember right."

"I do," he replied. "I love you."

"I love you, too. Good night."

"Sweet dreams." She waited until she heard a click on his side, and then pressed end on her phone.

Thursday, March 7, 2013

Lizzy walked wearily into the mudroom, took off her boots, and placed them against the wall before removing her overalls, which were immediately thrown in the washer. She was exhausted, and filthy, and melancholy. When William had said he was going to have to go on a business trip, she knew that she'd miss him, but she'd never imagined that she would have so much difficulty sleeping. Add to that an almost three-year-old, working, and extra time toiling over the handmade paper she was working on with Anita, and she was done in. Slipping on a pair of shorts and one of William's t-shirts that she'd seen folded in a clean clothes basket, she made a stop in the kitchen to pour herself a large glass of wine. Then she followed the sound of the television to the living room, where she found Mrs. Reynolds watching a movie.

"There you are, dear," said Mrs. Reynolds, as Lizzy came around to the front of the sofa.

She dropped down and took a long sip. "How'd Melly do tonight?"

"She had a bit of a tantrum when it came time to go to sleep, but it wasn't too bad," Mrs. Reynolds said in a concerned voice. "She kept asking for her daddy."

Lizzy realized what Mrs. Reynolds must have thought, and began to laugh uncontrollably. Attempting to control her mirth, she wiped the tears that had leaked from her eyes while Mrs. Reynolds regarded her strangely. "Melly calls William 'Daddy'."

"Oh?...Oh!" She chuckled for a moment. "She's been asking for him periodically since I've been here, and William had said that her biological father wasn't a part of her life. I just assumed that he once was, or she knew him." She waved her hand exasperatedly in front of her. "Oh, I don't know!"

"It's okay. I'm sorry to laugh so hard."

"Nonsense," she admonished, "you're exhausted. I know I've had extreme reactions like that when I'm so tired that I can't see straight. It just hadn't occurred to me that he'd already told her to call him that."

"There are several young couples who pick up their children at her school. I imagine that she's noticed the daddies are with mommies, and since William and I are together, she must have figured that made him Daddy. I'm not sure, but she decided, and we didn't fight it." Lizzy's laughter finally calmed and she took a sip of her wine as she shrugged. "William liked it as well."

"I've always said that he's a good boy," Mrs. Reynolds gushed proudly, while she turned off the TV. "Well, unless you need something, I think I'm going to go to bed."

"I'm fine, thanks." Lizzy smiled and stood as well. "I'll follow you upstairs, though. I really need to get this sawdust out of my hair." She heard the older woman chuckle as she turned out the light in the living room. They said good night and parted at the top of the stairs, when Lizzy entered her daughter's room to check on her.

Once she'd seen that Melanie was sleeping peacefully, she made her way to her room. She set her wine down on the bathroom counter and took a long, hot shower. When she felt that she was finally clean, she used her towel to remove as much water as she could from her hair so it would air-dry. She then put on her pajamas and returned downstairs to refill her glass before she returned to her room. Crawling into bed, she turned on a movie and sipped her wine until she answered William's call about twenty minutes later.

"Hey," he responded. "You sound tired. Or have you been drinking?"

"A bit of both actually," she said, finishing her wine.

"Sweetheart, are you well?"

That was all she needed. That one sincerely asked question was the catalyst that prompted her to break down into tears. "I miss you, I haven't been sleeping well, my hands are all dry and cracked from working on the paper, and I'm so tired."

"Oh, baby, I arrived in New York this evening, and I'm at the penthouse. I need to go to the office here for an hour or so tomorrow morning, and then I'll be on the company jet straight to Meryton. I should be there just after lunch."

She sobbed softly as he continued to try to soothe her. "I love you so much. I've missed you, too, and I haven't been sleeping well either. We'll have the entire weekend together. We can take Melly to the park and spoil her with television so we can be lazy in bed on Saturday morning."

Lizzy chuckled through a sob. "I feel so ridiculous."

"You aren't ridiculous, because I know how you feel. We both need a good night's sleep, so go to bed, and I'll be there as soon as I can. I promise."

"Okay," she sniffled. "I love you."

"I know. I love you, too, but we both need to try to get some sleep."

"Bye," she said softly. "Sweet dreams."

"You too. I'll be there soon," she heard before she heard the click that he had hung up. She then, once again, let her tears flow freely until she faded to sleep.

Friday, March 8, 2013

The next morning, Lizzy woke feeling like she'd been sucking on a sweat sock all night long. She rolled over and slowly opened her eyes, allowing herself to become accustomed to the light in the room. The bright orange numbers of the digital clock jumped out at her.

"Ten?" she groaned, "How could I have slept so late?"

Her head felt so heavy, but she managed to pull it up as she sat up on the side of the bed. She turned on the water in the tub, and while it was filling, made her way downstairs to the kitchen. She poured herself a glass of orange juice and yawned while she glanced out of a window, noticing Mrs. Reynolds walking outside with Melanie and Bear.

Charles had been correct. The old dog had warmed up to Mrs. Reynolds rather quickly, and Lizzy harbored a suspicion that the grandmotherly woman had been slipping him bits of food when she cooked. Over the last two weeks, he'd developed a fondness for being in the kitchen during breakfast, when in the past he'd preferred to be outside. The method had proven effective, which was fortunate, since it meant Lizzy didn't have to worry about them venturing outside of the house during the day.

When she returned upstairs, she took her time and soaked in the tub, sipping her juice while the hot water helped her to feel more human again. When her glass was empty, she carefully shaved her legs, ensuring that she didn't miss a spot and didn't cut herself.

After she'd toweled off, Lizzy rubbed in some of her favorite almond oil that William had given her for Christmas, and put on the lingerie she and Jane had found earlier in the week. She had brought the swirly decorative bag home and tried to secretly hand wash the items in the bathroom. The thought of Mrs. Reynolds knowing about her lingerie was mortifying, but unfortunately, Lizzy's fear became a reality when she left the unmentionables soaking in the sink. She'd come upstairs later to find her bathroom clean, as well as the items rinsed, and draped over hangers in the shower. Luckily, Mrs. Reynolds never mentioned it, so Lizzy decided just to follow suit, pretending that it never happened.

The set was definitely not risqué. She and Jane had decided to find some sexy undergarments that she might normally wear, but were fancier than the cotton panties he was accustomed to seeing. The bra had been a little of a puzzle. On their way into the department store, they'd found a black dress on a clearance rack that her sister had insisted William would love. The back consisted of a 'v' of sheer material that stretched almost to her waist, and they both agreed that a bra would not work. Fortunately, the woman in the lingerie department had a solution with an adhesive, strapless, backless bra in a black satin.

She put on everything, fumbling a bit with the fasteners on the garters, before slipping on the little black dress. She knew that she'd probably be overdressed for William's homecoming, especially considering he flew to New York first, and after a brief meeting there flew to Meryton, but she still owed him for Valentine's Day, and she wanted to surprise him.

After she brushed her teeth, she touched up her face with a bit of moisturizer and mascara. She then pulled her hair into a low bun with a few loose curls framing her face, so that William could easily view the back of the dress.

Her shoes were in the wardrobe, and she put them on before she made her way downstairs. As she reached the living room, she heard Mrs. Reynolds' voice reading one of Melanie's favorite books.

"The creature roared and growled, but Jack wasn't afraid."

Lizzy smiled at the variations in Mrs. Reynolds' voice, especially when she said the actions of the creature. Her voice would go deep, and sometimes a bit gravelly. She listened to her read the book until she recognized the end was coming.

"Jack and the creature became friends,
and they always explored the forest together."

When she heard the last line, she slipped into the room. Melanie was in Mrs. Reynolds' lap, and she was just closing the book.

"Another!" her daughter cried enthusiastically.

A floorboard creaked, and they both turned to see Lizzy in the door. "Mama!" she cried. "Pwetty!" She scooted from Mrs. Reynolds' lap and ran to her mother, who squatted down and let her daughter hug her around her neck.

242

"You must be hungry," said Mrs. Reynolds. "I made some chocolate croissants yesterday, and when I heard you, mulling around up there I made some coffee."

"Thank you," she replied. She'd tried to tell Mrs. Reynolds that she didn't have to be so extravagant with it just being the three of them in the house, but her protests had fallen on deaf ears. Mrs. Reynolds had baked, cooked, and cleaned for the entire two weeks. Lizzy was sure that Longbourn had never been so spotless; even the baseboards gleamed.

They moved into the kitchen, and Mrs. Reynolds placed the coffee, a small pot of heated milk, and the sugar bowl in front of her with a chocolate croissant. She prepared her cup, and then broke off a piece of the pastry and popped it in her mouth.

"Mmmmmm," she said as the flaky layers and chocolate melted in her mouth. "Mrs. Reynolds, these are wonderful."

"I'm glad you like them, dear. I have plenty more for you and William sealed in a bag in the pantry." She finished wiping the stove and took a seat. "I also have several dishes that just need to be warmed in the refrigerator."

"That certainly wasn't necessary, but I do appreciate it."

The older woman's face wore a knowing smile. "Oh, I remember what it was like to be young and in love. This way you have more time to be together, and you won't have to cook."

Lizzy hoped she hadn't noticed the blush that crossed her cheeks. She was interrupted in her thoughts when she noticed Mrs. Reynolds looking at her expectantly. "I'm sorry. What did you say?"

"Melanie is staying with the Bingleys, then?"

"Just tonight," she responded, "although, Jane's attempting to persuade me to let her spend tomorrow night, too."

"Why not?"

"I guess I've always felt a bit like I'd be pawning her off on someone, and Jane and Charles have always helped me with her a good bit."

Mrs. Reynolds gave her a motherly smile. "There's nothing wrong with you having a night, or even a weekend off here and there. I say take your sister up on her offer. It'll give you and William some time to yourselves. One day Melanie will grow up and move out, and it'll just be the two of you. There has to be a relationship between you and William that exists without your daughter." She glanced over to where Melanie was playing in the corner with her kitchen before looking back. "I know you and William have your dates and such, which is great, but I believe it'll be a good thing for both of you to have the rest of today and Saturday to yourselves. The two of you can then pick her up on Sunday and take her to do something special. If the weather's nice, William always loved the zoo."

Lizzy smiled at the idea of him as a child at the zoo. Only, the funny part was that she saw him as a child, but he was dressed in his suit, donning his stern, no-nonsense business demeanor.

"It's a good thing the weather is warmer today," Mrs. Reynolds commented. "Or else you'd be rather chilly in that dress. Of course, that's what a man's suit coat is for, isn't it?" She stood and patted her on the shoulder. "You tell him I said welcome home."

"Yes, ma'am," she responded, giving a small chuckle.

"Look at the time," she exclaimed. "You should get on the road if you're going to make it to the airport by twelve-thirty."

Lizzy gasped and stood. She cleaned her hands while Mrs. Reynolds put her coffee in a travel cup and pressed it into her hand. Grabbing her things and Melanie's overnight bag, the two ladies ensured the house was locked up and made their way to the garage.

"Mrs. Reynolds, what about your bags?"

"Oh, I loaded those in the car before Melanie woke this morning." She squatted down and put out her arms. "Do I get a hug, Princess Melanie?"

Melanie giggled as she gave her a bear hug and a smacking kiss. Lizzy strapped her into her car seat and then turned to Mrs. Reynolds, giving her a hug. "Thank you so much for everything."

The older woman waved her off. "It was nothing. I enjoyed it immensely. It's been a long time since I was able to take care of a family like this, and I do miss it."

Lizzy nodded, and they both got into their cars. Mrs. Reynolds pulled out first, and was soon on her way. They followed close behind until Lizzy watched Mrs. Reynolds' small car turn to head towards her house, while Lizzy continued on toward Netherfield.

Dropping Melanie off didn't take long, even with Jane and Charles making Lizzy twirl to show them her new dress. Jane renewed her offer to keep Melanie for Saturday night as well, and Lizzy agreed, with the stipulation that if her daughter became overly upset they would promise to call her so she could pick her up and bring her home

She'd never left Melanie for more than a day at work, so Lizzy walked out the door barely keeping her countenance. Jane must have noticed, because she followed her out to her car and hugged her tightly. "She'll be fine—I promise. And you'll get a chance to have a little vacation."

"I never considered Melly so tiring that I'd need a vacation."

"I know, but the last two weeks have been trying, with William away and all the extra work you've been putting in." Jane put her hands on Lizzy's cheeks and looked her in the eye. "Enjoy yourself the next two nights, and she'll be here Sunday when you come to pick her up. Just don't get here at the crack of dawn."

Lizzy smiled as Jane released her and opened her car door. "I'll call tomorrow to see how things are going." She noticed Jane smile while she nodded. Lizzy started the engine and pulled from the driveway, heading toward town. Her nerves were settling in as she neared her next stop, the airport where she would meet William.

Chapter Seventeen

"Mr. Darcy," said the pilot's voice over the intercom, "we'll be landing in a matter of minutes. I'd recommend buckling up if you aren't already."

William reached down and fastened his seat belt as he attempted to calm himself. He was going to see Lizzy, and soon. He knew being away would be difficult—that he'd miss her, but he had no idea the extent. His heart had torn when he heard her sobs last night. The wine had relaxed her natural reserve, and that had made her crying harder to hear, especially being so far away. He knew she was hurting, and he could do nothing to console her.

On the other hand, the idea of Lizzy waiting for him in the terminal was heart-warming, and he couldn't wait to disembark. Closing his eyes, he envisioned her wearing her red velvet dress, and hoped that she'd worn it today. He took a deep breath to calm himself, and, drumming his fingers on the armrest, turned to look out of the window at the airport becoming closer as they came in for the landing.

The jet jolted when the tires touched the runway, and soon he heard the brakes roar as the plane slowed on its way to the terminal. They taxied to the gate for private planes, where it stopped. William would've normally waited to rise and gather his things until he saw the stairs being aligned to the exit, but he was too anxious to disembark. Instead, he stood, and began moving his suitcase and laptop bag near the door. He'd been standing at the front of the plane with the attendant and the pilot for close to five minutes when they were finally able to open the door and exit.

He quickly made his way inside and through the building to the terminal where he impatiently scanned the lobby. His brow furrowed when he didn't see her, and he'd just begun a second sweep, when Lizzy emerged from behind a group of people to walk toward him. His breath hitched in his chest, and he paused to take in her appearance from head to toe. He'd expected her to be in jeans and a top, but she wasn't dressed as casually as he would've thought. She was wearing a black dress with an uneven hem that was longer on the sides than the middle. As he drew closer, he noticed that from her shoulders to the top of her chest was sheer, and she wore a moonstone necklace he hadn't seen before. The look was simple, but she was stunning.

She may not have been a classical beauty like her sister, Jane, but in her usual attire, she had more of a girl next-door kind of draw that he preferred. When she was dressed like this, however, she could stand toe to toe with Jane, and in his opinion, even surpass her. He felt she had a sultry sensuality that he loved.

Lizzy began to step forward, and he took a few strides to meet her in the middle. "Hi," she said a little awkwardly.

He set down the bag on his shoulder and stood his suitcase so he could take her in his arms. "You look beautiful," he whispered in her ear before he brushed his lips against her cheek.

She smiled shyly and kissed him briefly. "Thanks," she said softly. "Why don't we get your things to the car?"

He'd wanted to give her a more passionate kiss, but not in the terminal; that could wait until they were in the car, and not in the midst of so many people. He picked up his things, slinging his smaller bag over his shoulder, then placed his hand on her back. When he felt a different material than he'd expected with his thumb, he glanced behind her curiously.

At first glance, he'd thought the dress was a bit conservative for her tastes, but the dress was not just sheer in the front. There was also a 'v' of the same sheer material that ran down her back almost to her waist. The dress appeared new, and he was wondering if she'd bought it for his homecoming. He did have to admit that he was enjoying this style as much, if not more, than the red velvet he had always loved. The most intriguing part for him was that she did not appear to be wearing a bra from the back, but she did from the front.

"Is this a new dress?" he asked.

"Yes," she replied, beaming. "Jane and I went for a quick shopping trip during her lunch break earlier in the week."

"You didn't mention that on the phone." His tone was conversational, and he placed his hand on her lower back as they exited through the sliding doors that led to the parking lot.

"I wanted it to be a surprise." He grinned widely. She wanted to look nice for him, and the idea made him very happy.

"Are you tired?"

"Hmmm?" he asked, snapping from his thoughts.

"I just asked if you're tired. I thought we might go eat lunch somewhere." They walked up to the car, and she opened the back so he could load his suitcases. She handed him the keys, and he opened her door before he took his place in the driver's seat.

His hand ran down her temple to her cheek, turning her head towards him. "I missed you." She gripped his lapel and pulled him toward her. William took a deep breath as she kissed him, inhaling the almond scent that he had come to associate with her. Unable to resist, he deepened the kiss, tasting her for the first time in two weeks. He moaned and pulled back before he was tempted to go further right there in the airport parking lot.

"Did you say something about lunch?"

"Yes, or we can just go home. Mrs. Reynolds has probably stocked my refrigerator with casseroles and all kinds of things we just have to put in the oven."

"Things went well then?" he asked.

"She left before she could complete her quest of sterilizing Longbourn, but yes, things went well. I told her she didn't have to do so much cooking and cleaning, but she didn't listen to me."

He chuckled and faced the front to turn on the engine. "That does sound like her."

The car turned onto the main highway, and he moved to place a hand on her leg, caressing her stocking with his fingers as he drove. William glanced over to where she was seated. He definitely *did not* want to go to lunch. He wanted to drive straight to Longbourn and lock them in her room. The thought of skimming his fingers lightly up her skirt to see if she was wearing garters had crossed his mind, but if he did, he would lose the last bit of restraint he had.

As they neared town, he reluctantly decided that her dress deserved at least a lunch at a nice restaurant before they returned to Longbourn. They enjoyed a comfortable silence for the next few minutes, until he pulled into a spot downtown.

"I thought we were going home?"

"I decided that I do want to take you to lunch somewhere." He leaned over for a peck and then got out to walk around the car and open her door.

They strolled around the corner to reach the glass front of a restaurant named Coastal. "Have you ever been here?"

"No, but Jane and Charles usually go on their anniversary, so I've heard it's nice."

"It was my parents' favorite." He loved watching her smile at the significance of the restaurant to him. Opening the door, he gestured for her to enter, and followed close behind.

The manager happened to be at the front when they walked in, and immediately recognized him. As a result, they were seated quickly, with menus and glasses of water.

"What's good here?" she asked.

"I've never found anything that I didn't care for, but I do like the stuffed gulf flounder quite a bit. I've also enjoyed the braised rabbit."

"I don't know if I could eat a bunny," she laughed.

He allowed the melodic sound to wash over him, absorbing what he'd missed while he was gone before he turned his attention back to the menu. "I think I'm going to have the catch of the day. What about you?"

"I'm thinking about the eggplant casserole with shrimp and crabmeat. Have you ever had it?"

"Yes," he replied as the waiter arrived to take their order. "It's rich, but very good. Is that what you'd like?" She nodded, and he ordered for them, pointing out a bottle of wine for them to share.

"How did the papermaking go this week?" he asked, as the server walked away from the table.

"Tiring, but well. I have no idea how much we made, but we've made some books, a bit of paper art, and the rest is all bundled in sets. Anita said she would tally it up before the craft fair next month so we have a running idea of our inventory."

He glanced down at her hand, which was resting on the table, and noticed her cracked skin. He rubbed his thumb over her knuckles, wincing at how red and painful they appeared.

She shrugged a bit self-consciously. "It's not great for the skin. I tried to wear gloves most of the time, but between rinsing the pulp and making the actual sheets, my hands were in the water too much."

"Well then, I'll just have to give you some hand massages and ensure plenty of lotion is used."

He was enjoying the sweet smile his suggestion had prompted when their conversation was interrupted by a loud voice. "Darcy, I'd heard you weren't arriving back until Monday!" He looked up to find James Harrod, an executive who ran one of D&F's subsidiaries, striding up to the table.

Darcy stood and extended his hand, despite the fact that he abhorred the man. "I'd always intended to return today, but I'm out of the office until Monday," he corrected. Harrod's eyes roamed from William's to where Lizzy was sitting.

"And who's your lovely dining companion?" he asked in a voice that oozed an affected charm. His eyes remained glued to Lizzy.

"James Harrod, this is my girlfriend, Elizabeth Gardiner." He noticed her eyes dart to him when he said "Elizabeth," but he ignored it. The last thing he could take was Harrod addressing her as if they were friends.

"Girlfriend!" he exclaimed with a drawl. "Will wonders never cease? With that to welcome you home, it's no wonder that you won't be in until Monday."

250

"Yes, well," William began, becoming impatient with the interruption. "I *will* see you in the office on Monday. I hope you have a nice weekend."

A look of recognition passed the man's features as he heard his dismissal, and William witnessed the one last lecherous glance he gave Lizzy. "Of course, Monday. It was lovely to meet you."

"Have a nice weekend," she replied. William held in a laugh that threatened as he realized that she hadn't returned Harrod's pleasantry. With one last look at William, Harrod slunk off across the dining room to his own table.

William took his seat and Lizzy chuckled. "You don't like him," she observed softly.

"Not at all, but my father hired him, and I've never had a legitimate reason to fire him. In fact, he's a proficient manager."

A small smile appeared as she seemed to study him. "So, is it just his general sleaziness?"

"There's that, but he can't keep a secretary, *and* he's smarmy. He's also married, but it's commonly known that he'll sleep with anything in a skirt."

She nodded and leaned back as their food was placed in front of them. They chatted about the last two weeks as they ate, deciding to order dessert to go.

They took the long route back to the car, passing through the park with her arm looped through his. He adored the way she leaned against his side as they strolled, but at the same time, he did not dawdle, since he was impatient to get her alone.

When they reached the car, he opened her door. "Where do we pick up Melly?"

"She's spending the night with Jane and Charles, so unless you need something from the guest house, we can go straight to Longbourn."

William almost didn't hear the last part, because he was realizing that he had Lizzy to himself, no chance of interruptions for possibly the next twenty-four hours. He loved Melanie, but the thought of having Lizzy to himself was something that he couldn't help but anticipate.

She smiled mischievously at his expression and took her seat, watching as he walked around to take his own. "When do we have to pick her up?"

"Sunday."

Dear lord, did she say Sunday?

"Sunday?"

"Yes," she replied with a chuckle. "Are you okay?"

He grinned widely and leaned over to kiss her briefly on the lips. "I'm great, but are you sure you're comfortable with this?" As much as he looked forward to it being just the two of them, he didn't want her to be constantly worried about her daughter.

"I'll be fine. If it's okay, I'll probably call her tonight, and probably tomorrow as well."

Running the backs of his fingers down her cheek, he looked her directly in the eye, so she knew that he was serious. "You can call as much as you need. While I'm looking forward to spending these two days alone with you, neither of us would be able to enjoy it if you worried the entire time."

"Thank you." He was happy to see that the gratitude and reassurance in her eyes.

The trip back to Longbourn was swift, and soon they were stepping into the mudroom off the kitchen. The door closed behind William, and he dropped his things where he stood. He grasped Lizzy and pulled her back against his body, attacking her graceful neck where it was exposed by the style of her hair.

His hands moved of their own accord across her stomach, one moving to cup a breast as the other simply held her tightly to his body. Her rear was against him, and he was hardening at the feel of her. He nipped at the soft flesh where her shoulder and neck joined, and heard her breathing hitch as her head lolled back onto his shoulder.

He'd missed her so dearly—her company, the taste of her, and the way she felt pressed against him, surrounding him. Her arm was thrown over his other shoulder with her fingers threading through his hair, but he wanted more. Turning her abruptly, he finally claimed her mouth and caressed her tongue with his as he began steering her into the kitchen.

She came to a stop when her back hit the island, and he felt her hands work at his tie, followed by the buttons of his shirt, pulling it from the waist of his pants. Her small hands then made their way underneath the seam, where she began stroking his side and lower back.

He moaned as his hand grazed up her leg as it was riding up his thigh. His erection was painfully straining against the confines of his pants, and he had been giving serious thought to lifting her to the countertop when he felt something. Abruptly, he pulled back and pushed her dress higher.

"Is something wrong?"

He had no idea if she looked concerned or worried when she asked. His eyes were too busy feasting on the image of her perfect thigh adorned with garters. "No," he said, reverently running his fingers along the top of the stocking. Now there would be no quickie on the kitchen island. He had to see what she was wearing under the dress.

Running his other hand up that leg, he hiked up her skirt when he lifted her to wrap her legs around him. Then supporting her with his hands on her rounded behind, he carried her upstairs while she kissed his neck and suckled his ear lobe as if she'd been starved for him.

Lizzy collapsed against him and felt his body begin to relax, placing small kisses against his collarbone as she tucked her head into his neck. His hands traced along her rear, down her garters and she smiled.

William's reaction when he first saw the lingerie was a bit disconcerting. He just kept staring, but when they'd made it upstairs, she realized that she recognized that stare. The look in his eye wasn't disgust or even dislike. It was lust, pure and simple. He was just too engrossed in studying her body to speak.

"I need to get up for a few minutes." She knew it was ridiculous to blush, but she felt her cheeks warm at the admission.

"As much as I hate for you to take these off," he said, gesturing towards her lingerie. "I suppose you would be more comfortable."

She grinned widely at his pout as she rose from her comfortable spot on his chest and went to the bathroom. She'd just taken off her heels when there was a knock on the door. "Can I come in?"

"Yes," she called back through as she laughed. The door opened and he strode in.

"Do you need any help?" He lifted her to the countertop and began unfastening her stockings, sliding each down her leg with a long caress.

"Are you enjoying yourself?" she asked with an amused expression.

"Very much so. Are these new?" His hands roamed up to her hips and behind her back to unhook the garters.

"I bought them when I bought the dress. I did tell you that I'd make Valentine's Day up to you, remember?"

"President's Day, Valentine's Day, Christmas, my birthday. I'll take this any day," he said with a rakish grin.

"They aren't uncomfortable now that they're not rubbing like they were."

He was still beaming as he glanced up at her face. "I wouldn't want to take any chances. I think it would be better if we just leave them off."

She began to laugh again, and he smiled as he leaned in for a kiss. "I'm thinking no clothes at all until Sunday."

"I'm not cooking in the nude! I don't want to burn myself!"

"Okay," he conceded, "you can wear your robe while you cook."
Lizzy rolled her eyes at the large grin that adorned his face, and
wrapped her arms around him. She was so glad he was home.

Lizzy opened her eyes and peered up at William, who was still
sleeping soundly. The clock indicated it was ten in the morning, and
she wondered how much she'd truly slept.

Their joking around in the bathroom had led to a tryst on the
counter, followed by snacks and wine in bed before another round of
lovemaking. Then she was awakened at some point during the night
by William kissing her shoulder and caressing her body with a very
specific intent. There was no way she was going to say no.

Her mind was brought back to the present by the sound of her
stomach growling. Carefully shifting, she made it out of the bed
without waking William, donned her robe, went downstairs to let
out Bear outside, and quickly called Jane so she could check on
Melanie.

Once her sister assured her several times that her daughter was fine
and having a great time, she set to work fixing breakfast for her and
William. Mrs. Reynolds' chocolate croissants were still in the
pantry, so she arranged them on a plate with two coffee mugs and
some orange juice. She'd just begun slicing some fruit to go on the
side when she felt a pair of arms snake around her middle.

"You weren't supposed to leave me in bed alone," he whispered
seductively in her ear. Her skin tingled with the feel of his breath on
her neck, and she inhaled at the sensation.

"You aren't hungry? Her voice sounded weak to her ears, but she
was barely standing without the help of leaning against the counter.

His fingers deftly untied her robe and she gasped as one hand
slipped inside. The knife dropped from her hand to clang on the
counter, and she reached back to grasp his thighs behind her. Lizzy
lost herself to the pleasure he was giving her, eventually finding
herself on the countertop with her fingers gripping the edge. At
some point, the kettle had begun to whistle shrilly, but neither
noticed, nor cared, as they lost themselves in one another.

After, they simply lay on the counter as they recovered, her fingers gently sweeping his curls back as his face rested on her breasts. When their hearts had calmed to a more normal rate, he lifted his head and shifted. She glanced up to find him watching her intently, his chin resting on his hand.

"How's Melly this morning?" She smiled that he knew her so well, and brushed an errant curl back from his brow.

"She's fine. Jane says she's having a ball, which means they're spoiling her rotten." She could feel his chest vibrate as he laughed.

He carefully shifted off of her as she sat up, so he could remove the kettle and fill the French press. Then he moved back and pulled her to his body, embracing her. "I love you," he said softly while he brushed her nose with his. His lips claimed hers as he stroked her thigh. "I love you so much," William repeated, burying his face in her neck.

She ran her fingers through his hair as they just held each other. They would have this full day, just the two of them, before they picked up Melanie the next. He would then sleep over on Sunday night, and after going to work on Monday, he would stay at the guesthouse until Thursday night. The thing was, the idea of him staying somewhere else bothered her. She didn't want him to leave. She didn't want him to need the guesthouse. Lizzy gently kissed his ear and felt him shiver against her. Yep, he needed to be right here at Longbourn with her and Melanie—this was where he belonged.

"William?"

"Yes, sweetheart?"

"Why did you never buy a place of your own?" He pulled back to look at her curiously. "Why did you remain at the Netherfield guesthouse?"

He shrugged as his brow furrowed. "At first, I couldn't find anything that I liked, and I wasn't interested in building. I wanted something older that I could possibly remodel or renovate." He began delicately tracing her collarbone with his fingers as he followed the movement with his eyes. "I suppose that once we began seeing each other seriously, I was staying here more and more, so it seemed kind of a waste to purchase something I wasn't going to use. Jane and Charles were adamant that they didn't mind…"

He trailed off as his index finger found its way to her neck and was trailing up and down one side. She cupped his cheek in her hand and his eyes met hers. "Move in here with me."

The look of shock on his face was such that she worried for a moment that maybe she shouldn't have asked. "Unless you don't want to," she mumbled, backpedaling.

"Are you sure?" His finger had stopped its explorations, and she could tell that he was examining her expression to ensure she was serious. "You were worried at one time about moving too fast."

"It may be quick by some people's standards, but I'm positive," she responded, maintaining eye contact with him. "Melanie and I would love to have you."

He gathered her to him. "Then there's no other place I'd *ever* want to be."

Chapter Eighteen

<u>**Saturday, March 16, 2013**</u>

The week following William's return had been busy. On Sunday, the couple picked up Melanie from the Bingley's, and took her to the zoo for most of the day. They had a great time touring some of the exhibits before settling down to eat their picnic lunch in a pretty, wooded spot near the playground. As usual, Melanie was finished first, so she had a great time on the slide while William and Lizzy enjoyed the remainder of their meal.

When everything was packed up, they walked around for almost two more hours, letting Melanie wear herself out completely. She fell asleep on the ride to the guesthouse, where they packed up a carload of William's belongings to bring to Longbourn. Every day, he brought more, emptying the guesthouse by Thursday, so a professional service could go in and clean it on Friday.

They had yet to tell Jane and Charles of their plans, so they'd decided to invite them to dinner at Longbourn that Saturday, to inform them of the news and return the keys. Therefore, Lizzy found herself in the kitchen putting the potatoes in the oven to roast and mixing up her famous chocolate cake while William checked the chicken on the grill.

"I still can't believe we're cooking a chicken by sticking a can of beer up its ass," he said loudly, as he returned inside. He'd watched her prepare everything with a wary eye, but she kissed him on the cheek and told him not to worry, it would be great.

"You keep saying that," she laughed. "Just make sure you don't say ass in front of Melly. I really don't want her to pick up that habit."

"Yes, ma'am," he flirted, wrapping an arm around her from behind. He pushed her long curls over her shoulder with the other, and she felt his warm breath along the back of her neck, causing goose bumps to erupt along the sensitive flesh.

She inhaled sharply and closed her eyes. "William," she scolded in almost a moan, "Jane and Charles are going to be here soon, and you won't have time to finish what you're starting."

He rotated her around so they were facing, and ground his hips against hers. "We have time."

"No...no, we don't," she murmured while he brushed his lips under her ear. "Why do you like the back of my neck so much lately?"

"Because I can see you react physically to me. I enjoy feeling you shudder and seeing the little bumps break out across your skin."

She could feel him smiling against her cheek just before he claimed her lips. Their tongues began to intertwine, and her resolve was about to crumble when the doorbell rang.

His head dropped to her shoulder and she laughed. "I tried to warn you. Jane called me as they were leaving."

"You didn't tell me that part," he groaned.

"Well, you were kissing and blowing on the back of my neck. You make it very hard for a girl to think."

He smiled widely and gave her a quick peck. "You should probably take that batter out of the mixer."

She watched him turn toward the kitchen door, grabbing his rear before he moved too far away.

"Hey, now," he exclaimed, turning to back through the kitchen door. "Don't start something you won't be able to finish."

She grinned widely while she unhooked the bowl from the mixer, poured the batter into the pans, and placed them in the oven. Jane came in a moment later. "Hi, sis," she said as she gave her a quick kiss on the cheek. "It smells wonderful outside, chicken?"

"Yep. Where's Charles?" Lizzy looked behind her sister, expecting to find her brother-in-law.

Jane rolled her eyes and exhaled heavily. "Caroline called on the way here, and he hasn't been able to get her off of the phone."

"That bad?"

Lizzy simply couldn't resist. She had to hear the conversation and headed toward the living room, with Jane following close on her heels. She could hear Charles' frustrated voice from the dining room. "No, Caroline, I won't give you William's number." As she stepped into the room, she immediately saw Charles standing in front of the sofa, his cell phone to his ear, while William was emphatically shaking his head no.

"I'm telling you that he won't speak with you...I don't have to ask him, because I *know*!"

Charles became very quiet as he listened, and even as far away as Lizzy was, she could hear a high-pitched tone coming from the earpiece. Charles shook his head while he rubbed his temple with his free hand.

Lizzy could also make out William's frantically whispered pleas. "There's no way in hell," she could hear as well as a "No, no, fuck no!" Charles nodded in response.

"Stop yelling at me!" exclaimed Charles, as the voice over the phone became louder. "William dealt with you chasing after him for years, despite the fact that he'd made it perfectly clear he'd never date you, much less marry you. *I* told you. *I* had father speak with you, but *you* wouldn't listen, and you pushed and pushed until *William* asked me never to bring you with me when I visited. Then you began with the sneaking into his office and his family's penthouse."

More of the same irate cacophony erupted from the phone, and he held it away from his ear for a moment before beginning once more. "No, it wasn't his family that had you arrested, Caroline. *He* called the police and out of respect for our parents and me, he had the prosecutor offer you a deal." William dropped onto the sofa with his head in his hands as Charles, having lost his temper, finally began to yell. "I'm going to say this for the last time, Caroline! He doesn't want to speak with you or see you, despite what you have to say! There's also still a restraining order in effect—here, as well as in New York, so I would suggest that you do not test him! He'll have you arrested, and neither Dad nor I will help you this time! You *will* go to jail for stalking!"

Impressed, Lizzy's eyebrows lifted. She'd never heard Charles stand up to anyone that way, and was pleased to see he actually had it in him.

"I'm going to go check if all that yelling woke up Melly," whispered Jane, near her ear. Lizzy nodded as she watched Charles abruptly end the phone call.

"Thanks, Charles," William said, visibly relieved as he stood to clap a hand to his friend's back. "If he doesn't know already, your father needs to be told."

Charles sighed as he nodded. "He knows. Unfortunately, her usual therapist has been out of town for the last two weeks, and one of his colleagues saw her. He's a big proponent of apologizing, and has filled her head with the idea that she needs to tell you she's sorry. The whole situation has made me wonder if he thoroughly read her case."

"Please tell her that I accept her apology, and I forgive her, but I won't drop the restraining order and I won't see her."

Charles acknowledged William's statement as he again ran his hand through his hair. "Honestly, I wonder if she's using it as an excuse to see you."

"That was my thought when you were on the phone." William stood and glanced over at Lizzy. "I also wonder if we shouldn't have a restraining order in place so that she can't approach Lizzy or Melly."

"I'll check into it on Monday. Given her long-lasting obsession with you, I might be able to convince a judge."

Lizzy was stunned at the turn in the conversation. "Do you really think it's necessary?"

"I'd rather not take a chance," William reassured her, "but when she discovers that we're together, I have no idea what her reaction will be. I prefer to be prepared... *And* to change the subject, I think the chickens should be ready to come off the grill. Charles, would you mind giving me a hand? And when we're done, I'll get you a large tumbler of scotch—I think you've earned it!"

"Of course," exclaimed Charles happily. They all passed through the kitchen, and Lizzy pulled the salad from the refrigerator and began setting the food on the table as the guys went out the back door.

Jane entered the room with Melanie on her hip a few minutes later. "Where are the guys?"

"Apparently, it takes the two of them to pull the chickens off the grill." Her sister began to laugh while Melanie wiggled her way down to the floor.

"Kiss the baby!" she cried.

"Not right now, sweetie. I'm not sitting down." Lizzy began laughing when her daughter led Jane to a chair where she ordered her aunt to sit, and then kissed her bulging middle.

William and Charles returned through the mudroom, and stopped at the sound of all the laughter. "What's so funny?" asked Charles.

Jane's explanation was just as humorous as what had actually happened, and the men chuckled at Melanie's antics. They moved into the dining room, and all took their seats, but before Lizzy could pick her up, Melanie leaned forward to kiss her mother's stomach. "Kiss Mama's baby," she said proudly.

Lizzy was speechless, her face burning as she looked around the table for help. William wore a huge grin, while Jane and Charles were stifling their amusement, and she realized there would be no aid forthcoming.

"Sweetie," she said gently, "there's no baby in Mama's tummy—just Aunt Jay's."

Her daughter's brow furrowed, and she pointed to her stomach. "Baby in my tummy, too."

"Ummm...no, just Aunt Jay." She noticed Melanie's jaw set, and knew her little girl was going to argue the point, so she decided a distraction was in order. She put some food on her daughter's plate and put her in her booster seat. "Look, chicken, potatoes and green beans," she said as she pointed to each item.

When her daughter was happily eating, Lizzy faced the table, and everyone began serving themselves. William was still wearing the same ridiculous grin, and it was making her crazy. "What?"

262

"If she wants a little brother or sister that badly, I can help you with that."

Lizzy looked to her sister and Charles, who were watching like they should have a tub of popcorn between them, and then turned back to William. "I think we can wait a while on that, don't you?" Shrugging, he was still smiling as he put some potatoes on his plate.

The rest of the meal went smoothly, and when everyone rose to clear the table, William briefly disappeared. Lizzy had just begun to load the dishwasher when he came into the kitchen and placed the guesthouse key in front of Charles

"I want to thank you and Jane for allowing me to stay in the cottage, but I won't be needing it anymore. I'm completely moved out, and I've had the place professionally cleaned."

She turned off the water and, drying her hands, turned to see Jane's questioning gaze directed at her. Charles seemed to think for a moment before he glanced at Jane, who was staring at Lizzy, and suddenly understood. "Oh!" He looked down at the dish in front of him and said, "I'm going to go make sure we have everything from the dining room," and walked straight through the door. However, William remained, and Lizzy could tell by the look on his face that he intended to stay.

Jane turned toward him and before she could say anything, Lizzy interrupted, "You can say whatever you want, Jane. I don't have anything to hide from him."

Her gaze returned to Lizzy, and she took a deep breath. "Are you sure about this?"

"I'm positive," she replied. "I asked *him* to move in with me."

She could tell that Jane was surprised, but she didn't let it faze her. "I can't help it if I'm concerned. The two of you haven't been seeing each other that long, and you don't have much experience with men, Lizzy."

"You were so happy a few weeks ago when we talked about my relationship with William, and now you're doing a complete one-eighty."

"No," Jane defended adamantly, "I'm still very happy for both of you, but I never expected the two of you to progress so rapidly." Her shoulders dropped, and she reached over to take Lizzy's hand to hold it. "I just don't want you to get hurt."

"I know, but I realized when he was in England that I was tired of saying goodbye to him when he went home. I missed him, and frankly, we were almost living together before he left. He spent four nights here and three at the guesthouse."

"But if there was an argument or something, he still had a place to go."

"When there's an argument between us," interjected William, "I'm not going to go running away to wherever. I'm going to stay to work it out." He ran a hand through his hair and exhaled heavily. "We're adults, Jane, and this is what we want. I wanted to move in here before I left for England, but I wanted it to be right for Lizzy. Besides, if I recall correctly, you and Charles moved in together at about six months into your relationship. We're only two months ahead of you, which isn't a huge difference."

Jane turned red and stammered. "I can't believe you remember that!"

William began laughing, and moved over to place an arm around Lizzy's shoulders. "What, are you kidding me? Charles was driving me crazy because all he ever spoke about was his angel. The day he moved in was when he seemed to mellow out."

Lizzy began laughing, and Jane squeezed her hand. "Touché," she said softly with a smile.

Lizzy turned and hugged her sister. "I love you, Jane."

"I love you, too. I *am* aware that I'm sticking my big nose in your business, but I can't help but worry."

"You've been worrying for too long," Lizzy explained. "I feel like you put your life on hold, to be there if I needed you, and I never wanted you to do that. Don't get me wrong, I appreciate that you and Charles were there for me, but I need to be able to take care of myself and make my own decisions."

"I know you can take care of yourself," replied Jane softly. "I...I knew when you married...him...that it wouldn't turn out well, and I did make sure that if you needed a place to go that you could come to me. Aunt Mel said that you could live with her, if you ever showed up on my doorstep. Then I married Charles, and I made sure he knew all about you, and that I'd promised that I'd be there if you ever needed me. He understood, and helped me with Aunt Mel's trust documents, ensuring they were iron-clad, so Greg could never get his hands on any of Longbourn or the accounts that are there for its upkeep."

"Charles is very good at those little nuances," chimed William.

Jane smiled. "He is. Anyway, then Aunt Mel died, and I knew that Charles and I would have to be there to help you. We never gave up hope that you'd leave him one day. I just never expected you to be beaten and bloody on my doorstep." A tear trickled down Jane's cheek, and she gave a rueful smile. "That was the first time I'd ever seen Charles irate." Jane looked to William, who regarded her curiously. "He answered the door that morning—it was four-thirty, and Lizzy fell through the entry and passed out into his arms. He carried her inside and laid her on the sofa, while the cab driver followed him in, yelling about the money for the drive. I was attempting to wake her when he ushered the driver out of the door. Charles then angrily told him if he entered our home again, he would be arrested for trespassing. He actually called 911 and got dressed before he paid the man."

William had a surprised expression at a side of Charles he probably hadn't seen often.

"The funniest part, looking back, was the ambulance blocked his cab, and he couldn't leave until after Lizzy and I left to go to the hospital. The man was fuming, and had been complaining to the EMT's as they ran back and forth to the vehicle."

"Charles never mentioned any of this," William remarked.

"Your father and sister had died a month before, and you'd just returned to England. You had so much on your plate that he didn't want you to worry about us." She turned her attention back to Lizzy as Charles returned. "It's never been about the fact that you can't do it on your own, but that we wanted to help you. You were essentially alone for six years, and we'll never let you be that isolated again."

She seemed to look out at the night through the windows, and then back to directly into Elizabeth's eyes. "I know you felt like you were intruding, but you weren't. We loved having you stay with us, and we love having Melly visit. You were never a burden, and I'd do all of it over again if it was needed."

"I second that," exclaimed Charles, who wrapped an arm around his wife's waist. "Is everything okay?"

Jane nodded as she smiled. "I think everything is going to be wonderful from now on, don't you, Lizzy?

"Of course," she replied as she squeezed her hand, "we're all going to be great." She felt William kiss her temple, and she leaned further against him, glancing at Melanie, who was playing with her kitchen in the corner.

"I think we need more drinks as we clean up. What about you, Charles? You have Jane as a designated driver."

Charles glanced at Jane, who gave him a kiss on the cheek. "You go ahead. I don't mind driving home."

Beaming, he accepted, and William poured the two of them another tumbler of scotch and Lizzy a glass of cabernet as they got back to work. With four of them cleaning, the job didn't take long, and they were soon seated in the living room with pieces of chocolate cake and coffee.

"Isn't the craft fair next weekend?" asked Jane, before taking another bite.

"Yes, out at Longwood Plantation."

"I'd forgotten about the similarity of names," remarked William. "I don't think I've ever been in that home."

"It's really a very neat house," commented Jane. "The inside is unfinished, and the family only lived on the first floor. When they take you upstairs on the tour, there are still some of the old tools and such that you can see."

"It also has a lot of land for all of us to set up." Lizzy glanced at Melanie as she ate at the coffee table.

266

"Are you selling anything beyond the paper you made with Anita?" asked Charles.

"We made some small books from handmade paper, like small journals or sketch books, and a few collages. I'm also going to have the paintings that didn't sell at Christmas. Last year, I had some people ask about various types of watercolors for babies' rooms and such, so over the last year, I've worked on a series of butterflies and flowers. I also have photographs that I took over the course of the year."

Jane looked at her curiously. "The flowers?"

"Yes, the Magnolias especially, so I took several different angles this past summer, and I have several copies of each."

Charles placed his plate on the tray. "Do you need us to keep Melanie for the day?"

"Thanks, but no," responded William, "Mrs. Reynolds jumped at the chance when she heard. She's even spending the night before here, so we can get an early start that morning."

"So when is Mrs. R. going to become a permanent resident?" laughed Charles.

William smiled, leaned forward to put his plate on the tray, and then returned to put his arm around Lizzy. "I'd love for her to be here full time, but she'd need her own residence. There's no housekeeper's suite here, although, I was wondering about that old building behind the garage."

"That old thing needs to be torn down," commented Lizzy. "I don't think it can be salvaged anymore. There's also not enough money for a project like that in Longbourn's accounts."

"I'd pay for it," he offered. "She could keep Melly during the day, while you have class, and clean. You'd have more time to paint."

"She'd embark on a one woman crusade to sterilize Longbourn." He and Charles laughed, and she leaned her head back on his arm. "I kind of like that it's just us right now."

"We'd have to renovate that building first. I'm not talking about her moving in here tomorrow. Since it's spring and the south, there will be a fair amount of rain, so that alone could take a couple of months." She studied his expression, and knew that he'd be willing to speak about it later, so she let it go.

Not long after dessert, Jane claimed that she was getting tired, prompting her and Charles to call it a night. Lizzy kissed Melanie good night as William took her upstairs for her bath and to put her to bed, before she gathered the last of the dishes to return to the kitchen.

William stepped through the door of the kitchen to find Lizzy pressing start on the dishwasher. Wrapping his arms around her from behind, he kissed her ear as she leaned back against his chest. "Are you tired?"

"A little."

"Come on, then. I'll get you tucked in."

He took her hand, and leading her from the room, turned off all the lights as he brought her upstairs.

Once they were ensconced in the warm covers, they faced one another on their sides, their legs entwined. "Do you really want Mrs. Reynolds to come live with us?" asked Lizzy in a soft voice.

"I know she misses working for a family. She adores Melanie and has commented that she'd enjoy taking care of her more often, but I don't wish to force her on you. I just thought if we could fix up that building into a small home for her, she would live here, but have her own place."

He could see her hesitance, and reached to brush his fingers through her curls. "Let me at least get an architect to look at that building, and see what can be done. Then we'll have a long discussion about options. I think she'd be a good thing. She would keep up the house, and you'd have more time to spend with Melly or paint. You have to admit that you'd like that."

She nodded. "I would, but I just don't want anything to change right now. I like things the way they are."

"Like I said earlier, it wouldn't be for a few months, so let's see what the prognosis is on that building first." He ran his fingers along her face and then back into her hair.

"I've been wondering for a while now about the two empty bedrooms. Why is there no furniture? I can only assume that at one time, Melly's didn't have a bedroom set either."

By the tone of Lizzy's sigh, he knew he was not going to like the explanation one bit, but schooled his features.

"Aunt Mel, my great aunt, inherited Longbourn from her parents. My mother's father, Aunt Mel's brother, had died from a heart attack when my mother was a teenager, and my aunt said that my mother had never made it a secret that she wanted Longbourn. My grandparents knew she would never care for it the way my aunt did.

"It made sense that Aunt Mel inherited Longbourn though. She lived with my grandparents and took care of them. She was also their child. My aunt didn't want a rift in the family, so she gave my mother some of the furniture."

"Did that fix it?" he asked in a doubtful tone.

"With Olivia Bennet, never. She still complains that she should have this house because her father should've been the 'rightful heir' or some such archaic nonsense. She tried to get control of Longbourn when she realized that Aunt Mel left it to me, but she didn't get too far. I think my father refused to pay the lawyer's fees."

"What did your mother do with three antique bedroom sets?"

"She uses one of them, one is Jane's, that she's had moved to Netherfield, and the last is Lydia's."

He scooted closer, and began stroking his hand up and down her side. "I have more furniture in storage that we could move into those rooms," he suggested. "There's the furniture from my old room, and my parents' bedroom set is actually larger than this one."

"Would you want to move that set in here then, since the room is larger, and move this one into one of the other rooms?"

"As long as it's okay with you. We'd need to buy some new mattresses for them, as well as the bed you used for Melly's mattress, since you didn't buy her a new one."

"It was silly to buy a new mattress for her," explained Lizzy. "Diapers and training pants leak sometimes, and kids jump on beds even though they aren't allowed. There was no reason to buy her a brand new one that she'd ruin."

"No, I understand, but I think it would be nice to have the rooms set up in the event we ever do have guests. Richard and his parents used to visit my family years ago. Uncle Hugh even hinted that he might come sometime this spring, although you never know when he's teasing."

"Is that where Richard gets it from?"

"Most definitely," he remarked dryly. "I was also wondering..." she nodded, and he took it as permission to continue, "what that room is that's always locked up downstairs?"

"I'm not hiding anyone away in there." He chuckled at her tease. "It was the study or library at one time, but that was also furniture my mother took, and I was worried about Melly climbing the shelves..."

"So you closed it off."

"Yes, I didn't want to worry about her finding her way in when my back was turned. You know how fast she can be." He sat up and grabbed his robe, quickly donning it.

"What are you doing?" she asked. He pulled her to stand and dressed her quickly in her own robe.

"I want to see the room," he answered excitedly. He'd asked, hoping he could have it remodeled for a home office, but to find that the room was already what he wanted was intriguing. He pulled her down the stairs and into the living room. "Where's the key?"

"What if I said it's upstairs?"

270

He noticed the slight quirk to her lips, and smiled. She was teasing him. "Nice try, sweetheart."

She walked over to the mantle, and picked up a small ceramic jar and dropped something into her hand. When she returned, she held out the old fashioned key, flat on her palm. He grasped it in his hand and unlocked the door, quickly crossing the threshold and turning on the light.

Lizzy watched him as she leaned against one side of the double doors that matched the ones to the living room. He pivoted in a circle when he reached the center, to get an idea of what would need to be done. The walls needed a coat of paint, but he realized as he ran his hand on the dusty bookshelves that the finish was still in good condition. The room definitely needed a good cleaning.

There was an empty set of shelves, and he turned. "There are books missing?"

"My father took them. He loves to read, so Aunt Mel allowed him to have a few."

He nodded and returned, standing behind her as his arms enveloped her. "May I move my father's old office furniture into this room, and my books?"

"Of course," she replied, "I want you to be at home here. It'll take all week to sort the books that remain and dust everything."

"I could hire Mrs. Reynolds to do it. She'd have this place completely free of dust in a day. Do any of the rooms upstairs need paint like this one?"

"Yes, I'd planned to paint one this spring."

"I have a man who works in our maintenance department at D&F, who paints when we need it. I've heard through some people at work that he's having trouble making ends meet since his wife lost her job. I was thinking I could ask him if he'd want the opportunity."

"That's so nice," she whispered.

"We can go pick out colors one day this week, and I'll see if he wants to start next weekend. That way, the job is done before the furniture is moved."

She was being very quiet, and he began to worry that she was upset about him spending money. "Is that okay with you?"

She turned in his arms, beaming at him. "I think you making yourself at home sounds wonderful."

He hugged her tightly to him before he reluctantly withdrew to relock the door. The key was placed back in its hiding place, and he led her back upstairs where he held her close the rest of the night.

Chapter Nineteen

<u>**Saturday, March 23, 2013**</u>

The sun was just peeking over the horizon when Lizzy and William departed Longbourn to set up for the craft fair. Mrs. Reynolds had been up impossibly early that morning, ensuring they had a good breakfast and plenty of coffee to take with them. She'd also prepared a picnic basket and a small ice chest, so they would have lunch.

William was driving Lizzy's car, following the directions the GPS system was giving him, while she was still blearily drinking her coffee. He quickly glanced over, and wished the morning were warmer so she wouldn't be bundled in her sweater. She was wearing the same outfit as the first time he'd met her, and he loved the way the corset style top accentuated her figure. He'd been such an ass that day as he tried to come up with excuse after excuse to avoid a relationship with her—and even to avoid her at times. He'd been so worried that eventually he wouldn't be able to resist.

He'd also been grossly incorrect about the effect she would have on his life. He was happier than he'd been in years, and it followed through to his business as well. The hours he was putting in were fewer, but things were running more smoothly than he remembered, and profits were up. It could've been a coincidence, yet he was more inclined to think she'd made him a better person.

"I still can't believe that Mrs. Reynolds managed to get that room so clean so quickly," Lizzy said, breaking the silence.

He chuckled as he made the turn the automated voice had indicated. "She can be quite determined when she sets her mind to it. I think she's even planning to clean one of those empty upstairs bedrooms for Matthew to paint.

"How long did he think the painting would take?"

"He thought he would have the study and one of the bedrooms done this weekend. Since you weren't sure when the last time the walls were painted, he wants to prime them first."

"So he'll be working tomorrow too."

"Yes, he said he'll be over after church and lunch."

She nodded, and took a sip of her coffee as they pulled into the drive. Lizzy texted Anita, who let them know where they were setting up. Anita had driven her SUV with all of their paper products, while her husband Sean had transported the tent, tables, and chairs in his truck.

"Do they do these things often?" William asked when they pulled up, and he saw all of the equipment they'd begun to unload.

"They do four or five a year. He's a ceramic artist and sculptor, subsidizing his gallery work by making bowls, vases, cups, and such to sell at craft fairs."

He parked, and the two of them were soon helping, too. William was amazed at everything they'd brought. They had a large party canopy that was soon erected, and then Sean showed William how to set up some freestanding pegboard walls that would extend along the entire the back and one side of the tent.

Meanwhile, Lizzy and Anita set up the tables and began laying out the paper first, sorting it by type and color as they went. Once enough paper was set out for people to see, the extra was stored under the tables, and then small signs indicating what each paper was made of as well as the best uses for each variety were placed with the different stacks.

As they finished, William began taking artwork out from the car, so Lizzy could set everything up the way she wished. She had a sample of each photograph in a frame that would hang from a short hooked peg on the makeshift wall, and crates underneath on a table that had copies of each print wrapped in plastic, filed and labeled in different sizes.

She then mounted each of her watercolors, including the smaller more simple paintings of butterflies and flowers, which were separated to one side.

"How long have you been working on these?" he asked, as he scanned the wall that had various varieties of butterflies. He even recognized one or two that were species found in Britain. There were flowers as well, but he could tell that painting them wasn't as natural as some of the other subjects. Finally, she had some still life

274

works that each had a different kitchen theme. Some were wine bottles and glasses, some contained fruit as well.

"Since last year's show," she explained. "I had a few people ask me if I made simpler works—a couple were pregnant women who liked the look of a watercolor painting, but didn't want a landscape for their child's nursery. Some simply wanted kitchen décor. I like the butterflies and the wine bottles and the fruit, but the flowers drive me crazy."

He chuckled and wrapped his arm around her. "I think someone will like them more than you do."

The corner of her mouth quirked up as she looked at him. "I guess I'm my own worst critic."

He peered across to where Anita and her husband were finishing their set-up. Soon, people began trickling through, at first, other artists and artisans from nearby tents, followed by the general public as they began to arrive.

They both remained fairly busy. William offered to man the lock box so Lizzy could mingle and talk with the customers. He'd worried it would be confusing, since they were running everything as three different businesses. Lizzy's, the paper, and then Sean and Anita manned their own box, but fortunately, most of the patrons didn't seem to mind. He sat at the back on the side of the canopy where all of Lizzy's paintings were displayed, and took money for her work and the paper.

During lulls, he browsed through Sean and Anita's work. Sean had some metal work sculptures, as well as a plethora of ceramic bowls, cups, vases and the like. Anita, while Lizzy had said she liked to make handmade books, mostly had various prints, as well as what Lizzy had explained were altered book art. He found those fascinating, and even bought a copy of *20,000 Leagues Under the Sea* that had been made to appear as if a giant octopus was emerging from the pages to attack a small ship.

There was another slow period around lunch, and William took the opportunity to unpack the picnic basket Mrs. Reynolds had prepared. One thing he knew had never changed about Lyla Reynolds was that she didn't do anything halfway. There were two small bowls of an orzo pasta salad with feta cheese that he'd always loved, some smoked salmon and cucumber finger sandwiches, and a dish of tiramisu that was just enough for the two of them.

He laid everything out and pulled two bottles of a sparkling juice drink out of the cooler. Lizzy, who'd just sold a few butterfly pictures to a lady who was expecting, came over and took a seat.

"Things seem to be going well. I think a lot of the paper is gone."

"I just restocked some of it a little while ago, and probably two-thirds is gone. Did you speak with the one girl and her mother who bought the huge stack?" He shook his head because of the bite of food in his mouth. "She spends a lot of her free time making origami, and her mother preferred some of our paper to what she buys in the craft store."

"She'd given me her money, but I hadn't spoken to her at length. I was wondering why she'd bought so much."

"Her mother showed me photos of some of her creations on her phone. They're really good. Anyway, when her daughter wasn't paying attention, the mother asked me to put more aside. Her husband is supposed to come by later. They want to save it for a birthday or Christmas present."

He remembered the woman and the large, very expensive stack she'd purchased. He was surprised that they were returning for even more.

"Mrs. Reynolds must have been up at five this morning to make all of this," exclaimed Lizzy as she surveyed their lunch.

"I'd say she brought some of it with her when she arrived. I know I carried in a cooler bag that made a rather distinctive clinking noise. I'm sure she'd already made the salad and the dessert, but she was still probably up by five to get dressed and have it all packed for us to leave. She also mentioned having dinner ready for us when we got home."

"She was supposed to come and watch Melly. I didn't expect her to do all of this, too."

Lizzy appeared upset, and he placed a hand over hers. "Sweetheart, she enjoys taking care of people. Her children live nearby, but they

276

work and the kids are in school, so she enjoys coming in to help us. I think she sees me as another son, and by extension, Melly, another grandchild."

"That's very sweet of her."

"Do you know that I've tried to pay her for when she babysits, and she refuses to take it?"

He regretted telling her almost immediately when he saw her face. "I didn't know you were paying her."

"She wouldn't take it, Lizzy."

She put down her food and took a long hard look at him. "Did you pay her when you were in England?" He realized his face must have given her the answer, because she brushed her hands off on the napkin and rose from her seat. He leaned forward and grasped for her hand.

"I knew you were going to be busy, and I wanted you to have the help."

"You suggested it to save me money, but I didn't think it would be at your expense." He could see that she was hurt. Since he'd moved in, she'd refused to take any money for the utilities, and had been buying all of the groceries for the three of them. He occasionally stopped and bought some wine or things he knew they needed, but she'd been taking care of most of it.

There was no one nearby, so he stood and made an attempt to pull her close. "I just wanted to help. We both live at Longbourn, but you've paid all of the expenses so far."

"You paid Mrs. Reynolds to clean the study and the rooms to be painted, as well as the help to paint them. You're also thinking about renovating that old building behind the garage. Those aren't cheap projects."

"No, but I can afford them."

"So because I can't, I should just let you pay for everything. I want to pay for the utilities and groceries because it makes me feel like I'm doing something else to pay you back for the car."

He furrowed his brow. "You paid me for the car."

"No, I gave you a check for probably one-fifth of the purchase price, and I've managed to make you accept a couple of payments. It's not a significant amount when you consider the cost."

"It's added up to more than that, and I told you that I really wanted you to accept it as a gift." He ran his free hand through his hair and an idea came to mind. "If we were married, would you still be so bound and determined to keep things so even financially?"

"I doubt it, but that's different."

He turned her face to look him straight in the eyes. "It isn't any different in my mind."

Some people walked under the canopy and began to browse. Lizzy pulled herself free and grabbed a finger sandwich to nibble on while she waited to see if they required her help. He remained where she left him until a gentleman approached him with some paper and he accepted the payment.

Taking his seat, he ended up watching her for the remainder of the day. During lulls, she finished her salad and finger sandwiches, but she mostly mingled with the people who came into the tent while he felt as if he was watching her from afar, which bothered him immensely.

Lizzy spent the afternoon wondering why something that was trivial to William would mean so much to her. She also felt guilty. Mrs. Reynolds had likely spent a good deal of time making that lunch, and Lizzy was so preoccupied, she barely tasted it. Now it sat like a rock in her stomach. Fortunately, the sparkling juice drink settled the discomfort to a certain degree, although she still avoided William for the remainder of the afternoon. She didn't want to have the conversation or argument, whichever it was, in such a public place.

The father she'd discussed with William had indeed returned a few hours later. He not only purchased what the mother had asked to be set aside, but also most of their remaining stock that Lizzy and Anita indicated would fold well.

278

Once he'd left, Lizzy began organizing, and they removed the empty tables. Overall, the day was a resounding success, and they left out the last of the stock as William and Sean packed up the canopy. She'd been happy that she'd sold most of the butterflies, all of the still life works, and all of her photographs. She'd also sold three of the four landscapes that had been leftover from the Christmas exhibition at The Depot.

Since William had never seen the inside of Longwood, Anita and Sean offered to watch over what was left, so they could go on the tour before the house closed. She felt awkward, but he took her hand, lacing his fingers with hers as they made their way across the grounds.

It was evident by William's expression that he found the tour fascinating, but they didn't tarry long, so they were soon walking back toward the booth. "Are you ever going to speak to me?" he asked with a rather forlorn expression.

"I've just always wanted to stand on my own two feet..."

"You do, but everyone needs some help now and then. There's no shame in accepting it." He tugged her arm so that she turned to face him. "I'm not trying to take away your independence—I love that about you. I would also never want you to just accept anything I say as if it were a command." He brushed her hair over her shoulder. "I don't like seeing you worry over something I can solve without difficulty."

Her shoulders dropped, and he must have sensed an opening because he pulled her into his arms. "You don't need to pay me back for anything. As a matter of fact, the money you gave me went into a trust for Melly."

"I should've known," she mumbled into his chest while he chuckled.

He leaned in close to her ear. "I love you, and I have big plans that eventually include a ring and forever. I'm not worried about a car, groceries, and paying Mrs. Reynolds—especially the food and Mrs. Reynolds. I would be paying for those if I'd found a home when I returned to Meryton." He lifted her face and she could see his earnest expression. "I feel I am contributing to our life—the life we're building together."

"Just be upfront with me, so I can at least argue with you about it," she responded. She smiled when he did, and she heard the low rumble of him laughing. The sound helped to relieve the weight that she'd been carrying since the argument.

"You've got a deal. I like arguing with you, as long as you're not really mad."

She felt his lips graze her forehead, and they continued their trek, watching people from the other booths wander around to see what remained so they could make a few last minute purchases. When they returned where they had set up, Sean and Anita were packing up what was left of his ceramics and her prints.

"The woman from the booth next to us came and bought the last of the plant fiber paper," called out Anita when she saw them. "All we have left is a partial box of the recycled paper."

"That's all yours then," replied Lizzy. "I have no plans to do another fair in the next few months."

Anita nodded and grabbed the box to place in her SUV. Meanwhile, William went to the car where he wouldn't be out in the open, and counted out the paper proceeds. He put half in an envelope that he returned to Lizzy, who had just finished packing up the last few items she had remaining. She added what she owed for the rental of the spot for their tent, and gave the money to Anita.

The sun was going down, so once William helped Sean finish loading up the pegboard walls, he and Lizzy left, heading back toward Longbourn. The drive passed quickly, so Lizzy was surprised when William pulled into the drive where he stopped, and turned off the lights by the lake.

"What are you doing?"

"We never ate the dessert, and I thought we could finish our picnic while we watched the moonlight on the lake." They stepped out, and William pulled a blanket from under the basket. "Mrs. Reynolds had put that there for earlier, but since you still had customers, we didn't use it."

He spread the quilt, and they took a seat under the trees while Lizzy took in her surroundings. The front porch lights were on, as well as some garden lights that were meant to illuminate the old home when the reception hall was in use, as it was tonight. Glancing back, she found William holding out the bowl of tiramisu. She took a bite and was surprised it was still cold. "Did she put cold packs in the basket?"

"She did, but I moved this to the cooler."

"Oh," she replied, and he pulled her so that her back was to his chest. She took another bite and enjoyed the creamy concoction melting in her mouth. "This is really good." William reached down for the spoon they were sharing, and she leaned against his chest.

"This has always been my favorite dessert that she makes."

They slowly savored the dish bite by bite until it was gone. Lizzy then placed the bowl next to her on the blanket, and relaxed in William's arms.

"Don't fall asleep."

She laughed a bit. "I hadn't planned on it." She watched the lights reflect off of the water and gave a contented sigh. "It really is a lovely evening. I'm glad you thought of this." When she glanced back, he leaned forward and his lips lightly caressed hers.

His lips were soft as they spread small kisses on her eyes and nose. She smiled and he reclaimed her mouth, leaning her back on the quilt. They did nothing more than kiss, but Lizzy never relaxed, which William eventually noticed when he was brushing his lips down her neck.

"Are you nervous?" he whispered near her ear.

"I keep worrying about a snake finding us." His head shot up from her neck, and she chuckled.

"You've never mentioned snakes before."

"It's the south and I have a pond on my property. Everything stays mowed down, which helps, but it doesn't mean there aren't any around. We're also down on the swampier end of the water." She shrugged and followed as he sat up. "Most of the snakes I've seen on this property have been down here."

281

"You could've told me that before I set things up."

"I honestly didn't think about it at first. It wasn't until you laid us down on the quilt that it came to my mind." He glanced around them and gathered the dishes.

"Perhaps we should go ahead to the house. Mrs. Reynolds will be expecting us soon."

Lizzy stood carefully, taking the container and utensils while he gathered the blanket. "I'm sorry if I ruined any ideas you had."

William shook his head. "I can't stand snakes," he confided.

"For what it's worth, I'm not fond of them myself."

He took her hand as he led her back to the car. "So, I don't ever have to worry about you wanting a pet snake?"

"No," she said, laughing. "I can guarantee you that I'll never, ever want a pet snake."

They drove around to the garage, and after unloading what was left, made their way into the kitchen.

Mrs. Reynolds was laying out a small dinner for them as a pajama-clad Melly came running and jumped at William, "Daddy!"

"How was your day?" He settled her on his hip, and she wrapped her arm around his shoulders.

"Nana read to me!"

"Anything else?" he asked, chuckling at her use of the nickname for Mrs. Reynolds. He had called her Grandma Reynolds and Melanie had picked up Nana, which the older lady loved. At that moment, she was beaming proudly.

Melanie thought for a moment at the question. "Colored."

"What else?"

"Went outside." She gave William a kiss on the lips and scooted down in an attempt to go play.

"Oh no you don't, young lady," said Mrs. Reynolds as she scooped her up. "You didn't take a nap today, so I think it's time to go lie down now that Mama and Daddy are home."

"She didn't take a nap?" Lizzy asked.

"She lay there for an hour and never fell asleep, so I let her get up." Lizzy shook her head, and Mrs. Reynolds' face showed some worry that perhaps she had erred.

"No, that's fine. I'm just surprised." Lizzy smiled warmly as Mrs. Reynolds seemed to relax.

The older woman bounced Melanie on her hips a bit. "She slept until nine this morning, so that could've been a factor."

Putting her hand to her daughter's forehead, Lizzy checked her temperature before she kissed her. "I hope she's not getting sick."

Mrs. Reynolds shrugged. "It's possible, but she may not have slept as well last night. You never know. Now, I have a small dinner laid out, so you two eat and I'll get her settled in for the evening."

"Thanks, Mrs. Reynolds," said William as he gave her a kiss on the cheek. "You do know that you're not driving home this late, don't you?"

"I'll be perfectly fine."

"No, you'll stay here one more night. You can go home after breakfast tomorrow. I insist."

Lizzy found it adorable when the woman blushed and patted William on the cheek. "You're such a sweet boy." He reddened at her compliment, and Lizzy grinned at his embarrassment.

Mrs. Reynolds bustled from the kitchen while the two of them took their seats, and didn't return until they were finished with their dinner. Lizzy had just stood to begin cleaning up the table when Mrs. Reynolds stopped her. "No, dear, you've had a long day, and I'm sure you must be tired. Why don't the two of you go get cleaned up and ready for bed. I'll finish up down here."

"I can't let you do that," Lizzy exclaimed.

"I don't mind. In fact, I insist."

William came up behind her, and she felt his arms snake around her stomach. "I'll make sure she goes upstairs," he commented, gently pushing her toward the door. "I told you she likes taking care of people, so let her," he whispered in her ear as they went.

"You want to go to bed at nine?" she asked while the door swung closed behind them.

"No, I want to get you into the shower, because you are a dirty, dirty girl."

Lizzy burst into peals of laughter.

"Shhhh, you'll wake Melly."

She pulled away from him, turned, and slowly began backing her way up the stairs in front of him. "Do you want to lather my body with soap?" She ran her hand down her side to her hip, trying to act sultry. He smiled, and she wondered if she looked as ridiculous as she felt. Reaching back up, Lizzy pulled the first two hooks free on the front of her top as his eyes widened. She then unhooked enough so that he could see she wore no bra underneath, and turned and ran for her room.

She could hear his long legs behind her as she made the door, when he scooped her up around her middle with one arm and kicked the door closed behind him. "Come here, you little tease!"

"Oh, I think you know that I'm no tease..." she laughed as he placed her feet on the floor. She backed away from him, continuing to unfasten her top while she moved farther and farther away from him. "At least for you, I'm not." With the last word, she slid the straps down her arms, baring her chest, and turned into the bathroom as she dropped her skirt.

Lizzy couldn't help but laugh when he strode through the door a minute later as naked as the day he was born.

The next morning, Lizzy woke rather early, and snuggled into William's warmth as she attempted to fall back to sleep. When she was unsuccessful, she carefully freed herself from his embrace to put on her pajamas and robe.

She peered in on Melanie, who was still sleeping soundly, sprawled out on top of the covers, before she walked downstairs to let out Bear. Mrs. Reynolds was not yet in the kitchen, so she began rummaging through the refrigerator and pantry to see what she could make for breakfast, when Mrs. Reynolds came through the door.

"Oh!" she cried with a start. "You startled me! I didn't realize anyone else was awake yet."

Lizzy smiled as she set the coffee on the kitchen counter and began putting it in the grinder as she shrugged. "I couldn't go back to sleep."

"I never asked you how the craft fair went yesterday?"

"Good, I sold most of my work, so I'm very happy."

She smiled widely. "That's wonderful, dear. I hope the two of you had a nice time."

"William helped most of the day, since we were pretty busy, and then he and I toured the house. I think he enjoyed it. It's different than most of the Antebellum homes around here."

Mrs. Reynolds nodded, and gestured toward the living room. "The study looks lovely with the new paint. Have you seen it yet?"

"No," Lizzy responded while she put the coffee in the French press, "I'll have to take a look when I get a chance."

"I'd be happy to come this week and clean those other two bedrooms upstairs so Matthew can paint them next weekend." Lizzy stopped what she was doing and looked up at Mrs. Reynolds.

"I couldn't ask you to do that."

"You didn't ask. I offered. I could also keep Melanie for the day, and you'd have some time to run any errands you might like before or after your classes." Mrs. Reynolds appraised her for a few moments, making Lizzy a bit uncomfortable. "I heard William tell you last night that I like to take care of people."

Lizzy's eyes widened, caught off guard by the blunt statement, and the older woman chuckled. "I do, you know. I don't mind helping one bit. I suppose that was why I took the job with the Darcys in the beginning. Mrs. Darcy was pregnant with William, and they wanted someone who would be at the house all day. My youngest had just begun elementary school, and I was at home by myself."

Lizzy heard the kettle whistle, and poured the water in the French press. As she prepared the coffee, Mrs. Reynolds continued, "I know that William wants me to come work here for the two of you, but if you aren't comfortable, I won't be offended."

"You don't make me uncomfortable," she clarified. "It's simply that he just moved in, and I like things as they are. I guess I'm not ready for anything to change."

"There's nothing wrong with that, dear. The last thing I'd ever want is for you to feel like I'm intruding on the three of you."

She fit the lid on the press and looked up. "If you did work for us, how would you propose we do that?"

"Well, I could mainly help out during the week. I could have meals prepared, unless you wish to cook, of course. I could keep Melanie as well, so you don't have to pay for the day care center on campus, and keep things cleaned up. You would have more time for William and Melanie, as well as to paint, if you like."

"I guess I just need some time to adjust to the idea. I knew that you wanted to work for William again when he found his own home, but I hadn't really considered it until he mentioned it recently."

"That's fine, dear. I'm happy being a part-time babysitter. Melly is such a precious little girl."

Lizzy smiled. "Thanks, you've been wonderful for her." She poured the milk in her cup of coffee and took a sip.

"Okay, we'll have none of that sappy stuff," Mrs. Reynolds said suddenly, causing Lizzy to chuckle. "What are we going to make for breakfast? I didn't know that William would insist I stay last night, or I would've prepped something."

Lizzy began pulling ingredients out of the pantry. "I can make biscuits, if you'll make the eggs and bacon."

Mrs. Reynolds smiled as she poured herself a cup of coffee. "Sounds like a plan to me."

They began cooking. Mrs. Reynolds took out the things Lizzy would require before she needed them, and then cleaned up behind her. When the biscuits were in the oven, they swapped roles, with Lizzy, after checking on her daughter, cleaning up and preparing more coffee for William when he came down.

He came through the door just as everything was ready. Melanie was in his arms, and he inhaled deeply when he came into the kitchen. "It smells wonderful in here."

"I hope you're hungry," said Mrs. Reynolds, as she placed the last of the food on the table.

He gave her a wide smile. "Famished."

They all took their seats. William insisted Mrs. Reynolds join them when it appeared she wouldn't. Breakfast was lively, and despite Lizzy's hesitation to Mrs. Reynolds becoming their live-in housekeeper, she was becoming more open to the idea than she was before.

Chapter Twenty

Lizzy took a step out into the cool night air. She could see the last of her students, who'd walked out of the sculpture lab, half way across the parking lot, and turned to lock the door to the building, a campus security guard patiently waiting behind her.

The officer, Scotty, had offered at the beginning of the semester to escort her to her car every Thursday night and to this day, he'd never been late. She was thankful that he was a sixty-year-old man, and not younger, or else William might have been a little jealous. As it was, she knew that William would appreciate the guard's dedication.

They walked across the street to the faculty parking, and he stepped ahead and made a quick circle around her car. She couldn't explain it, but she felt as if someone was watching her. Looking all around her, she saw no one, before she turned to see the officer looking back at her. "You have a good night, Ms. Gardiner."

"Thanks, Scotty, you have a good evening, too."

"Yes, ma'am." Scotty watched her get into her car and lock the door. Lizzy took one last long look at the surrounding area, and started when there was a knock at the window. She rolled down the glass and he leaned over. "Are you all right?"

"I can't explain it. I just feel like someone is watching us."

He stood straight up and scanned the area carefully, his eyes narrowing at a copse of trees across the street. "I'll check it out. Why don't you go on home?"

"You'll let me know if you find anything?"

"Yes, ma'am," he responded.

After thanking him once more, she rolled up her window and pulled out of the parking lot. For the life of her, Lizzy couldn't explain the feeling, but it made her check her rearview mirror more often on the way out of campus, as well as the highway home.

By the time she arrived at Longbourn, she no longer felt so strange, but she still clutched her cell phone in her hands as she walked from the garage to the back door. She ensured the door was locked behind her, and after stripping her dirty clothes off to her shirt and a pair of cotton shorts, she found William in the living room, and climbed into his lap.

A part of her wanted to tell him, but she refrained, deciding she was probably being paranoid. What good would it do to make him worry all of the time, when it was sure to be nothing?

She dismissed it to such an extent that when she received a call on Saturday, where the person on the other end of the line hung up, she passed it off as a wrong number.

In fact, Lizzy had dismissed the event that night to such an extent that she was surprised to see Scotty when he came by during her watercolor class on Tuesday and knocked on the doorframe. Everyone was working independently, so she had a few minutes and stepped outside in the hall. "Good morning."

"Good morning, Ms. Gardiner," he responded, "You asked me to let you know if I found anything Thursday night."

"Oh, that," she laughed, "I was being so paranoid. I'm sure it was probably nothing."

"It may have been, but I thought I saw someone in that cluster of trees across the street. As soon as you pulled out, I took a look-see, but there was no one there. However, there *were* footprints where I'd seen the shadow." He handed her a card with a long series of numbers and a phone number. "This is the report I filed with the university. It may seem a bit presumptuous, but I'd rather have it documented in the event the situation arises again."

"Isn't it possible that it was a coincidence?"

"It may be nothing, but I'd rather not take a chance. I'll be there with at least one other security guard this Thursday, so please don't leave that building without us. If your class happens to let out early, call me at the phone number on the card. That's the cell phone that I carry with me.

"Thank you, but I don't plan on leaving the building alone. My boyfriend would never forgive me."

"Good, I'm glad to know that someone's looking out for you."

"I appreciate this, but I need to get back in there," she said, gesturing toward the classroom.

"Yes, ma'am," he responded, and she returned back inside, where a student was waiting with a question.

Saturday, April 6, 2013

Lizzy returned downstairs after her shower, dressed in a pair of jeans and a short-sleeved, cowl neck blouse that was one of her favorite and most comfortable tops. She made herself a second cup of coffee and went in search of William and Melanie, finding them in the backyard. William was sitting on the steps of the back porch, while her daughter was having a ball on the enormous play set now erected on the left side of the courtyard. William had insisted Melanie needed the monstrosity for an Easter present, and at Lizzy's insistence, an early birthday present also.

Quietly closing the door behind her, she took a few steps before she noticed Bear, who was sitting on William's other side. The dog was perched directly next to him as he seemed to watch Melanie like William did. She smiled widely as she made her way over to them.

"Are both of the men in my life guarding over Melly?"

William started and chuckled. "He was leaning against me a few minutes ago, and actually let me pet him."

"I told you it may take a while, but he'd warm up to you." She settled herself on the step next to William and glanced over to see her daughter squealing as she came down the slide. She felt Bear sit down next to her and lean against her side. "Hi, Bear." She patted his head and gave him a scratch around the ears.

"I see I've been deserted." She chuckled before she realized that William suddenly had a strange look on his face. "Lizzy, what's he doing?"

290

She turned to see one side of Bear's lips lift to reveal his teeth. "Haven't you ever seen a dog try to smile," she asked. She laughed as the dog put his paw on her leg, resting it there for a while as they watched him. William began laughing with her, and reached over to give the dog a scratch to the side of the head.

"I would be violently jealous if he were a man."

She smiled widely and gave William a peck on the cheek. "He's done this for as long as I've known him."

"How old is he? He doesn't seem to be a young dog."

"No, we think he's about eleven." she responded. "Aunt Mel took him in from a friend who'd rescued him. The people who owned him before used him to train Pitt Bulls for fighting."

"That's disgusting!" She could see the horror on his face and sympathized.

"If animal control had taken him, he would've been put down. My aunt thought he was not an inherently mean dog, so she decided to adopt him." She smiled as she recalled the first time she'd ever seen him. "I remember that my father thought he could pet him, and cornered him. He was bitten on the hand and immediately came to the conclusion that Bear was violent and should be euthanized. I was beside myself at the idea, so I went outside and called him to me. He was a bit skittish, but he came up and let me pet him." She shrugged, reaching up to give Bear another scratch behind the ear. "Once he was secure and knew no one would hurt him, he was an excellent watch dog. We just have to ensure we keep him close to the house when there are functions at the reception hall across the lake."

"I've noticed that he doesn't like it."

"Not at all, but he's become more accustomed to it." She turned back, checked Melanie and then turned toward William. "If you hadn't noticed, the fence that separates the part of the property behind the lake is a six foot privacy fence. There are also 'Beware of Dog' signs plastered all over the other side, as well as one on the gate to this side of the bridge. Luckily, Bear minds me when I call him back."

"You don't ever worry about Melly being around him?"

"He's never been anything but patient with her. She's still never been alone with him, though. He'd rather be outside, and she's never out here by herself."

William nodded, and rubbed his hand up and down her leg that was next to him. "In several years, you could allow her to play on the porch or in the yard while you keep an eye on her from the window. We'll have to figure out something."

"We have a while before we need to worry about that."

"True," William began, but was interrupted by his cell phone ringing.

"Hi, Richard."

Lizzy watched her daughter as she listened to William's side of the conversation.

"Describe it to me...No, I know the photo. It was taken at a gallery opening last week for the society page of the local newspaper, and made it to the Meryton Herald's website. They must have found the information there." He paused while Richard must have been speaking. "No, it doesn't bother me, unless they send a horde of paparazzi to Meryton...I will. Thanks, Richard...Sure, I'll speak to you about it on Monday...Bye."

He hit end on the phone and turned, kissing her on the temple while she placed her coffee cup on the porch next to her. "You're now famous in Britain for scooping up London's most eligible bachelor."

"Richard?" she asked with fake innocence.

She heard his low growl as he turned and began tickling her, causing her to roll down onto her back. She was wrestling back while she laughed raucously and Bear began licking her face. "Ewwwww!" The next thing she knew, her daughter had jumped and landed on her lower stomach, straddling her waist, while she also began digging into her mother's sides.

"Are you sorry?" William said while Melly was giggling uproariously.

292

"No," she choked out between her uncontrolled reactions to the tickling. "You...you should've seen...the look...on your face!"

He reapplied his efforts until she was hiccupping and crying, "I surrender!" William stopped his tickling while he drew back and helped her to sit up. Meanwhile, Melanie, who'd realized the fun was over, had gone to resume her playing. Brushing herself off, Lizzy rose and began walking back toward the back door.

"Where are you going?" called William after her.

"I've seen what Bear eats in the yard, and he was licking my face. I'm going to wash it."

She saw him chuckle as she went through a door that led through a hall directly to the foyer. Her face was quickly scrubbed and she applied moisturizer before she returned to her seat beside William. They were quiet, simply watching her daughter for a while, when he interrupted the silence.

"You need to be sure to tell me if you ever feel threatened in any way."

She faced him, to see a distressed expression on his face. The statement hadn't come out of the blue. He'd mentioned it earlier in the week when Charles had called to inform them that Caroline was now aware of their relationship. The same photograph Richard called about had been taken at a friend's gallery opening, and then from there spread to other newspapers—now including the overseas tabloids. Caroline's reaction wasn't that of a stable woman, and the elder Mr. Bingley had called William at work to ensure he was fully aware of her ranting.

Lizzy shook her head. "I think all this worrying has made me paranoid. I felt as though someone was watching me Thursday night after class."

She didn't know how it was possible, but he looked even more disturbed than he had before. "I'll come and pick you up after class from now on."

"One of the campus security officers escorts me to my car every night. Because of my silly paranoia, he's said he won't be the sole officer there this week. I *need* you to be here with Melly."

Exhaling heavily, he leaned his forehead on her shoulder. "I just worry."

"You fret like an old woman," she teased. "If I held on to that much anxiety, I'd have blown a few hang-ups way out of proportion this week."

His head shot up. "You're getting crank calls?"

"Probably wrong numbers," she said dismissively. "I shouldn't have brought it up."

"Of course you should! On the home phone or your cell?"

Her brow furrowed as she thought about it. "Both, if I remember correctly."

"How many calls?"

"I don't know, four or five?"

"When was the last one?"

"Yesterday," she replied. "It's probably just a coincidence."

By the end of the day, she'd wished that she'd kept her mouth shut. William insisted she file a police report, and the police officer had seemed to agree that it was all a bit suspicious. She'd even pulled the phone numbers from her cell phone and the caller ID for the paperwork.

He also called Mrs. Reynolds and enlisted her to keep Melanie at Longbourn for the week, rather than have her travelling around town with Lizzy and at school. Regardless of the childcare center's policies for a child pick up, he wanted someone he trusted keeping his little girl.

That night, William made love to her like she would disappear at any minute, and then held her to him tightly while they lay spooned with their legs entwined. "Promise me," he whispered.

"Promise you what?" she asked groggily.

"That if you get one more of those calls, you'll tell me."

"I promise," she whispered back as she drifted off to sleep.

Friday, April 12, 2013

William placed the phone receiver on the base, and glanced at a photograph of Lizzy and Melanie that had graced his desktop since around New Years. He'd just ended a call with the contractor who was going to convert the building behind the garage into a small cottage for Mrs. Reynolds. The final product wouldn't be much more than a small studio-type apartment, but Mrs. Reynolds had only had a bedroom when she'd lived with his parents. He thought she would be rather pleased with her new and more spacious accommodations once everything was completed.

Although she still had reservations, Lizzy was slowly warming to the idea of Mrs. Reynolds, and he hoped that by the time the renovations were completed they would have everything worked out so that she was happy. Regardless of the outcome, the small building had been an eyesore, and it was also dangerous. Melanie was already sneaking away at times within the house and hiding from them. What would happen if she made her way out of Longbourn and tried to hide in there?

He was just settling back to his papers when his assistant, Owen, buzzed him. "Mr. Darcy, Mr. Jameson from the district attorney's office is here requesting a meeting."

"Of course," he replied. "Please show him in." He couldn't help but wonder why the district attorney himself would show up at his office without an appointment.

He stood from his seat and walked around to the front of his desk just as Owen opened his door. "Thank you," said Mr. Jameson when he entered. He looked over and extended his hand to William, and they shook hands. "Mr. Darcy, I appreciate you seeing me on such short notice."

"Of course," replied William, gesturing towards a chair, "please have a seat."

At that moment, his assistant stepped forward. "May I get you some coffee or water, Mr. Jameson?"

"No, no thank you."

Owen returned to his desk, leaving them in privacy, and William took his own seat. "I enjoyed meeting your wife and children at the Christmas tree lighting. I hope they're well."

"Yes, they are, thank you for asking," Mr. Jameson responded.

William leaned back in his seat as he appraised the man sitting across from him. "You do have me very curious about what's brought you to my office. It isn't an election year, so I know that isn't the reason."

The gentleman smiled uneasily. "No, I'm not here to ask for a contribution for anything. I was actually given some information this morning, and I wished to convey the news myself rather than sending someone else."

William furrowed his brow and leaned forward on to his desk. "This sounds ominous."

"I wouldn't call it ominous, but things aren't as neat and tidy as I would've liked. There's no easy way to say this," he began as he shifted in his chair, "but we've discovered the identity of the man who committed the hit and run that killed your father and your younger sister."

"What?" Of all the things the district attorney could've said, that was the last one he expected. Roughly three years had passed since the accident, and he'd given up hope that they would ever apprehend the culprit. He still wasn't quite thinking clearly when he muttered. "How?"

Mr. Jameson reached down to grasp the briefcase that he'd set on the floor. "A man was recently arrested across the river in Vidalia for possession. They suspect he's been dealing, and hoped to get him for intent to distribute, but he only had one joint on him at the time of arrest." He took some folders from the bag and then returned it to its previous spot. "However, when they were processing him at the station, he had an outstanding warrant for a domestic violence issue, so they held him through his initial arraignment and bail hearing. During that time, a DNA sample was taken, which matched the blood in the stolen car that was involved in the accident."

"So they still have this man in custody?"

"No, unfortunately, he made bail and was released pending trial before the DNA test came back positive. The investigator..."

"Detective Carver," interjected William.

"Yes, Detective Carver went to Vidalia, and they went to the address provided on the bail documents, but he wasn't there. There have been other attempts to locate him, but they've been unsuccessful."

William stood and walked to the large wall-length window that looked over the river. They'd come so close. They had a name, but would he ever see this...this... "Mr. Jameson, I don't remember you ever mentioning this man's name."

"Oh, I guess I was so wrapped up in the particulars that I left out that part. His name is Wickham...Gregory Wickham."

"What?" he asked incredulously as he jerked back to face the D.A.

"I said his name is Gregory Matthew Wickham."

Fuck! thought William as he covered his face with his hands, then running his fingers through his hair.

"Mr. Darcy, are you okay? I expected you to be stunned, but not to this extent."

"You said this man was wanted for domestic violence?"

"Oh...yes, several weeks after the accident, he beat his pregnant wife, now ex-wife, severely. According to the police report, he broke several ribs, her arm, *and* caused her to deliver her baby prematurely. He's charged with second degree assault, but if they can't find him, they can't try him."

He no longer had any doubts it was the same Greg Wickham. What cruel twist of fate had him practically engaged to the ex-wife of the man who had so carelessly killed his father and little sister?

"Are the police still actively looking for him?" he asked, attempting to keep thoughts of Lizzy separate at that moment.

"Now that we know he's in the area, or was as of a week ago, Vidalia and Meryton police forces are on the lookout for him. Detective Carver is following up the leads that he found in Vidalia as well."

William suddenly had a sickening feeling. Did Lizzy know that Wickham had been caught? The police would have to notify her, would they not? "Do you know if they've notified his ex-wife of his arrest?"

"She should've been notified through her attorney. Her sister is actually a prominent lawyer here in Meryton."

He was so preoccupied in his own thoughts that he only heard bits and pieces of what followed.

"I promise you, Mr. Darcy..."

"I'll do everything I can..."

"...isn't dropped."

Mr. Jameson finally stood and walked over to where Darcy was standing, handing him a photo. William looked down to see the mug shot of what he could tell was once a handsome man, who now looked haggard and menacing. Wickham looked incredibly angry, and he shuddered to think this was the man who was once married to the Lizzy he loved so much. This was the man whose blood ran through little Melanie's veins. He stared at the face until he noticed Jameson's hand held out.

He returned the photo and walked as if in a daze to his desk. He took a seat heavily in his chair, looking up at Jameson. "The police had been watching this man for a while?"

"He's been seen around the area off and on over last few months. Wickham has several aliases, so until he was picked up, no one really knew what his name actually was. His identification was in his wallet though, and they've matched it to DMV records, so it is him." He placed the picture in the folder and returned to his seat. "Carver went out and interviewed the witnesses and checked to see if they recognized the mug shot. He was positively identified by those who were closest to the car."

"They couldn't help with a drawing, but they can tell it's him in that photo?" William asked doubtfully. "Will that hold up in court?"

"I think with the DNA evidence, yes." He paused for a moment as if internally debating something and then leaned forward to ensure William was looking him in the eye. "The man is a monster. If you'd seen the pictures of the woman he beat, you'd understand. I don't know how she's not disfigured. She was practically unrecognizable."

"You have those pictures?" he asked, not sure why he wanted to see them.

Jameson appeared taken aback. "You *want* to see them? Why?"

"I don't know. I guess morbid curiosity?"

He shifted in his seat as Jameson pulled another folder from his briefcase and placed it in front of him. "I would prefer that you didn't tell people I showed these to you. I know they will be on display in the courtroom during the trial, but I don't just go showing victim's photos to people."

"I understand," he said softly, as he clenched his teeth and opened the cover. Everything in him revolted at the sight in front of him, and he had to restrain himself not to cry out or visibly react at the image in front of him.

Lizzy, his Lizzy was…good God, she didn't even look like herself. She had two black eyes that were swollen so badly he was unsure if she would've been able to see if she'd been conscious. As he slowly flipped through each of the pictures, he was amazed that she'd lived. He couldn't comprehend how she'd lived. There were bruises everywhere.

Feeling something burning at the bottom of his throat, he handed Jameson back the folder. "Thank you for coming to tell me in person. I appreciate the courtesy."

"Think nothing of it, Darcy. I'll keep you apprised of any progress."

"Of course, thank you."

William was holding his emotions so tightly in check that he didn't notice Jameson leaving until the sound of the door closing startled him. He rose from his chair and went into his private bathroom, finally surrendering the control he'd been struggling to maintain by losing his lunch in the toilet.

He leaned over the seat until he was sure he was finished, and then sat back on the floor with his head in his hands. How? How could he face Lizzy? He didn't blame her, but could he continue to have a relationship with her, knowing she had been married to that man?

He'd known that Greg Wickham was a monster, just not the monster that had killed the last of his remaining family. What was he going to do?

Chapter Twenty-one

<u>**Friday, April 12 cont...**</u>

Lizzy glanced at the grandfather clock and wondered what could be keeping William. He'd checked in with her around lunchtime, but she hadn't heard a peep from him since, which was unusual. Since the suspicious calls had begun, he typically checked in with her when her classes were over, ensuring she was heading to Longbourn and asking if she was making stops, but the sun was beginning to set and he wasn't home. He had always called in the past if he was going to be late, and she was beginning to worry.

Bear was jumping, barking, and whining at the front door, so Lizzy let him out, watching as he bulleted across the yard while continuing to bark loudly. She shook her head before she shut and locked the door. He must have seen some kind of animal through the window.

She turned to look at Melanie, who was sitting and watching a cartoon with her stuffed cat hugged in her little arms. She hadn't taken her nap that day, and was fighting tooth and nail to stay awake, the exhaustion clearly visible in the dark circles under her eyes. Lizzy had already given her a bath and dressed her in her pajamas, so she turned off the television and lifted her daughter into her arms. "Let's go upstairs, Melly."

"Read me a story?" the little girl asked tiredly against her mother's shoulder.

"Of course." Lizzy made her way to Melanie's room, where she tucked her into the covers and perched herself on the side of the bed. "What would you like to hear?"

"That one," she mumbled, pointing to a book on the nightstand. Lizzy smiled as she recognized the book William had brought home a few days ago and opened the hard cover to read to her until she was fast asleep.

Melly was out like a light, and realizing Bear was still outside, she went to the front door and turned on the porch lights. "Bear, come here boy!" Lizzy called over the wide expanse of land that was her front yard. She scanned the view before her and called again, but he didn't come like he usually did, so Lizzy secured the door, worried.

She didn't want to go out hunting for him without William at home. He probably would insist on doing the searching, and make Lizzy wait within the house. She was just picking up the phone to call him when she suddenly saw a shadow through the sheer drapes of the front window.

Her heart dropped to her stomach, and she began to shake as she pressed the button to turn on the home phone, only to find there was no dial tone. Quickly, she hurried to the kitchen where she'd left her purse, grabbed her cell phone, and pressed send to pull up her recent calls. She saw the same silhouette through the kitchen windows, and what sounded like Bear growling and barking. Frightened, she ran upstairs and locked herself in Melanie's dark room. She then looked down to find William's cell number was first on the list of numbers, so she pressed send and prayed he would answer.

William sat on the floor of his office bathroom for what felt like hours before he decided that he needed to get out and do something, so he asked Owen to reschedule a late meeting he had that day. Then he got into his car and just drove.

He wasn't aware how long he'd been on the road, or how he found himself at Netherfield, but not stopping to think about it, he got out of his car and strode up to the door. Charles answered the doorbell a few minutes later.

"William! I didn't expect to see you here this evening."

"I really hadn't planned it, but I need to talk something out." He ran his hand through his hair and shifted uncomfortably. "Do you have a minute...or an hour?"

Charles ushered him inside and led the way to his study. "This seems serious."

"Yes...I think so..." He groaned, and again, ran his hand through his hair. "I don't know!"

His friend studied him for a moment. "Why don't we sit, and you can tell me exactly what happened that has you so upset." He pointed towards the shelf where he kept the liquor. "How about a little scotch?" William took a seat and leaned forward onto his knees.

"I don't know if that's a good idea."

"Not enough so that you can't drive. Just enough to sip while you talk."

William nodded, and soon found himself with a glass in his hand. He took a sip and swallowed, welcoming the comforting burn of the liquid as it went down. Tears welled in his eyes, and he attempted to shake them off.

"William," said Charles as he regarded him curiously, "what *is* going on?"

"I had a visit from Mr. Jameson today." His friend's eyebrows lifted.

"The district attorney?"

"The very one. There's been a match to the DNA found in the car that killed my father and Ana." He looked up and saw Charles' wide-eyed expression just before he dropped into his own seat.

"I can't believe after three years they finally have that man identified," he said with an almost awed expression to his voice.

"I know. I think I was just as shocked as you are."

Charles leaned forward with his elbows on his knees, and his tumbler cradled in his hands before him, similar to William's earlier position. "So, how? Where is the scumbag? When will he go on trial?"

William then told him the particulars of the arrest, just as the DA had until Charles stopped him. "Did he give you a name at least?"

"Oh, yeah," said William, taking the last large gulp of his drink.

"So...don't leave me in suspense, man. Spit it out!"

William looked him straight in the eye without blinking once. "Gregory Wickham."

"Fuck me," murmured Charles. He rose to get himself another glass of scotch, pouring it to the brim before looking back at William. "They're sure?"

"The DA himself came to tell me, Charles. I don't think there's any doubt."

He placed both arms on the bar, leaning heavily. "I can't believe they didn't call Jane to tell her that they had that scumbag in custody!"

William nodded. "I must admit that I'd wondered about that. I think something fell through the cracks somewhere." He put his glass on the coffee table, and watched Charles as he began pacing back and forth.

"Now I understand why you're so agitated. At first, I thought perhaps that you and Lizzy had argued, and I was finding everything rather humorous. I owe you an apology for that."

Shrugging, he shifted in his seat. "You didn't laugh. I would've never known if you hadn't told me."

"How are you going to tell Lizzy? She's going to be overwrought. You do know that?"

"That's the problem. What am I going to do?" William put his head in his hands.

Charles took a long hard look, and sat down in his chair. "You aren't going to let this come between the two of you, *are you?*"

"What if I can't get past this?" he asked sorrowfully. "What if I can and she can't?"

"William, look at me." He looked up to find Charles watching him intently. "You both happen to be victims of the same man. She had nothing to do with your family's deaths, and she never knew anything about it either. I can guarantee it."

"No, I know she didn't have any knowledge of this."

Charles sighed. "I'll never forget the moment when I opened that door and saw her there. He beat her so badly. I still don't know how she and Melly lived."

The images the D.A. had let him see suddenly came to mind, and William grimaced. "I wasn't supposed to say anything, but Jameson showed me the pictures."

"He had the pictures of her from that night?" Charles looked shocked, and William hoped that Jane didn't become angry enough to confront Jameson.

"Yes, they were..." He shook his head as if to clear it. "How does someone do something like that to a pregnant woman?"

Charles returned to his seat and leaned forward. "Wickham never loved her. She was a means to an end in the beginning—a way for his father to pay his living expenses—and then I don't think he had any money to divorce her."

"You should see his mug shot."

His friend's eyebrows lifted. "He looks rough?"

"Well, I don't know what he looked like before."

Charles stood, walked around his desk, and opened a drawer. "Lizzy wanted to get rid of her wedding album, but Jane kept a few of the pictures in the event Melly ever wished to see them." He took out a manila envelope and handed it to William.

He slipped his fingers inside flap and pulled out the largest. Lizzy was dressed in a bouffant, frilly, white dress, obviously picked out by Mrs. Bennet, and was uncomfortably held in the arms of a dark haired man who was standing behind her. He was good looking, smiling at the camera in a charming manner.

"If you hadn't told me this was Wickham, I never would've guessed based on the picture I saw earlier." William's heart clenched to see her in the arms of another man, even if they didn't appear natural together.

Turning his attention back to Lizzy, he examined the expression on her face, and noticed that the smile didn't reach her eyes. He'd seen her truly happy, and she wasn't happy in the photo. Anyone who really knew or cared about her would be able to see that she was faking it.

"What am I supposed to do?" He placed the picture back in the envelope and passed it back to Charles.

"Speak to her. This isn't going to be easy, but the two of you love each other. Isn't she worth trying to get past this?"

"Of course she is!" exclaimed William.

"Then stop questioning everything."

William stopped to think while Charles took a sip of his drink, watching him carefully. He was finding it hard to control his emotions, and rubbed his hands up his face to rid himself of the tear that had fallen from his eye.

His cell phone ringing pierced the silence. The screen showed Lizzy's name and number. Suddenly noticing it was dark outside, he realized she must be worried, and answered without thought.

William?" she cried frantically.

"Lizzy, I'm okay…"

"There's someone outside. I saw a shadow pass outside of the window. I let Bear out…"

"Whoa, what do you mean there's someone outside?" His heart began to pound and he glanced at Charles, who jumped up and grabbed his phone from the desk. William put on the speakerphone so Charles could hear.

"Bear was freaking out at the door earlier, so I let him out. After I put Melly to bed, I went back downstairs and called him, but he never came."

"Did you lock the door?"

"Yes, and I went into the living room, and that's when I saw a shadow pass in front of the living room window. I tried to call you on the home phone, but it doesn't work. I went into the kitchen to

306

get my cell phone, and I think I saw someone by the door to the laundry room."

William looked up and saw Charles dialing what he was sure was 911, so he grabbed his keys off the table.

"Lizzy, I'm with Charles. He's calling the police, and I'm leaving right now." Charles glanced up and acknowledged that his friend was leaving, so William swiftly walked through the house as he continued. "I'm on my way. I'm going out to my car right now."

"I'm scared." Her voice cracked, and the sound of her fear only increased his.

"I know. I want you to go get Melly and lock yourself in your bathroom."

"I locked myself in her room."

"How long have you been in there?" he asked, while he pulled out of the driveway.

"I called you just after I locked the door."

"Okay, just stay there then."

He knew Melly's bathroom didn't have a lock, otherwise he'd have her behind two locked doors rather than one. She couldn't leave the room, though. What if the person was now in the house? He sucked in a shuddering breath while his heart beat a mile a minute. He was terrified. What if something happened to her or Melanie? Greg Wickham and the accident that had previously dominated his mind completely vacated his thoughts. Only Lizzy and Melanie, and the overwhelming fear that something would happen to the family he'd finally found remained.

"I'm on my way. I'm turning on to the highway now."

"Please hurry," she said.

"Just stay on the phone with me. Can you do that?"

"I'm not going anywhere," she joked pitifully.

"What did you and Melly do today?" he asked, hoping to calm her some.

Lizzy was speaking softly through the receiver, recounting how Melly had helped her make bread, when a pair of sheriff's cars came speeding up behind him. Their lights were going and their sirens were blaring, so he pulled to the side and allowed them to pass, speeding up a bit when he pulled back on the road in the hopes they were going to Longbourn.

"I think I'm behind a pair sheriff's cars heading your way," he said, praying it would help alleviate some of her fears. He knew his wouldn't abate until he was holding Lizzy and Melanie in his arms.

"Where are you?"

"Less than five minutes away, and they've pulled way ahead of me."

"Don't drive too fast. I don't want you to get hurt."

He suppressed a nervous chuckle. Lizzy was probably the only woman he knew who would fret that he was going to get injured coming to her rescue.

"I'm almost there, don't worry about me."

He pulled into the drive, and quickly cleared the trees to see three cruisers parked in front of Longbourn with their lights still glowing.

"Lizzy, honey, the sheriff's department is outside."

"I can see the lights flashing on the trees outside the window."

"Stay where you are until they've ensured the house is clear."

"Okay," she said softly. She sounded a bit more hopeful than a few minutes earlier, during what he felt had been the longest ride of his life.

William pulled in front of the house as a deputy came up to the car. He parked and stepped out.

"Sir, I'm going to have to ask you to get back in the car."

"I live here. My girlfriend is locked upstairs in one of the bedrooms with our daughter. I have her on the phone."

"Do you have a key?"

"Yes," he said as he pulled his keys out of the ignition and handed them to the officer, with the house key isolated in his fingers.

"Which bedroom are they hiding in?"

"Second door on the left when you go up the stairs."

"Tell her we're going to ensure the house is clear, and then you can go in to confirm for yourself that she's okay."

William nodded, and locked himself back in the car. "Did you hear?"

"I did. I'm just glad this is almost over."

He could tell she was in tears, and hoped to distract her. "How's Melly?"

"She stirred a bit with the sirens, but she's still asleep. She was exhausted when I put her to bed—she wouldn't take a nap today."

"Again?"

"Yep, I think she's outgrowing them. You know how late she's begun staying up when she takes one. I'm beginning to think the nap isn't worth it." She fell silent for a moment. "William, are they in the house?"

"Yes, they went in after I gave them the key."

"Where could Bear be? What if the person hurt him?" He was worried about Bear too, but he couldn't help but hope that the old dog had gone after the intruder.

"Then he'll get a steak dinner for trying to protect you."

He managed to get her to speak more about the day until he heard a knock on the door through the phone. "Ma'am, I'm Deputy Grant. There's no one inside the house."

"He slid his ID under the door," she whispered.

"They just want you to be sure before you come out." He heard her open the door. "I'll be up there as soon as I can, sweetheart."

"I know. I'm going to hang up."

"Okay," he responded. "I love you."

"I love you, too."

When the sheriff's deputies finally let him into Longbourn, William grabbed Lizzy, and gripped her to him as she began to cry. More officers arrived, and they all began walking outside with flashlights and their weapons as they swept the grounds.

The two of them just stood there embraced for a long time, until William broke the silence. "I need to see Melanie."

She nodded, and led him upstairs, where he sat beside the sleeping little girl on the bed. He kissed her softly on the forehead as he ran his hand through her curls. Pulling Lizzy over, he wrapped an arm around her waist to pull her into his lap.

"We should probably go downstairs, in case we're needed for something," she said, leaning against his shoulder.

He could feel that Lizzy was still shaking, and rubbed his hand up and down her arm. "I know. I just needed to see her, and now I don't want to let either of you out of my sight."

Lizzy straightened some. "She'll be fine," she soothed. William's cell phone rang, so they quickly moved out into the hall, allowing the call to be answered without further disruption to Melanie. They weren't sure how she'd continued to sleep through all of the commotion, but they weren't going to tempt fate.

"William, thank god!" exclaimed Charles. "Are they okay?"

"The deputies have cleared the house, and they're now checking the grounds. Lizzy and Melanie are both fine." He heard Charles relay the information to Jane, who began sobbing in the background.

310

"Can Jane speak to Lizzy?"

"Of course," he answered before he handed the phone over.

Lizzy remained wrapped in his arms, with her forehead against his chest as she answered each of Jane's questions. The next thing he knew, she was dissuading Jane from coming over. "No, you don't need to come out. We're all fine. William's here, and you need to get your rest."

She paused for a moment, and he heard someone clearing their throat behind him. William turned to find Deputy Grant as he heard Lizzy attempting to end the call. "Jane, there's nothing you can do, and I'd rather you take care of yourself and the baby. Yes, I'm sure. I have to go, though. A deputy just came up the stairs and needs to speak with us...I love you, too...I will...I promise."

She hung up the phone and stepped around William, so they could both face the officer. "I apologize. My sister was very worried."

"I understand, ma'am. I just wanted to let you know that the phone line has been cut, and we've found blood with some fabric toward the back of the property. I know that you had the door unlocked while we looked, but I think it'd be best if you keep it secured for now. We'll keep you updated and provide our identification to gain entry if it's required. I have a few of my men ensuring all the doors and windows are locked on the first floor."

"Thank you," they both replied.

He'd turned and was preparing to return back downstairs when Lizzy stepped forward. "Sir, my dog...I let him out before I saw the shadow on the porch. I haven't seen him since."

The expression on the officer's face wasn't promising, and William put his arm around her. "I'm sure they'll let you know if they find him or he's hurt."

William looked up at the deputy while he continued to almost grip Lizzy to him. "He isn't very friendly with strangers, so if you find him, you may want to come and get one of us."

"I understand," Grant responded. "We have a few dogs on the way to help us track whoever this was, so hopefully we'll have some answers for you soon."

They both nodded and followed him downstairs. The last of his men reported that everything was secure, and William locked the door behind them as they continued their work. He had just turned back to face Lizzy when something occurred to him.

"Did you have the windows open upstairs today?"

She looked at him oddly. "Yes, it was a lovely day, why?"

"I may be overdoing it, but perhaps we should make sure they're all locked as well." He took her hand, and once they'd double-checked everything on the second floor, he led her to the kitchen. "I could use a drink. What about you?" Her face was doubtful, but he could still feel a tremor in her hands, and felt they could both stand to relax a bit.

"Don't you think now isn't the greatest time?"

"We aren't getting drunk, Lizzy. Today has been..." he trailed off, running his hand through his hair. He knew he'd have to tell Lizzy about the D.A.'s visit, but he was unsure if he should do it now or later.

"I'm sorry, you had a rough day." She lightly brushed a curl back from his face, placing her hand against his cheek.

He'd craved an almost constant connection with her since he'd arrived at the house, so he took her in his arms and held her tightly against him, his forehead touching hers as tears began to pour down his cheeks.

How could he have thought that Greg Wickham's evil would make a difference in their relationship? He'd been so unhinged at discovering the connection that he'd questioned everything— thought that somehow it mattered. Charles was correct. The only things that had any significance were his feelings for Lizzy, and hers for him. He'd understood that they'd both been victims earlier, but to end his relationship due to that man's actions would only give Greg Wickham the power to hurt them both further. No, *that* wasn't going to happen—*that* would never happen again.

312

He kissed her passionately, attempting to convey everything he felt for her in one kiss. Once their lips parted, he brought her head to his chest and held her close as they both cried out their fears over what could've happened that night.

They simply took comfort from one another without regard for time. William felt Lizzy relax against him and his own tension began to ease until she startled him by carefully pulling away to pour him a glass of scotch and herself a glass of cabernet. The only light on in the kitchen was a small one over the stove, which made the room dim, but also allowed them to see the flashlights as they made their way around the yard, bobbing so that the light flickered like fireflies.

William stood to her side and they watched what they could through the small crack in the sheers as they sipped their drinks. He wrapped his arm back around her, and she leaned in to him. She seemed to need the feeling of safety and security that he was providing just as much as he needed to have contact with her.

They saw dogs making their way across the yard, and he heard her choke back a sob.

"What is it?"

"I'm worried about Bear. It isn't like him to not come back."

"I know. I'm worried, too."

"The deputy said they found blood. Do you think that's why whoever it was never got into the house? Bear stopped him?"

"I think it's probably the explanation, sweetheart."

She began to cry again, and he pulled her closer. "You and your aunt gave him a happy home for a long time. He was thankful for that, and chose to protect you. If that's truly the case, I can only be grateful in return."

They continued to stand there in silence until they heard a knock on the front door and went to see who it was. Deputy Grant was outside, showing his badge, so they quickly opened the door.

"Ma'am, the sheriff is out searching with the K-9 unit, but he asked me to come and inform you that we found your dog."

He saw her expression brighten, and she stepped forward. "You did! Where?" She then turned to see another officer, his dog trailing closely behind him as he carried a bundle in his arms. She gave a strangled cry and made to run out, but William grabbed her around the waist.

The deputy's face showed his sympathy, and he stepped in front of her. "I'm very sorry. We have one group that's currently tracking a torn shirt they found behind the house, near the tree line. The other group tracked from the blood we found on the back porch to your dog."

She inhaled sharply. "When the phone wouldn't work in the living room, I went to the kitchen. I saw the shadow and I thought I heard Bear, but I went upstairs." She began to cry. "If I'd only..."

"Ma'am, if you'd opened the door, you probably would've let the person who killed him into the house."

"I want to see him," she demanded. The deputy gave William a look, and he glanced back at the bundle that was being wrapped in a plastic tarp, seeing blood staining the material.

"I don't think that's a good idea," William said softly.

"I just want to say goodbye."

"The men from the K-9 unit will take good care of him for you," interjected the deputy. "In fact, the deputies who found him were talking of chipping in for his cremation, and would like to bury him for you."

"Is that something they do often?" asked William, genuinely surprised.

"No, but they're considering him killed in the line of duty, and would like to treat him as one of their own."

Lizzy began to sob, and left him to head toward the living room. "Please tell them thank you," he said softly. "We appreciate the consideration."

314

Grant looked in the direction that Lizzy had walked, and replied in a low voice. "He was stabbed and beaten badly. They also have reason to believe he did injure whoever did this before he died."

William closed his eyes, thanking God for Bear's love of Lizzy and Melanie. "You'll let us know if you find anything else?"

"Yes, of course." The deputy gave a sad smile and stepped off the porch, walking toward the K-9 officer's car.

He closed and locked the door so he could return to Lizzy. Taking a seat next to her on the sofa, she leaned against him as she sniffled. "He was really a good dog."

"He was. I'm sorry that he's gone."

"Me, too."

With that, she dissolved into further tears, crying until she fell asleep.

Chapter Twenty-two

Saturday, April 13, 2013

Lizzy startled awake at the sound of a loud knock on the front door. Lifting herself up from where she was lying nestled against William's side on the sofa, she blinked wearily as he turned his head to face her.

"Was that a knock?" he asked groggily.

"I think so."

They both rose, and she glanced at the grandfather clock as she passed, vaguely registering that it was six in the morning. When she reached the door, she pulled it open to find the sheriff, Harold Brandon, standing on the front porch.

"I apologize for waking you, but Deputy Grant indicated that you wished to be kept abreast of what was going on."

"Yes, of course," replied William, who reached around Lizzy to open the door further. "Won't you come in?"

He thanked them, and they brought him into the living room where they all took a seat.

"Would you like some coffee?" asked Lizzy.

"No, thank you, ma'am. I'm sure you'd have to make it, and I don't want to put you out so early in the morning." She nodded as William sat beside her and took her hand. "We managed to track the man who was attempting to break into your home last night to an old stolen truck that he'd parked on a dirt road to the north of the property."

William leaned forward with a look of dread and anticipation. "So you have him in custody?"

"Yes, sir, he had to be brought straight to the emergency room, though. That dog of yours took a good chunk out of his arm, as well as his leg. Both wounds required stitches, and the arm was broken. They were just transporting him to the station when I returned out here."

316

"Who, why..." began Lizzy.

"All I know at the moment, is that his name is Greg Wickham."

Lizzy gasped as her head began to spin, only instead of crying, she became angry—very angry.

"I understood from the 911 call that you know the man?" he asked.

"He's my ex-husband, and there's a restraining order as well as an outstanding warrant for his arrest in Vidalia."

"Actually," interrupted William, "I learned something yesterday, but with everything, I hadn't had a chance to tell you." Puzzled, she turned towards him, trying to understand what he could've learned that would be important at that moment. "The DA came by my office yesterday. Greg Wickham was arrested for possession recently in Vidalia. They had an initial arraignment and let him out on bail, then he disappeared."

Lizzy was confused. "They'd charged him for the night he beat me, and I wasn't notified?" She suddenly started. "Wait, how would you know?"

"Because they took a DNA sample while he was in custody. The sample matched the one of the man who killed my father and sister."

She felt like she was either going to faint or vomit, and placed her hand on the sofa cushion in order to prop herself up. "No!" she exclaimed weakly.

William nodded. "I only discovered this yesterday, and I'd gone to talk to Charles when you called me. With everything going on, there was never a good time to tell you." He gave her a slight shrug of one shoulder. "I'm sorry."

As angry as she was with Greg, she could only be truly worried at William's reaction to the news. He hadn't come straight to her—he'd gone to speak with Charles. Was it possible for her to ever have any semblance of a life without Greg ruining it?

"What will happen now?" she asked herself weakly.

The sheriff glanced between the two of them and cleared his throat in an awkward manner. "Well, we've contacted the police department in Vidalia, and I'm sure we'll hear from the D.A. very soon. I promise that I'll keep you up to date as much as possible."

William placed a hand on her back, but she barely felt it, she was so numb. "I appreciate that, Sheriff."

"Of course, but I feel like I should get back. My K-9 deputies will get in touch with you to arrange for the burial of your dog. Based on the ranting Wickham was doing when we found him, he saved the lives of you and your daughter, ma'am. My men were very impressed with him."

She nodded and vaguely registered William standing and showing the sheriff out. She heard the sound of the door, and William speaking softly before he returned. He came and sat down next to her, scooting close beside her.

"Why don't we go upstairs? I'm sure you're exhausted. We barely slept, and even when you did manage to fall asleep, you were plagued by nightmares."

"Melanie's going to be up in about an hour."

"Then I'll call Mrs. Reynolds. She'll be happy to help out." He took out his phone, and she listened as he briefly explained the previous evening and asked if she'd be able to come take care of Melanie for the day. The conversation was quickly concluded with Mrs. Reynolds' acceptance, so they simply remained cuddled together on the couch until Lizzy voiced the thoughts in her head aloud, ending the silence.

"Am I allowed to have a life that he doesn't try to ruin?"

"Sweetheart..."

"No," she said angrily, pulling away from his side and sitting up. "I admit that it was my stupidity that led me to be married to *that man* in the first place, but every time I'd ever thought he wasn't going to return or I was free, he'd come back to ruin things. Now, on top of everything, he's the one responsible for the last of your family being killed."

318

"You know that I don't blame you, don't you?" She could see his expression, imploring her to believe him, and felt her shoulders slump.

"How can you not? How can you want to have anything to do with us anymore?"

He placed a hand on the side of her face and lifted so that she was looking into his eyes. "Because *you* didn't steal that car. *You* didn't drive that car while intoxicated. I remember that he hadn't contacted you in months when he returned and beat you that night, and that was what...I think a few weeks after the accident. You weren't truly a part of his life, but you're just as much of a victim of his actions as I am."

She began to shake her head, and he pulled her to him. "I'm not going anywhere, Lizzy Gardiner. Do you have any idea how terrified I was that I was going to lose you last night?" He began rubbing her back, and she melted into his embrace. He drew back and put his finger under her chin. "I love *you*. I *want* to marry you."

Her heart wanted to jump with joy, but she still had too many concerns. "But how can you want to marry me? You wouldn't resent me?"

"Not for something *he* did! Don't let his actions keep us apart! He wins at completely destroying your life that way. I won't be his victim for the rest of my life. Will you?"

She could see the truth in his eyes. He was also right. She'd spent the last three years refusing to be Greg Wickham's victim any longer, but here she was allowing it once more. Why was she giving him that power again?

"Lizzy?"

Nodding, she placed her hand on his cheek. "You're right," she said calmly. He leaned forward and placed a firm kiss on her forehead. "Yes."

He drew back with a puzzled expression. "Yes?"

The corner of her mouth quirked up, "Yes, I'll marry you."

His eyes bulged, and she began to laugh for the first time since everything began the day before. "Oh my! That was a statement, not a proposal," exclaimed Lizzy.

"No!" he cried emphatically. "I'll take the yes. I thought you'd want more time."

She shook her head. "No, not unless you do."

He pulled her across his lap and gently brushed his lips against hers. "No, I know exactly what I want."

"You're sure that Greg doesn't matter?"

"I'll admit that when I first found out, I panicked. That's why I was with Charles—I needed to talk. But then you called. You needed me, and all of that flew out of the window. I *knew*." She gazed at the expression that she was sure she would never forget. "I *knew* that none of it mattered. I *knew* I couldn't live without you."

She wrapped her arms around his shoulders and held him tightly. "I love you, too."

He kissed her hair and her cheek, pulling back so they were face to face again. "I want to adopt Melly, too."

"Are you serious?"

He nodded. "You did say that Wickham signed away any rights to her, didn't you?"

"Yes, but..."

"No, there are no buts. I don't want to be just the man she calls daddy, I want to actually be her father in whatever ways are possible. Does that make sense?" Before she could answer, he continued, "As far as she's concerned, I'm her father, and this way, I would be legally, as well. The only thing I couldn't be is biologically, and frankly, I've learned that it doesn't matter. In my heart, she's already mine."

Lizzy felt a tear run down her face as she nodded. One of the most beautiful smiles she'd ever seen appeared on his face, and he hugged her to him tightly. "You're my family. You and Melly," he whispered in her ear. He leaned into the cushions of the sofa while they just held each other. They were just beginning to doze off once more when there was another knock on the door.

"That would be Mrs. Reynolds," William said groggily as he rose to open the door.

William stood and let in the older woman, who was already fussing over them as she came inside.

"There are all kinds of theories bounding through the news about what happened out here. Did you know that press vans are parked out along the highway? It's a good thing you own all this land, or they'd almost be on your doorstep."

"I wonder if the sheriff had to drive through them earlier?" William thought aloud.

"I should say so. He has two deputies at the end of the driveway to ensure they don't block the entrance."

William grabbed his cell phone and made a call, while Lizzy told Mrs. Reynolds in more detail what had occurred the night before. The last thing she explained was what had happened to Bear.

"Oh, the poor dear," she said mournfully. "He was such a sweet thing." Then her eyes returned to Lizzy as a different expression crossed her face. "I'm glad he hurt Wickham though. If only he'd bitten him between the legs. That man deserves to lose a testicle or two."

Lizzy was unable to suppress her chuckle, and Mrs. Reynolds smiled. "Don't worry about Melanie. You and William catch up on your rest."

"Thank you," she replied as her cell phone rang.

"You get that, dear, and I'll go see what I can whip up for breakfast."

The call was from Jane, who hadn't yet heard about Wickham's current arrest. Charles had evidently told her last night of Greg's arrest earlier in the month, as well as his now known link to the Darcy case. As a result, Jane was livid, and was calling to check on her sister before venturing down to the station. She was adamant that she would help put Greg Wickham behind bars for as long as possible.

By the time Jane was off the phone, and William had ended his call, Melanie was awake. Lizzy cuddled with her a bit before Mrs. Reynolds took her to the kitchen for breakfast, so she and William could sneak upstairs.

"I have a security detail coming out to keep the reporters off the property," said William, once they were comfortably situated in bed.

She propped her head on his chest. "Do you really think that's necessary?"

"I hope not, but I'd rather hire someone than have the county pay for it. While the story would make news, the press wouldn't be camped outside of the driveway if the Darcy name wasn't tied to it."

He rolled so they were face to face with their heads on the pillows, their legs entwined. "Do you want a large wedding?"

She smiled, knowing that he wanted to discuss happier topics. "No, I've always dreamed of something small and intimate. My mother insisted on a monstrosity of a wedding eight years ago—puffy, meringue dress and all."

He chuckled and brushed the backs of his fingers down her cheek. "I just wanted to be sure. So, you'd want Jane and Charles? What about any of your friends?"

"No, I think family is good. Would you want to invite your family?"

"Yes, but I'd still marry you without them. Then I wouldn't have to choose between Charles and Richard for my best man."

She slid up next to him and wrapped her leg around his hip, his lip quirked up as she leaned in to tug first his top lip and then his bottom with her own. Meanwhile, his fingers found their way under the bottom edge of her tank top, and he caressed his way to her back, one hand reaching down to cup her rear. Pressing herself as close as she could to his body, she could feel him becoming aroused.

"Are you sure?" he murmured against her lips.

322

"Yes," she whispered, as she again claimed his lips. He groaned and pulled her on top of him.

Despite the proposal and his words, she needed him. She needed reassurance physically of everything he'd said that morning, to lose herself in what they had together.

With the warmer weather she'd been forgoing the pajama pants, so he began removing her panties. Urgent to feel the heat of his skin against hers, she peeled off her top and pressed herself to his body, running her fingers through his hair as he kissed and nibbled his way to her breasts. He lingered there, suckling and nipping until she couldn't take it anymore and whispered his name. His eyes met hers, and he began moving back toward her face, trailing his lips up her neck as she guided his face to hers for an all-consuming kiss. Their tongues tasted and explored while she took his solid length in her hand, running her hand from the base, to the tip, where she gently squeezed.

"Lizzy," he moaned, lifting her to join them together.

She could barely contain her emotions as they began to move with each other. One of her tears fell to his cheekbone, and she kissed it away. "I love you," she whispered near his ear. She scraped her teeth along the lobe and heard him inhale sharply as he began to thrust a bit faster.

"Look at me," he groaned. She pulled back, and they held one another's gaze until her eyes reflexively closed and she dropped her head to his shoulder, biting him to prevent herself from crying out. She barely registered his muted vocalizations as he reached his orgasm.

When they'd recovered, they shifted so that Lizzy was curled against his side with one leg thrown over his, and they remained entwined in that manner while they drifted off to sleep.

Lizzy woke abruptly to find William gone. She lifted herself to sit up, and heard the shower running. Without worrying about a robe, she got out of bed and made her way to the bathroom, smiling when she saw his silhouette through the frosted glass. Carefully, she opened the door just enough to watch him as he stood, his arms against the wall, letting the water run down his back. He opened his eyes and startled.

"I thought you were still asleep."

"I just woke up a minute ago. I missed you."

He smiled, and tugged her in to the running water with him. "That's a problem we can easily solve."

The warm water felt so good on her skin as he held her tightly in his arms. She picked up the bar of soap and lovingly bathed him before he returned the favor, stroking every inch of her skin.

William smiled warmly when he turned off the water. He grabbed a towel and wrapped it around himself before he gently did the same for her. She removed the tangles from her hair with a wide-toothed comb, and then went into the bedroom to select some clothes.

After she pulled on her underclothes, she decided on a pair of jeans and a brown wrap top from the closet. She was fastening her belt around her hips when she felt William's arms snake around her middle.

What captured her attention was not him kissing her shoulder or anything physical. Her line of sight was pulled to a black jewelry box that he was holding in front of her.

"Elizabeth Grace Gardiner," he began softly near her ear. "I love you, and I've come to realize that the one thing that would make me happiest is to have you as my wife."

She felt tears welling in her eyes. "Will you do me the honor of marrying me?"

She turned in his arms, so she could look directly into the brilliant blue of his eyes. "Yes, I'll marry you." He leaned in and kissed her softly yet meaningfully. "You do know that I meant it this morning, don't you?" she quipped with her eyebrow raised.

He laughed as he pulled his arms around her to take the ring out of the box. "I do, but I thought you deserved a real proposal, too."

She was always amazed with how sweet he could be. He slipped the band on her finger, and she looked down so she could examine it. The ring was white gold with three diamonds, the center and largest stone a squared princess cut with two smaller triangular shaped diamonds on either side. The gemstones were beautiful and shone in the sunlight coming through the window.

"William, you shouldn't have bought something so extravagant."

He smiled, running his thumb across the top of the setting. "It was my mother's. I've had it cleaned, and the setting checked and repaired so it would be ready. I hid it here when I moved in."

"I'm surprised it just happens to fit," she commented.

"I had them size it, too."

"But how did you know?"

He began laughing. "The jeweler let me borrow a set of those rings they use, and I checked one night after you fell asleep."

"My, aren't you sneaky." She smiled as she used her most teasing voice.

"Only when I want to surprise you. So, when do you want to get married?"

"Perhaps this summer? I'm not teaching any classes, so we'll have a free schedule for me starting in May."

He nodded. "That makes sense. I'll be the only one who has to make arrangements for work." He scratched the back of his neck. "They're supposed to finish renovating that building behind the garage by mid to late May, so perhaps the end of May? Early June?"

"I think I'd prefer May. Why don't we begin planning for the thirty-first? Since we're only planning a small ceremony—us, Jane, Charles, and I would imagine Mrs. Reynolds, it should be very simple."

"We could travel to England and have the honeymoon at Pemberley. I'm sure Uncle Arthur and Aunt Adelaide would like to meet you, in the event they can't make it here. Mrs. Reynolds and Melly could come with us."

"You want Melly along?"

"Of course, although do not doubt that Mrs. Reynolds will be there so we can have plenty of time to ourselves."

She rolled her eyes with a smile. "I should've known."

"We could also go for a week or two in France or Italy while Melly stays with Mrs. Reynolds at Pemberley."

"An entire week?" she asked rather discomfited at the idea of leaving her little girl for so long.

"We wouldn't be far, and the family owns a jet that we can use, so if she needs us, we'll be able to reach her faster than if she were here." He leaned over so that he was looking at her face. "You can call to check up on her as much as you wish."

"I'm sorry. I truly look forward to that, but I've never left her longer than that weekend when she was with Jane."

"We can worry about the honeymoon later. Why don't we begin planning for those dates. Perhaps we can invite Jane and Charles tomorrow, so we can discuss it with them."

"That sounds good." She looked around. "I think my cell phone is downstairs with Mrs. Reynolds."

They made their way down to the kitchen hand in hand, where they found the lady herself cooking what appeared to be a huge meal.

"Oh, there you two are," she exclaimed as she put something in the oven. Melanie was playing with her kitchen in the corner by the table. "I hope you caught up on some sleep."

"I hope this isn't all for us," said Lizzy, surveying everything on the countertop.

"Your sister called a few hours ago—such a sweet thing. She wanted to see you, so I invited her and Charles to dinner. I hope you don't mind."

326

"No," interjected Lizzy quickly, "of course they're welcome." She felt William kiss her on the head before he walked over and sat on the floor next to Melanie to play with her. "Is there something I can help you with?" She placed her hands on the counter and noticed the woman's eyes grow wide. "Mrs. Reynolds?"

"Oh, dear! I'm so happy for the two of you," she exclaimed before she embraced Lizzy. "I'd hoped, but I didn't think he'd ask so quickly!"

She turned and began walking towards William with her finger pointing. "William Bryan Darcy, you should've known that I'd recognize that ring! You could've given this old woman a heart attack by surprising me this way!"

He laughed and stood to hug her. "We only became engaged this morning. I just couldn't wait to put the ring on her finger."

"Your mother and father would be so proud of you," she said when she'd pulled back from the embrace. "And they'd love Lizzy and this little munchkin." She tickled Melanie, who giggled happily. "Have you discussed a date?"

"We're thinking May thirty-first," he said. "The apartment will be finished, and Lizzy has agreed that you should definitely move in and help out here."

Mrs. Reynolds looked hopefully at Lizzy. "You're sure?"

She shrugged and gave a small smile. "Yes, everything seems to work out well when you're here, so I don't see how that'll change."

"As long as you let me know if you wish to cook, or if I'm stepping on your toes, then nothing will. You've had no problems discussing things with me so far."

"No, ma'am, I don't."

Mrs. Reynolds walked back to the counter to work. "When do they estimate the work finished? I'll need to give notice to my landlord."

"Probably by the end of May, and I think the contractor is giving me that date with the expectation of some rain." He didn't mention that he'd already offered a bonus for completion, as long as the building finished to his satisfaction before June.

They began speaking of the particulars that William and Lizzy had previously discussed for the wedding, including Mrs. Reynolds accompanying them to England. She was happy to do it, and helped promote William's idea of a week in Italy or France for the two of them.

By the time Charles and Jane were due to arrive, the smell of dinner was permeating the old home. William and Lizzy had spent the afternoon with Melanie, playing different games and walking outside, so when the doorbell rang, the three of them went to the foyer to greet Jane and Charles. As Jane followed Charles inside, she lunged forward when she saw Lizzy, hugging her tightly.

"I'm so glad you're all right!"

They separated not long after, when Melanie grabbed her aunt's hand and pulled. Laughing, Jane allowed herself to be led to the living room, where she was told to sit, so Melanie could kiss her stomach. Jane then put her niece's hand on her abdomen so she could feel the baby kick.

"Do you feel that?" asked Jane. Lizzy chuckled at her daughter's wide eyes. The curious child was just reaching down to lift Jane's shirt, so she could try to see what she was feeling, when Mrs. Reynolds interrupted her exploration.

"Melly, would you like to help me with dinner?" Distracted from her endeavor, Melanie slid off the sofa and jumped up and down.

"Yay!" she cried, as she grabbed Mrs. Reynolds' hand. Lizzy caught the happy smile on Mrs. Reynolds' face while her daughter escorted her Nana to the kitchen.

With Melanie gone, the adults turned serious once again. Lizzy scooted closer to Jane. "I'm fine. Let's just hope that Greg stays in jail this time."

Jane grimaced. "I don't think there's much chance of him making bail. The D.A. here is going to request he be held for trial because he left Vidalia and violated the restraining order against you. He thinks he can convince a judge that Wickham is a flight risk, and that he

328

poses further danger to you." She glanced over at Charles. "Honey, would you mind bringing me my briefcase. I forgot it in the car."

Charles chuckled. "I'd never realized forgetfulness was a symptom of pregnancy."

"Hey!" Lizzy and Jane cried while William laughed.

Lizzy, surprised by her sister's information, redirected the conversation back to Greg. "You spoke with the D.A. on a Saturday?"

"When he got word that the man who killed Andrew and Ana Darcy had been brought into custody, he immediately went down to ensure nothing was passed over. The arraignment is first thing on Monday."

Leaning forward in his seat, William took a deep breath. "Did Wickham say what he had planned last night? I mean, he had to have a reason for all of this."

Tears began pooling in Jane's eyes. "I..."

"What is it, Jane?" asked Lizzy. "Just tell me."

"He began ranting and raving like a lunatic when he was taken into custody, screaming how he was going to kill you and 'your brat.' The deputies who drove him to the hospital said he didn't stop the entire ride." A tear fell from Jane's eye. "He's been hiding from creditors, and hadn't realized you'd ever pressed charges."

"How could he not understand that?" asked William incredulously. "Wasn't he served with the restraining order?"

"He was, along with the divorce papers. When I spoke with him today, he claimed that he'd thought that was the end of it. He had no problems staying away." She sighed and leaned back into the sofa. "Apparently, his arrest in Vidalia prompted all of this. When he realized he was facing jail time for beating you, he began thinking of revenge. He even admitted that he'd bribed someone at the University for your phone number." She shook her head. "Anyway, they found meth on him, and they're pretty sure he was high as a kite last night."

"I can't say that it surprises me," muttered Lizzy. "Did the police tell you that he killed Bear?"

Jane's eyes filled with tears and she nodded. "They did. The officers who work with the K-9 unit were pooling their money while I was there." Lizzy felt her sister's hand wrap around her own.

Charles was shaking his head. "I just wish I could get a moment alone with that bastard—for you and for Bear."

"I know, Charles. I feel the same way," William said, nodding.

"I don't want either of you getting in trouble for revenge. Greg Wickham is simply not worth the time or effort." Lizzy caught William's eyes and held them. "Melly and I want you here, with us, and not rotting in some jail cell because you beat the tar out of Greg." She turned toward Charles and pointed her finger. "And you, you have a baby on the way." Charles was nodding his head when Jane's voice gained her attention.

"I doubt you would recognize Greg if you saw him. He's...well, he's a lot different."

"That began the last year or so before Melly was born." She was speaking softly as she shook her head.

"It still surprised me. I'm *still* upset that neither of us was notified. I can only guess that because it's been a few years, we fell through the cracks." Jane reached over and took Lizzy's hand. "I'm just relieved you're okay. I was so terrified last night." Lizzy felt her sister's finger cross her engagement ring, and she glanced up to see Jane start and her eyes widen as she looked down. "Ummm...Lizzy, is that an engagement ring?"

Lizzy smiled. "We were going to invite you over to tell you, but Mrs. Reynolds beat us to it."

"I'm so happy for you," she gushed as she embraced Lizzy, tears again streaming down her face. "When did this happen?" She stood to hug William, who'd moved closer in expectation of Jane's congratulatory gesture.

"This morning," he explained. "We've tentatively set a date for the end of May."

"You'll be my matron of honor won't you?"

"I was last time, despite my reservations, so you know that this time, I wouldn't miss it for the world." Jane placed her hand on her bulging belly. "You could've waited a bit so I wouldn't be a beached whale."

"You look lovely, Jane."

"We'll need to go dress shopping," said Jane, with a gleam in her eye. "This time you can choose something you like, versus Mom's taste."

"I'd like that." Lizzy rolled her eyes.

Charles returned through the doors and Jane pivoted. "They're engaged!"

He stopped in place with a stupefied expression on his face. "What? When?"

"This morning," explained William. "I was hoping you'd be my best man."

"Of course," he replied as he began to chuckle. "I guess I shouldn't be surprised. Once either of you gets an idea in your head, you go for it. Congratulations." A wide smile broke out across his face. He set down the briefcase and gave William a slapping hug on the back. "Have the two of you decided on a date?"

William informed him of what they'd already planned, and then discussed the ideas for the wedding until Mrs. Reynolds came in to tell them dinner was ready. Melanie joined them in the dining room, pulling Mrs. Reynolds with her, despite the older woman's protests that she belonged in the kitchen. At William and Lizzy's insistence, Mrs. Reynolds joined them for their celebration, and then returned behind the swinging door to take care of the mess. Lizzy had to admit, when the evening was over, that she didn't miss doing the dishes or cleaning the kitchen at all.

Chapter Twenty-three

<u>Friday, April 26, 2013</u>

"I can't believe you're trying on something with ruffles, Lizzy. Are you sure you don't want mom here to shop with you?" teased Jane, who was comfortably ensconced in a plush armchair while her sister changed.

Lizzy opened the door to the dressing room to see her sister's wide smile and laughed. "Bite your tongue! It isn't a big frou frou mess like she'd pick out."

"No, it definitely lacks the scads of lace that she'd prefer, but it *is* different than anything you've ever liked in the past."

Lizzy stepped up on to a podium that stood in front of the large three-way mirror, and surveyed her reflection from head to toe. "What do you think?" She tilted her head and looked critically at the gown. The style was off the shoulder with a sleek bodice that led to an asymmetrical waistline, a flower or star shaped pin accenting the higher end where the floor-length skirt then descended in layers of filmy organza ruffles. The effect was not gaudy, but elegant. She looked at Jane's reflection in time to catch her wiping a tear before it ruined her mascara.

"It doesn't matter what I think, even if I happen to think it's beautiful and perfect. Do you like it?"

"I really do." Lizzy allowed her face to break out in a large smile. "I probably would've never tried it on if the sales girl hadn't suggested it, but I love it." Her expression changed to show a bit of doubt. "But do you think it's a bit much for just a few people?"

Her sister pulled herself up and waddled around to stand between Lizzy and the mirror. "It doesn't matter how many people will be there. This is *the* day—the one you dreamed of as a little girl, and you did have a dream because I remember you telling me." She took her hand and squeezed. "You get whatever dress you want, even if it's the most ornate one in this place."

Lizzy laughed. "I don't think so." She pivoted so she could see the back, which was similar to the front, except for the row of decorative buttons that concealed the zipper.

Jane returned to her plush chair and plopped down as gracefully as she could. "I only hope that I can get my body back like you did once this little guy is out in the world."

"I'm sure—wait, did you say little guy?"

Biting her lip, Jane did all she could not to smile. "I'm really not supposed to tell. Charles and I agreed to keep it a secret."

Lizzy put her hand on her hip. "And I'm your best and favorite sister, we don't keep secrets."

"Yes," she said, rolling her eyes with a huge smile, "we're having a boy."

"Oh!" Lizzy stepped down and hugged her sister tightly. "I'm so happy for you!" When she was standing straight once again, she clapped her hands together. "So, what's the theme for the baby's room? You know I'm going to paint him a whole room full of artwork."

Jane laughed. "We've decided on trains. Charles put together the furniture last week, and I have a conductor's hat and a few decorative engines I found. Some paintings would be wonderful, though."

"I'll have to pick up a couple of canvases and some extra acrylics on my way home today. Are you using pastels or darker colors?"

Jane shook her head. "More of a lighter muted shade of most of the colors. I prefer blues and greens though.

"Oh!" Jane exclaimed. "I meant to tell you earlier. I've heard back from family court. The hearing is scheduled for July twenty-fifth."

"That's good. We'll have plenty of time before we need to be back from England. Although, I'm sure we'll be back for the birth."

"Good, because I want you here," exclaimed Jane. "I'm so happy that everything worked out between the two of you. He's such a good guy. Both of you deserved to find each other."

Rachel, the sales girl, came walking back in. "What do you think?"

Both ladies smiled. "It's perfect," replied Lizzy.

The young woman grinned widely as she came to a stop before them. "Then I guess we should go look at some veils."

Lizzy looked over to Jane and lifted her eyebrows. "Veils? Do I want a veil?"

"Of course, Perhaps we could put your hair up in some kind of up do and the veil could hang from underneath—understated, elegant."

"I'll have to check and see what hairstyles I can find on the internet," Lizzy thought aloud as they began following Rachel toward where the veils were on display.

"We also have a portion of the boutique dedicated to bridal lingerie, if you care to take a look," Rachel said as she led the way.

"What do you think, Lizzy?"

Lizzy smiled widely with a hint of a blush on her face. "Why not?"

William walked in after work to find Mrs. Reynolds cooking in the kitchen. Smiling, he placed his suit coat over a chair, and his briefcase on the floor against the wall.

"Something smells wonderful," he said as she bustled over to grab his things. "I'll do that in a bit. I wanted to greet Lizzy and Melly first."

"Now, you know I don't mind." He picked up his satchel so she wouldn't have to bend over. "The chili will be ready in thirty minutes. The ladies are in the studio."

He grinned widely. Since the incident just before Melanie's birthday, he'd discussed his preference of having their daughter at home with Mrs. Reynolds, as opposed to the campus childcare center. He felt with what happened, she was safer, and she most certainly wasn't suffering for it.

Jane had called a few days ago to inform them that the Vidalia prosecutor had offered Wickham a plea deal for the assault against

334

Lizzy, so all they were waiting on were the trials in Meryton. On top of everything, Charles let them know that Caroline had been hospitalized again. Their worries were diminishing by the day.

Mrs. Reynolds moved toward the front of the house, and he turned to make his way through the back mudroom and laundry room to Lizzy's studio. When he walked through the door, Melanie was on the floor with a cup of water and a paint with water book.

He gave her a quick kiss on the cheek as she continued to ignore him, engrossed in smearing all of the colors of the kitten together on the page, but when he crept up behind Lizzy, he could see her working on a small canvas.

"You don't normally paint on those," he commented.

"They're for the baby," she said, happily. "Jane confessed today that they're having a boy."

"So the two of you discussed more than dresses while you shopped?"

She smiled. "Yes, we did. She let the sex slip, and I told her that I wanted to paint something for the baby's room for a gift, so she let me know what they liked."

"A train?"

"The things she's picked out for bedding and decor are all trains and such, so I'm going to paint a series of things for all over the room. I have a watercolor drying before I can add more detail, and I am also making a few paintings on canvas."

"You're going all out," he said with a smile.

"Well, they did a lot for me when Melly was born, and it's not everyday that we become godparents." He heard the defensive tone of Lizzy's voice, and realized she hadn't understood that he was simply making a comment.

"I wasn't criticizing, sweetheart. I think it's wonderful." She turned and looked up at him with a happy smile, and unable to resist, he leaned down to give her a lingering kiss. "Is my name also going on the card?"

"I was thinking it would be from both of us," she responded with a frown. "Unless you have a different gift you'd like to give."

"No, I was hoping you were including me, but I wanted to be sure. I didn't want there to be nothing from his godfather."

She picked up her brushes and stood. "I still want to get him an outfit, but I thought I'd wait until closer to the birth." He followed as she went to the sink in the laundry room and began rinsing her brushes. "Would you get Melly's water so I can dump it out? I think she's soaked those pages long enough."

He chuckled and retrieved the cup. As Melanie stood, she looked at William.

"I wanna play with Bear."

She'd asked a few days after the scare with Wickham, and they'd explained that Bear had needed to go away, but she still brought it up from time to time.

"Sweetheart," he began gently. "Bear loves you and misses you very much, but he had to go away, remember?"

"I want Bear!" she exclaimed petulantly.

"I know. We all miss him, but he can't come to play. I'm sorry."

Lizzy came up behind him and sat on her knees. "I want a hug from my Melly Belly." Her daughter turned and wrapped her arms around her mother, as Lizzy whispered in her ear. "Nana said there are cookies for after dinner."

Melanie abruptly pulled back from her mother's embrace. "Cookies?"

"Why don't you go find her, and tell her we're ready for dinner." They watched as she ran on her tiptoes from the room. Lizzy turned to William. "I think we need to begin redirecting her when she asks."

"I don't want to avoid things because it's difficult."

"We're not. She's too young to understand death, and as far as she's concerned, he should be able to come back and play with her. We've explained to her that he had to go away and that he loves her more than once." She entwined her fingers with William's as she stepped closer. "We're not being unfeeling by avoiding it. She's just too young to really understand."

He nodded sadly. "I feel so bad when she asks. Perhaps we should find a puppy to replace him."

"I feel bad too, but I don't know. Maybe after we return from Europe. I don't want to drop an untrained puppy on Charles and Jane while we're away." Realizing she was correct, he nodded. "Melly is asking about Bear less than she was. She'll be okay." Lizzy bent over to begin picking up Melanie's mess, and he joined her. When everything was cleaned up, the two of them made their way to the kitchen for dinner. Wanting to lighten the mood, William thought about the wedding and smiled.

"You didn't tell me if you found a dress today."

"Perhaps," she said, beaming.

"You won't tell me?"

"I want it to be a surprise, so I don't want to unknowingly give you any hints." She leaned in to his ear as she whispered. "Although, I will say that we also shopped for lingerie for the wedding night." She took a few steps backward into the kitchen as she gave him a flirtatious look.

He chuckled, glancing to see that Mrs. Reynolds had returned, and shook his head. She'd known he couldn't retaliate for her tease. He enjoyed that she seemed to be becoming a bit bolder, and seemingly more confident with him. He took it as a sign that she felt more comfortable with their relationship. Time and his presence would be the only cure to the insecurities that remained, but he had plenty of both, and he surely wasn't going anywhere.

They took their seats around the table, and he took a bite just as he felt Lizzy's bare foot slide up his calf to his knee, and then between his legs. He peered over to see her trying not to smile while she watched his reaction. One thing he was learning quickly, life with Lizzy would definitely never be boring.

Mrs. Reynolds left for her own home after she'd cleaned up the mess from dinner. William gave Melanie her bath, and after she was in her pajamas, they both tucked her into bed for the night. When she was finally fast asleep, William pulled Lizzy to him and softly kissed her neck.

"I thought we could turn in early tonight," he whispered against her ear. He felt her shiver in response and smiled. "Unless you have something you'd rather do?"

"No, but we should make sure all the lights are out and the doors are locked."

All day, William had been looking forward to pressing Lizzy down into the plush mattress and making her writhe beneath him, and she'd only made things worse with her game of footsie at the table. Once they were sure everything was secure for the night, he led her up the stairs, where they undressed one another and fell into bed. Lizzy didn't disappoint, and he found it very difficult to hold back, letting himself go only after she cried out in release. When he was completely spent, he rolled off of her and pulled her close.

"I've been thinking about that all day."

She smiled as she brushed some hair back from his face. "I'll bet that made for an interesting time at work. I hope none of your meetings noticed."

He laughed and pinched her behind.

"Ow! I had some news, but if you're going to pinch me, I don't know if I should tell," she pouted while she removed a hand from his side to rub her rear.

"You can't tell me that and then not share."

"What do I get if I do?" Her arm slinked back along his side. He smiled, thoroughly enjoying the raised eyebrow and the suggestive tone she used.

"I'm sure something would come up," he replied in a husky voice.

"Jane told me that we have our court date."

His heart jumped and a smile came to his lips. "When?"

"July twenty-fifth," she responded.

"So, we can definitely have the whole month of June in England." He was happy they wouldn't have to return in a hurry. He wanted a chance to relax for a few weeks, and then spend a week in the London office before their return. "That's great! That'll allow me to spend a week working over there as well. Oh! I meant to tell you that I heard from Uncle Arthur today."

"Do they want to come for the wedding?"

"Yes, they'd like to see Longbourn, and Uncle Arthur wants to visit the offices here. He hasn't been in some time."

She nodded. "We'll have to get new linens and such for the spare bedrooms. Neither Aunt Mel, nor I ever entertained many guests."

"That shouldn't be a problem. We can go this weekend if you'd like." William loved spoiling Lizzy and, despite her resistance, looked forward to taking her shopping. "The progress on Mrs. Reynolds' apartment is going well, so she should be moved in by then. I'm glad you agreed to let her begin working now. I like knowing Melly is here with her."

"Eventually, she'll have to start school, you know."

"I know, but that's not for another two years, and she has a few friends with that tadpole swimming class you take her to periodically. Besides, Meryton Academy isn't far from here, and it's much smaller than the local public schools."

"It's also a small fortune," gasped Lizzy with wide eyes.

"She'll have the best education there, and I like that it isn't large." He watched as Lizzy shook her head and smiled. "I can't help it if I want the two of you to have the best."

"It's very sweet," she replied, kissing him softly.

Saturday, May 11, 2013

William waved goodbye as Charles' car pulled away from Longbourn early that morning. He'd managed to wake and rise earlier than usual without rousing Lizzy. Fortunately, Melanie wasn't sleeping heavily, so he was able to get her up quickly, exciting her with the prospect of a slumber party with Aunt Jane and Uncle Charles.

Melanie hadn't spent a night apart from Lizzy since William had returned from his business trip in March, and he really wanted to surprise Lizzy with some alone time for her birthday. So, he'd asked Charles and Jane if they would mind keeping her, and since they were always happy to spend time with Melanie, they quickly agreed.

He crept back inside and into the kitchen. Mrs. Reynolds, another co-conspirator, had prepared a quiche that he'd already put in the oven to warm as per her instructions. Checking the pantry, he found the tray that he'd purchased to use that day; it was still hidden on the top shelf in the very back corner. William chuckled to himself, proud of the perfect hiding spot he'd found. Lizzy wasn't short, but she didn't like taking out the stepladder, so she only had things that she rarely used up there.

Once the tray was washed and dried, he placed the quiche with some strawberries on a plate. He placed her cup of coffee on the tray, followed by some fresh pink roses and calla lilies in a crystal bud vase he'd found in the china cabinet. He'd thanked Charles profusely that morning when he'd arrived with the blooms in hand. William had been worried about his ability to hide them, and had enlisted Charles to hold them at Netherfield for the night.

He turned everything off, and carefully carried everything upstairs, but once he opened the door, he frowned to see that Lizzy wasn't in bed. A minute later, she emerged from the bathroom and stopped.

"What are you up to?" she asked with an enormous smile.

"Happy Birthday, sweetheart."

She laughed, and reached down to the bed for her pajama pants. "This is beautiful, but Melly will be up soon. Perhaps we should take it to the kitchen?"

The tray was quickly placed on the foot of the bed, and he moved to take her in his arms. "Melly is with Uncle Charles and Aunt Jane." He watched her eyes grow wide, and worried that perhaps he had been a bit presumptuous.

"When...How?"

"I asked them last week, and they agreed. Charles was here at seven this morning to pick her up." He combed some of her hair from her face with his fingers. "Are you mad?"

She jumped a bit as if she was thinking about something else. "No, I'm just surprised is all. When are we due to go get her?"

"Tomorrow," he replied tentatively. "Jane and Charles have a special dinner planned, so you can have a birthday with Melly, too." He leaned in and brushed his lips softly against hers. She responded, and he knew that she was not truly angry.

"Are you hungry?" he asked as he pulled back.

"Yes, it smells wonderful!"

He pulled her over to the bed, and had her return under the covers. The tray was placed on her lap, and she picked up the flowers, smelling them and putting them on her bedside table.

"I love roses and lilies. They're beautiful, thank you."

"Not nearly as beautiful as you."

She laughed. "You've been practicing your smooth compliments."

"Of course," he replied in a cocky manner. She smiled and rolled her eyes just before she took a bite of her food.

"This is really good," she moaned. "Have you eaten?"

"Did you think I'd brought almost half a quiche just for you?"

She smiled saucily. "I'd hoped."

He shook his head and chuckled as she held her fork in front of him, offering him a bite. They leisurely ate their breakfast, and when they were done, he moved the tray to the floor, so they could cuddle under the covers.

She began laughing when he pulled off the sweatpants and t-shirt he was wearing. "Too many clothes," he complained, and began unceremoniously ridding her of her pajamas and panties. When they were situated once more, he entwined his legs with hers and began caressing her thigh.

"Lizzy," he began pulling her a bit closer. "What would you think about getting off the pill now and trying to get pregnant?"

"You're full of surprises this morning." She began to trace her fingers along his chest as she watched, avoiding his eyes. He knew that it wasn't a good sign. "Eventually, I want to have another baby, perhaps two, but not right now."

He put his bent index finger under her chin, and lifted it so their eyes met. "I hope you don't think I'd be angry if you said no?"

"No, it's not that, but I didn't want to see you disappointed."

His fingers traced her jawline and into her hair. "I want another child with you, but not at the expense of your happiness. Just know that I'm ready whenever you are."

She gave a small smile. "I'm not ready to split our time more than it already is. We get so little of it that's just the two of us, and that will virtually disappear with another child."

"We'd still have our dates, so that wouldn't change."

"It would at first, while I recuperate, and because we'll be up at all hours of the night with diapers and feedings. Then there's the possibility that the baby will refuse to take a bottle, so then we'd be limited even more."

"You worked while Melly was a baby, so she obviously took a bottle."

"She hated them. The ladies at the center sometimes managed to get her to take one, but I usually had to feed her just before my class, and then I'd have a three to four hour window before I had to return."

342

He nodded, and pulled her flush to his body. "So, we're just going to keep practicing then?"

Lizzy grinned. "We should be very proficient when the time comes."

"That's the basic idea." He claimed her lips, alternating between the top and bottom, softly caressing them. Her hand cupped his face, and he pulled back to look into her eyes.

"You aren't going to have any crazy rules like no sex for a week or two before the wedding, are you?" he asked.

She chuckled and lowered herself so her face was against his shoulder. "Before I met you, I probably wouldn't have minded, but now—no way."

He understood what she was implying without explanation, and kissed her shoulder before he lifted her face up so he could see her eyes. "I love you."

She smiled beautifully. "I love you, too."

"Do you want your birthday present?" he asked, no longer able to wait.

She rolled off of him and cuddled up under the covers. "I thought I told you that you didn't have to buy anything."

"You knew that I wouldn't accept that."

"I did, but I wanted to try," she explained, smiling.

He leaned over the side of the bed and pulled a package from underneath, placing it in her lap when he was situated once more. She gave him a sideways glance as she pulled the ribbon and the paper before opening the box inside to reveal a set of paintbrushes.

She examined several of the brushes, touching the bristles and lightly running them on her hand. "These are sable. William, I love sable brushes, but they're expensive. Camel or squirrel work well also, and are significantly cheaper."

"I asked the woman at the supply store which the best were, and these were the ones she indicated. Besides, you need them. I've noticed that yours are getting pretty worn." He picked up a brush that looked a lot like a fan, due to the way the bristles were arranged. "They only had camel in a couple, so they aren't all sable."

"*One* isn't," she laughed. "I do need them, and I was putting off buying more, so thank you." She leaned forward and kissed him softly. "It was a very thoughtful gift."

He took the box and reached into his bedside table for another. "One more." He placed the wrapped jewelry box in her lap. "I know you love gifts, so open it."

She smiled as she pulled the wrapping paper away, and then opened the deep burgundy velvet box. He heard with satisfaction her small gasp when she laid eyes on the pearl and diamond necklace.

"It's lovely," she gushed softly. "Is it an antique?"

"It was my grandmother's. I thought you might like it."

"I love it." She fingered the large pearl surrounded by a sunburst pattern with small diamonds. "Especially since it's a family heirloom."

He handed her an unwrapped box that she opened to reveal a smaller set of pearl earrings with a small diamond accent at the top. "My mother bought these to go with it. I don't know what you planned to wear with your dress at the wedding, but I wanted you to have the option."

She closed the boxes and placed them on the bedside table. Rolling back against him, she wrapped her legs around his hips and thanked him liberally with her actions, rather than words.

Chapter Twenty-four

Lizzy adjusted the bow on her daughter's ponytail and combed her fingers through her curls, attempting to loosen them a bit. She had liked to wear pretty clothes when she was little, but not to the extent Melanie did. The little girl now only wanted dresses, and refused to wear any kind of pants, shorts, or even skirts. Lizzy was sometimes frustrated by her recalcitrance, especially when her daughter wished to play outside, but the little girl couldn't be persuaded to wear anything else. William was no help either. He'd only seen something he could indulge in her, and had taken to coming home with a new dress or pretty bow from time to time, thoroughly enjoying the light that came into his daughter's eyes at the gift.

She sighed as she looked down at her daughter. Today's white sundress was a perfect example. The garment was adorable with the eyelet pattern around the hem, but Lizzy would've *never* bought white. She wondered if the dress would even make it beyond today, because as soon as Melly went outside, she was sure to find mud or smear pollen on it from the flowers in the courtyard. Mrs. Reynolds had fussed over the new dress and how pretty Melanie would look in it, but then she would probably be bleach-happy when it came to keeping it true to color.

She stood and walked around in front of where Melanie was sitting on the bed, looking down as she played with her stuffed animal.

"Are you ready?

"Yes! I want to play with Nana!" She scooted off the bed and ran on her tiptoes for her bedroom door. Her daughter was thrilled when Mrs. Reynolds had finally moved into the renovated one-room cottage behind the garage a few days ago. The contractors had endured very few delays, thanks to the cooperative weather and long workdays, so the progress had been swift. The grandmotherly woman sometimes made an adventure out of taking Melanie back there for a game, or simply to fetch something she required.

"Nana is busy cooking. Do you want to go outside and pick pansies?"

"Yeah!"

Lizzy was relieved she agreed so easily. Mrs. Reynolds always seemed to cook copious amounts of food, but judging by the supplies spread out on the island this morning, she was preparing more than usual.

William's uncle and aunt, along with their son, Richard, were arriving today, and Mrs. Reynolds had begun working on dinner just after she cleaned up the mess from breakfast. Lizzy was nervous, and looked carefully at Melanie's little summer dress, hoping she, at the very least, didn't become filthy before William returned with his family. Perhaps if she smeared her dirty fingers on it, he would then understand why white was such a bad idea.

When they reached the kitchen, Mrs. Reynolds looked up from rolling out piecrust and grinned. "Don't you look like a princess!" she exclaimed, prompting Melanie to twirl and put her little hand on her hip.

Lizzy could see the older woman suppressing a chuckle as their eyes met. "The two of you are going outside?"

"I'm going to let Melly pick some pansies and perhaps we'll take a walk through the dogwoods."

Mrs. Reynolds looked wistfully through the back window. "The dogwoods were so beautiful when they bloomed. I only wish they'd lasted longer."

"I know," replied Lizzy. "My aunt and I would make that comment every year."

"I've never seen as many as you have back there growing on their own. I've seen clusters that have been planted, but not just naturally occurring."

Lizzy looked down and found her daughter pulling at her hand. "Mommmmaa, let's go," she exclaimed in an exasperated voice. Biting her lip, she waved at Mrs. Reynolds and followed Melanie to the mudroom, where they both put on their sandals and exited the back door to the porch.

Pansies were always one of her favorite flowers to plant, and she had them lining several of the beds. She helped Melanie pick a few, and then they walked through the backyard for a little while. When it

346

became close to lunchtime, they returned to the courtyard, so her daughter could pick some more pansies to put inside a small vase.

Melanie had just about finished picking a small cluster when Lizzy's attention was drawn up by the sound of the back door opening.

The car William hired for the drive to the airport and back pulled up into the circle in front of Longbourn.

"This is lovely," his Aunt Adelaide commented as she scanned the house and the front yard. A small smile graced her face as she took in the pansies that lined the drive.

"It's been in the Gardiner family for over two hundred years." He opened the door and exited, holding out his hand for his aunt, who followed. "Lizzy, her sister, Jane, and her great aunt have done everything they can to keep it in the family." He knew his aunt and uncle could appreciate the thought, since it was something they'd all strived to do with Pemberley and Matlock.

His uncle stood, surveying the property while they waited for Richard. "There's no Gardiner son or grandson to keep the name with the estate?"

"No, Lizzy's mother was the last born Gardiner."

"But Lizzy's last name is Gardiner," Richard commented, from where he stood next to his father.

"She changed her name after her divorce. Her relationship with her parents has never been good, and she always felt her aunt was more of a mother to her than her own."

His cousin raised his eyebrows. "I'd just assumed Jane's maiden name was Gardiner."

"No, Jane used her father's name of Bennet until she married Bingley."

They paid and tipped the driver, who unloaded the bags as William and Richard moved them, placing them in the appropriate rooms so Mrs. Reynolds wouldn't insist upon taking on the task herself. Once everything was in the house, William joined his family, who were mulling around the foyer and living room.

"The Bingleys should be here around four," he said, glancing at the grandfather clock that read quarter after twelve. "Mrs. Reynolds told me she would have a light lunch prepared, and then there should be plenty of time to rest before dinner."

Mrs. Reynolds came bustling out of the kitchen and grinned widely. "I thought I heard someone out here. It's a pleasure to see you again, Lord and Lady Matlock."

"I thought we cleared that up years ago, Lyla," said Adelaide Fitzwilliam with a huff. "There's no need to be so formal with us."

"We had, but like you said, it's been years." She turned her attention to William. "Lizzy is in the courtyard with Melly, picking flowers." William beamed as Mrs. Reynolds bustled back into the kitchen.

"Would you like to meet Lizzy and Melanie?"

"That's why they're here, isn't it?" quipped Richard dryly.

His uncle gave a snort, and his aunt rolled her eyes. "Perhaps you should find someone of your own, and stop giving your cousin a difficult time. What was the name of that last girl you dated?" Richard turned a few shades of red, and William grinned widely, leaning against the banister to watch.

Aunt Adelaide gave a rather satisfied smile. "That's right, I believe it was Penelope. She was barely twenty, according to the tabloid reports of your *dates*."

William smiled smugly, and Richard turned to glare at him. "Oh, shut up. She was very entertaining."

But his aunt was unfazed. "I don't care to hear your ideas of entertainment. Find someone closer to your own age, and get your bum out of the headlines."

Richard laughed incredulously. "What did I do to deserve this?"

348

"Your cousin has kept his private life out of the papers, and he's found someone he loves and is settling down. You don't have to tease him about it."

"He knows I'm having a bit of fun with him, don't you?" Richard looked to William, who was having a difficult time controlling his laughter, to back him up.

"I do, Aunt," he managed to get out. "I'm used to it."

His aunt's expression was still doubtful. "When he begins behaving as an adult, then he can tease you for already being one."

"What's the fun in that?" asked Richard while his father joined his cousin laughing.

William offered his aunt his arm, and he led them through the hall. He could see Lizzy bending over to help Melanie through the glass of the French doors, and he turned the knob, leading his family outside to the porch.

When she looked up, she stole his breath away. She was dressed in a simple red sundress, with her hair flowing in long curly locks around her shoulders. He was still reeling at the idea that they would be married in less than a week. She took Melanie's hand as they stepped forward.

"It's good to see you again, Lizzy," greeted Richard warmly. He kissed her cheek and then looked at William, surprised that he wasn't scowling.

"She may find you amusing from time to time, but she's marrying me," William quipped, much to his aunt and uncle's entertainment. He placed his arm around her shoulders, and held out his hand gesturing towards his relations.

"Lizzy, this is my Uncle Arthur and my Aunt Adelaide Fitzwilliam, Richard's parents."

She smiled as she took his uncle's proffered hand, and then greeted his aunt, who took his fiancée's hand with both of hers. "It's lovely to finally meet you, dear."

"Yes, it's nice to finally meet you as well. William speaks of you often."

"He's always been such a sweet boy. We're just glad to see him so happy."

William noticed Melanie as she took to ducking behind her mother's skirt, and whisked her into his arms. "I'd also like you to meet our daughter, Melanie."

He'd told his aunt and uncle a little of Melanie's father, but informed them that she'd taken to calling him Daddy, as well as the pending adoption, so they wouldn't be taken by surprise. They both greeted the toddler, despite the fact that she was, for some reason, being shy, hiding her face against William's broad shoulders.

Mrs. Reynolds called them inside, and they were soon seated in the dining room where she'd set a light luncheon of bread, cheese, and fruit, so no one was overstuffed for the large dinner that evening.

"I understand you're an artist?" asked his aunt as they began to eat.

Lizzy placed some cheese and fruit on Melanie's plate. "I am. I predominantly paint watercolor landscapes."

"She did a wonderful rendering of Pemberley. You'll need to come by the office one day this week so you can see it."

His aunt smiled warmly. "There are plenty of lovely views in Derbyshire. Perhaps William can take you to view some of them while you're in England."

"He's mentioned it. I plan on bringing my camera and lenses, so I can take plenty of pictures." Her excitement showed in her eyes, and William suppressed a chuckle at the image of him following her around with her bag while she took photographs of everything.

"You don't prefer to work like the Impressionists?" His aunt had a teasing smile on her face, and despite her friendly appearance, William knew that she was testing Lizzy to see if she was just someone who knew how to paint pretty pictures or truly knew about art.

350

"No, I'm not one for working outdoors," Lizzy laughed. "I like to take my time, and the lighting isn't constant. I much prefer a still photo that I can make larger on my computer."

"Aren't you limited by the printer on the size?" inquired Uncle Arthur.

"There are websites where you can make a poster, and it prints out in sections on regular letter size paper, though they omit small sections of the photo at the margins, which can be problematic. I've also gone to the local office supply store and made larger printouts."

His uncle nodded and, not one to be overly interested in art, changed the subject. "William was telling us about the wedding venue across the pond. I would be very interested to hear more."

"Jane, Lizzy's sister, and their friend, Charlotte Lucas, began the operation."

"William's correct. I actually have very little to do with any of that. I have a key to the premises, if you'd care for a tour, but if you're more concerned with the business side, you'll have to ask Jane when she comes tonight."

"I'd like a tour," he clarified. "As long as you have some time for it today."

"Of course," Lizzy responded.

Uncle Arthur sat back in his seat. "We tried a few weddings at Matlock, but…"

"Arthur doesn't mind the tours during the day, but he abhorred the noise from the wedding reception," Aunt Adelaide interjected.

"Exactly," continued Uncle Arthur, "we no longer use the stables, so when William mentioned that your reception hall resembled a barn, I began to consider a renovation."

"I understand," said Lizzy, as she nodded. "There are many antebellum homes in the area that have tours, but I don't wish for people coming in and out of Longbourn all day long. This is a way to fund the upkeep of the property without all the traffic."

"Unfortunately, Matlock and Pemberley are much bigger and older," explained William. "The upkeep and renovations required to keep them in good repair are costly. We're also able to close sections of the homes and isolate ourselves from the tourists. It would be harder to do that here."

"I can definitely understand how the cost of renovating them might be so high. Longbourn's upkeep is rather expensive, and I'm sure it doesn't entail even half of what your estates require."

Richard, who was sitting across from Melanie, leaned down to catch the little girl's eye and winked. "Do you remember me?"

Melanie must have become a bit more comfortable since she practically batted her eyelashes at Richard and giggled.

"Not while she's eating," scolded Aunt Adelaide.

"I was just saying hello."

"Yes, but she could've decided to be shy, and then not eat for the remainder of the meal."

Richard rolled his eyes while everyone else chuckled. He glanced around and then looked up. "By the way, what *is* that?" He pointed up to a carved wooden piece hanging from the ceiling. "I've been sitting here trying to figure it out, and the purpose just escapes me."

Lizzy laughed. "It's a fan. Before air conditioning, someone would stand over on the side of the room, there." She pointed to a place on the wall where a rope was hanging disguised against the drapes, "and pull the rope causing it to sway back and forth, creating a slight breeze."

"So, something like fanning with palm fronds," he joked with a smirk.

"I would think the palm works better," Lizzy smiled.

William took in everyone at the table. The conversation remained light as the Fitzwilliams and Lizzy learned about one another. The introduction had gone better than he'd expected, and he only hoped his aunt and uncle would truly like Lizzy. They were inclined to accept her, but that wasn't the same.

Just after the meal, Uncle Arthur again expressed an interest in seeing the reception hall, and Lizzy retrieved the key. William observed Aunt Adelaide stop when she saw some of Melanie's books on an end table.

"What an interesting book," she said to Melanie, as she picked it up. "I don't believe I've ever read this one. Would you like to read it with me?"

Melanie climbed up on the sofa and sat beside his aunt, as she began to recite the words on the page. The book wasn't long, so by the time Lizzy returned, they were on their second.

"She'll be fine," he whispered.

"I'd prefer Mrs. Reynolds knows that they're out here. Just in case Melanie freaks out that we've left."

He nodded, and quickly informed the housekeeper before his uncle and Richard followed them out of the door. Charlotte's staff happened to be there setting up for an evening wedding, so they hadn't needed a key. Uncle Arthur took his time as he and Richard examined the operation, making comments here and there. They also were glad to see the coordinators and caterers preparing for the event.

They returned to the house an hour later to find Aunt Adelaide dozing on the sofa with an open book in her lap, and Melanie in the kitchen with Mrs. Reynolds. The Fitzwilliams all retired to their rooms for a little while to rest until the Bingley's arrival later in the day.

Dinner that evening was an enormous success. William's uncle and aunt were thrilled to finally meet Charles' wife, since they were out of the country when the Bingleys were in England, and that she was Lizzy's sister only seemed to make things better.

Charles and Jane left early, due to Jane's fatigue, and the Fitzwilliams went to bed soon after due to jet lag.

The next morning, Lizzy made her way down to the kitchen early. Mrs. Reynolds' grandson was having a birthday, and, despite her protestations, both William and Lizzy were insistent that she take the day off. She attempted to be stubborn, stating she only required enough time for the party, but in the end they succeeded and so she had the entire day at her disposal.

Lizzy chuckled when she saw the large plastic containers of homemade croissants and biscuits awaiting her on the island. Taking out the French press, she set out to make the coffee, removing two large insulated carafes they'd found in William's stored belongings that had been moved into Longbourn.

As she was finished filling the first carafe, Aunt Adelaide came through the door. "Good morning," said Lizzy, screwing on the cap.

"Good morning. I was hoping I could get a cup of tea." She looked around at the large kitchen before settling on Lizzy. "Do you have any?"

"I usually have several types, but William bought these recently." She placed two tins that she removed from the pantry on to the counter. "Since he doesn't drink tea, I can only imagine they must be for you."

"That dear boy," she said. "He knows I cannot abide coffee, and this is my favorite."

"That sounds like William." She pulled the kettle from the stove and filled a cup that she placed in front of his aunt.

His aunt began to open the packaging as she studied Lizzy. "I'm glad that you were able to see beyond his mistakes when you met."

Lizzy regarded her questioningly.

"When he returned, Richard told us all about you. I think he was actually impressed that you turned my nephew down." Aunt Adelaide chuckled at what Lizzy assumed was the memory of the story.

Lizzy filled the kettle and set it back on the stove. "Why's that?"

"Not many women would've refused him." Lizzy could see her honest expression as she dunked her tea bag. "I think that's part of the reason he stopped dating. He was tired of so many women being the same—having identical motives and pursuing him."

"Well, I look at it this way," said Lizzy frankly, "I married a man because it was expected of me, and to garner my parents' acceptance, not because I loved him. It was a disaster. This time I'll marry William because I love him." Her lip quirked upward on one side. "Although, sometimes I wonder if happiness in marriage is simply nothing more than a matter of chance."

"That seems a bit cynical for one so young." His aunt had her head tilted to the side, and Lizzy knew she was definitely evaluating her.

Lizzy placed a bowl of sugar and a small pitcher of milk on the island. "Perhaps it is cynical." She poured more milk and began heating it for her coffee. "I know that I'm happy now, and I know with certainty that William will do everything he can to ensure that doesn't change, but then, I'd do the same for him."

"Richard never mentioned the particulars of your previous marriage, but perhaps that is the primary difference between this relationship and your last?" asked Aunt Adelaide, looking at Lizzy thoughtfully.

"I'd say it's all the difference," she responded softly. Feeling rather uncomfortable—exposed—she moved to the refrigerator and took out eggs, bacon and sausage, placing them on the island.

"Arthur's cholesterol will be high as a kite when we return," Aunt Adelaide murmured as she scanned the counter.

Laughing, Lizzy wrapped the biscuits and croissants in foil, and put them in the oven at a low temperature for them to warm while she cooked the remainder of breakfast. "We don't eat like this every day. Mrs. Reynolds also makes steel cut oats and sometimes we just eat cereal."

"Well, that's a relief. The doctor put him on a diet several years ago, and, since then, I'm continually catching him with foods he's not supposed to eat. He hides them all over the house." Aunt Adelaide let out an exasperated sigh. "I've caught him with biscuits on several occasions, and I've also found bags of crisps. He'd been hiding them in a chimney flue that we never use."

She had a vision of her scolding William for a similar transgression when they were older, and smiled widely. "How do you keep him from eating badly at the office?"

"He comes home saying he ate salads and such, but I don't believe that load of rubbish." Lizzy bit her lip to keep from chuckling at the woman's expression and tone of voice.

"Richard supports him, and claims they go to lunch together. They think they have me fooled," she said, pointing her finger, "but my son isn't a man to eat salads. He's just like his father." She took a sip of her tea and leaned forward as she whispered conspiratorially. "I think they go get fish and chips most days."

Lizzy couldn't help but begin chuckling madly. "I'm sorry. I just find it funny."

"It's absolutely ridiculous if you ask me," the older woman retorted.

William walked in holding a still pajama-clad Melanie. "What's so funny?" he asked when he saw the way Lizzy was laughing.

"Oh, I was telling her about your uncle, and how he hides biscuits, and crisps, and lies about what he eats at lunch."

Smiling widely, William set Melanie down to go play with her kitchen. "You mean the fish and chips Richard brings him a couple of times a week?"

Aunt Adelaide pointed toward Lizzy as she placed the sausage and bacon in pans on the stove. "I told you he was sneaking around."

"My question is how did you find out?" asked William. "He thinks he's pulling one over on you."

"Of course he does." She shook her head. "I've been married to that man for thirty-seven years. He'll need to try harder if he wants to keep something like that a secret." She set down her cup and looked at her watch. "I should go make sure he's getting dressed, so he doesn't miss breakfast."

She bustled out of the kitchen, and William wrapped his arms around Lizzy from behind. "I thought you'd wait until I was ready to come down."

356

"I needed to get the coffee brewing. I wanted to have it ready in the event they rose early."

"I think you really only need to worry about my aunt when it comes to early risers. Richard and my uncle aren't ones to wake at the crack of dawn." He kissed her where her neck and shoulder met, causing goose bumps to erupt along her neck and upper back.

"And your aunt doesn't drink coffee."

"Exactly."

She turned, and wrapped her arms around his neck. "Mrs. Reynolds will be here for the remainder of their visit, so you'll have more time in the mornings before Melanie wakes."

"Good," he said, punctuating it with a kiss to her nose. "I didn't like waking up to an empty bed. Then, I didn't even get to shower with you."

She smiled at his pout, and ran her thumb along his bottom lip. "You poor thing. I dare say you'll survive."

"I want to do more than survive," he said huskily, pulling her to him.

She began to melt into him a bit before she heard the bacon popping in the pan behind her. "Oh," she exclaimed as she turned to begin tending to her cooking. She'd lowered the temperature on the stove, and flipped the bacon, when another pop caused some grease to hit the back of her hand. "Crap!"

"Did you burn yourself?"

She washed it off with cold water, and moved back when William wrapped an arm around her while he tended the stove. "I've got it from here. Why don't you get the plates and utensils out?"

"Are you sure?"

"Positive. I don't want you burning yourself again."

Lizzy raised herself on her toes and brushed her lips against his, just as the door behind her swung open.

"Gah!" Richard interrupted loudly. "There's a child in the room! Behave!"

"Are you referring to Melanie or yourself, son?" Aunt Adelaide quipped, pushing past him to pick up her cup of tea.

Richard rolled his eyes and put his arm around his mother, giving her a kiss on the cheek. "I wouldn't want my delicate sensibilities scarred." His mother gave a small snort.

William and Lizzy laughed as Lizzy mixed her coffee. She then began removing plates from the cabinet, surprised when William's aunt picked them up and began setting the table in the kitchen.

"I'd thought we'd use the dining room," commented Lizzy.

The older woman looked up at her. "Would you normally eat breakfast in there?"

"No, but..."

"We're family, and we would normally eat at our kitchen table if we were at home, so why do anything different?"

Not really sure what to say, Lizzy shrugged and began following, setting the knives, forks and spoons around the plates. She finished the table and noticed that William had removed the sausage and bacon from the stove, so she made the eggs and took the pastries from the oven.

Soon, they were all seated around the table, enjoying their breakfast. Lizzy glanced around at everyone while she ate, thinking about how she truly liked William's relatives. They were what she'd always thought of as a family, and Aunt Adelaide's blunt wit was exceedingly entertaining.

She watched as William took a seat next to her. "Is there anything special you would like to do while you're here?" he asked his aunt and uncle. With that question, the assembled family began discussing the week ahead. Plans were made for the day, as well as some other excursions around Meryton during the week. Uncle Arthur and Richard wanted to check in at the local D&F offices, and Aunt Adelaide was eager to see how paper was made, resulting in a scheme to go up to the University of Meryton campus so Lizzy could use the facilities to show her.

Once everyone was happy with the arrangements, their discussion turned to other topics, as William's family continued to learn more about the new additions to their family.

Chapter Twenty-five

William sat behind his desk in the D&F offices, watching as his uncle pressed end on his cell phone and sighed. "I still wonder at times if Catherine was adopted," he groused.

Chuckling, William leaned back in his seat. "I take it from the conversation that she was having a fit about my wedding?"

"A fit is an understatement. I would say she was spitting mad." His uncle plopped down into one of the chairs on the other side of William's desk. "She's still livid that you passed over the wife she'd hand-picked for you."

"Anne?"

"Don't worry, I fully understand," his uncle commiserated as he frowned. "That woman is as false as they come." William nodded. "She began going on—something about Lizzy's ex-husband being the man who killed Ana and Andrew."

William grimaced and shifted uncomfortably for a moment. "It's not the way it sounds."

His uncle blanched. "Dear God, do you mean it's true? I just thought she was on one of her rampages." He leaned forward in his seat. "Are you sure about this girl? As much as I hate to agree with Catherine..."

"Before you say anything else, Uncle, she hadn't seen him in almost two months when the accident occurred. The next time she saw him—a few weeks after the accident—he beat her so badly that he nearly killed her and Melanie." His uncle eyed him doubtfully. "She had no idea until about a month ago—at about the same time that he tried to kill her again."

"What?" His uncle's face reflected his shock.

He then laid out the particulars of the night Melanie was born, as well as the near miss they had endured in April.

"It's not that I don't trust you, but there's D&F, as well as your assets to protect," said his uncle. William regarded him warily. "Charles will corroborate all of this?"

"Yes, he was married to Jane at the time, and answered the door the night Lizzy showed up on their doorstep." William leaned forward, his forearms on the desk. "If it makes you feel better, Lizzy insisted on a pre-nup. She was concerned about the family considering her to be... How did Aunt Catherine put it in her letter to me? 'A gold-digging harlot.'"

His uncle nodded. "I'm sorry, William, but I had to ask. I'd hate to have you taken in by someone."

"No, I completely understand. I knew Lizzy didn't know about Wickham's involvement in the accident, but I panicked and questioned everything, until I knew she was in danger. Then none of it mattered. I realized that if I let Wickham stand in our way, I'd only be allowing him to cause further havoc in my life."

"You refuse to be his victim again." Uncle Arthur nodded his head in understanding.

"Exactly," said William. "Lizzy decided a long time ago that she would no longer allow him any further power over her life. I happen to agree with her."

The phone on his desk buzzed and he pressed the speakerphone. "Yes?"

"Sir, Lady Matlock and Ms. Gardiner are here for your lunch appointment."

"Of course, Owen, please send them in."

A minute later, his assistant opened the door to show his aunt and Lizzy into his office. His aunt, who hadn't been in the room for years, scanned her surroundings with interest.

"Is this your painting, Lizzy?" she asked, as she walked to stand before it.

"It is." William walked over to stand not far behind while she looked over the work.

"This is lovely." Her aunt turned and smiled warmly at Lizzy. "She brought me to the campus this morning, and I met her friend Anita. I saw an exhibition of art made from handmade paper last year, and I've wanted to learn a bit about it. Lizzy's friend was kind enough to offer a demonstration."

"It's a lot of work, isn't it?" asked William. "I went with Lizzy a few weeks ago, because she wanted to make a batch of paper. I only watched her form sheets, and I was convinced that it was easy—I was definitely mistaken on that!"

Lizzy began laughing. "The art world is definitely not missing anything."

A wide smile on her face, Aunt Adelaide turned to face Lizzy. "I take it that William's paper was bad?"

"He was so impatient, and shook the mold and deckle too much. He also tore his sheets after I pulled them out of the hydraulic press."

"I never claimed to be an artist." Lizzy could tell that he wasn't as offended as he appeared.

"No, but I can enjoy that you do *something* badly."

"He's definitely lacking when it comes to meeting people," said Richard, as he strode into the room. He looked with humor at Lizzy. "You should know that better than anyone." William rolled his eyes and placed his arm around his fiancée's waist.

"You missed Catherine's call," Uncle Arthur said to his wife.

Aunt Adelaide's face clearly expressed her unspoken opinion of her sister-in-law. "She was furious when she realized the reason we were travelling here was for William's wedding, so I can't say that I'm surprised."

William felt his fiancée tense beside him, and realized he hadn't thought that his aunt and uncle might bring the situation to light in front of her. "Your aunt is angry because you're marrying me?" she asked with a hurt expression.

"Dear, don't worry about Catherine," said his aunt as she took Lizzy's hand. "She wanted to marry Sir Louis deBourgh when she

362

was a young woman. Only, he discovered that she was mental, and married someone else instead. When Louis and his wife only had a daughter, Catherine decided that William should marry the girl."

"She's angry because you refused?" She was now studying his expression with an odd look on her face.

"I told her numerous times that I had no interest in Anne deBourgh, but she refused to listen. She called me a month ago, and began yelling through the phone that I needed to return to England and arrange for my marriage to Anne, but I hung up on her."

His uncle chortled. "Good for you, son. I would've paid money to see her face when she realized you were no longer on the line." His expression soon turned serious once more. "Lizzy, you should know she's had you investigated. I wouldn't put it past her to have you followed, so just keep an eye out."

"We'll all be leaving for England the day after the wedding, so it's kind of a moot point." William began rubbing her side with his thumb, in the hopes that she might relax. "I've already hired a security detail for her, as well as Melly for the duration of our stay in the UK. Hopefully, we won't need it for our honeymoon."

"Mrs. Reynolds and Melanie are more than welcome to stay with us at Matlock, if it's needed," Aunt Adelaide chimed in with a smile.

"You just want to spoil that little girl," said Richard, who then pointed to Lizzy. "Don't do it. Melanie will be rotten by the time you return."

"Shush," his mother scolded.

"I doubt a week or two will make a brat out of her." Lizzy finally wrapped an arm around William as she cocked an eyebrow at his cousin.

"You're taking her side then?" asked Richard with some amusement.

Aunt Adelaide grinned widely. "I love you, son, but you're a fun target. I've told you that for years."

"Getting back to this Aunt Catherine," said Lizzy worriedly.

"Dear," his aunt continued, "don't let an embittered old spinster worry you. Arthur and I will pay the nosey old battle-axe a visit when we return. She lives on one of our properties, so if she persists in bothering the two of you, or even investigating you, she'll just find herself without a place to live."

"You'd do that?" Lizzy was wide eyed.

"Once William's married, she'll probably do everything she can think of to cause problems between the two of you, while she begins pushing Anne on Richard."

Richard's eyes grew wide as he turned to his father. "There's no way I would *ever* touch that slag."

"Language!" his mother scolded.

"She is! I've seen her out, and I've heard what she's done!"

"If it's enough to make you call her a slag, then none of us want to hear it." Aunt Adelaide's nose scrunched, showing her distaste.

"I think we should head to lunch," interjected Uncle Arthur, "I'm famished."

His wife gave him the evil eye as she turned to leave the room. "You can get your mind off of the fried prawns and chips. I'm sure they have some kind of broiled or grilled fish that you can eat."

"Whatever you say, dear."

William had to do everything to suppress his laughter. His uncle's voice was cheerful and complying, but as he walked behind his wife, William saw him grimace. Lizzy must've also seen it, because he could feel her shaking with silent laughter as they followed Richard.

His hand moved from her waist to entwine his fingers with hers, and he squeezed gently. She glanced up at him, beaming happily, and stepped a bit closer. He found his arm pressing against the side of her breast a bit maddening, since he could do nothing about it, but wouldn't have had her move for the world.

Thursday, May 30, 2013

"Jane, this is silly. William lives here, so why was Charles so insistent to cart him off to Netherfield?"

Her sister smiled her serene smile that Lizzy knew indicated she was up to something. "He can't see the bride before the wedding. It's bad luck. Besides, it's only one night, Lizzy."

Lizzy grimaced at the slightly scolding tone of the last sentence, and then narrowed her eyes at Jane. "I know you have something up your sleeve, so spill."

"There's nothing to spill. Tonight is the last night before you get married to a man you love, and whether you've been living together or not, you'll adhere to tradition."

Her eyes narrowed suspiciously. "Is Charles taking him to Twin Peaks?"

Jane sputtered. "Why on earth would my husband take William to a strip club?"

"Oh, I don't know." Lizzy rolled her eyes. "Perhaps as a bachelor party? Richard went with them, so I wouldn't put it past him to plan it, and Charles to go along for the ride."

Her sister put her hands on her shoulders and looked her directly in the eye. "I swear to you that they aren't going to a strip club. Does that help?"

Eyeing her warily, Lizzy nodded. "I know you're up to some kind of mischief. You only have that fake smile when you're up to something."

"Now isn't the time, Lizzy. We have reservations at Acadiana in forty-five minutes." She walked over to the closet and pulled out a garment bag. "Don't forget that you're wearing this." The bag was placed on the bed, and Jane turned to face her sister. "Do you need any help?"

"I think I can manage."

"Good, I'll be waiting with Aunt Adelaide." Lizzy smiled, watching her sister waddle from the room. While Jane was a tall five foot nine, she'd always been very thin and willowy. The baby was causing big changes to her figure, as well as her gait. Not to say that Lizzy had never waddled when she was pregnant, but it definitely wasn't to the extent or as early as Jane began.

She slowly walked over to the bed and unzipped the bag to reveal the emerald green halter-top dress inside. Aunt Adelaide had wanted to go shopping in the boutiques in the old part of town, and Lizzy had found it in the last store they browsed. Jane made her try it on, and then she and William's aunt gushed how perfect it was for her. Before Lizzy could protest, Aunt Adelaide was asking the sales woman to wrap it up, and whether they had shoes, insisting she was buying it as an early wedding present.

"The two of you definitely don't need anything for the house, so I'll buy you a dress. You can wear it on your honeymoon." She gave Lizzy a knowing smile. "I'm sure William will take you to dinner a few times."

As soon as she donned the dress, she attempted to tame her curls a bit, and applied her mascara before she ventured to her jewelry box, pulling a pair of earrings William and Melanie had picked out for Mother's Day. The white gold Celtic knot drop earrings with emeralds matched perfectly. She then located and slipped on the silver strappy heels Jane had bought to complete the look before she ventured downstairs.

"You look lovely," Aunt Adelaide gushed when she noticed Lizzy entering the living room. "Are we ready to go?"

"Yes," replied Lizzy, "but let me go say bye to Melly."

Her daughter was engrossed with her toys in the corner of the kitchen while Mrs. Reynolds cleaned for the evening, so Lizzy only received a quick peck.

The drive to Acadiana didn't take long, but she was confused when they began to lead her upstairs to the club area where they'd been dancing almost six months ago.

"Where are we going? The entrance to the restaurant is over there."

"Trust me, Lizzy," entreated Jane.

She followed her up the steps where her sister opened the door and put a hand between her shoulder blades to gently propel her inside.

"Surprise!" called Charlotte, Anita, and Joslyn.

Lizzy jumped and turned to her sister as she laughed. "You said we were going to dinner, and you never mentioned the girls."

"We are going to eat, but this is your bachelorette party." She leaned in and whispered, "*I* didn't hire a stripper, but I can't guarantee about Joslyn."

She stifled a chuckle and moved to hug all the ladies as she thanked them for coming. Then Jane and Aunt Adelaide had her seated at the head of the table with a glass of her favorite moscato and a tiara on her head.

"A tiara?"

"It's your party, so you're the queen. Whatever you say goes," responded Charlotte.

She hugged her childhood friend. "I'm sorry we haven't spent more time together recently."

Charlotte shrugged. "You've been busy, and so have I." Lizzy noticed the small smile at the corner of her lips and regarded her curiously. "I'm getting married."

"What? When did this happen? To whom?"

"Billy Collins and I began seeing each other after we began a conversation at the church's 'Trunk or Treat' last Halloween." Lizzy knew that she was gaping and quickly stopped to take a gulp of her wine. "We've been seeing more and more of each other, and he proposed, last week on my birthday."

"We've bumped into each other at the store, and you've called me a few times about the reception hall, but you never told me?"

"It never seemed the right time, and I know how you feel about him, so I didn't want to defend my choice until it was necessary."

Lizzy placed her hand over her friend's. "Are you happy, Charlotte?"

She beamed. "I'm very happy."

"Then that's all that matters. I just wish you'd trusted me enough to tell me." She squeezed her hand, and tears gathered in Charlotte's eyes.

"I'm sorry. I just know that you don't like Billy, so I assumed..."

"I had an issue with things he said to me, but that has nothing to do with the two of you."

"So, you'll come to the wedding?" Charlotte gave her a hopeful look.

"Have you set a date already?"

"We're thinking New Years. Daddy offered The Depot for the reception, and he's talking about a big fireworks show at midnight."

She bit back a laugh at Mr. Lucas, knowing he was probably attempting to make his daughter's wedding the social event of the year. "William and I will be there."

A waiter came up to deliver some appetizers to the table, as well as to ensure whether they needed anything else before making himself scarce. The ladies drank wine—except Jane, who drank a sparkling fruit drink—nibbled on hors d'oeuvres, and chatted until Jane announced that it was time for gifts.

Aunt Adelaide looked to Lizzy with a smirk. "We know you don't need china or towels, so we decided to do something different."

Lizzy furrowed her brow. "Different how?"

"You'll see," sang Joslyn as Jane handed her a gift.

The small card on the package indicated it was from her sister, and Lizzy eyed her warily as she pulled the ribbon and removed the lid, lifting away the tissue to reveal an almost see-through baby doll negligee.

"Jane!" she exclaimed, snapping the lid back on the box. All the ladies at the table roared with laughter while Lizzy blushed.

"Let's see it," said her sister. When Lizzy looked at her incredulously, she smiled. "Honey, what's wrong?"

"What if the waiter comes back in?"

"Oh, we actually have two servers tonight, and one is female. I warned her that we'd be giving you lingerie, so the guy won't be back until she gives him the all clear."

"Okay, what about Aunt Adelaide?" she whispered with about as much tact as her mother.

Her husband's aunt grinned mischievously. "Don't worry about me, dear. You haven't seen my gift yet."

Everyone laughed raucously, and Lizzy held up the negligee for all to see. She then hurried to place it back in the box. Charlotte took the present and put it on a table close by while Jane handed her another.

Anita's gift of some lacy boy shorts with a fitted lace top was accompanied by some of her handmade paper that was adorned with a watermark featuring Elizabeth's future initials. Lizzy thanked her warmly, and opened Charlotte's gift, a beautiful white silk nightgown with a matching robe, before opening Aunt Adelaide's gift.

Based on the older woman's comment earlier, Lizzy smiled nervously while she pulled the tissue from the bag. At first, she thought William's aunt had been joking, because it looked like bath products, but when she looked closer, she noticed they were, in fact, edible massage oils and other assorted edible products.

If everyone thought Lizzy had blushed before, the slight pink color that she wore earlier couldn't compare to the beet red that was now suffusing her cheeks.

"You might not want to tell William who gave you those." Aunt Adelaide wore a broad grin, and Lizzy shook her head as she chuckled.

"Definitely not," she responded.

"Saved the best for last," called out Joslyn, placing a large box in front of Lizzy.

"Perhaps I should save this for later." Lizzy picked it up and began to hand it to Jane, who pushed it back down to the table.

"Oh, no you don't."

She groaned and finished the last of her wine, prompting the waitress to refill the glass. She drank another large gulp, and then began to unwrap the gift as if it might bite her through the wrapping.

When she had removed the last of the paper, she gingerly opened the box and peered inside. "Dear Lord!"

Joslyn clapped her hands, laughing, as Lizzy surveyed everything: a set of fuzzy leopard print handcuffs, a black leather bustier and boy short set, a riding crop, several books, and some items that she had no clue as to their function—and wasn't sure she wanted the knowledge. "I *am not* holding this up." At her pronouncement, Jane began chuckling and took the box to pass around the table.

"Jos, I'd thank you, but I'm not sure if I should," Lizzy teased. Joslyn playfully pouted, and Lizzy began to laugh as she hugged her friend. She noticed Aunt Adelaide blush when she looked in the box, and began to laugh harder.

"I think we need a dessert," said Jane. "I haven't been able to drink, but I can at least have something decadent."

The waitress heard her sister's cue, and disappeared for a moment only to return with a bakery box containing a very chocolate, very rich looking torte. The ladies all leaned forward in their seats.

"It's a flourless chocolate torte that I heard of from one of the paralegals at the firm. She recommended the bakery as well as the dessert."

"That looks amazing," Lizzy commented as Jane sliced a piece and put it on her sister's plate. Charlotte stood and walked around the table next to her.

"Jane, why don't you go and sit down? I'll serve everyone."

"I don't mind."

Charlotte pushed at Jane's back, propelling her toward her seat. "Save your ankles and rest for a bit. I can handle cutting a cake."

Lizzy enjoyed herself immensely, and was exceedingly tipsy by the time Jane and Aunt Adelaide led her out to the car. She dozed on the return trip to Longbourn, where Jane woke her to get her inside and up the stairs. As soon as her bedroom door closed, she stripped, throwing everything on her dresser before she burrowed into the covers and drifted back to sleep.

Netherfield was rather quiet, and not as raucous as most bachelor parties. Charles grilled steaks and shrimp for their dinner, before they were to settle in to a long night of scotch and poker. They had just finished their meals when the doorbell rang, and Charles jumped up to answer it.

William, hoping it was the ladies, followed close behind, but was sorely disappointed when the door was opened to reveal the Bennets. Mrs. Bennet reached for the screen door as Charles stepped closer and pulled the handle toward him, effectively barring anyone from entering.

"Olivia, David, we weren't expecting you tonight."

"We know we're always welcome in Jane's home, and we have business in the area, so we're here to stay for a few days."

Charles looked to Mr. Bennet for support, but William noticed the expectant look with the quirk of an upturned lip that indicated there would be no help forthcoming.

"As a matter of fact, if you'd only called first, Jane and I both would've told you that we'd be unable to welcome company until Saturday night."

She looked at Charles as if he were being silly. "What is this? Of course we're welcome." She attempted to pull the screen, but only managed to open it a bit before Charles blocked it bodily. "Where's Jane? She'll let me inside."

"Jane isn't here, and I'm having a party for a friend, which is why you can't possibly stay here tonight."

"Well, this just won't do. You simply must call Jane and have her come home. We need her to help us with this predicament that my poor, dear Lydia is in."

"And what predicament would that be?" asked Charles, taking a long look at his sister-in-law. Lydia rolled her eyes before she began studying her fingernails.

"If you'd let us inside, I'd tell you." Mrs. Bennet was becoming visibly irritated, noticeable by the higher pitch of her voice, and the fierce grip she had on the door. William was sure she was probably pulling a bit, but Charles wasn't budging.

"You'll have to tell me here, because I have company and you aren't going to intrude on the party."

"Party?" she exclaimed. "The only person I see is your disagreeable friend here."

Charles turned and saw William, who stepped forward. "Charles is telling the truth. Jane isn't presently at home, and there are indeed other guests."

"Over the last year and a half, you've taken to showing up on our doorstep unannounced," said Charles sternly. "You wreaked havoc on Thanksgiving, and now you turn up during a party." He pointed a finger in Olivia's face. "You *will* call before you decide to travel here again, and I won't have you guilt Jane into staying ever again, especially now that the baby is coming."

Mrs. Bennet was evidently affronted. "David, can you believe this? My daughter would always welcome me into her home!"

"I'm going to ask you one more time before I close the door. Why exactly do you need Jane's help?"

She huffed. "She needs to get Greg Wickham out of jail."

"Excuse me?" interjected William. "And why would she do that?"

372

"Because he was in Atlanta almost four months ago, and Lydia is pregnant."

Charles exhaled heavily. "Olivia, he pled a deal on beating Lizzy, and he's serving time for that at the moment." Mrs. Bennet rolled her eyes, displaying the distinct resemblance between her and her youngest daughter.

"That's just ridiculous. Why would he serve time for something he didn't do?"

Charles became angrier than William had ever seen him, and was shocked by the bright red color that suffused his cheeks. "Because whether any of you want to admit it or not, he could've killed Lizzy and Melanie. He also was drunk when he hit another car a few years ago, and killed both its occupants. The D.A. has DNA evidence, as well as eyewitness accounts that identify him as the driver. He also returned here in April, and attempted to break into Longbourn. By his *own* confession, he was there to kill Lizzy!" His voice had continued to rise until he was yelling by the end.

Mr. Bennet's expression was one of shock. "Charles, are you serious?"

"Do you honestly think I'd lie? We've never lied about that man, but it's evident that you chose to believe what you wanted!" William heard a sound behind him, and saw Richard and his uncle at the end of the hall. He put up his hand, but it was obvious that they were remaining where they were should he or Charles need them.

"His father was a good man! How were we to know?" Mr. Bennet was becoming irate at his son-in-law's verbal tirade, and William was thankful that a few acres separated Netherfield from their nearest neighbors. The Bennets had finally seemed to push Charles too far.

"Perhaps if you hadn't decided to discard your daughter when she decided to live her own dream and not yours, you would've known that she was only marrying the man to please you! She thought she'd finally earned your approval, and she stayed for five years— *Five years!*—Because she knew that you'd berate her, and not believe her reasons if she left! After his father died, that sleaze would disappear for days, then weeks, and finally months on end.

Money disappeared, and he took out a mortgage on the home Mr. Wickham bought for them. Then the bank foreclosed."

Lydia scoffed, and Charles became even more irate. "Lizzy worked to keep a roof over her head, and sent anything she owned of value to us so Greg wouldn't sell it!"

William placed a hand on Charles' shoulder, and directed his speech at Lydia. "He wouldn't have cared if you were pregnant. He came home drunk four months after Lizzy became pregnant, and laughed at her because he thought she was fat. The next time he saw her was when she was eight months along, and he realized that she wasn't just fat. That was when he beat her."

Charles looked between Lydia and Olivia Bennet. "He broke her wrist, cracked three ribs, and Melanie was born early!"

"As if Melanie is actually Greg's!" Lydia mumbled haughtily.

Charles peered around his mother-in-law. "I can get DNA proof that Melanie is biologically Greg Wickham's, if that would finally shut you up!"

"That man won't be released from jail for a very long time," interceded William once more. "He was also high on meth when he was arrested."

David Bennet's head whipped around to glare at Lydia. "Have you been doing drugs with him?" Lydia refused to answer, returning her attention to her fingernails. He then turned to face Charles. "I want to hear this from Elizabeth."

"No," replied William.

"Excuse me? Who do you think you are?"

"Lizzy's husband. I'll let her know that you wish to speak with her, but I can't guarantee that she'll agree to it."

"Since when are you her husband?" Mr. Bennet scoffed.

"That's none of your business." William was implacable, and didn't give an inch while his future father-in-law was attempting to stare him down.

"We're going to Longbourn." Mr. Bennet turned, but before he could take a step William halted his movement with his next statement.

"If you step one toe on Longbourn property without being invited there, I'll see to it that you're arrested for trespassing."

"You would prevent *my* daughter from seeing me?" he yelled, outraged.

"No," William replied in a deceptively calm voice. "The choice is up to her, but I *will* protect her from you if that is *her* wish." He watched the man clench his jaw fiercely. "Lizzy has never wished to spend time with you or have you around her daughter. I'll take her feelings into consideration before I give any credence to yours."

"Longbourn should be mine," huffed Olivia under her breath.

William heard her muttered comment and wouldn't let it go unanswered. "Obviously, your grandparents felt that your aunt would take better care of the home, since they left it to her. Aunt Mel then chose the person who not only needed it the most, but also would ensure that it remained in the family for as long as possible."

"Rather than selling it piece by piece," added Charles.

Mrs. Bennet's eyes widened and she scoffed. "Just you wait until I tell Jane! She'll..."

"Speaking of Jane," Charles interrupted, "I'll tell her that you came by, and have her call you, but I doubt that it'll be before Saturday. We have a busy day planned tomorrow." He began to shut the door. "Good bye," he said to Mrs. Bennet, and she was forced to take a step back as the large oak panel closed in her face.

"Thank you for not disagreeing with me that I'm Lizzy's husband." William spoke softly, in the hopes that his voice wouldn't carry through the door.

"Tomorrow only makes it official, and they don't need to know about the wedding. They might decide to show up at Longbourn if they knew about the ceremony."

"I'm sure if Lizzy had been here to see it, she'd be thanking you for standing up to them for her."

Charles shook his head. "I should've done it a long time ago. I'm not entirely happy with revealing as much as I did, but I couldn't let Lizzy and Jane's relationship suffer because I couldn't stand up to them."

"You didn't reveal anything too personal," replied William, placing a hand on his shoulder. "I'm sure she'll be okay with it."

As Charles moved to a window to be sure the Bennets were leaving, William pulled his cell phone from his pocket, and with the touch of a few buttons was speaking to Mrs. Reynolds, giving instructions in the event the Bennets disregarded his warning and paid a visit to Longbourn. The next call was to a local security firm that William used in Meryton to arrange for a detail to be assigned to Longbourn. He required assurance that the wedding and their plans would not be interrupted.

Once everything had been settled, they met up with Richard and Uncle Arthur at the end of the hall, where they began walking toward Charles' study. "I'd say a drink is in order after that scene," said William's uncle.

Charles poured them all glasses of Macallan, and Richard raised his glass. "To Lizzy who, with hopefully a long jail term, will always have her freedom from that shit-for-brains!"

"Hear hear!"

Several hours after the Bennets' abrupt showing at Netherfield, William waited for his uncle to place his bet, while Charles downed the rest of his scotch. He hadn't particularly cared to have a bachelor party, but he appreciated his friend's effort nonetheless. He was only thankful that Charles hadn't allowed Richard to have a hand in the planning.

He glanced over at his cousin, who was busy puffing on a cigar. "I wish you'd put that revolting thing out." His mood had deteriorated since the Bennets departed Netherfield, and his mind was preoccupied with Lizzy. He was still worried his future in-laws might decide to show up at Longbourn's door.

"Why would I do that?" he asked casually. "You're the only one bothered by it."

"Put it out, son."

"Why?"

Uncle Arthur gave his son an exasperated look. "Because it's his party."

"This isn't much of a party. Charles insisted that I couldn't hire a stripper."

"Thank you, Charles," said William. "It's good to know that *he* at least thought about what I'd want." He looked at his cousin while he spoke.

"It would've been so much fun to watch you squirm." Richard smirked as he leaned toward Charles. "I found this woman, Rafaella, who's working as an exotic dancer to pay for her Ph.D. She's spec-tac-u-lar!" He practically sang the last bit. "She dances in her lab coat, and has this pink stuffed monkey that she uses to…"

"Seriously?" William asked as he rolled his eyes. "I'll be sure to hire a stripper to embarrass you for your bachelor party. Will that suffice?"

His cousin shrugged with a grin. "Sounds good to me."

Uncle Arthur put down his cards. "I fold."

Richard threw some chips into the pile. "I'll call." He threw down his cards to reveal a flush.

Smiling, William slowly put down his four of a kind, and carefully stood, so he didn't fall over from the amount of scotch he'd imbibed over the course of the evening. "Good night, gentlemen…oh, and you too, Richard."

He stumbled up to his room, and sat on the bed while he considered his options. Charles had informed him earlier that he was supposed to spend the night at Netherfield, but that was the last place he wished to be. He wanted to be at home with his wife. Well, she may not be his wife until the next day, but as far as he was concerned, she'd already filled the position.

He took out his phone and called Meryton taxi, requesting a car to pick him up, and for them not to honk, he didn't want anyone to know he was making his escape. The steps weren't easy to navigate quietly while drunk, but he made it down and tiptoed out of the kitchen door. The taxi pulled up five minutes after his trek to the end of the drive, and he hurriedly climbed in just before they drove away with no one the wiser.

The moon was full, and the lake was glistening in the moonlight when they pulled up to the front door of Longbourn. Money was swiftly was passed to the driver, and he tried as best he could to close the car door with some stealth. William then cursed the difficulty his hands had unlocking the door, but he was soon inside and crawling up the stairs.

As he closed the bedroom door behind him, he drank in the vision of Lizzy curled onto her side with her hair strewn across the pillows. His clothes were discarded haphazardly as he made his way to the bed and slid between the sheets, sidling up to her back and wrapping an arm around her waist.

"Mmmmm, William?" she murmured groggily.

He felt her naked bottom against him, and began running his hand up and down her thigh, his lips exploring her shoulder as she turned to face him.

"I didn't think you'd be home tonight."

"I escaped." He had not planned on anything other than holding her as she slept, but she just felt so good that he couldn't help himself. She laughed at his response as he eagerly claimed her lips.

He rolled her on top of him and slipped easily into her warmth. They rocked for a few minutes, when William, thinking how blissfully perfect this was, faded to sleep.

Chapter Twenty-six

Friday, May 31, 2013

Lizzy was having difficulty opening her eyes as she grimaced at the dry, foul taste in her mouth. She felt like she'd been sucking interminably on a cotton ball, and her head felt so heavy. When she finally managed to open her eyes a bit, she realized she was wrapped in William's embrace, the hair of his chest tickling her nose.

Pressing the hair down softly with her hand, she cuddled closer to his warmth, while he began to stir. He groaned as his hand stroked up her bare back. She placed a small kiss over his heart and pulled back to see his eyes open blearily.

"I'm so glad that our room is on the west side of the house."

She smiled, reaching out to caress from his forehead to his temple. "How much did you have to drink?"

"I'm not sure. Charles and Richard kept topping off my glass, so I was never able to keep track." Lizzy could tell he was studying her expression. "You had more than you're accustomed to as well?"

"Oh, yeah," she drawled. "I would imagine that Charles told you what Jane planned for last night."

He gave a short nod. "He did, but I didn't want to sleep at Netherfield. I wanted you in my arms. I hope you don't mind."

"I never expected or wanted you to spend the night at Netherfield last night. That was strictly the idea of my sister and her husband."

William kissed her on the temple and gave her a wan smile. "I feel I owe you an apology for last night."

She regarded him with a confused expression. "I have no idea why."

"Well, considering I only remember starting, the sex couldn't have been good. I was entirely too drunk."

Lizzy searched her mind, trying to remember anything after she collapsed into her bed. "I don't even remember you coming in last night. We had sex?" She said the last softly and a bit warily.

"You were awake. You said my name and kissed me."

"Jane used to say that I could hold a conversation in my sleep, or perhaps I was awake and I don't remember." She began to chuckle hysterically as she buried her head in his chest.

"I'm glad to know that it was so memorable for you," he said dryly. She only began laughing harder, and he began to chuckle as well. "I suppose I should be thankful you aren't angry with me."

She drew back, puzzled and trying to restrain her laughter. "Why would I be angry?"

"I think some women might be upset."

"Obviously, I was a willing participant up until one or both of us passed out; besides, I *know* you would never do anything to me against my will." She looked him in the eye while she said it, but after they regarded each other seriously for a few moments they both began laughing.

"This is mortifying," he managed.

"We'll be the only people to know, and my part is equally embarrassing."

He ran the backs of his fingers down her cheek, and leaned in when she put her finger over his lips. "I love you, but I'm sure my breath reeks as bad as yours does. I think this morning we should brush our teeth before we inflict that on one another."

They both quickly went to the bathroom and took care of their morning breath before they snuggled back under the covers. William was just leaning in to claim Lizzy's lips when someone began jiggling the handle of the door, prompting them to jump apart.

"Lizzy?" they heard Jane call through the door. "When did you lock the door?"

Lizzy quirked an eyebrow as she raised herself onto her elbow. "How do you know it wasn't locked?"

380

"I've never seen you so drunk, so I checked on you before I went to bed. If you'll open the door, I have some water, orange juice and ibuprofen."

A cell phone rang, and she heard Jane set something down on the ornamental table at the top of the stairs. Her voice was muffled for a minute before she must have moved back to the other side of the door.

"Lizzy, is William in there with you?"

Smirking, she sat up in bed and felt William wrap his arms around her as he scooted up behind. His chin was resting on her shoulder. "Why would he be here? He's supposed to be at Netherfield."

"Charles is on the phone. He says that William isn't there." While the worry in Jane's voice wouldn't be discernible to everyone, Lizzy heard it, and grabbed her robe from the foot of the bed. Following her lead, William rose and donned his own before he unlocked and opened the door.

Jane jumped, and was obviously relieved when she saw him. "He's here," she said into her cell phone. "I love you, too. See you in a bit." She put her phone in the pocket of her robe and placed her hands on her hips, reminding Lizzy of their mother. "Do you know what you just did to my nerves?"

"Okay, Livvy," responded Lizzy.

"Ha.Ha. Seriously, what if something happened to you coming over here in the middle of the night?"

"Well, *Mom*, I took a cab, and I was still in possession of enough of my faculties to remember Longbourn's address."

"Jane, everything's fine. No one is missing or injured. Might I suggest that you ask before you decide that people are going to spend the night apart? Neither of us wanted to be separated last night, and it wasn't necessary over a silly superstition."

Her sister's shoulders dropped a bit. "I just wanted you to have a bit of something traditional, since you aren't having a large or ornate ceremony."

"I had one of those, remember? The size of a wedding isn't indicative of the couple's feelings. William doesn't like big events if he can help it, and I know from experience that a large wedding can mean absolutely nothing. We're having the ceremony we want." She noticed that Jane looked upset. "I enjoyed my bachelorette party last night. It was great to have a girls night out, but I just would've enjoyed coming home to William instead of an empty bed."

"I agree with her," piped in William. "I would've been in a much better mood last night if I'd been here, and hadn't been told that I was going to sleep at Netherfield. Charles told me that Lizzy wanted me to stay there."

"He did?" asked Lizzy, and he nodded in response. "I never said that."

"No, she didn't. Charles probably felt it was the only way to get you to put in an appearance."

Lizzy wrapped her arms around Jane from the side, since her belly was in the way. "We both appreciate that you wanted to do something nice for us, but we both would've been more than willing to go to our respective parties if you'd just explained everything."

"The two of you are really quite ridiculous," Jane said with a quirk to her lips.

"What's that supposed to mean?" Lizzy dropped one arm, leaving the arm draped around her sister's shoulders.

"You can't spend *one* night apart?"

"No, we can spend a night apart, but we don't see the point if it's not necessary." She looked over at William, who was chuckling. "You don't agree with me?"

"I do. I just think all of this is funny."

"You should both get dressed," said Jane, with a hitch to her voice. "Father Ben will be here in a few hours." She turned and picked up the small tray and handed it to William before she returned downstairs.

When the door was closed, William turned to Lizzy. "Is it me, or does it not make sense why she's so upset about last night?"

"I think the hormones are making her act like our mother." She took the water and the bottle of ibuprofen, taking two before handing the glass and a dose to William. He then sat her down and informed her about the Bennets' unexpected visit to Netherfield, and her father's wish to see her.

"I'm not sure what I want to do. I don't think he's sorry for the way he's been in the past. He probably just wants verification of what Charles said."

"You have all the time in the world to decide what you wish to do. A phone call when we return might be the solution. You could call him from the office or Jane's cell phone, so he won't have our personal numbers." He kissed her on the temple and held her for a moment.

"I'll tell Jane that I'd like to think about it. That way my dad will know that you told me."

"Sweetheart, I'm not worried whether he knows I told you or not."

She shrugged and handed him the glass of orange juice that they shared before they put on some pajamas so they could go down to the kitchen, where Mrs. Reynolds prepared a variety of baked goods and coffee. They ate with Jane, Melanie, and Aunt Adelaide before they were required to get dressed for the ceremony at noon.

Lizzy turned to look at herself in the full-length mirror. She'd made arrangements to have her hairdresser, Jude, come out to the house and style her hair. She'd also done Lizzy's makeup, since she rarely wore more than a bit of lip-gloss and mascara. When her friend was finished, Lizzy just stood, staring at herself in the mirror.

"Lizzy?" Jane placed a hand on her back as she peered around her, a worried expression on her face.

"I'm okay. I guess I'm just a bit overwhelmed." Tears pooled in her eyes, but she managed to stifle them before they fell.

"Don't you dare ruin my makeup job," Jude threatened from the side. "We don't have enough time to fix it." Lizzy smiled as she rolled her eyes.

"It's different, I would imagine." Jane adjusted her sister's veil a bit, as she carefully studied the look in her eye.

"I was resigned last time, and I think I was busy convincing myself that I'd always be happy. Today, I'm excited and happy...and I'm finding it hard to control my emotions." She looked toward Jane. "I honestly wondered if I'd ever have a relationship like this."

Her sister adjusted a curl from her forehead. "Of course you would've. You've just been alone for so long." She corrected herself before Lizzy could speak. "I know you had Melanie, but there was no one caring for you for years before she came along."

Mrs. Reynolds poked her head in and smiled. "Everyone's ready when you are." She pulled a hand forward, where Melanie came through all decked out in her frilly flower girl dress with a circle of roses on her head. Her long curls were hanging past her shoulders.

"Hi, sweetheart," said Lizzy as she bent down. Her daughter came running over and hugged her.

"You're pwetty!"

"Thank you, so are you."

"Tank you," said Melanie, as she twirled and Lizzy looked up to see Jane grin.

"Have you seen Daddy?"

"He's downstairs. He looks pwetty, too."

Everyone laughed, and Lizzy looked up to Mrs. Reynolds. "Are we really ready?"

"When you are, dear."

Lizzy strode over to the box where the flowers were, and handed Melanie her little basket of rose petals, before she took her bouquet of lilies and pink roses. Jane took her small cluster before they headed out to the front door. Her sister kissed her on the cheek before she headed outside and Charles scooted inside the door.

"We're ready to go then, I take it?" He rubbed his hands together with a huge grin on his face.

"I'm ready," said Lizzy.

He leaned over and whispered to Melanie, guiding her out onto the porch. They peered through the leaded glass as she walked to where Charlotte, who'd helped out by planning the details, was waiting on the other side of the drive. Charlotte pointed to the two oaks near the lake, where they were having the ceremony, and Charles and Lizzy began to chuckle when Melanie took off running.

Charles extended his arm. "Let's go get you married!"

Lizzy kissed him on the cheek and then used her thumb to wipe off the lipstick. "Thank you."

"For what?"

"For being the best brother I could ever ask for."

He chuckled. "I'm the only brother, but I'll take it anyway."

He led the way outside, and she crossed to where Charlotte was standing. "You look beautiful, Lizzy." They hugged briefly, and as she pulled back, Lizzy's eyes caught William standing where the branches of the two oaks met. He'd picked up Melanie, and held her to his side. When his face turned from speaking with their daughter, his eyes widened, the soft smile he'd had for Melanie broadened, and his happiness seemed to radiate from him.

Her breath caught in her throat, and she gravitated toward him. Charles must have noticed her body shift, and began to lead her in that direction. She knew that her expression probably rivaled William's, but she was shaking like a leaf, which she hoped wouldn't last throughout the ceremony. One good look at William enabled her to see that he was attempting valiantly to keep control of his emotions as well.

When she finally reached where he was standing, She noticed Father Ben, who was also wearing a broad smile. As the priest in the church where she was raised, he was disappointed when the Wickhams had insisted on her marrying in their church, but he was thrilled when he learned that she wished him to marry her and William.

"Dearly beloved: We have come together in the presence of God to witness and bless the joining together of this man and this woman in Holy Matrimony..."*

Lizzy was angled toward William, and Father Ben's words were tuned out as the two of them held each other's eyes. Melanie must have decided that she didn't wish to be held anymore, because she began to wiggle to get down. They watched as she skipped over to Mrs. Reynolds, and grasped her hand while Aunt Adelaide walked over by Father Ben and began to read from Song of Solomon. William placed an arm around Lizzy as they listened.

When she was done, Aunt Adelaide flipped the pages the Bible, and handed it to Jane, who began to recite the next reading. "If I speak in the tongues of men and of angels..."** Lizzy turned to face her, and felt William's arms snake around her middle.

Jane's reading went well until she began to read, "Love is patient, love is kind" and her eyes welled with tears. Lizzy knew that her sister loved the verse, which is why she wanted her to read it, but she hadn't expected her to cry.

"It is not rude, it is not self-seeking, it is not easily angered, it keeps not record of wrongs. Love does not delight in evil but rejoices with the truth."

Lizzy noticed Jane look at her intently, as a tear dropped down her cheek.

"It *always* protects, *always* trusts, *always* hopes, *always* perseveres. *Love* never fails."

She felt William shift as he leaned down to kiss her shoulder, and she used a finger to stop a tear that was threatening to fall from her own eye. Lizzy knew that in her own way, Jane was applying the reading to their relationship. They'd been sisters and best friends for as long as Lizzy could remember. Jane loved her, and that because of love, Lizzy would always have Jane, no matter the circumstances—just as Lizzy would now always have William.

"And now these three remain: faith, hope and love. But the greatest of these is love."**

Jane closed the Bible and turned to Charles, who was holding out a tissue. She chuckled and took it to dab her eyes.

William and Lizzy's attention was brought back to Father Ben as he looked to William and began the vows. She caught William's gaze, and they both smiled when he took her right hand in his.

"In the Name of God, I William Bryan Darcy, take you, Elizabeth Grace Gardiner, to be my wife, to have and to hold from this day forward, for better for worse, for richer for poorer, in sickness and in health, to love and to cherish, until we are parted by death. This is my solemn vow."

Lizzy beamed while she listened the vows she was to repeat, their hands adjusting so she could take his right hand in hers.

"In the Name of God, I Elizabeth Grace Gardiner, take you, William Bryan Darcy, to be my husband, to have and to hold from this day forward, for better for worse, for richer for poorer, in sickness and in health, to love and to cherish, until we are parted by death. This is my solemn vow."

Father Ben gave a blessing, and then William took her left hand, holding the circle of diamonds that was her wedding ring. "Elizabeth, I give you this ring as a symbol of my vow, and with all that I am and all that I have, I honor you, in the Name of the Father, and of the Son, and of the Holy Spirit."

She then took his ring from the silver tray and placed it on his finger as she repeated the same vow. From there, the remainder of the ceremony was somewhat of a blur. There were prayers and blessings before she heard Father Ben say, "Those whom God has joined together let no one put asunder."

William wore a large smile when he leaned in to give her a soft lingering kiss. When he pulled back, he brushed a tear from beside her eye with his thumb. "Don't cry yet. We still have pictures to take."

He brushed his lips against her temple, shook Father Ben's hand, and then wrapped an arm around her as they faced her family and his. Congratulations were exchanged all around, and then everyone posed for pictures as Maria, a local photographer friend of Joslyn's, directed everyone with the ease of a professional.

When they were done with the photos, William picked up Melanie, and they walked around the house to the courtyard, where a table had been set up on the porch. Soft music filtered out through speakers that were arranged outside, and they all took seats.

A light luncheon was served, and the new family spent the time conversing and laughing. Lizzy leaned against William when the meal was over, and felt him place a kiss to her hair. "You're so beautiful," he whispered. "I'm glad you wouldn't let me see the dress. I was amazed when I saw you come around the azalea bush."

She smiled widely, and gazed at his face as she cupped his cheek. "You're very handsome in your tuxedo—very James Bond." He blushed, and she grinned at his response. Richard standing drew their attention, and they both turned to face him.

"I've known William for as long as I can remember, and despite the fact that he's rather uptight..." he began with a smirk. Aunt Adelaide smacked his arm, and he rolled his eyes. "He's smiled more lately than I've ever seen, and I know that it's a direct result of Lizzy's presence in his life. All of us in the family are overjoyed to see him as happy as he is, and we only hope that your joy will grow as time goes by. The fact that Melanie joins the family as a result of this marriage is only icing on the cake." He raised his glass. "To Lizzy, may she always have the ability to handle William, because someone should be able to."

Everyone chuckled as Uncle Arthur raised his glass. "To Lizzy and William!"

"To Lizzy and William," everyone chorused as they took sips of their champagne.

Charles stood while Richard took his seat.

"I'm honored to be acting as father of the bride today. I'll never forget the young woman I met almost five years ago. In some ways, Lizzy is much the same as she was then—beautiful and caring, but over the past two years, she's shown how resilient she is. I've rooted for William from the beginning, and I'm overjoyed that my best friend is now truly my brother. Their feelings grew quickly, but they love each other fiercely, and I know, in my heart, that they were meant to be. I ask y'all to raise your glasses to the happy couple."

"To Lizzy and William," everyone chorused once more. Everyone clinked glasses with those around them, and Lizzy laughed when Melanie lifted her sippy cup to toast with the adults.

"The two of you need to dance," said Jane.

She was surprised at her sister's statement. Lizzy hadn't planned to dance while the family watched. "We hardly have a dance floor, Jane."

Jane scoffed. "We don't need one. There's plenty of room on the porch, and then there's the courtyard. I'm sure someone will turn up the music a bit."

William leaned in to her ear. "If you're avoiding this for me, don't worry about it. I don't mind."

"Are you sure?" Lizzy asked skeptically.

"Yes, I actually enjoy dancing with you."

William stood and walked around her. He held out his hand, which Lizzy grasped firmly while she rose, and he then led her out to the center of the courtyard near the fountain. The volume of the music became a bit louder, and he smiled as he placed the song, recognizing it as one they'd danced to that night at The Balcony. The piano played the intro, and William pulled Lizzy into his arms where she belonged.

It was a song that had several renditions by different vocalists, but the one playing was the closest to the way it had sounded that night at the club. He glanced over Lizzy's shoulder, and saw Jane and Charlotte standing next to each other on the porch, wiping tears from the corners of their eyes. They'd both been there that evening, and obviously played that version intentionally.

He placed a kiss to her temple and felt her sigh. "Do you remember this song?"

"Of course. Have you seen Charlotte and Jane? Despite the tears, they each look like the cat that's just swallowed the canary." He heard her laugh.

"I do love this song," she breathed against his neck.

Melanie broke away from Aunt Adelaide and came running up. William scooped her into his embrace, and placed one of his arms back around Lizzy as he continued dancing. He had his family in his arms, and for the first time in a long time, he was completely happy and content.

*Wedding ceremony from the *Book of Common Prayer*.

**Corinthians13:1-13

Epilogue

February 20, almost two years later

William shifted on his makeshift sofa bed, attempting to become comfortable as he watched the television mounted on the wall in front of him. He had been flipping through the channels, aimlessly searching for something to watch when he stumbled across a travel show featuring Italy. He stopped channel surfing to enjoy the familiar views and scenery, smiling at the memory of his and Lizzy's honeymoon.

Prior to the wedding, he'd casually asked her several times about travel to Europe, hoping she would slip and mention a destination she dreamed of visiting. Instead of naming a specific location, she told him her dream of almost vagabonding across Europe by train, stopping at different towns to see the museums and architecture as she travelled.

The planning had been tricky but he'd tried to make the arrangements so that she would feel as though she were travelling the way she'd always wanted, while still maintaining an itinerary. He managed to fly her to Venice in his jet, without telling her where they were going until they boarded the water taxi to reach the hotel. He'd never forget the expression on her face when he revealed their location.

They spent three days in Venice, where Lizzy took him through any old building, museum, and art gallery she could find by day. Mostly they spent the evenings in their hotel rooms, enjoying room service and each other.

After Venice, they boarded a train for Florence. There they spent hours touring the Uffizi before they went to the Galleria dell'Accademia that housed Michelangelo's David. William restrained a chuckle at the remembrance of her teasing when they'd viewed that sculpture.

> *"William," she whispered in his ear with a coy smile.*
>
> *"Yes."*
>
> *"Turn around."*
>
> *"Why?"*

"I want to compare your ass to David's."

He raised his eyebrows as he watched her struggle to restrain her laughter. "I don't think so." Her small fingers lightly pinched his rear, and she kissed him on the cheek.

"I'm sure yours is nicer. Perhaps I can get a better look later?"

William smiled as he shook his head. "Only if I can have a nice long look at yours for myself?"

"I'm all yours, hon!" she responded in a low voice.

He just hadn't expected Lizzy to inform him that after three days in Rome, she was ready to move on to their next destination—a place he didn't have on their schedule.

"I want to go to Naples and then Reggio Calabria." A surprised William watched her incredulously as she was placing her things in a bag.

"But we still have reservations for three more days in Rome."

Lizzy waltzed up to him and wrapped her arms around his neck. "This honeymoon has been wonderful, and I'm sure we'd have a wonderful time in Rome for the next three days. But I've wanted to see Pompeii and the Riace bronze warriors since I took an ancient art history class in college."

He gave her a skeptical look. "The warriors sound like art, but Pompeii? Isn't that nothing but ruins and petrified bodies?" William had wanted her to see whatever she desired, but he'd looked forward to a leisurely few days before they returned to England.

"Yes, Pompeii," she said emphatically. "There are still frescos that you can see. They deteriorate all the time, and it's unknown how long they will last. There's another city that was destroyed by Vesuvius called Herculaneum. Its frescos are better preserved, and I've seen photographs of mosaics that are inside the bathhouses. We should see it now, because who knows how long the artwork will be there?"

He sighed and gave a small smile. It was impossible to say no to her when she had that excited glint in her eyes.

In the end, Lizzy was very persuasive, so they packed up their things and took a train to Naples the next morning. They spent the remainder of the day exploring Pompeii, and the next touring Herculaneum before they boarded another train for Reggio Calabria. He had to admit that he found it all very interesting, and in the end, decided that her method of traveling had its advantages as well.

The best part for William was Lizzy's expressions of wonder and excitement as she studied art she'd only read about or seen images of in a book or on a computer monitor. One day, he was going to take her to Crete and Greece. She'd love all of the ruins and old artwork there.

Overall, their trip to Italy had lasted two idyllic weeks. Every day, he'd awoken worried that Lizzy would be overwrought and want to return home to Melanie. God knew, he'd missed the little rugrat, but while Lizzy missed her daughter, she made do with speaking to her on the phone twice daily. He also had to give credit to Mrs. Reynolds, who was very adept at persuading his wife that her daughter was fine and to enjoy herself.

Once they were back in England, they spent another two weeks before they returned to Meryton, in time for the arrival of the newest Bingley. Little Jacob Bingley (although weighing in at 9lbs 8oz, one could hardly call him little) was almost two weeks late when he finally made his appearance, but Lizzy was thankful that his tardiness allowed her to be there for his birth.

A few weeks later, William and Lizzy were officially made Jacob's godparents in a private christening ceremony. After the Bennets' scene at the door to Netherfield during William's bachelor party, Charles and Jane opted for a more intimate ceremony, and invited the Bennets the following weekend. Father Ben had happily performed a blessing the next Sunday at church to help appease Mrs. Bennet, who was very put out that she wasn't allowed to attend her first grandchild's baptism.

Mr. Bennet had been insistent to speak with Lizzy, and attempted to contact her for several months after their marriage to discuss Wickham, but she'd been hesitant to meet with any of the Bennets. Eventually, realizing her father wouldn't quit until he had his say, Lizzy agreed to meet with him at Netherfield. Much to David Bennet's consternation, William was by his wife's side throughout the entire interview, with the intention of removing her at the first sign of her abuse. Mr. Bennet simply asked questions about the elder Mr. Wickham and his son, but no apology was tendered. When they were finished, he simply thanked her for her time and rose to leave. William had been disappointed, but Lizzy wasn't surprised in the least. It had never been in her father's nature to admit when he was wrong.

From that point, there had been no mention of the Bennets until Lydia gave birth to a premature baby boy that fall. Jane let them know of the birth, and Lydia's subsequent abandonment of the child, Landon, three months later. She'd decided motherhood wasn't what she wanted out of life, and fled to the Mississippi gulf coast, where she was working as a cocktail waitress in one of the casinos.

Deciding she would do what she could to raise Melly and her sibling together, Lizzy appealed to William, who sent one of his lawyers in an attempt to adopt the little boy. However, Mrs. Bennet wouldn't relinquish her "Lydia's precious baby boy" to her least favorite daughter and her snob of a husband, so Lizzy and William continued on with their lives.

A small cry and a sucking noise stirred William from his memories. He rose and took a step to the clear plastic bassinet nearby. Inside, his daughter of less than a day was furiously sucking on the heel of her hand. He glanced at the clock, noting that it hadn't even been two hours since her last feeding.

"There's no way you're hungry again, sweetie," he crooned softly. "Come here."

He picked up the swaddled baby carefully and cradled her to his chest. "Let's let Momma have a bit more sleep before we wake her."

He returned to his seat and studied his newborn daughter's face. He'd done it several times since she was born the night before, but he couldn't imagine it ever getting old. William trailed a finger down the downy softness of her cheek, and she turned, opening her mouth wide to try to nurse his finger.

"Nope, that's not a nipple. I'm sorry." He gave her a light kiss on the forehead.

Lizzy was convinced that she was a lot like him, but all he could see when he looked into his new daughter's face was his wife's features. Only time would tell, of course, but the baby already had one large curl just above her forehead, and he was crossing his fingers that it would become a large mass of curls just like her mother.

Lizzy. She still had the ability to turn his head when she entered a room, and he could pick out her laugh in a crowd of people. His love for her had only grown, and he'd always be eternally thankful that she'd offered him a second chance to win her heart. She never ceased to amaze him.

The last two years had been quite a transition, and she'd handled all of it without blinking an eye. Her career had undergone quite a few changes. Her class schedule at the university, as promised, no longer contained 3-D design, and the spring before, she'd requested to only teach watercolor in the future. The department head, realizing that either he'd agree or he'd lose her completely, capitulated. William couldn't imagine her having the confidence for the maneuvering she'd accomplished with her employer before their marriage.

As a result of her school schedule, not only was she painting more, but she was also making paper with Anita year-round for the craft fair in the spring. Lizzy staunchly refused to take part in more, but didn't want to give up the Longwood event. They had received some press coverage the year prior, and thanks to the publicity, she'd received a call from a gallery in Jackson, interested in her work.

Her occasional nightmares from her time with Greg had slowly disappeared with her new found confidence as well. The fall after their marriage, Greg had been found guilty of vehicular manslaughter for the deaths of Andrew and Ana Darcy. He was also convicted of crimes related to stalking Lizzy, and the attempted break-in at Longbourn. Not long after his incarceration, he was involved in a scuffle in the local lock-up, that resulted in the death of another inmate. Greg Wickham was now on death row; he'd never again be a free man. William couldn't rejoice in a loss of life, but the thought of never dealing with Greg Wickham again brought a peace to his thoughts of the future that he knew Lizzy shared as well.

Lizzy's life had just seemed to fall into place, and even Jane was thrilled with her sister's transformation. His sister-in-law made sure to confide in William that Lizzy was the happiest she'd ever seen her.

After the discussion about getting pregnant, William had left the decision for the timing of children to Lizzy. He'd been ready to have a baby since before he'd said "I do", but Lizzy wanted some time to work out her career. With her lighter workload, Lizzy made the decision to surprise him with a pregnancy rather than letting him in on her plan, so during their trip to France last summer, she'd gone off birth control without his knowledge. He remembered with a large smile, his shock when he came home from work almost a month later to find Melanie wearing a shirt that said "Big Sister! February, 2015."

When he'd finally understood what the shirt said, he'd turned toward the laughing behind him to find Lizzy and Mrs. Reynolds, the latter holding a video camera to record his reaction as he took his wife in his arms.

Glancing up, he studied a hand drawn picture of their family that was taped to the wall next to Lizzy's bed. Melanie, whose adoption was finalized the fall after they were married, was now a very precocious five-year-old. She was excelling in kindergarten, and so very excited to become a big sister. The work now proudly on display was one of hers, a gift for her little sister to teach her about their family, which included an energetic and happy Springer Spaniel puppy she'd named Maisy.

The baby let out a small cry, and William stood to walk around while he swayed her back and forth. He checked to ensure Lizzy was still asleep, and breathed a sigh of relief. Her hormones, combined with the memories of Melanie's birth, had made her very emotional since she began having contractions. She'd shed happy tears when they placed the new baby on her chest, all wet and crying furiously, but when it was all over, everything was calm, and they were alone, she had sobbed over having missed the experience with Melanie.

"Is she hungry?"

He turned to Lizzy, who was using the controls to raise the head of her hospital bed into a better position to nurse.

"She was sucking on her hand, but it hadn't quite been two hours. I wanted you to get a bit more sleep." She smiled softly as he carefully transferred the baby to her arms before scooting onto the mattress beside her.

"So are we agreed on her name?" he asked, while Lizzy opened the front panel on her nightgown.

"I thought you liked Ella Ashlynn."

"I do, but I just wanted to be sure that you did."

"Yes, I do." She helped the baby latch on, and after a few long draws, he could hear the now familiar sound of Ella feeding.

He placed an arm around Lizzy's shoulders, and leaned his cheek on her hair. "Well, at least you didn't have a silly nickname for Ella like you did all the other names." He knew Lizzy would recognize the teasing tone of his voice, and waited for her response.

"Little does he know, does he, my little Ella Bean," she crooned.

"Ella Bean?" He lifted his head and looked down at her. Her green eyes were shining brightly despite how tired she was.

"Yeah, like vanilla bean, but Ella Bean."

He laughed heavily and kissed her softly. "I love you," he said against her lips.

"I love you, too." She turned, and continued to nurse their daughter while his head returned to rest on her head as he watched.

They had another daughter. Perhaps they'd have only girls like the Bennets. His eyes grew wide at the thought. Could he spend the rest of his life surrounded by a houseful of beautiful women? Of course, they'd have to be beautiful, because Lizzy was their mother.

He smiled at the thought, deciding it would be no hardship at all. He'd be quite content.

Little did he know that in three years, the birth of a very mischievous little Andrew Darcy would change *everything*.

The End

After completing *A Matter of Chance*, I had some inspiration at home that helped me write this short story that takes place nine years after the story. I hope you enjoy it!

A Matter of Chance Vignette - A Funeral for Lobsty

(Lizzy and William have been married for 9 years, Melly is 12, Ella is 7, and Andrew is 4)

For a late Sunday morning, Longbourn wasn't any noisier than it usually was. Lizzy Darcy relaxed in bed with her morning cup of café au lait and her laptop, browsing through the online stores for Christmas present ideas for the children. Her husband of nine years, William was propped up on pillows beside her while he poured over something for work on his own laptop. She was just taking a steaming sip when her seven-year-old daughter, Ella, came running into the room with a four-year-old Andrew following close behind.

"Look what Layla did!" she exclaimed, pushing her cupped hands filled with red fluff and pieces of pipe cleaners in Lizzy's face. Layla was their nine-month-old Springer Spaniel puppy that they'd adopted from a rescue organization, and she was always getting into something.

Lizzy stared at the pile intently, attempting to figure out what the mass of trash was in her daughter's hands. "What is it?"

Ella gave an exasperated exhale. "It's Drew's lobster!" Her hands thrust forward a bit with each word in an attempt to emphasize scope of the tragedy. The puppy then came trotting in and plopped down beside Ella, panting and looking like she was grinning widely.

She turned back to the mess and looked again, finally seeing the resemblance to the craft project she and her son had made a few months ago. She looked up into his face and smiled softly in sympathy.

"I'm sorry, sweetheart. We'll have to break out the craft kit and make you another animal."

Drew looked at her sadly. "I want to make another Lobsty."

"But we can't," she began carefully, "there aren't any more red puffballs and pipe cleaners in the kit. If we find the directions, then you can pick out a new design, and we'll make that one."

Little Drew's face reflected his skepticism of that idea, and Lizzy fought a smile. Suddenly, Layla made a jump for the mass of fluff, and Ella raised her hands to keep it away from her. "Why don't the two of you go throw what's left away before Layla finds it again and eats it."

"I think that's a good idea," came William's voice from behind Lizzy. "We wouldn't want her to get sick."

That was when Ella's face perked up. "We can have a funeral for him!"

Lizzy was sure her eyes widened, but she tried to behave unfazed. "A funeral?" she asked, the doubtful tone that was in her head coming through in her voice.

"Yeah! Let's go, Drew!" The two of them bounded out of the door, where she could hear the pounding of their feet as they ran around the upstairs.

She looked to William. "A funeral?" He only smiled widely, shrugged, and went back to his work.

Looking back at the monitor, Lizzy began browsing once more while she listened to the voices outside of her door. She was sure she heard the word casket, but most of the time the kids sounded like they were in Drew's room. Maybe twenty minutes later, Ella and her brother came running back into the room.

"Daddy!" they yelled, "look at the casket we made!" Lizzy's head shot up to see what looked like a short tray made out of Legos with Lobsty's remains perched on top.

"That's nice, but it's not really a casket," explained William. After that, she really didn't hear what her husband was saying since she was too busy staring at "The Casket". She hoped that he was attempting to straighten out their idea because she was worried they would want to bury the thing. The last thing she wanted to do was to have to dig it up later when Drew wanted his blocks back.

The children disappeared again, but reappeared about fifteen minutes later. "We're ready for the funeral, come on!" Ella and Drew called out from the doorway.

"Really?" she asked, regarding William warily.

"Really," he responded before kissing her quickly on the lips. "Let's go, Mama." Her husband pulled her out of bed, and laced his fingers with hers as they followed the children down the stairs to the kitchen. There were three barstools set up a few feet in front of the pull out that contained the trashcan, and Mrs. Reynolds was already seated in one of them. Melanie, who'd thus far been absent from the lobster saga, was standing beside the cabinet with the "coffin," holding Lobsty in her hands. Ella and Drew joined her, the latter wearing a Jedi tunic made out of brown felt that he'd gotten at a friend's birthday party.

"What's with the Jedi robes?" asked William, chuckling.

"Funeral clothes?" ventured Lizzy. She felt something soft brush her foot and looked down to see their older Springer, Maisy, lay down next to her foot. Layla was standing beside Melanie, waiting for Lobsty's remains to fall at her feet. One would've thought she was holding a steak the way the puppy was sitting and staring at the cotton fuzz.

Ella seemed to wait patiently until they were all comfortably situated, and she raised some pages torn out of an old composition notebook that were covered in a purple crayon handwriting.

"First we will have a speech, then Melanie will dump him, then there will be a prayer."

Lizzy couldn't hold it in any longer. The absurdity of it all combined with what her daughter had just said made her erupt in a fit of laughter. She wasn't alone. Mrs. Reynolds and William were both laughing, and when she looked up, the children were laughing as well. Once their chuckles were back under control, Lizzy apologized.

"I'm sorry, but when you said that Melanie would dump him, I couldn't help it." She could hear William beside her now fighting to control his chuckles as Ella raised the papers and began again.

400

"This lobster was very special to me and my brother, Drew. Lobsty was the best lobster I've ever seen. My mom and Drew built this lobster from puffballs, pipe cleaners, and glue. That's my vulnerable speech." Her husband snorted from beside her, and she grabbed his hand, squeezing it gently.

"Do you mean venerable, Ella bean?" Her daughter shook her head and furrowed her eyebrows.

"Did you really mean vulnerable?" asked William. She smiled widely and nodded before turning to face her sister.

"Now, Melanie will dump Lobsty," said Ella in a very official tone as she opened the cabinet. Their oldest turned the tray over into the trashcan, and the mass of red fluff dropped into the white plastic bag, covering whatever Mrs. Reynolds had put in there last. Once the cabinet was closed, they all turned back to Ella.

"Now for the prayer." She flipped the papers and produced a new page also written in purple crayon.

"It was once a pile of puffballs, and a little boy came along. He put the puffballs together, and made a lobster. And then a dog came along and chewed it all up. And that's what brought us here today."

During the "prayer," the three adult spectators couldn't control themselves any more and began laughing again. By the time Ella had read it all, Lizzy and Mrs. Reynolds were laughing so hard they were crying, and the children had joined them.

Lizzy stood and kissed and hugged each of her children. She looked over her son's head as she embraced him, seeing William wiping his eyes as he hugged Ella. Beside her daughter, on the counter were the sheets of paper with the purple crayon writing. Lizzy picked them up and read them, finding the actual speech and prayer from the funeral written out on them.

When the hugs were passed all around, Melanie went off to read the latest book she was engrossed in, and Ella and Drew went to return the Legos to his room. Lizzy quickly pocketed Ella's papers and returned upstairs with William to lounge around with him some more.

When they were once again comfy in the bed, Lizzy called Jane and described the entire event to her, including reading the speeches from Ella's notes. Jane was giggling madly by the time Lizzy had recited the entire episode.

"They're so creative," her sister gushed. "Just like their mom. "You'll have to scan those pages and email them to me. I want to tell Charles, but it won't be the same if I don't have the words right."

"I can type it out and email it quicker, if you want."

"That'll work. Thanks, sis!"

"You're still coming over this afternoon to grill, right?"

"Oh yeah, we'll be there," responded Jane. "Jacob and Sarah are so excited. You know they love playing at Longbourn. Apparently, Netherfield just isn't as cool."

Lizzy laughed. "I don't know about all that. I happen to think Netherfield is a neat house, but I should get going so I can get some work done before y'all come over.

"Okay, Bye Lizzy."

"Bye," she said and hung up.

"What did Jane say?" asked William as he closed his laptop and scooted closer to her.

"She said that they're so creative... just like me."

"She's correct, you know."

Lizzy rolled her eyes. "I think they've got some of my intelligence along with you're massive brains, and we're going to be lucky to keep up with them." She felt William's hand caress up her leg as he leaned over to kiss her softly on the lips. He dipped down, and she felt his soft lips brush her neck.

"I'm thinking that perhaps we should begin working on another."

Her eyes widened as he lifted up and looked down at her. "Another?" she squeaked. His hand roamed up to stroke her stomach, and she squirmed. "William, the door is open." She heard and felt his low chuckle.

"Then perhaps you should go close and lock it."

Acknowledgements

While it's easy to read a book on your own, writing one is a different story, and I definitely have people to thank.

I'd like to recognize Jane Austen for writing such amazing characters that two hundred years later we're still inspired to use them over and over again.

I'd like to thank my husband and children who've been my biggest cheerleaders, supporters, and fans. I'm their biggest fans and I couldn't have written this book without being their mom. There is so much of them in Melly, Ella, and Andrew.

To be honest, I can't say enough to express my thanks to Lisa Toth, Kristi Rawley, Suzan Lauder and Debra Anne Watson. These talented women took time out of their lives to read and edit my story for nothing more than my thanks. They each have their own strengths that I've come to rely on and they definitely made this story readable. Thanks ladies!

I'd like to give a bit thanks to the Chat Chits, who make me laugh and certainly can brighten my day. They are also some of the most supportive women I've had the pleasure of knowing. When I have problems, they're there to encourage me to keep going. They're a great bunch!

For those who wondered, I did have a dog named Bear when I was younger. His backstory is the same as the Bear in the story, only he bit my cousin and not my dad. I will say that Bear lived to be a very old dog, dying of old age. He was one of the smartest and best dogs I've even known.

I'd lastly like to thank those who read my stories and left me their comments! Comments may not seem like much when you're reading a new story, but they help us know that we're doing a good job and what could stand to be looked at again. Thanks!

If you'd like to know what I'm currently up to, follow me here –

facebook.com/LLDiamond
twitter.com/LLDiamond2
lldiamondwrites.com

Made in the USA
Charleston, SC
13 February 2015